ALSO BY OWEN LAUKKANEN

The Professionals
Criminal Enterprise

KILL FEE

A graduate of the University of British Columbia's Creative Writing Program, Owen Laukkanen spent three years in the world of professional poker reporting before turning to fiction. He currently lives in Vancouver.

KILL FEE

OWEN LAUKKANEN

CORVUS

First published in the United States in 2014 by G. P. Putnam's Sons, a division of the Penguin Group, part of the Penguin Random House Company.

First published in paperback in 2015 in Great Britain by Corvus, an imprint of Atlantic Books Ltd.

Book design by Gretchen Achilles

10 9 8 7 6 5 4 3 2 1
A CIP catalogue record for this book is available from the British Library.

E-book ISBN: 978 1 78239 602 4
Paperback ISBN: 978 1 78239 601 7

Printed in Great Britain.

Corvus
An imprint of Atlantic Books Ltd
Ormond House
26–27 Boswell Street
London
WC1N 3JZ

www.corvus-books.co.uk

FOR ANDREW AND TERRY

KILL FEE

I

The billionaire picked a heck of a day to die.

It was a sunny Saturday in early April, a beautiful afternoon in downtown Saint Paul, the kind of day that seemed to chase away any memory of the long Minnesota winter just passed. It was not the kind of afternoon for a murder.

An hour before the billionaire met his end, a plain-looking man and a beautiful woman met for a greasy lunch at the old dining car on West 7th Street, and when they'd finished, dawdled slowly along St. Peter toward the Mississippi River.

They made an odd couple. He was paunchy and balding, pale and comfortably middle-aged. She was brown-skinned, statuesque, and maybe even a little severe, more than a decade his junior. And though they walked close beside each other, talked easily, and laughed quickly, there was a slight hesitation in their manner, an unresolved tension. They were something more than simply passing friends.

They reached 5th Street and turned west, walked past the stately old Saint Paul Hotel and into Rice Park, an oasis of calm amid the rush of the city. The day was sunny but still crisp, and the park was filled with families and other couples, native Minnesotans and tourists alike. The man and the woman walked aimlessly, took a leisurely tack past the Landmark Center, with its pink granite towers and turrets, and then crossed through the park toward the vast Central Library. They bought coffees inside the Saint Paul Hotel, and then wandered back out and found a bench in Rice Park. It was a Saturday afternoon, and neither Kirk Stevens nor Carla Windermere had anywhere else to be.

In truth, they looked forward to these meetings, Stevens and Windermere both. They weren't always so languid—work, the Minnesota weather, and the demands of Stevens's family made routines a fantasy—but they happened, a couple times a month, maybe, and that was almost enough.

Windermere sipped her coffee and tilted her head skyward, basking in the sun's warmth. "This is what I'm talking about, Stevens," she said. "This is what I've been waiting for. Sunlight. Warmth. Vitamin D."

Stevens grinned at her. "Summer's coming," he said. "You survived another winter. You're practically a Minnesotan now."

"Like hell." Windermere glanced at him sideways. "I'm a warm-weather girl, always will be. No matter how many snowstorms I live through."

"You like it up here, though," he said. "Kind of. Admit it."

"Maybe. It ain't the weather, though."

He cocked his head. "Then what is it?"

Windermere shook her head, the hint of a smile on her lips. She took another sip of coffee and set the cup down on the bench between them. Then she looked around the park.

People milled about, enjoying the sunshine, taking pictures of the fountain, the Landmark Center, the hotel, the statues of the characters from the comic strip *Peanuts*—homage to its creator, Charles Schulz, a Twin Cities native. Windermere watched a family crowd around Charlie Brown, all of them smiling wide, posing for the camera, laughing and jostling one another. She waited until the picture had been taken and the family had wandered off before she turned back to Stevens.

"It ain't you, either," she said. "So don't get any ideas. It's not the food, or the scenery, or the nightlife. Miami's got Minnesota beat every time."

"Then it must be the work," Stevens said. "Is that it?"

"The work." Windermere pursed her lips. "Yeah, I guess so, Stevens. It must be the work."

TWO AND A HALF YEARS EARLIER. Kirk Stevens had driven from Saint Paul to the FBI's regional headquarters in downtown Minneapolis, where he'd met a woman with bewitching eyes and a slight southern accent who'd sat him down in her cubicle in the Criminal Investigative Division and listened as he outlined a sensational theory about a group of nomadic young kidnappers. The woman was Windermere, and Stevens, a Special Agent with the Minnesota Bureau of Criminal Apprehension, needed her help tracking the kidnappers out of state.

He'd intended to drop the case in Windermere's lap and forget about it—he was, after all, just a state policeman—but Windermere had insisted he join her, put in a special request, and Stevens had found himself on a plane to Chicago less than a day later. It was the start of the rollercoaster ride of Stevens's career.

A year or so later, it happened again. Carter Tomlin, a wealthy Saint Paul accountant-turned-bank-robber, an acquaintance of Stevens's. Windermere sniffed him out. Stevens hadn't believed her. Neither had her FBI partner, or her superiors, not until Tomlin had started to kill. Not until he'd dragged Stevens and his family into the middle of his murderous spree.

They'd drifted apart after that first kidnapping case. The second time, after Tomlin, they stayed close. Even amid the awful terror and the adrenaline rush, the sickening race against time and Tomlin's dwindling sanity, Stevens had missed Agent Windermere. And though the FBI agent was about as prickly as a sea urchin, Stevens knew she felt the same.

So now here they were, a year after Carter Tomlin, sharing a park bench in downtown Saint Paul, drinking coffee and enjoying the sun, talking and laughing like lifelong friends. It was, Stevens thought as he looked around at the park, an almost perfect day.

ACROSS THE STREET, a silver Bentley sedan turned in to the driveway in front of the Saint Paul Hotel. Stevens watched it glide to a stop outside the building's ivy-covered façade. Windermere nudged him. "Check it out," she said. "Maybe it's Prince."

"I get it." Stevens shook his head. "Because this is Minnesota, right? Everybody in a nice car has to be Prince."

"Or F. Scott Fitzgerald. But I don't think he rolls in a Bentley."

"I don't think he rolls, period," said Stevens. "I figure at this point he's pretty much stationary."

They watched as the driver climbed out of the Bentley and circled around to open the rear passenger door. A short, white-haired man in an expensive suit stepped out to the pavement.

"Fitzgerald," said Windermere. "What did I tell you?"

Stevens squinted across the driveway. "He looks old enough, anyway."

The white-haired man leaned on a cane as he stepped away from the big sedan and started slowly toward the hotel's front doors. Windermere cast an eye at her companion. "Barely looks older than you, Stevens."

Stevens arched an eyebrow. Started to reply, but never got the words out. A shot cracked out from somewhere, cutting him off. Someone screamed. A split second later, the white-haired man collapsed to the pavement.

2

Windermere was on her feet before the white-haired man hit the ground. She ran across the cobblestone street and up the hotel driveway, dodging angry taxicabs as horns blared. Someone was still screaming. Bystanders ducked for cover.

The man was dead; Windermere knew it instantly. He'd taken the shot to the back of his head, just behind his right ear, and the results were not pretty. There was blood, lots of it. Bone, too. Gore spattered the driveway. Windermere dashed toward the hotel doors and ducked behind the big Bentley, wishing she'd brought her service Glock. *"Everybody stay down,"* she said. *"And someone call 9-1-1."*

Stevens crashed in beside her, breathing hard. Looked across at the white-haired man. "Shit," he said. "Where's the shooter?"

Windermere crouched low and played the scene back in her head. Heard the shot again; watched the white-haired man fall. Pictured the entry wound and tried to map the bullet's trajectory. "Sniper," she said.

Stevens got it immediately. He twisted around and peered across the back of the big sedan. Behind them, the Landmark Center loomed, its myriad turrets and towers excellent vantage points for any would-be killer with a rifle and a scope. Stevens nudged her. *"Up there."*

3

Lind dropped the rifle as soon as the target fell. He pulled the window closed and walked out of the room and onto the balcony surrounding the inner courtyard.

Already there were sirens outside. Word was spreading. People stood on the balcony, their office doors open, cell phones and paperwork still clutched in their hands. They shot quizzical looks in Lind's direction. He ignored them and walked along the balcony to the stairs.

The sirens grew louder as he descended to ground level. The stairwell was crowded. Clerks. Secretaries. Librarians and curators from the museums housed inside the center. Lind walked past a tour group and descended quickly to the main level, then crossed the courtyard to the building's front doors. He slipped around another group of confused workers and hurried out into daylight, passing a man and a woman on the front stairs, a black woman and an older white man, their jaws set, both of them moving quickly. Lind didn't slow down. He turned right on 5th Street, away from the swarm of police cars outside the hotel, and kept walking.

» » »

STEVENS AND WINDERMERE hurried into the Landmark Center, dodging scared civilians every step of the way. It was chaos inside, people everywhere. Stevens pushed through to the inner courtyard, Windermere right behind him. "The towers," Stevens said. "How do we get up there?"

Windermere searched the courtyard. Spotted a set of stairs. "Come on."

A woman flew out of the stairwell just as they approached. Nearly collided with Stevens, her eyes wide and wild. Windermere caught her. "Whoa," she said. "Slow down. What's the rush?"

The woman squirmed. Fought Windermere's grasp. *"Let me go,"* she said. "I have to find the police."

"We're police," Stevens told her. "BCA. FBI. What's the story?"

The woman looked at Windermere. Then at Stevens's badge. "Thank God," she said, pointing across the courtyard. "He went that way."

"Who?" said Windermere.

"The shooter. He went that way. I followed him down."

Windermere swapped glances with Stevens. "Describe him," she said.

"A smaller guy. Brown hair in a buzz cut. Young. Mid-twenties, maybe." She looked at them, her expression urgent. "He's getting *away.*"

"We passed him," said Stevens. "On the steps. We walked right past him."

Windermere was already halfway across the courtyard. "You coming or what, Stevens?"

4

They left the woman in the Landmark Center and burst out onto 5th Street, Windermere in the lead, moving fast. She turned right and kept running. Stevens struggled to follow. He kept himself in decent shape, mostly, but Windermere was a heck of a lot younger. Plus she'd been some kind of track star back home in Mississippi.

Windermere reached the end of the block and slowed to look up and down Washington. Then, just as Stevens caught up, she took off again. Stevens paused, caught his breath. Then he hurried after her.

» » »

LIND WALKED WEST down 5th Street, skirting the high, windowless brick walls of the stadium where the pro hockey team played. He walked quicker now on the empty sidewalks, the sirens and the chaos retreating into the background. He walked quicker, but he didn't run. Running would attract undue attention.

He circled the arena until he reached 7th Street, and then cut across the busy intersection, toward the bus station. Downtown was behind him now; the land here was vacant—event parking for the hockey arena, mostly. In the distance, he could see the spire of the Cathedral of Saint Paul.

Lind cut through a thin copse of trees lining 7th and came out into a half-empty parking lot. He walked across the dusty gravel until he reached his car, and was about to climb in when someone called out behind him.

Lind turned and saw the black woman from outside the Landmark Center hurrying toward him. Her companion followed, about thirty feet back, both of them running hard, their faces determined. Lind watched them approach.

» » »

"STOP!" Windermere called across the parking lot. The kid did as he was told. He straightened. Turned from his little hatchback and looked at her. Windermere met his gaze and felt a chill run through her.

He was a normal-looking guy, just as the woman at the Landmark Center had described. Probably five seven or five eight, he had close-cut brown hair and was dressed like your everyday rube. He looked normal. Except that he didn't. He didn't look normal at all.

It was his face. His *eyes*. It was his slack expression, the way he studied her with no hint of malice, no fear, barely any comprehension at all. Windermere slowed, involuntarily, wishing again that she'd remembered her Glock.

The kid looked at her for a couple seconds. Then he turned around—calm, deliberate. Slid into the car and turned the engine over and drove out of the lot.

5

Stevens caught up to Windermere. "Why'd you slow down?" he said. "You had him."

Ahead of them, the car reached the end of the parking lot and pulled out onto 7th Street. It drove fast, but not wild. Not out of control.

"Chevy, right?" Stevens said, pulling out his cell phone. "An Aveo, I think. You get the plates?"

"Yeah," Windermere said. "I got them."

Stevens had his phone to his ear. "Crowson," he said. "Get a pen. The shooting downtown, the Saint Paul Hotel. We make the shooter's ride."

He handed Windermere the phone. Windermere recited the plate number and handed the phone back to Stevens.

"Get that to Saint Paul PD," Stevens told Crowson. "It's a little Chevy hatchback, gray, an Aveo, most likely. Get them looking." Stevens ended the call and turned back to Windermere. "So what the hell happened?"

Windermere looked out to where the gray car had disappeared into traffic. Didn't answer a moment. "I just lost it, Stevens," she said finally. "The kid looked at me and I spooked."

"Spooked. What the heck do you mean?"

"I just lost it." She shrugged. "It's like I was a potted plant, the way he looked at me. A cloud or something, insignificant. Like I wasn't a cop and he wasn't a killer."

"You didn't show him your badge," said Stevens, "or your gun. Maybe he didn't make you for a cop."

Windermere shook her head. "It was more than that," she said. "He just murdered somebody. He was making his escape. And he looked at me like he was waiting for a bus."

She frowned, staring across the parking lot toward 7th Street, where the traffic slipped past, normal, like nothing had happened at all.

THEY WALKED BACK along 5th Street toward Rice Park and the Landmark Center and the Saint Paul Hotel. There were police everywhere now, and ambulances and the rest. TV news trucks. Bystanders. Like a movie scene.

Here we go again. Stevens flashed back to the kidnappers, Arthur Pender and his gang. Carter Tomlin and his team of bank robbers. He felt a brief twinge of excitement, and nursed it as long as he dared. Then he chased it from his mind.

Not your case, he thought. *Not Windermere's, either. This is Saint Paul PD all the way.*

They waded back into the mix. Showed their badges to the uniform holding the line outside the hotel's driveway. Then they walked up to the entrance, where the white-haired man's body still lay on the pavement.

Uniforms lurked at the margins. Forensic techs combed the body. A couple dour-faced men in rumpled suits stood by the Bentley, sipping coffee, watching the techs. Every now and then one of them would crack a joke and the other would laugh a little, grim. Homicide cops.

Windermere flashed her badge at them. "Windermere, FBI," she said. "Who's working point?"

The men glanced at each other. Then the older guy stepped forward. "Parent," he said. "Remember me?"

"The Tomlin case," Windermere said, nodding. "You worked that poker game, right? This one yours, too?"

"At least until the FBI takes it off my hands."

"No such luck. We're just witnesses, Detective. This one's yours." She introduced Stevens.

Parent looked at them both. "Witnesses, huh? The two of you together?"

"Interdepartmental bonding," said Stevens. "We saw the shooting from that bench over there. Got a look at your suspect and the plates off his car."

"No shit." Parent glanced back at the body. Then he pulled out a notepad. "Well, all right, witnesses," he said. "Tell me what you know."

6

Lind drove the speed limit southwest down 7th Street, trying to blend in with traffic. Trying to ignore the little pinprick of panic that had started to itch in his mind.

The black woman would have memorized his plates. She would have called them in to the police. Right now, the police would be looking for the car.

Remove yourself from the scene without being detected. Don't attract undue attention. Secondary objective.

Lind checked the road for police cars. Checked his rearview mirror, oncoming traffic, the parking lots that lined the road. He saw a couple cruisers. They didn't follow him. He kept driving.

He followed 7th Street until it merged with the highway and turned south to cross the Mississippi River, and he drove past the lakes and the grassland and forest until he reached the airport turnoff. He parked in the rental car lot and waited as a man scanned something off the windshield. The man grinned at Lind. "Enjoy your visit?"

Lind didn't answer. The man frowned and handed Lind a receipt, glanced back at him once before hurrying away. Lind was already walking to the terminal. He found a garbage can and tore up the receipt, just like he'd been taught. Then he rode the concourse tram to the main terminal building and found the Delta line.

The woman at the counter frowned when she read his alias off the computer. Lind felt the little niggle of panic return. "You're a frequent flier, you know," the woman said finally. "You could have skipped this whole line."

Lind relaxed. "Next time," he said. He took his ticket and walked to the security lineup. The guard waved him through. The metal detector didn't beep.

He boarded the plane with the frequent fliers and the first-class passengers in the priority lane. Sat in his window seat as the plane slowly filled, as it taxied from the gate, as it careened down the runway and reached a safe cruising altitude. He didn't look out the window. He didn't read the in-flight magazine. He sat in his seat and wondered if the black woman and her companion constituted undue attention.

Two and a half hours later, the plane landed in Philadelphia. It was dark outside, and raining. Lind walked off the plane and out through the terminal to the parking garage, where he retrieved his car and drove away from the airport.

He drove along Interstate 95 over the Schuylkill River and into downtown Philadelphia, navigated the busy, rainy streets, and parked in an underground garage and rode the elevator to the apartments above.

He stepped off the elevator to his apartment on the building's top floor. Kicked off his shoes and then moved from room to room, turning on every light he could find. When the whole place was daytime bright, he went into the living area and turned on the television and turned up the volume. Took a TV dinner from the kitchen freezer and heated it in the microwave, brewed a strong pot of coffee, and brought the dinner and the coffee into the living area.

It was dark out, and rainy. The city's sounds were muted far below. Lind ate his dinner and drank from his coffee mug, sat on his couch in the middle of his bright living room, watching the television play an endless loop of movie previews. He sat on his couch all night, drinking coffee and watching the TV, praying his phone would ring again soon.

7

The dead man's name was Spenser Pyatt, and he was very rich.

"Media conglomerations," Detective Parent told Stevens and Windermere. "Satellite TV. Built an empire from a radio station out in the hinterlands."

"I've heard of him," Stevens said. "Fergus Falls. That's where he started." Windermere looked at him funny, and he shrugged. "Kind of a state treasure, I guess. Made a billion dollars with his own two hands."

"I get it," said Windermere. "This guy here's the state hero."

"Hero's a bit strong," said Parent. "He's just a good story."

Windermere looked across the driveway to where the Ramsey County medical examiner was loading Pyatt's body into the back of the van. "Not so much with the happy ending, though."

Stevens and Parent followed her gaze. Then Stevens cleared his throat. "You need anything else?" he asked Parent.

"Not unless the BCA wants to take this thing off my hands."

"Not on your life." Stevens shook the detective's hand. Turned to Windermere. "Guess I'll head home."

Windermere looked at him. "Really?"

"Told Nancy I'd be home for dinner. And JJ's got soccer tonight."

"It's not even four, Stevens. You don't want to see how this plays out?"

Stevens glanced back at Parent, at the medical examiner's van, at the big silver Bentley and the spattered blood on the sidewalk. He pictured the killer, saw the little Chevy slip away into traffic, and, yeah, maybe he wanted to stick around a little. But he shook his head. "Not our case, Carla."

"Maybe not technically," she said, "but we saw this guy, Stevens. We know what he looks like. We know who he is. Maybe we can help somehow." She caught his expression and laughed. "Don't even try to pretend you're not feeling this, partner. You're as pumped up about this whole thing as I am."

Stevens was trying to think up an answer, something diplomatic that wouldn't paint him as some boring has-been, when a uniform broke through the line and came running at Parent.

"*Detective,*" she said, huffing and puffing, cheeks red. "Word from dispatch. They found the shooter's car."

Stevens swapped glances with Windermere. Turned to listen.

"A gray Chevy hatchback," the uniform told them, "as advertised. It's a rental, Liberty Cars. They found it at the airport."

Parent frowned. "They get a name off it?"

"Name, flight, everything. Guy took off out of state in a hell of a hurry."

Windermere grinned at Stevens. "Out of state, partner. You know what that means." She started back toward Parent, pulling her cell phone from her pocket. "Mathers," she told the phone. "Hold up one second."

She turned to Parent. "Maybe the FBI can help, after all, Detective. What's our shooter's name?" She raised her phone again before Parent could answer. "Mathers," she said. "You there? What are the odds we ground every flight at MSP within the next fifteen minutes?"

She listened. "Yeah, well," she said. "Try it anyway. There's a killer on the loose."

She hung up the phone. Turned back to Parent. Parent opened his mouth. Windermere held up one finger. Turned back to Stevens, still grinning. "Sure you don't want to stick around?"

8

Parkerson took a late-afternoon break to check the news on his computer. He found what he was looking for and read with interest, a satisfied smile growing on his face. When he'd finished the article, he closed his Internet browser and reached for his phone. Then he paused.

He stood and walked to the door of his office, closed and locked it. It was Saturday afternoon; the plant was nearly empty. Still, you couldn't be too careful.

Satisfied, Parkerson sat down again and reached for the phone. He dialed the number by heart and waited.

A man picked up. "Is this line secure?"

"As it ever was," Parkerson told him. "The job's done."

There was a pause. "You're sure?"

"Check the news. The job's done."

"Okay." The man exhaled. "Okay."

"I'll be expecting payment," said Parkerson. "You know what to do."

"He's dead," the man said.

Parkerson sighed. "Dead and gone. Your wish came true. Now you pay me." There was another long pause. *"Okay?"*

"Okay," the man said. "Okay. I'll get you your money."

Parkerson hung up the phone. Opened a spreadsheet file and settled back in to work—or tried to, anyway. Within five minutes, the phone was ringing again. Parkerson answered. *"What?"*

"I killed him." The man moaned like a wounded animal. "Christ, they'll hang me for this."

"You didn't kill him," Parkerson said. "I told you, you're clean. No ties to the job whatsoever. You're safe. Now settle your tab." He hung up the phone again and sat in the stillness of his office for a minute or two. Stared at the phone, thinking.

An amateur, the guy was. A ticking time bomb. A liability. Parkerson studied the phone a minute longer. Then he picked up the handset again.

9

The visions came back. They always came back.

Lind stayed awake for as long as he could. He sat on the couch with every light on around him, the TV blaring movie previews until the neighbors beat on the walls. The rain drizzled down outside and the night slowly passed, and Lind sat on his couch and drank coffee and didn't move.

Morning came. The rain didn't stop. The sky turned light in the east and gradually the day came, a miserable, dripping, tarnished-steel day. Lind hardly noticed the bleak light. He waited for the phone to ring and prayed the visions wouldn't come back.

They came back. They always did.

He held them off as long as he could. Felt his eyelids grow heavy and, with the fatigue, the rising panic. He fought it. Drank more coffee. Stood and paced the room. It didn't work. Nothing worked. The visions always came back.

He fell asleep around noon. Lay down on the couch and curled himself inward and surrendered, gave in. Then, just like that, he was out.

HE WAS THERE AGAIN. *Over there.* He was riding with Showtime and Hang Ten and the rest. The heat was unbearable; he was sweating through his gear, big, itchy drops of sweat trickling down to the small of his back. The truck barreled through the desert. The sun, high above, was relentless. The place was like hell without the fire.

He could hear the big engine rumbling. Could feel the vibrations. He could see Showtime beside him, at the wheel, laughing about something. Hang Ten's girlfriend, probably. She'd sent a picture that morning: a white sandy beach, a bikini. Showtime got a hold of it. *"Jee-sus,"* he said, laughing, fending off Hang Ten. "Why the hell'd you ever come over here, man?"

Hang Ten was up top, in the turret. Mini-Me and Slowpoke in the back. Through the front windshield, Lind could see Rambo's Humvee ahead, and he knew there was a third truck behind. There was a journalist back there, some wannabe hard-ass. A taste of the shit for all the readers back home. A routine patrol through the wasteland.

He could see it all. He could hear it. He was *there*. The trucks rumbled along, kicking up dust and sand, jostling over uneven terrain. The convoy motored past civilians, kids who stopped kicking soccer balls to run over and wave at the trucks, dark-eyed older men in white robes and head scarves—*ghatra*—who glared at the convoy, suspicious. The city shimmered in the heat in the distance.

They were halfway through the city when the world disappeared. On some narrow, misbegotten street. Showtime was still needling Hang Ten. Took one hand off the wheel and made a rude gesture. Hang Ten leaned down to see it. Lind was laughing despite the tension. Maybe *because* of the tension, the whole goddamn scenario. Every damned patrol was the same, a 450-day game of Russian roulette.

Then it happened.

In the visions, it only came back in fragments. An explosion. Screaming. The truck shaking like a child's matchbox toy. Showtime holding up a stump of arm, laughing, manic. Fire, everywhere fire. An unbearable heat.

He felt himself dragged away from the truck. Someone grabbed him by the back and hauled him away on his ass. He watched his legs trail behind him, making twin tracks in the dirt. He watched the truck burn as other soldiers swarmed around it, Rambo pounding on Mini-Me's door, Hang Ten slumped over his turret.

He didn't feel any pain.

Then he was in another truck, rumbling back across the desert. Someone was yelling at him, shaking him. Rambo. The truck jostled. Rambo disappeared.

He was in a room somewhere. Doctors everywhere. They stared at him. Talked to him. He tried to reply. He still felt no pain.

They loaded him onto a plane, a big C-17. Wheeled him on board with seventy-five other soldiers, and he lay there and stared at the roof as the plane rumbled down the runway and took to the air. He stared at the roof until the plane landed somewhere, somewhere the air was cool and the sun wasn't so harsh, somewhere with more white rooms and more doctors. He stayed there for months, and every day they talked to him and asked questions and he didn't say much. They looked at him with concerned eyes and whispered to one another. Still, he didn't feel any pain.

Then he was on another plane. This time, he sat upright, in a jump seat, and stared at the jump seat across from him and saw the desert and Showtime and Hang Ten and Mini-Me burning, and he must have cried out or said something, because a medic came with a needle and then Showtime and Mini-Me and Hang Ten were gone. And then he wasn't there anymore, either.

He was in another room, a doctor's office inside a large hospital. Couches and comfortable chairs. A woman watched him from across a coffee table, her eyes friendly, concerned. She spoke to Lind, but Lind didn't hear her. She watched him stand, followed him to the door. She called out to him as he walked away.

There was a man waiting outside the hospital. He stood in the sunny parking lot in a blue baseball cap and sunglasses, and he straightened as Lind approached. Smiled at him. Talked to him. Took his arm and led him to a big gray car, buckled his seat belt and said something and laughed.

Lind went with the man. He tried to listen. He still hadn't felt any pain.

10

According to the Saint Paul Police Department, the suspect's name was Allen Bryce Salazar, and he had boarded a Delta regional flight to Omaha, Nebraska, just after the shooting. Windermere passed the information back to Derek Mathers in the FBI's Minneapolis field office, along with instructions to ground the plane, if possible. Mathers called back a few minutes later.

"No can do," he told Windermere. "Flight's in the air, and they won't turn around. I have agents in Omaha waiting on the tarmac."

"Shit," said Windermere. "Wanted to bring him down myself. Tell Omaha to ship him back our way so I can get my hands on him."

Mathers laughed. "I feel sorry for this guy already."

Windermere pocketed her phone and surveyed the crime scene. The crowd had diminished, now that the body was gone. The news trucks had filed their reports. There were a few cops, and a few crime-scene techs, and the hotel's concierge peered out from the door. Windermere wondered how long it would take for business to return to normal. Before the whole tawdry affair was a tourist attraction. Stevens caught her eye. "Get your man?"

"Just about." She checked her watch. "Give it an hour or two. Then he's mine."

"Poor bastard."

Windermere cocked her head. "Mathers said the same thing, Stevens. Am I unpleasant to deal with or something?"

Stevens laughed. "You?" he said. "Nah."

STEVENS SURVEYED the Landmark Center from the crime scene. They'd found the suspect's rifle in an empty room overlooking 5th and Market Streets, a clear shot at the Saint Paul Hotel. The gun itself was unremarkable; a Remington 700 bolt-action hunting rifle with a scope, it would have had no trouble covering the eighty-yard range between window and target. Still, it was a skilled shot. Not exactly amateur work.

Windermere elbowed Stevens. "You're trying to figure out the why again, aren't you?"

Stevens glanced at her. Laughed. "Maybe," he said. "I mean, it's the most interesting part, isn't it?"

"You know how I feel about motive," she said.

"Sure do," Stevens said. "Heard it all before. We know the who and the how, so who cares about the why?"

"Exactly. I just want to catch the bastard, Stevens."

"I just think it's interesting." He gestured back at the empty Bentley. "This was a targeted killing. The shooter knew our man would be here. He camped out and waited and sniped him. Then he walked. Didn't run. He *walked* to his car, got in, and drove back to the airport. Boarded a flight home. Why?"

"Guess I'm going to find out." Windermere grinned at him. "You want I should keep you posted? Or maybe you'd like to come over and see the new headquarters. You can ask Salazar yourself why he done it."

Stevens shook his head. "Any chance you can get, huh?"

Windermere kept her smile pasted. Didn't say anything.

"I'm too old for your FBI work and you know it," he said. "I'm not G-man material."

"So you keep saying."

"So my wife keeps saying," Stevens said, and instantly regretted it. He sighed and checked his watch. "Speaking of which, I'd better go."

"I'll keep you posted." Windermere punched his arm. "First thing I'll ask Salazar is why."

STEVENS LEFT WINDERMERE and walked back through Saint Paul until he found his old Cherokee parked by a curb. He fired up the engine and drove west and out of the city center. His route took him past Rice Park again, a few blocks to the south, and he caught himself glancing up Market Street for another glimpse of the excitement.

Stevens had been a BCA agent for more than seventeen years now. Before that, he'd been a Duluth city cop. He liked police work, liked untying the knots, the impossible riddles. Mostly, he worked cold cases, spent his time in an office. It was a quiet existence, or it had been until Windermere came along.

That first kidnapping case with Windermere had been the most action Kirk Stevens had tasted in years, and though he was loath to admit it, he'd enjoyed the excitement. Hell, he'd even enjoyed some of the notoriety, the press attention that followed. It was nice to get a little recognition. An adrenaline rush. The whole case had been a heck of a lot of fun.

It had also been very dangerous.

Stevens knew Windermere thought he was wasting his talents at the BCA. "Come join the FBI," she told him after the Tomlin case was over.

"Work with me. We'll partner up. We'll eat takeout and chase bad guys full-time. You'll love it."

A part of him *would* love it, Stevens knew, as he piloted the Cherokee west along the interstate toward his home in Lexington-Hamline. A part of him longed for more of that excitement. It was the same part, maybe, that felt an electric little thrill whenever Windermere turned those big bewitching eyes on him. It was a dangerous urge to indulge.

Stevens turned off the interstate and navigated along the surface roads, the streets getting quieter and the rush of the city fading into the background. He slowed in front of a tidy green craftsman home and pulled into the slim driveway, climbed out of the Jeep and walked around his small patch of lawn, and surveyed the house before climbing the front steps to the door.

Stevens paused on the porch, his hand on the doorknob. Through the front window he could hear his daughter laughing with her friends in the kitchen. He could see his young son in the hallway, chasing his big German shepherd up the stairs. And he didn't need to look in the living room window to imagine his wife spread out on her favorite chair, brow furrowed as she worked through a mountain of paperwork, as pretty now as the day he'd married her.

This was the other part of his life. This was the part that didn't need the excitement, the adrenaline rush, the profiles in the *Star Tribune*. This was reality. This was what was important. Stevens paused at the front door, indulging the moment. Then he turned the doorknob and rejoined his family.

▌▌

Windermere knew two things about Allen Bryce Salazar within minutes of his arrival in the Criminal Investigative Division. First, she knew he was very angry. Then she knew he wasn't her guy.

She was back at her desk in the new FBI building in Brooklyn Center, northwest of Minneapolis, when Mathers brought him in from the airport. Heard him as soon as the elevator doors opened, listened to him swear a blue streak from the elevators to the interview room. Mathers set him up, and then came over to Windermere, a sardonic smile on his face.

"Mr. Salazar is very displeased," he said. "He's using foul language. Mentioned a lawsuit. Even threw a government-issue chair."

"I heard the commotion," said Windermere. "You couldn't calm him down?"

Mathers shrugged. "Cuffed him to the table. Took long enough." His smile grew. "Had to get Doughty in there to hold the guy down."

"Bet he loved that."

"Doughty? Or the guy?"

"Doughty," said Windermere. "Bet he'd cursed my name about seventy-five times before he got the poor bastard detained."

"I lost count." Mathers gestured down the hall. "Guy's ready for you, anyway."

Windermere thanked him and walked through CID toward the interview rooms. The office was long and low, carpet and cubicles, set up like an accounting firm, and she could see across the vast room to Bob Doughty's private office on the other side. The door was closed, thank God.

Windermere had partnered with Doughty on the Carter Tomlin

investigation. It hadn't been a particularly successful pairing, and though Windermere knew she wasn't exactly easy to get along with, she still figured the senior agent shouldered much of the blame. In the end, he'd filed a formal complaint and put in for reassignment, and in the months since, he'd said not word one to his former partner, work-related or otherwise.

If Doughty was half as good a cop as Stevens, we'd have gotten on fine, Windermere thought. *And since he isn't, good riddance.* She pushed Doughty from her mind as she approached the interview room. She could hear Salazar shouting through the heavy door, something thumping in there.

Windermere paused outside the door. She let Salazar have his little tantrum, and when he'd calmed down she peeked through the small window and had a look at the guy. Then she stepped back.

It wasn't her man.

The shooter had been slight, pale, almost sickly in appearance. Allen Bryce Salazar was none of those things. Windermere studied the man through the window again. He was a big guy, swarthy, a lot of muscle. He looked nothing like the man who'd driven off in that Chevy.

Windermere spun on her heel and crossed the office to Mathers's desk. "Not my guy, Derek," she said. "Someone screwed up."

Mathers looked up from his computer. "That's Salazar," he said. "Omaha picked him up the minute he got off that plane. ID checks out. That's your guy."

"Bullshit," said Windermere. "I *saw* the shooter. He was shorter than this guy. He was *whiter*. This isn't our guy."

Mathers shrugged. "That's Allen Bryce Salazar," he said. "What can I tell you?"

12

Salazar turned out to be a decent guy, after he'd calmed down a little.

Windermere walked into the interview room with a Coke and a Quarter Pounder with cheese. Sat down and slid the food across the table, told Salazar she'd uncuff him if he promised to be good. Told him she'd kick his ass if he tried to get cute. Salazar stared at her, baleful and suspicious. Windermere held his gaze until he looked away. "Fine," he said.

Windermere uncuffed him. Watched him scarf down the burger. Waited until she heard the rattle of ice in his Coke. Then she leaned forward. "Okay," she said. "So who are you?"

Salazar wiped his mouth with the back of his hand. "You know who I am," he said. "My name is Allen Bryce Salazar. I live at 82 Poplar Street in Council Bluffs, Iowa. Married, no kids." He looked down at his hands. "My wife's probably losing her shit right now."

"We'll get word to your wife that you're fine," Windermere told him. "If you're as clean as you say, you'll be home by tomorrow. So let's figure this out. What brought you to Saint Paul?"

"Trade show," said Salazar. "I sell fertilizer. Farm-grade."

"Fertilizer."

"My wife tells me I'm real good at peddling bullshit." He met her eyes. "It's a job. There was an agricultural trade fair all week, downtown at the RiverCentre. I came in Tuesday evening. Was supposed to get home tonight."

Windermere studied his face. The RiverCentre was within a block of Rice Park and the Saint Paul Hotel. A two-minute walk to the Landmark

Center. Except Salazar wasn't the man she'd seen climbing into the little gray Chevy. He wasn't the man she'd passed on the Landmark Center steps.

She fixed her eyes on him. "You come with a partner?"

Salazar frowned. "What?"

"Did you bring a friend? To the trade fair. You work with a partner, or what?"

"Just me," said Salazar. "It's a pretty small business. Mom-and-pop, I guess you'd call it. Just trying to get our foot in the door."

"Yeah," said Windermere. "Listen, here's the thing: A man was shot this afternoon at the Saint Paul Hotel. Somebody with a sniper rifle. You know where the hotel is? Like, a half a minute away from the RiverCentre. Literally across the street."

Salazar's eyes got wide. "Whoa," he said. "I didn't—"

"Hold up." Windermere held up her hands. "I chased the shooter," she said. "He got away in a little gray Chevy hatchback, a Liberty rental car. Rented from the airport by one Allen Bryce Salazar of Council Bluffs, Iowa. That's you."

"Bullshit." Salazar shoved his chair back and stood, his eyes wild. "That's bullshit, lady. I never rented that car."

Windermere held his gaze. "Liberty says you did."

"They're lying," he said. "They're fucking liars."

"Prove it."

Salazar stared at her, breathing heavy. "Prove it?" he said. "Okay, I will. I'm an Emerald Club member. *National Car Rental.* I rented a mid-size sedan on Tuesday. Upgraded for free to a Chrysler 300, white. Brought it back this afternoon just before my flight. What the hell would I want with some shitty hatchback?"

Windermere said nothing. She studied Salazar and sucked her teeth, thinking. A computer would straighten out Salazar's story. A quick call to National and she'd know if he was lying. He wasn't acting guilty, though.

He didn't look like he knew a damn thing about Chevy Aveos. And that meant this easy case was about to get hard.

If Salazar wasn't the guy—if he was one hundred percent clean—then who'd mixed him up in the game? More to the point, who was the kid in the little Chevy hatchback? Who was the killer, and where the hell did he go?

Windermere pushed back from the table and stood. Salazar watched her. "Where are you going?"

He didn't sound tough anymore. He sounded confused. Scared, even. Windermere shook her head. "Gotta call National," she said. "Corroborate your story." She looked at him. "I'd get comfortable. This might take a while."

13

The phone rang again on Monday morning.

It was nearly noon. Lind was sitting on his couch, upright, trying to keep his eyes open. He hadn't slept all night. He'd finished all the coffee. He was just slipping away, giving in, when the phone rang.

It jolted him awake.

He stood on unsteady legs and walked to the window and looked out over the city. It was still raining outside. It was still gray. The cars on the street were smeared brake lights against the wet glass.

The phone kept ringing. Lind tried to ignore it. He was awake now. He didn't need to answer the phone.

Except that wasn't right. If he didn't answer, the phone would stop ringing. Sooner or later, it would stop ringing for good. And then he would be alone with the visions, with nobody to help him. Nobody to make the visions go away.

Lind shivered. Felt the first wave of panic insinuate itself into his brain. It grew there, a pounding blackness, just behind his eyes. Quickly, Lind crossed from the window and picked up the phone.

"Hello," he said. "I'm ready."

TEN MINUTES LATER. Lind drove out of the parking garage and back through the city to the airport. He parked in the short-term lot and walked into the terminal to the Delta Airlines counters. He waited in the frequent-flier line, and when he reached the front, the girl at the counter smiled and waved him over. "Hi," she said. "On the road again?"

She was a pretty girl. She had big eyes and clear, pale skin, mahogany hair that fell just to her shoulders. There was a hint of mischief in her smile.

"Duluth." Lind slid his fake ID across the counter. "Richard O'Brien."

The girl smiled at Lind another moment. Then she blinked and shook her head a little, looked down at her computer, and started to type something. She stopped and looked up again.

"It's just I've seen you before." She looked away quickly, blushing. "You're always flying somewhere. What kind of business are you in?"

Lind shifted his weight and looked around the terminal. Felt the jackhammer panic inside his skull again. He squinted. Closed his eyes. Rubbed his temples. "Insurance," he lied. "That's what I do."

"I'm sorry." The girl's whole face was bright red now. "I just wanted to— I was just making conversation. I'm sorry."

She thrust a ticket into Lind's hands. Lind grabbed it. Forced a smile and then walked away quickly. He could feel her eyes following him as he hurried toward security.

14

tevens was at his desk at the BCA headquarters in Saint Paul when his phone started to ring. He was typing a report, hunt-and-peck style, a cold case he'd just closed on Friday. It seemed to be taking forever.

Distraction, he thought as the phone rattled beside him. *Thank God.* He reached for the handset.

"Stevens?"

Stevens sat up straight. "Carla."

"The one and only." Windermere paused. "Listen, I hate to take you away from whatever it is you BCA people do over there, but I need you in Brooklyn Center for a while."

Stevens frowned. Looked around the Investigations department. It was pretty quiet for a Monday. Not much going on. "What's up?"

"Long story," said Windermere. "Anyway, listen, I'll get you back to work in an hour or two, tops. Just come on in, would you?"

Stevens looked at the report on his desk, and then across the office to Tim Lesley's door. Lesley was the Special Agent in Charge of Investigations, and he'd be waiting on the report. Right now, though, Stevens figured he could use a break. "Sure," he said. "On my way."

"Good. And, Stevens?"

Stevens paused. "Yeah?"

"Bring lunch."

FORTY-FIVE MINUTES LATER. Stevens parked his Cherokee in front of the FBI's regional headquarters in Brooklyn Center. An imposing, five-story structure ringed with high fences and security checkpoints, the building was markedly more secure than the Bureau's old offices, housed as they were in a commercial skyscraper in downtown Minneapolis. The FBI had just moved in a month or so prior, and Stevens was halfway into the city before he realized his mistake.

Was a hell of a time finding the place anyway. Stevens missed his exit off I-94, had to retrace his route along surface roads, past a couple truck-stop motels and light industrial warehouses before he found the place. He parked, showed his badge to a couple security guards, navigated the metal detector, and rode the elevator up to Criminal Investigations and cut through the office to Windermere's cubicle. Set a paper bag of takeout Thai on her desk and grinned at her. "Brand-new building and they still can't get you a real office, huh?"

Windermere scowled. "Nope. I took down Arthur Pender and Carter Tomlin and I still can't get any privacy, Stevens."

"Wait a second," said Stevens. "*We* took down Pender and Tomlin. I think I helped a little."

"You got an office yet? I rest my case." Windermere eyed the bag. "What'd you bring me?"

"Pad Thai," said Stevens. "It's decent."

Windermere rolled her eyes. "It's Minnesota, Stevens."

"Better than Taco Bell. What's the story?"

"Yeah." Windermere unpacked the bag. Set a foil takeout plate on her desk and removed the cardboard top. Studied the contents for a moment, her face impassive. Then she glanced at him. "Pull up a chair."

Stevens pulled a chair over. Sat down and listened as Windermere explained the situation in between bites of pad Thai.

"So the rental car guy, Salazar," she said, chewing, "he's not the shooter. Omaha brought him in, flew him back here. He had a little tantrum in the interview room. Broke an FBI chair, but he never killed anyone."

"But he rented the car."

Windermere shook her head. "He didn't even. And he got pretty mad when I had the gall to suggest he would ever rent from Liberty. Apparently he's an Emerald Club member, whatever that means."

"National?"

"Rented a white Chrysler 300C," said Windermere. "Had it all week. Brought it back a half hour before our shooter returned his Chevy hatchback."

Stevens reached into the bag and pulled out a second foil container. Cashew chicken. "A half hour."

"A half hour, Stevens. Right about the time our shooter was giving me the cold shoulder in the parking lot."

"So what's Salazar's play? How does he fit?"

"He doesn't," she said. "He swears he's innocent. Right now, I have no reason to suspect otherwise."

"You account for his whereabouts on Saturday? Do a background check, all that? Look for any ties to Spenser Pyatt?"

Windermere pointed across the office to a young kid bent over a computer. "Mathers's on it," she said. "We're working this case. So far, we have nothing. Salazar spent the whole week selling manure at some trade show. Has witnesses putting him at the RiverCentre all Saturday morning. And then he was in transit at the time of the shooting."

"Guy's got a clean background." Stevens looked up to find Windermere's new partner standing beside him. Mathers, she'd called him. The kid was clean-cut and damned tall. He nodded at Stevens and then turned to Windermere. "No criminal record anywhere. No ties to Pyatt, at least not superficially. Maybe there's something in his background."

"Keep looking," said Windermere. "A Minnesota TV billionaire and a fertilizer salesman from Iowa. Who the hell knows?"

Mathers nodded again and walked back to his workstation. Stevens watched him go. "Your new partner?" he asked Windermere.

Windermere grinned at him.

"Where'd you find him, the Bureau day care?"

"He's a good kid," she said. "Kind of goofy, but he saves me the grunt work." Her smile faded. "Anyway, Stevens, this damn case is starting to give me a headache. I can't hold Salazar, and I'm not sure I want to."

"You think he's clean."

She nodded. "My instinct says yes."

"You check out the airport? Maybe they have something on tape."

"Just about to," she said. "Was just waiting on you."

Stevens stared at her. "That's why you called me in? To ride out to the airport?"

Windermere shook her head. "No," she said. "I need a statement. You witnessed the shooting, remember?" She grinned at him. "I just figured maybe I'd take your statement in the car."

15

Lind returned to Minneapolis on a Delta Airlines A319. It was sunny when the plane landed, early afternoon. Lind barely noticed. He walked off the plane and through the terminal to another gate, where he boarded a Delta regional jet for the quick flight northeast to Duluth.

He walked off the small plane when it touched down in Duluth and found the Liberty counter inside the terminal. Rented a blue Kia Rio and asked for a map of the city, which he studied in the driver's seat of the Kia outside the terminal. When he'd found his destination, he folded the map closed and drove east from the airport, toward Lake Superior and a quiet, tree-lined street in Congdon Park. It was a posh neighborhood north of the city, the houses large and set back from the road.

The house Lind was looking for was nearly hidden amid the trees that surrounded it. It wasn't nearly as large as many he'd passed; it looked old and dark, neglected. Lind drove past the house to the end of the block, parked the Kia around the corner, and waited until he was sure the street was deserted. Then he climbed out of the car and set out through the trees toward the house.

It was quiet in the forest. Very still. Lind's footsteps cracked twigs and rustled the underbrush. Above him, birds called to one another. A car passed in the distance, unseen. Lind kept walking.

He found the house and crouched in the brush, surveying the building across the vast lawn. There was a car in the driveway, a dented Mercedes, but the house looked empty. There were no signs of life—of potential threats—anywhere.

Lind waited until the birds stopped calling above him. Until the whole forest seemed to forget he was there. He knelt in the brush, and from his pocket removed a pair of black gloves, which he pulled over his hands before crossing the lawn, fast and low, to the house.

The back door was locked. Lind punched out a small window and the glass made a tinkling sound on the carpet. He opened the door from inside and slipped into the house and waited. Heard voices, tinny music: a television somewhere. He crept through the house, room to room.

The television was playing in the living room. There was a man watching from a worn couch. There was an empty plate beside him, a half-empty bottle. The man didn't hear Lind come into the room.

Lind crept behind the man, quickly, his shoes making whispers on the carpet. He reached down and took the man's neck in his hands. The man stiffened. He fought. Lind squeezed his neck tighter. The man thrashed on the worn couch, clawing at Lind's shirt. Lind let him fight.

The man was much older than Lind. He was weaker. He fought, and then he stopped fighting, and when he went still, Lind eased him back down to the couch.

The man's eyes were wide open and sightless, his mouth wrenched in a last gasp for air. He'd kicked at the table, knocked over the bottle. Its contents had spilled onto the carpet.

Lind waited until he was sure the man was dead. Then he turned and retraced his steps through the house and out onto the lawn. He hurried back through the forest to the little blue Kia, climbed in, and turned the key. Then he stopped. Across the street, in front of a bungalow, a little boy chased a large rubber ball toward the road. The boy caught up to the ball, picked it up. Then he noticed Lind.

Remove yourself from the scene without being detected. Don't attract undue attention. Secondary objective.

The boy studied Lind intently, and Lind held the boy's gaze, wondering if he'd have to kill him. Then the boy looked down at the ball. Turned and threw it back toward the bungalow and gave chase, laughing, on stubby legs. Lind watched the boy play until he was sure the kid had forgotten him. Then, slowly, he pulled away from the house.

He drove back to the airport, stopping along the way at a gas station, where he stuffed the gloves and his sweater into a garbage bin, just as he'd been taught. Then he drove the Kia back to the Liberty rental lot, returned the keys to the woman at the counter, and walked into the terminal and through the security checkpoint to the lounge, where he waited to board the next flight to Minneapolis.

16

Parkerson was going over last month's reports with his secretary when he felt his burner phone start to ring. He'd pulled it from his pocket, a cheap pay-as-you-go flip phone, before he realized what he was doing.

Jamie frowned from the door. "Thought you had a BlackBerry."

"In the shop," he lied. Flashed the burner phone, rueful. "This is the piece of shit they gave me as a loaner."

"Phone companies." Jamie shook her head. "The worst. I'll leave you alone." She ducked out of the room, closing the door behind her. Parkerson waited until he heard the lock engage.

Shit, he thought. *That was close.* He brought the phone to his ear. "Yeah."

There was a pause. Parkerson could hear breathing. Then: "I've completed the assignment."

Done. Parkerson felt his whole body relax. He stared at his computer and exhaled, long and slow. "Good."

There was no answer.

"You're on your way home?"

Another pause. "I'm in transit."

"Good," Parkerson said. "Thanks for calling. We'll be in touch soon."

"You're welcome." Nothing else. The call disconnected. Parkerson put the phone down and leaned back in his chair. Swiveled around until he was staring out his vast picture window at the forest beyond, feeling the tension dissipate.

Parkerson replayed the Saturday phone call in his head and wondered again if the job had been worth the risk. The client had sounded desperate, unhinged. Parkerson hadn't liked the way his voice had wavered. He'd sounded irrational, barely clinging to sanity. He'd sounded like he was on the verge of making a mess.

Parkerson hated messes. He dealt with numbers, with absolutes. Coordinates. Code. Dollars, in and out. He preferred the cleanliness that numbers offered. The perfection. One or two. Yes or no. Paid or unpaid.

Humanity, with its tendency toward imperfection, made him uncomfortable. The client had purchased a kill. Parkerson had completed the contract. The job should have been over. Finished. No headaches. No messes.

The client, though, was unable to see the contract with Parkerson's clarity, though he'd shown an appealing lack of remorse when he'd ordered the kill. Parkerson had no time to deal with remorse, or morality, or any other human imperfection. This was numbers. Money, in and out. A contract fulfilled.

It had personally cost Parkerson to terminate the client. He'd had to allocate his own capital to fly the asset to Duluth, rent the car, finance the kill. Not an insignificant cost, but in the end, a necessary investment. Better to pay up front for security than to risk the program on one man's crippling weakness. Besides, Parkerson thought with a smile, the client had already paid his fee. The money had been transferred. The numbers made sense.

Parkerson heard his door open behind him. He turned in his chair and saw Jamie peering in at him. "Everything okay?" she asked him.

Parkerson smiled at her, wide, genuine. "Everything's fine." He winked at her. "Just some kind of crank."

17

"Well, god damn it." Windermere threw up her hands. "That was useless."

She'd just emerged from the airport police department at Minneapolis–Saint Paul International. Stevens and Mathers waited for her in the crowded terminal building. Even from twenty feet away, Stevens could tell his former partner was frustrated. "Dead end?"

Windermere snorted. "They have security tapes for the whole building. Rental car offices to the departure gates."

"Yeah, and?"

"And we can't see them. It's a TSA situation, they said. And the TSA doesn't want to play nice."

Mathers shook his head. "I don't get it."

"We could have full coverage of this guy walking into the airport, dropping off his rental car, and boarding a plane. We could figure out where he landed and work the tapes from his arrival airport as well. Hell, we might get lucky and get another license plate number, or a positive ID. But unless I come correct with TSA approval from on high, boys, we're not seeing those tapes."

Stevens scratched his head. "So how do we get TSA approval?"

Windermere sighed. "I don't know, Stevens," she said. "Maybe if we write our congressman."

NOBODY AT THE LIBERTY RENTAL DESK proved to be of any help, either. "Saturday, right?" the manager said. "Busy day. Heck, they're all busy. Some brown-haired kid isn't going to make an impression."

"The Chevy Aveo." Windermere read off the license plate. "Who rented it?"

The manager frowned. "Thought you knew this already."

"Humor me, Bob."

The manager typed something into his computer. Read it. "Here it is," he said. "Allen Bryce Salazar. Council Bluffs, Iowa."

Windermere swapped glances with Stevens. "You ever deal with this guy before? He rent from you guys in the past?"

The manager squinted. "Doesn't look like it."

"What about credit card information?"

The manager squinted some more. Leaned down and peered at his screen. "Looks like a corporate card." He looked up at Windermere. "Triple A Industries. That sound familiar?"

Mathers shook his head. "Salazar calls his company Wrong End Incorporated. I've never heard of Triple A before."

Windermere looked at Mathers. Then she looked at Stevens. Stevens shrugged. "Triple A Industries," she said finally. "I guess it'll have to do."

18

It was dark when Lind landed in Minneapolis. He walked off the plane and through the terminal to the Delta lounge, where he ate three packets of cheese and crackers before he boarded his flight back to Philadelphia.

He sat on board the big Delta airliner and stared at the seat back in front of him, trying to keep from thinking about Showtime and Hang Ten and that big Army C-17 as the plane taxied and took off into the night. Every flight was the same. Every stomach-lurching launch down the runway and every turbulent shuck and jive. If he closed his eyes, he'd be back on that transport plane with the rest of the lucky ones.

There was an older woman in the aisle seat beside him. Lind could feel her eyes on him. He stared at the seat back and tried to ignore her. She kept staring. "Business or pleasure?" she said at last.

Lind exhaled, long, and turned slowly to face her. She was a white-haired woman, mid-sixties or so. She smiled at him, friendly. Lind tried to calm the racing thoughts in his head. Tried to maintain some illusion of normalcy.

"I'm visiting my son," the woman said. "He's a doctor, or he will be. He just finished his residency."

Lind kept the smile pasted to his face. He nodded politely. He'd been trained for situations like this. *Be civil,* the man had told him. *Don't volunteer information. Extricate yourself from the conversation as quickly as you can.*

Lind looked around the airplane. Every seat was full. The canned air seemed suffocating, the atmosphere unbearable. He wished he were back at his apartment. He wished the man was there to help him.

"He's a surgeon, my son," the woman continued. "A general surgeon, but a surgeon nonetheless." She looked at him. "I bet he's probably about your age."

Lind nodded again. He was gripping the armrests tight, so tight he could have wrenched them loose if he'd tried. "My name is Richard O'Brien," he said at last.

"Glenda." The woman held out her hand. "Glenda Regis."

Lind looked at the woman's hand. He unpeeled his own hand from the armrest and gripped hers. The woman winced a little, but her smile stayed fixed on him. "Nervous flier?"

Lind nodded.

"Why don't you try sleeping? The time always goes quicker when you're asleep."

Lind let go of the woman's hand and turned to face the seat back in front of him. He could feel her eyes on him, but he didn't look at her. He stared at the seat back and tried to relax. "It doesn't work that way," he said. "Not for me."

19

"Triple A Industries," Mathers told Windermere, "is a joke."

They were back in the office, having dropped Stevens at his Cherokee and returned to CID to try and hammer out the shooter's credit card situation. Windermere left Mathers at his computer while she focused on grilling Salazar, who continued to claim innocence.

"I sell fertilizer," he told her, shadows under his eyes and two days' stubble on his cheeks. "I never heard of this guy Pyatt before in my life, I told you."

"Triple A Industries," said Windermere.

Salazar stared back at her, blank-faced. "Yeah?"

"What do you know about it?"

Salazar sighed and sat back, shaking his head. "I know nothing," he said. "What do you want me to say? I never heard of it in my life."

Windermere studied his face for a long time. He wasn't lying, she decided. There was no way she could prove it, but she was pretty damned sure at this point that Allen Bryce Salazar had nothing to do with Spenser Pyatt's shooting. Somehow, though, somebody had thrown him into the mix.

Salazar leaned forward and ran his hands through his hair. "My wife," he said. "I just want to go home."

"I know," Windermere told him. "I'm working on it."

She left the big man in the interview room and walked back out into CID proper. By now it was evening, and the office had mostly cleared out; only Mathers and a few diehards remained at their cubicles. The whole place was quiet.

Mathers looked up from his computer as Windermere approached. "Nothing," he said. "Triple A Industries is a joke."

Windermere pulled up a chair. "Explain."

Mathers gestured to his screen. "I traced the company back. It's nothing but a P.O. box in Richmond, Virginia. The company itself is a wholly owned subsidiary of a numbered offshore corporation based in the Cayman Islands."

"So who owns the numbered company?" said Windermere. "We follow the trail long enough, there's bound to be a person at the end of the line."

"Yeah," said Mathers, "except there's no following any further." He gestured at his screen again. This time, Windermere turned to look.

The screen was blue. There was a government seal in the background, a log-in prompt center stage. Windermere blinked. "I don't get it," she said.

"Department of Defense," said Mathers. "Access restricted."

"You're saying you traced Triple A to this numbered company, and when you tried to go deeper, the Defense Department stonewalled you?" Windermere stared at the screen. "How does that make any sense?"

Mathers shrugged. "Either the government's got a stake in Triple A, or someone inside doesn't want us to look further. Either way, this is some conspiracy-level shit."

"Essentially, the Defense Department rented our shooter a car. That's what you're saying."

Mathers held up his hands. "I don't know," he said. "That's kinda what it looks like."

"Christ." Windermere looked around the office, feeling her frustration start to mount. "Nothing's ever simple in this job, is it?"

20

Stevens wasn't at BCA headquarters longer than fifteen minutes Tuesday morning before Tim Lesley summoned him into his office.

"Kirk." The SAC motioned across his desk to a chair. "Come on in and sit down."

Stevens sat, feeling a sort of familiar dread as he did. A former homicide cop, Tim Lesley was lean and tough as a piece of old jerky, and his glare could silence even the hardest state cop.

"The Springfield report," Stevens said. "I'll have it for you first thing. Just polishing her off this morning."

Lesley held up his hand. Stared at Stevens over thin, wire-rimmed glasses. "Heard you paid the FBI a visit yesterday. Saw your friend Windermere."

Stevens nodded. "Sir. She needed to take a formal statement as regards the Spenser Pyatt shooting. The FBI's taken over the case."

Lesley nodded. "You give it to her?"

"Yes, sir."

Lesley tented his fingers. Didn't say anything. Stevens waited. The SAC's disdain for his federal counterparts was well documented, and he'd allowed Stevens to join Windermere on that first kidnapping case only grudgingly. He'd been even less thrilled with Stevens's involvement in the Carter Tomlin fiasco, and now Stevens chose his words carefully, knowing that Windermere's name was tantamount to blasphemy in Tim Lesley's office.

"Sir, I'm not looking to get involved in Agent Windermere's case," Stevens said finally. "As far as I'm concerned, I've played my part. The FBI can solve their own case this time around."

Lesley pursed his lips. Showed the hint of a smile. "Funny you should say that, Agent Stevens."

"Sir?"

"I happen to be friends with Spenser Pyatt's son," Lesley said. "Mickey Pyatt. Old classmate. He called me just now."

Stevens frowned. "Sure."

Lesley gave it a beat. "There was a murder yesterday," he said finally, "in Duluth. A cousin of Spenser's, Elias Cody, was found strangled to death in his home."

Now Stevens sat forward, almost despite himself. "Strangled," he said. "A home invasion?"

"No sign of a robbery," said Lesley. "Nothing else disturbed. The killer gained entry by breaking a window and unlocking the back door. Local homicide figures he walked in, killed Cody, and walked out again."

"Jesus. Motive?"

Lesley shook his head. "Mickey Pyatt was, understandably, quite concerned. Two relatives murdered in the span of three days."

"He thinks someone's targeting his family."

"He's scared," said Lesley. "He asked me for help. That's where you come in." Lesley studied Stevens across his vast desk. "This Cody thing, it's probably a coincidence. I want you to check it out anyway, see what you make of it. Decide if the Pyatts are in any real danger. Then report back."

"Sure," said Stevens. "Yes, sir."

Lesley paused again. "You're my top agent," he said. "That's half of why I'm giving you this assignment. I'm sure you can figure out the rest."

Stevens looked at his boss. "Windermere."

"Exactly. You're close with the Feds, Stevens. This is their investigation, but I want you beside them, at least until you can determine that the Pyatts are safe." Lesley gave Stevens the hint of another smile. "I don't imagine that will pose any problems for you."

Stevens grinned back. "No, sir," he said. "I don't reckon it will."

"Good." Lesley stood. "Then get moving. You're on the next flight to Duluth."

21

Lind woke with screams echoing in his ears. He sat up on the couch. It was morning. Gray, gloomy light filtered in through the windows. The rain drizzled down outside. His heart pounded.

He'd been dreaming again. Despite his best efforts, he'd fallen asleep. The visions had returned. They always did.

Lind pushed himself off the couch. Stood and, rubbing his face, walked to the window. Then he turned away. The view was the same. It was always the same.

He stood in the center of the room and waited for his heart to slow down. Tried not to replay the visions he'd seen in his dreams. Even when he was awake, they were inescapable. He remembered.

He remembered Showtime screaming. Hang Ten's limp body. He remembered, also, the man from the house in Duluth, struggling in his grasp. Dying in his hands.

Lind blinked. Looked across the apartment, seeing nothing. Feeling a coldness like ice water start to seep through his body.

He'd dreamed of the man in Duluth. He'd seen the man's liquor bottle topple just as clearly as he'd seen Mini-Me burning inside the Humvee. Heard the man gasping for breath, choking, the same as he'd heard Showtime's crazy laughter. It wasn't just the man in Duluth, either. He'd dreamed of them all.

The white-haired man in Saint Paul, just a crumpled newspaper picture and a speck in the sniper scope. The woman in Manhattan, the adulteress and her sexy young fling. The movie executive in Los Angeles, that Mulholland Drive mansion, the roar of the gun. Lind remembered. He'd dreamed of them all.

Above all, he'd dreamed of the first. His first target. It was the target's desperate screams that had rung in his ears as he jolted awake. It was those screams he could hear even now.

Lind closed his eyes. Shook his head. Ran his hands through his hair and tore at his face. He sank down to the floor and gave in to the visions again.

That face, that smiling face. The man who had taken him from the doctor's office out to that gray sedan, who had driven him away into blackness. That man. That face. He was smiling. He was holding a gun.

A revolver.

He pressed it into Lind's palm. Wrapped his fingers around it, firm. He was speaking to Lind, soft and incessant. He was promising things.

He was promising safety, relief. His promises were a mantra. He never stopped smiling.

The man waited until Lind gripped the gun. Then he stepped back. He took Lind by the shoulders and turned him around. Gentle, like a father. Lind let himself turn. Lind gripped the gun. He let the smiling man turn him to face the target.

The target.

The target was a young man, about the same age as Lind. His head was shaved close. There was a scar on his face, a thin line down his cheek. He was chained to a bloody concrete wall.

The smiling man's voice was like syrup in Lind's ear. He kept speaking, kept promising wonderful things. Lind couldn't escape it. Couldn't fight it. He felt himself giving in. Felt himself start to obey the smiling man.

He felt himself raising the gun.

The young man's eyes went wide. He struggled against the chains, shouting at Lind, pleading. Lind blinked. Shook his head. Couldn't escape the voice. The voice promised relief. The voice told him to pull the trigger. He did.

The young man screamed. He kept screaming. He screamed every night until Lind jolted awake.

22

The plane to Duluth was tiny, a cramped regional jet that rattled and shuddered its way slowly north. Stevens folded himself into a window seat and gripped the armrests tight, feeling every turbulent gust like a palm tree in a hurricane, praying for a safe landing.

There was a plainclothes city cop waiting for Stevens inside the terminal in Duluth. She grinned wide when she saw him. "Kirk Stevens," she said. "Back from the big city at last."

Stevens stopped and stared. "McNaughton," he said. "Holy shit."

The cop laughed and held out her hand. Stevens shook it, studying her face as he did. It had been nearly twenty years since he'd shared a shift with Donna McNaughton in West Duluth, and though she'd aged somewhat in her path up the ranks, Stevens still remembered the Cheshire cat grin—and the finger-busting grip. He took his hand back and wrung it gingerly as he followed his old colleague out to an unmarked Crown Vic.

"So what gives?" he asked her. "They kick you out of your squad car?"

McNaughton shot him the finger. "Violent crimes," she said, grinning back at him. "Downtown, baby. Going on ten years."

"No kidding?" said Stevens. "I mean, congratulations."

"Nothing like your life," McNaughton said as she slid behind the steering wheel. "I mean, with those FBI cases and all. But it works. Met a girl, settled down." She shrugged. "It's a life."

"More than a life," Stevens said. "You've done well for yourself."

McNaughton waved him away. "Shut up," she said. "Anyway, you're back. And we're working together again for a while."

Stevens nodded. "Elias Cody."

"The hermit." McNaughton glanced at him as she drove away from the terminal. "Guy had rich parents. Kind of coasted through life. Fell off the map about twenty years back. More of a neighborhood bogeyman than anything else."

Stevens blinked. "I remember," he said. "Family owned a grain elevator or something. He never left his house."

"Definitely a weirdo. You guys think his killer's the same guy who did Spenser Pyatt?"

Stevens gazed out the window as Duluth came into view. Felt his nerves finally starting to calm. "Don't know," he said. "Guess I'll try to find out."

HAD STEVENS APPROACHED Elias Cody's home at night, he might have been forgiven for suspecting it was haunted. The place was your classic scary-movie locale: a dreary, run-down old relic on a lonely side street, cut off from the neighbors and hidden from the road by a thick, gloomy forest. Anytime after dark and the place would have been spooky. As it was, it simply looked sad.

McNaughton parked the Crown Vic at the foot of the driveway. "Forensics came and went," she said. "Body's gone, but I can show you pictures."

"Sure," Stevens said. "Who called it in?"

"Housekeeper. Said she came by weekly to bring groceries and tidy the place. Probably the only human contact our man had."

They climbed out of the sedan and walked up the long driveway. There was a beat-up brown Mercedes parked by the house. "Cody's," said McNaughton.

"Seen better days."

"Be surprised if she still runs at all." The cop dug a key from her pocket and unlocked the front door. Stevens followed her inside the dark house.

"So here's the place." McNaughton led Stevens through a dismal front foyer and into the back of the house. "Guy broke a window and unlocked the back door. Found his way to the living room, where Cody was watching TV."

Stevens followed his colleague through the house to a living room, where a cracked leather couch faced a dusty TV. There was a table and an empty plate and a spilled bottle of whiskey.

"Snuck up behind him, we figure," said McNaughton. "Strangled him from behind. Cody kicked over the whiskey before he kicked the bucket."

Stevens looked around the room. "Forensics find anything?"

"Still early, but the victim had fabric in his fingernails. Like he was clawing at our killer's shirt. Maybe we get lucky and we find some skin in there, too."

"Sure," Stevens nodded. "Anything else?"

"Our killer wore gloves," McNaughton said. "There's some dirt by the back door, but not enough for a tread pattern. A couple leaves and some pine needles, like he came through the forest."

"Witnesses?"

"Not that we know of."

Stevens nodded again. "Huh," he said. He surveyed the living room a little longer, and then walked back out to the hall. "This guy have any enemies?"

"No enemies. No friends, either. Nobody to care whether he lived or died."

"He had money, though."

McNaughton shook her head. "Not really. Sold the grain elevator around the time you skipped town. Lived off the proceeds, but all indications are they're pretty much gone."

"And he wasn't robbed." Stevens wandered into a dining room. "You guys are pretty sure about that."

McNaughton nodded. "Housekeeper said nothing's disturbed."

"She have an alibi?"

"She's about four foot eleven, but, yeah. She cleans office buildings, too. Was downtown all day."

Stevens circled the dining room table. The room looked like it hadn't seen a meal in months. A window looked out onto the front lawn. There were pictures hung around the walls. Stevens looked at them. "Who's this?"

McNaughton came over. "My eyes," she said, squinting. "Getting old sucks. That's Spenser Pyatt. Must be fifty years ago, easy."

"Yeah," said Stevens. "And the woman?"

McNaughton grinned at him. "You're the big BCA guy. Figure it out."

Stevens studied the picture, frowning. The woman with Pyatt was a pretty blonde, young and vibrant. She stood close to the billionaire, both of them smiling, on some lake somewhere. She was in other pictures, too. Not all of them featured Pyatt. In many of them, the woman was alone.

She'd aged gracefully. The pictures were arranged in chronological order. At the end, another picture with Pyatt. She was much older now; both of them were. Her hair was shorter, and white, and her face was lined with age. There were still signs, though, of the beauty she'd been.

Suddenly, Stevens recognized her. "That's Paige Pyatt. Spenser's wife."

McNaughton nodded. "Exactly," she said. "So why is she here?"

"Had a crush on her, I guess. Kind of weird."

McNaughton stepped back from the wall. "Everything about Cody was weird, Kirk," she said. "You're just clueing in?"

23

Stevens walked through the house. "Humor me," he told McNaughton. "I want to figure this stuff out for myself."

McNaughton rolled her eyes, but she followed, and an hour or so later, Stevens was forced to admit his former colleague was right: there was no sign, anywhere, that Elias Cody had been robbed.

There were, however, more pictures of Paige Pyatt, and not all of them so neatly framed. Many of them were torn from magazines or newspapers. They lay in a stack beside Cody's bed, and amid vast reams of paper strewn across his office. Stevens examined the pictures and felt something start to gnaw at the back of his mind. Tim Lesley's words echoed in his ears, and he thought about Mickey Pyatt and his fear that his family was in danger.

Maybe not the whole clan, Stevens thought, studying a picture of Paige Pyatt torn from the *Star Tribune, but at least one family member was in deeper than expected.*

He walked through the rest of the house and out the back door, and stood in the sunlight and surveyed the yard. The forest seemed to creep nearly to the house, walling in the property and isolating it almost completely. Birds chirped and sang high in the trees, and a few early-bird bugs motored past, but otherwise, the whole place was silent.

Stevens turned to McNaughton. "What's through there?" he asked her. "How far back does it go?"

McNaughton shrugged. "Not as far as you'd think. There's a house directly behind this one about a hundred yards. A road about fifty yards to the right."

Stevens looked around. "Nobody saw the killer come in," he said. "No mysterious cars parked in the driveway?"

"Just the Benz."

"And the shooter left dirt and leaves by the back door, huh?" Stevens stepped off the porch and crossed the yard to the forest. There was underbrush, but the terrain was passable, and Stevens pushed his way into the woods as, behind him, McNaughton struggled to keep up.

"Christ," she said, between breaths. "Forgot you were the outdoorsy type."

They walked through the forest until they reached the road. It was a quiet side road, no curb. Stevens hopped across a slight ditch and stood on the crumbled pavement, looking around.

There were houses nearby, on the opposite side of the street. Older bungalows, not as big as Cody's. The trees weren't as thick. Stevens walked the shoulder until he found what he was looking for. It had rained recently, and the grass was still damp. There was an imprint of two tires in the mud.

Directly across the street, a child played with a ball on a grassy front lawn. He was a little boy, maybe six. Stevens crossed the street toward him.

"Hi there," he called. The boy froze. Looked at him once and then booked it around the house. Stevens walked to the front door and knocked. A minute or two later, the door swung open and a teenage girl peered out at him, a baby in her arms. Stevens showed her his badge. "Hi," he said. "BCA. Looking into what happened across the way. I wondered if you might have seen anything."

The girl shook her head. "I didn't."

"You were here yesterday?"

She nodded.

"Any chance the little guy was playing outside?"

The girl thought about it. "Yeah, actually, he was. You want to talk to him?"

She disappeared into the house before Stevens could answer. Came back a couple minutes later with the little boy in tow. Stevens hunched down at eye level, introduced himself. The kid hid behind his babysitter's legs and peered out at him.

"You see anything yesterday, guy?" Stevens asked him. "A car, maybe? Somebody walking in the forest?"

The kid stared at Stevens, his face solemn. Then he nodded. Stevens nodded back. "What did you see?"

"A man went into the forest," the boy said. "Then he came back and went away in his car."

Bingo. "What—" Stevens paused. "What color was the car?"

"Blue," said the boy. "It was a blue car."

"Big car? Little?"

"Little."

"What about the man? Was he young or old?"

The kid turned away and buried his face in his babysitter's jeans. "Okay," said Stevens. "Did he have light skin or dark?"

The little boy didn't answer. He twisted away and hid his face. His babysitter clucked her tongue. "He gets anxious," she said. "He doesn't like strangers."

Stevens stood. "That's okay," he said. He handed the girl a business card. "Tell the parents I stopped by. Duluth PD might need a statement."

The girl took the card. "Sure."

"Sure," said Stevens. "Okay." He told the girl good-bye and walked back to the road, where McNaughton stood on the shoulder, waiting. The cop raised an eyebrow as he approached.

"Anything?"

"Got a guy coming out of the forest," said Stevens.

"Nice," said McNaughton. "What else?"

Stevens looked up and down the empty road. "Got a car," he said. "Got a little blue car."

24

Parkerson finished work for the day and stood up from his desk. He walked around to his door and peered out. The office was nearly empty; it was a quarter past six. Almost everyone had gone home.

Jamie was pulling her coat on by her desk. She smiled at Parkerson. "Need anything before I go, Mr. P?"

Parkerson let his eyes wander over her body for a moment. Admired her smile, her long, coltish legs. "I'm fine," he said, shaking his head. "Get out of here already."

Jamie winked and tossed him a little wave. Then she turned to go. Parkerson watched her until she'd disappeared down the hallway. Then he ducked back into his office.

He sat down again in front of his computer. Shut down all of his work windows and opened the VPN he'd created, a virtual private network that would hide his activities from the office servers. He turned on a program he'd devised to cloak his IP address, thus preventing any prying eyes out in cyberspace from figuring out his location. Then, satisfied, he logged into the database.

There had been some activity since Saturday's job. Three new applications, all of them interesting in one way or another, each of them potentially lucrative. One was time-sensitive—a week on the outside. The other two could percolate.

Three new jobs. And no sign of any slowdown. The program was a success, just as Parkerson had always known it would be.

It had been six or seven years now since he'd dreamt up the scheme. Since he'd first recognized the profit potential in murder. The country was at war, and the economy was thriving. Death, Parkerson realized, was a commodity like anything else. There would always be a market. The trick was to exploit it.

Murder for hire. The connotations were ugly. Some shady back-alley thug with a pistol and a duffel bag filled with dirty money. Some sad sack killing his wife for the insurance payoff. Sleaze. Desperation. And, above all, incredible risk.

These days, though, a man could do anything from ordering pizza to finding a girlfriend online. Why not make killing just as simple? Quick and easy. Mitigate the risk. Murder with the click of a mouse.

Parkerson devised a business model. An online database, efficient and anonymous. He'd farm out the killing. Keep his own hands clean. Let someone else do the risky stuff while he counted his money in the background.

He'd searched for months for suitable assets. Common criminals wouldn't do; they'd get greedy, or scared. They'd make mistakes, freak out at the first complication. Too imperfect. Too *human*. Parkerson needed better.

He needed drones: cold, clinical, and totally malleable, capable of carrying out instructions quickly and self-sufficiently without ever compromising the program at large. What he needed were trained killing machines.

He found them in steady supply. Two wars were raging. Young men and women were returning from the combat zones by the planeload, many of them psychologically scarred and extremely vulnerable.

It had taken some time, but he'd perfected the formula. Young veterans, loners, traumatized by the war. He found them at veterans' centers and army hospitals and reeducated them. It was a messy procedure, fraught with risk. Some assets didn't take to the training, and Parkerson had realized very quickly that though he'd hoped to run the program without ever having to actually kill anyone himself, the assets' seemingly boundless capacity for failure meant he was going to have to get his hands dirty, and often.

The first candidate had hanged himself within hours of meeting Parkerson. The second had possessed a frustrating immunity to the reeducation process, and an equally frustrating tendency toward attempts at escape. Parkerson had rewarded both men with unmarked graves, and in those early, messy months he'd buried defective asset after defective asset, all of them either too fucked up in the head or not quite fucked up enough for the job.

Little by little, though, Parkerson had learned how to choose the right candidates. Mastered the training regimen. Slowly but surely, the attrition level dwindled. And, just as surely, the program began to thrive.

Still, even the good assets came with expiry dates, no matter how good they were. This current kid, Lind, was on his fifth kill, geriatric in asset years, and Parkerson knew it was almost time to start looking for a replacement. In the meantime, though . . .

Parkerson clicked on the first application, the time-sensitive client, and set about confirming the kill.

25

Stevens played a hunch and tried the Liberty counter first. It paid off. The clerk was a middle-aged woman. She smiled at Stevens, wide and friendly, as he approached the counter. Her smile faded somewhat when he showed her his badge. "Officer," she said. "Geez. What can I do for you?"

"I'm hoping you can find me a car," Stevens told her. "A little blue car. Returned yesterday."

The woman frowned. "Make and model?"

"Afraid not," Stevens said. "Would have been rented sometime between Saturday and Monday morning. Probably to a young guy, brown hair, medium build."

The woman punched something into her computer. Then she stopped. "Wait a second," she said. "The skinny kid, right? Really pale, rented a Kia?"

Stevens shrugged. "You tell me."

She nodded. "Has to be. This guy flew in yesterday afternoon. Rented a little Kia, blue, like you said. Dropped it back a couple hours later and flew out again."

Stevens couldn't help grinning. "Couple hours, you said?"

"Three hours, at the most. He was twenty-five, maybe. Nice guy, I guess. Didn't seem to want to say much, though. And his eyes." She looked at Stevens. "There was something spooky about him, I remember it now. Like he was looking through me, you know?"

"That's our guy. You have his reservation on file?"

"Yes, sir." The woman typed something else into her computer. Then she frowned. "That's strange," she said. "I could have sworn *this* guy rented a minivan."

Stevens peered over her shoulder. "But he didn't."

"Not according to the file, he didn't." She squinted at the screen. "Whatever. In any case, his name's Alex Kent. Lives in Chicago."

Alex Kent, Chicago. Allen Bryce Salazar, Council Bluffs. Another alias, maybe. Windermere would want it, regardless. "You mind printing that out for me?" Stevens said.

"Not at all." The clerk pressed a button and her printer fired up beside her. She stared at her computer for a second. Then she looked at Stevens. "What's this about, anyway?"

Stevens met her eyes. "Murder," he said. "A man was killed yesterday. We think this kid here's the perpetrator."

The woman gasped. "My Lord."

"You said it." Stevens took the printout. "Anyway, much obliged. You figure this Kent guy flew home to Chicago?"

"Chicago?" The woman frowned again. "No, that's the other thing. I snuck a glance at his itinerary when he dropped off the car. I'm quite certain the young man was headed back to Minneapolis."

26

The Criminal Investigative Division was all but empty. Windermere sat in her cubicle, where she'd sat for most of the day, staring at her computer screen and trying to figure out a way around the Department of Defense's involvement in Triple A Industries.

As Windermere had told Stevens the day Spenser Pyatt was murdered, she wasn't much of a motive person. Where Stevens found endless fascination in exploring the reasons why a criminal committed his particular crimes, Windermere had long ago decided she couldn't care less, as long as the right person was arrested.

Now, though, with the question of who at an impasse, Windermere found herself circling back to the why. Spenser Pyatt had been murdered, shot by an anonymous sniper. The sniper had disappeared and left a maze of disjointed clues behind him. So maybe it was time to focus on why Spenser Pyatt had died. Who stood to gain from his death?

The elevator doors dinged across the office. Windermere ignored them. Mathers, probably, returning with dinner. Windermere's stomach growled its anticipation. She ignored it, too.

Spenser Pyatt had controlled a media empire. He'd been a very rich man. It was natural to suspect that his wealth had played a role in his demise. From what Windermere and Mathers could figure, though, the guy was crystal clean: in fifty years of business, he'd never once been linked to any untoward activity, illegal or otherwise, and his will had remained unchanged for over a decade. Pyatt's wife and children would divide up his empire; there were no unusual life insurance policies or spurned lovers looking for payouts. By any account, Spenser Pyatt had been a remarkably simple man, and scrupulously honest to boot.

A shadow loomed above Windermere, blocking her light. "You bring the peanut sauce?" Windermere said.

"Must have forgotten it." A new voice. Not Mathers's. Windermere looked up and saw Kirk Stevens standing above her. He flashed her a grin. "Mind if I sit?"

Windermere felt her breath catch, involuntarily. Hated herself for it. Hated the fact that a married, middle-aged cop could get her off her game. She blinked and shook her head. "Be my guest," she said, pulling a chair over. "You get lost or something? What are you doing all the way out here, Stevens?"

Stevens dropped a piece of paper on her desk. Then he sat and waited. Windermere tried to stare him down before curiosity got the better of her. She picked up the paper and read it. "I don't get it."

It was a printout from a Liberty rental agency in Duluth. The airport, it looked like. Some guy from Chicago had rented a Kia for a couple hours yesterday. Alex Kent. Windermere scanned the page. Found the payment information and stopped cold. "Triple A Industries," she said. "Holy shit."

Stevens frowned. "Wait, what?"

"Who is this guy, Stevens?" she said. "What's his story? How'd you find him?"

"Triple A Industries," he said. "What does that mean?"

Windermere exhaled, impatient. "This guy paid with a corporate credit card registered to Triple A Industries. So did Allen Salazar, though he swears he's never heard of the company. And Triple A's in some shady business. So what gives? How did *you* get in on this?"

Stevens leaned forward, his brow furrowed. "I don't know about Triple A," he said, "but that guy Kent murdered Spenser Pyatt's cousin up in Duluth yesterday."

"What?" Windermere stared at him. "You kidding me, Stevens?"

"Or maybe he didn't," Stevens said. "Probably he's just like Salazar, a scapegoat. Either way, Pyatt's cousin was murdered. Strangled to death, and it looks like the same killer as Pyatt. And that's not even the weird part."

Windermere pushed back her chair. "Hold up," she said. "Back to the beginning. You working this case?"

"My SAC's good friends with Pyatt's son, Mickey," Stevens told her. "Mickey called in a favor. SAC sent me to Duluth to look things over, see if the family's in any danger."

Windermere raised an eyebrow. "And?"

"And I don't know, Carla. None of this makes sense." He shook his head. "But I found out a couple of things. First off, Elias Cody—Pyatt's cousin—had a major crush on Pyatt's wife. Like, obsession."

"Okay," said Windermere, "and the second?"

"The second." Stevens grinned. "After killing Cody, our murderer flew back to Minneapolis."

27

I don't get it," said Mathers. "Does this mean you guys are partners again?"

The junior agent had returned with dinner a few minutes after Stevens's arrival and found the BCA agent in deep conversation with Windermere. Now he studied the two agents over fried rice and chicken chop suey, his brow furrowed.

Stevens glanced at Windermere. "Not exactly," he said. "The BCA has an interest in the case. Mickey Pyatt's pressing my boss to protect his family. And to find his dad's killer. My boss knows I work well with Windermere. He wants me to keep an eye on your progress."

Windermere grinned at him. "So you're a spy."

"Something like that." Stevens shrugged. "Anyway, I'm here. And I brought you Kent, so I can't be all bad."

"So where do we take this?" said Mathers. "What's our play?"

Windermere and Stevens swapped another glance. "I'm going to check on Paige Pyatt," said Stevens. "Eli Cody had a hell of a collection of pictures."

Windermere nodded. "We'll head to Chicago, check on Alex Kent. Odds are he's just another scapegoat, like you say. But we'd better have a look."

"Good call," said Stevens. "Save me the flying."

Windermere laughed. "How'd you get to Duluth, you big baby?"

"Slowly and painfully." Stevens stood. "I'd better get home. Nancy's waiting. And it sounds like we're all back on the road tomorrow."

Windermere took a bite of sweet-and-sour pork. "Get out of here, Stevens," she said, chewing. "Keep us posted."

She watched him cross the office toward the elevators. When he'd pressed the call button he glanced back, and she grinned. "Good to have you back, partner."

Stevens smiled back, sheepish, and shot her a wave. Then the elevator doors opened and he climbed aboard.

"So what's the story?" said Mathers, when Stevens was gone. "You guys hook up or something?"

Windermere straightened. "What? The guy's married, Mathers."

Mathers cocked his head. "Okay . . ."

"He's like ten years older than me, dummy," she said. "Got a wife and kids. Anyway, no. We just work well together."

"Okay." Mathers turned back to his dinner. "Whatever you say."

Windermere stared at him for a moment. Then she turned back to her own food. "Never happen," she said, shaking her head. "You big goof."

Mathers nodded. Didn't say anything. Windermere stole another glance at him, though. Caught the shit-eating smirk on his face.

28

Stevens let himself in through the front door and bent down to untie his shoes as Triceratops, JJ's big German shepherd, padded in from the living room, tail wagging, his big eyes inquisitive. The dog nuzzled

Stevens, coating his face with slobber, and Stevens kicked off his shoes and pushed the dog gently away. "Okay, okay," he said. "Where is everyone?"

The dog looked at him. Stevens stood in the hallway and listened. He could hear explosions upstairs: JJ killing his video game monsters. Otherwise, the house was silent.

Stevens hung up his coat and walked into the living room, the dog padding softly behind. His wife groaned and sat up on the couch as he entered. "Agent Stevens," she said, yawning. "Where've you been?"

Stevens sank into the couch beside her. "Duluth," he said.

Nancy Stevens frowned. "But of course."

"Caught a case," he told her. "A murder. Ran into Donna McNaughton. She works violent crimes now."

Nancy sat up. "Doesn't work them too well, I guess," she said, "if they had to drag your butt all the way up there."

"Favor for Tim Lesley." Stevens hesitated. "It ties into that shooting this weekend, Spenser Pyatt, downtown."

"How so?"

Stevens explained it. Pyatt, Cody, Windermere. When he was finished, Nancy sighed. "So you're working with the FBI again."

"Not exactly," he said. "In fact, probably not. I'm working the family angle. Windermere's catching the killer."

"Huh." Nancy looked up at Stevens. "Did you ask for this assignment?"

Stevens shook his head. "Of course not. It's just Lesley wants eyes on the FBI side of things, I guess so he can bring something back to Mickey Pyatt. He knows Windermere's on the case."

"And you're friends with Windermere."

"Exactly." He grinned. "I'm kind of a spy."

His wife leaned against him. Stevens put his arm around her, and she craned her neck up and kissed him. "I always liked spies," she said.

"That so?"

Nancy kissed him again. Then she pulled back. "So long as James Bond comes back to me in the end."

"Every time." Stevens pulled her close again. "Don't you worry about that."

He kissed her, deeper this time, felt her body rise to meet his. Then the dog stiffened beside them and the front door slammed open. Stevens pulled back from his wife just in time to see his teenage daughter appear in the doorway.

"Gross." Andrea Stevens looked from her father to her mother and back again. "You guys were making out, weren't you?"

Nancy giggled. "Maybe."

"*Gross.*" Andrea groaned and disappeared down the hall. "Get a room."

Stevens stood, pulling Nancy up beside him. Held her close and kissed her again. "I'd say she's onto something," he said, grinning. "Wouldn't you?"

29

Stevens woke up early Wednesday morning. He lay in bed, staring at the ceiling and planning his day, until Nancy shifted beside him and groaned, rubbing her eyes. "Morning already?"

Stevens sat up and admired her, her tousled hair and her sleepy eyes. She was beautiful even now, the woman of his dreams, and though he'd grown used to waking up beside her, there were mornings, still, when he felt like a lottery winner.

Nancy cocked her head at him. "What are you looking at?"

"You." He leaned over and kissed her. "That a problem?"

His wife squirmed away. "Ugh," she said. "Morning breath." She held back a moment, teasing him. Then she leaned in and kissed him again.

"You like it," he said.

"I do not. But I'll suffer."

"A martyr. How noble."

She kissed him harder, slid her hand beneath the sheets. "You going to lie there and crack wise all morning, Agent Stevens, or do you have something better to do?"

Stevens grinned at her. "Something much better," he said, reaching for the drawstring on her pajamas. "Just you wait and see."

AFTERWARD, Nancy Stevens smiled at her husband and sat up in bed. "Well, all right, James Bond. You got the girl, now go save the world."

He ran his hand along the curve of her body. "You in a hurry?"

"As a matter of fact, yes," she said, pushing the sheets aside and standing. "I'm due at the office in an hour. Got some paperwork to go through before the hearing."

"Cripes."

"No rest for the wicked. That counts you and me both. You planning on coming home for dinner?"

"Not sure," he said. "Got a long drive ahead of me."

Nancy circled the bed. Leaned down and kissed him. "Stay safe," she said. Then she pulled back and grinned at him. "Don't be afraid to ask for directions."

STEVENS DRESSED and ate a quick breakfast before piling his son in the Cherokee and dropping him at school. JJ barely waited until the Jeep had pulled to a stop before unbuckling his seat belt and dashing from the car, calling back a good-bye over his shoulder. Stevens watched his son until he'd disappeared amid a clump of friends. Then he shifted into gear and drove out to the highway.

He spent the morning on Interstate 94, stopping for gas and a coffee in Sauk Centre before continuing northwest to Fergus Falls, sixty miles short of Fargo and the North Dakota border, nearly two hundred miles from home.

Stevens pulled off the highway into town, drove up the main drag, and stopped and pulled out a map book to check his bearings. Then he drove east again, away from city hall to a lake just past the town limits, and a large home on the shore.

It looked more like a hunting resort than a single home, Stevens thought as he pulled up the gravel driveway toward the front door. Certainly it was more mansion than rustic cabin in the woods.

There was a black Range Rover parked at the head of the driveway, a red BMW roadster beside it. Stevens parked his Cherokee alongside the two cars and climbed out.

It was quiet outside, and quite peaceful. Beyond the house, Stevens could see the lake, shimmering bright blue in the spring sunlight. The forest was alive with birds and insects, and the air itself smelled clean and fragrant. Stevens inhaled, stretching his arms high above his head, feeling the numbness in mind and body disappear. When he was limber again, he turned and walked across the driveway to the house.

The front door opened after his second knock, almost like it had been waiting for him. It was a heavy wooden door, and it swung open slowly. On the other side was the woman from Eli Cody's photographs.

"Agent Stevens," she said. "I'm Paige Pyatt. Please, come in."

30

Windermere and Mathers took the first flight to Chicago O'Hare Wednesday morning. An FBI agent waited for them in the arrivals terminal. Windermere recognized him instantly.

"Wintergreen," he said, flashing her a wide smile. "Didn't we do this before, you and I?"

"Good morning, Agent Davis," she said, ignoring the way his hand seemed to linger on hers. "Back for another try, are you?"

Davis snorted. "I could say the same for you. We going to find us a real bad guy this time?"

"Probably not," Windermere told him, "but we're hopeful. This is Agent Mathers."

Davis gave Mathers an appraising look. His smile faded somewhat. "I'm outside," he said, and led them through the terminal to an FBI-issue Yukon double-parked at the curb.

Mathers stole a glance at Windermere as they walked. "You know this guy?"

"Pender case," Windermere told him.

"He sounds like he missed you."

She rolled her eyes. "He offered to give me a tour of Chicago last time I was in town. I respectfully declined. He didn't take it so well."

Mathers glanced at Davis. Then he grinned. "Respectfully, huh?"

Windermere grinned back. They climbed into Davis's SUV, and the Chicago agent drove away from the terminal. "Our suspect's name is Alex Kent," Windermere told him. "Lives in Logan Square. We don't think he's dangerous, but we can't be certain."

"So long as he's home," said Davis. "That's all I'm asking."

They drove away from the airport and into Chicagoland. Davis took the Kennedy Expressway into the city, got off in Logan Square, and drove past a couple gas stations and strip malls before turning down a short residential street. He parked the Yukon across from a narrow, two-story brick house, and glanced over at Windermere. "Address?"

Windermere looked out at the house. "That's the place."

"No tactical this time," said Davis. "You cool with that?"

"Should be fine. But guns drawn. Mathers, go around back."

"Roger."

Windermere studied the house some more. It was a nice little place. Well taken care of. A white railing ringed the porch. It looked bright, freshly painted. "Okay," she said, reaching for her sidearm. "Let's go find Alex Kent."

31

Alex Kent was home, anyway. That was a positive. It was about the only positive of the day.

As with Allen Salazar before him, one look at Kent was all it took to convince Windermere she'd been fooled. Kent was a tall man, in his late forties, dignified. And he was black.

He stood in his doorway, eyes dinner-plate wide, staring at Windermere and Davis and their guns. He held up his hands and lay flat on the ground, and let Davis handcuff him and take him out to the Yukon.

"This is a mistake," he said. Then he said it again. "What is it that you think I've done?"

Davis eyed him in the rearview. "When was the last time you were arrested?"

Kent shook his head. "I beg your pardon?"

"You heard me. What did they book you for last?"

"I'm a history teacher," Kent told him. "I've never been arrested in my life."

Davis smirked in the front seat. "We'll see."

THEY DROVE KENT to the FBI office on Roosevelt Road, just west of downtown. Found an interview room and left him alone for an hour. Then Windermere unlocked the door and went in. "You hungry?" she asked him.

Kent looked up at her, eyes fierce. It only lasted a moment. His head dropped and he looked away. He nodded, wordless.

"My partner's making a sandwich run. Roast beef okay?"

Kent nodded again. Windermere studied his face. He stared at a point over her left shoulder, his eyes wide, his shoulders hunched. Scared. Windermere sighed. Somewhere inside, she felt for the man. "You were in Duluth on Monday," she said. "Why?"

Kent opened his mouth. Hesitated. "My sister," he said finally. "She was sick. Pneumonia. I went to help care for her kids."

Windermere made a note. "How long were you there?"

"Three days. I left Friday afternoon. What is this about?"

"You rented a car?"

Kent nodded. "My sister—she doesn't drive. Her ex-husband took the car."

"Who'd you rent from?" said Windermere. "What kind of car?"

"It was a minivan," he said. "A Dodge. For the kids. The Grand Caravan. I rented from Liberty."

"From Liberty."

Kent dared to make eye contact. He shied away quickly. "I'm sorry," he said. "What is it you think I've done?"

Windermere shook her head. "Your name's tied to a murder," she said. "I'm going to take a wild guess you don't know a damn thing about it."

Kent shook his head. "My God," he said. "No. Lord, have mercy."

"You didn't rent a blue Kia Rio on Monday, either."

"What? I rented a minivan. Red."

"And you've never heard of Triple A Industries."

Again Kent shook his head. He sagged like a beat dog. "Never in my life," he said. "I'm a history teacher. I went to Duluth to help my sister. You can call and ask her. I didn't kill anybody, I swear it."

Windermere watched him. Searched his eyes. Then she sat back and stared up at the ceiling. "Okay," she said, sighing. "Let me check on that sandwich."

32

Stevens followed Paige Pyatt back through the house and into a bright sunroom overlooking the lake. He recognized the view from one of Cody's pictures. It was a beautiful spot, breathtaking. Pyatt pulled out a chair. "Coffee?"

Stevens sat down. "Sure," he said.

Pyatt walked into the adjacent kitchen and started to fiddle with a coffee machine. She glanced back at Stevens. "Mickey said we should expect you," she said. "He's worried about us."

"Should he be?" Stevens asked her.

"Oh, probably." Pyatt shrugged. "Anytime you have money, people will want to take it from you. It's a fact of life, Agent. Cream and sugar?"

"Please. You think Spenser's murder was related to money?"

"I don't know what I think," Pyatt said. She returned to the sunroom with two steaming mugs of coffee. "Certainly, Spenser had enemies."

"Anyone who stood to gain from his death?"

"All of them," she said, "in one way or another. If not financially, then in other ways. Spenser was a great man, Agent Stevens. The weak will always try to pull people like him down."

Stevens took the coffee. Sipped it. "You came back to Fergus Falls," he said. "I'd heard you lived in Minneapolis now."

Pyatt nodded. "We did," she said. "We do. It's just Mickey panicked. He thinks the family's a target."

"Elias Cody was murdered. Monday afternoon."

Pyatt's face clouded. She stared into her coffee. "Yes," she said. "Yes, I know."

"He seemed to have a bit of a fixation on you."

"Fixation." Pyatt paused. "An understatement, maybe."

"Yeah?"

Pyatt didn't answer for a long moment. Didn't look up. Then she stood, slowly. "It's easier if I show you," she said. "I'll be right back." She walked out of the sunroom and disappeared into the house. When she returned a few minutes later, she was carrying a stack of papers.

"Spenser didn't know I kept these," she said. "Though I don't know why I did." She set them down before Stevens. Letters, he saw, all of them. Faded envelopes. Faded handwriting. All addressed to Paige Sinisalo. "My maiden name," Pyatt told him. "Eli never quite accepted that I'd married Spenser."

"All this time."

Pyatt nodded. "He wrote passionately. Certainly with more fire than I ever saw in his person. He was a slight man. Shy, unbecoming. But in his letters . . ."

Stevens examined an envelope. Peered inside. "He was in love with you."

"Madly," she said. "He never forgave Spenser."

"For marrying you?"

"For stealing me." Pyatt looked at Stevens. "Eli always believed I was his by right. He'd known me first, you see, and he already saw Spenser as a rival, a threat. He hated his cousin for taking me from him."

Something in her tone triggered an alarm in Stevens's mind. "*Hate* is a strong word," he said.

Pyatt nodded. "It's the right word, Agent Stevens. Eli blamed Spenser for all of his life's misfortunes, and he never let go of that blame. You must have seen his house. He withered away."

"Were you in contact with him?" Stevens gestured to the letters. "Did you keep writing?"

Pyatt shook her head. "Spenser found out. He forbade me. Of course, I could see his point. I was a married woman."

"How long ago did you stop?"

"About twenty years ago, I'd say." She looked away, out over the lake. "I didn't even love Eli. I suppose I just enjoyed the attention."

Stevens watched her. She was somewhere else, somewhere in the past, and he let her stay there for a few minutes. Then he cleared his throat. "Can you think of anyone who would have wanted to kill Eli?"

Paige Pyatt shook her head sadly. "I can't think of many people who knew he was alive."

33

The kill was set.

Parkerson checked the database on Wednesday afternoon. Found a message from the client. "Funds delivered," it read. "Final half on completion."

Parkerson checked the Killswitch account and verified the payment: A hundred-thousand-dollar transfer had completed three hours earlier. Parkerson stared at the account balance, savored the moment. Then he logged out of the database and the account. Squared up to his computer. He had work to do.

The client had forwarded a profile of the target, including a schedule of the target's probable movements and a list of suggested kill spots. Parkerson had printed it when Jamie was at lunch. Now he examined it, scanning each page, and beginning to formulate a plan.

THE PLANNING WAS THE FUN PART. The checklist. A weapon. A rental car and a hotel room. A bank account number. All of the logistics, the cogs in the machine. Parkerson relished the cleanliness of the operation, the fulfillment of a hundred distinct tasks that would, when completed, result in some poor bastard's demise.

It wasn't the killing itself that interested Parkerson. In fact, the messiness of murder fairly sickened him: the blood and bile, the shit and piss and decay, the abject and utter *filthiness* of death—it was enough to turn a man's stomach. No, what fascinated Parkerson was the machine itself. The money came in. The cars were rented. The weapons procured. The assets mobilized and the targets destroyed. Clean and automatic. An ultramodern mechanism for destruction.

He'd spent hours in his room as a boy, dismantling things. Radios. Toaster ovens. TV sets. Anything he could scrounge up. He'd grown up alone, the product of parents who fought from the day he was born to the day his mother walked out. His father, a mechanic, had encouraged his son's curiosity. Parkerson had been a quiet child, not athletic, uninterested in girls. Machines were about the only interest he had in common with his father.

Later, Parkerson discovered computers. He was instantly enthralled. Where cars and appliances needed grease, and oil, and were prone to mechanical failure, computers were clean and sterile. Fast. Predictable. Reliable. In computers, Parkerson found the perfection that humanity sorely lacked.

He studied computers, obsessed over them. Devoted his life to working with them. Found a career that rewarded his diligence, an industry that welcomed his particular collection of interests. He'd worked hard and been compensated well. Had built a life for himself that outwardly appeared normal. A family. Friends. A nice house, a wife.

Inside, though, Parkerson knew it was all just a part of the game. A man needed to do certain things to succeed in the world. He needed a family. He needed to dress well, and tell jokes, and flirt with his secretary. Attributes. Objectives. Life was simple when reduced to its component parts.

Parkerson had played the game for years. He'd advanced through the company. Made friends. Earned respect. Inside, though, he was stultified. He'd won the game.

Then Killswitch came along. A new game to play: more challenges, higher stakes. The work was fulfilling, the rewards exhilarating. These days, Parkerson hardly ever got bored.

34

Parkerson booked a return airline ticket to Miami in Richard O'Brien's name, a nice hotel on the beach. And a rental car—Liberty.

He'd discovered the weakness in Liberty's reservation software a few weeks after he'd launched the Killswitch database. Rather, an enterprising young hacker had discovered the loophole. That hacker was now dead, and any remnants of his work rested solely with Parkerson, who'd worked hard to scrub the young anarchist's boasts from the litany of Internet forums he'd frequented. Now, as far as Parkerson knew, the Liberty loophole was secret once more, safe from mischievous teenagers—and from the Liberty IT geeks themselves.

It was a simple play, really. Parkerson had taught himself over the course of a weekend. Log in to the reservation software, and with a couple keystrokes, swap out the asset's name for that of another customer. Sometimes Parkerson used Liberty clients. Sometimes he just used names pruned from FAA passenger manifests—another anonymous hacker's contribution to Killswitch.

Parkerson had hoped that his computer chicanery would remain an unnecessary precaution, but, judging from the response to the Minnesota job, he'd been smart to implement the protocol when he did. The asset had been careless; the FBI had tailed him and copied down his plates. Now some poor Iowa manure salesman was in federal custody, while the asset skated free with no worries.

Parkerson scouted the client's proposed kill spots and settled on a suitable locale. Then he printed a briefing for the asset and reminded himself to overnight a weapon to the asset's hotel in the morning.

As with the rental cars, Parkerson found the Internet made securing guns for his assets a simple procedure. Any sucker with a counterfeit ID could fake a purchase permit, and online retailers would happily ship as much ammunition as an army of assets could use. A weapon's serial numbers could be filed, rendering the gun untraceable, and there were plenty of second-tier courier services willing to ship packages across the country quick and cheap, no questions asked. Running a contract killing operation, Parkerson had found, was almost shockingly easy.

Parkerson reviewed his plans for inconsistencies. For needless risk. Found nothing unsatisfactory, and shut down his computer, stood, and pulled on his coat. Locked up the office and went home for the night.

35

Windermere played a hunch and let Alex Kent walk. "Had to do it," she told Davis. "We don't have enough to hold him, anyway."

"Accessory to murder?" said Davis. "He rented a car for a killer."

Windermere shook her head. "Identity theft. Kent doesn't know a damn thing about any murders."

"Your case," Davis said, shrugging. "Hope it doesn't come back to bite you."

Me, too, Windermere thought. "Don't make me an asshole," she told Kent as she dropped him outside his house. "Stick around. We might need to bring you back in for more questioning. Got it?"

The guy practically tore the door off the car. "Thank you," he told Windermere, scrambling out to the sidewalk. "No problem. Thank you."

To his credit, Davis didn't suggest any more tours of Chicago—or anything else, for that matter. He drove Windermere and Mathers back to O'Hare in silence, and it was only as he dropped them at the United terminal that he spoke.

"You're making a mistake," he said. "That guy was a suspect. You should have charged him with something and let him stew on it."

"He's a history teacher, Davis," said Windermere. "Anyway, soon as he called a lawyer he'd have been gone. There's something else going on here. Something bigger than Kent."

Davis shook his head. "Good to see you again, Agent. Next time maybe we'll actually *do* something."

"Look forward to it." Windermere slammed the door closed. Mathers climbed out to the sidewalk beside her.

"So what happens next, Supercop?" he asked her.

Windermere watched Davis's big SUV pull away from the curb. "The hell if I know," she said, sighing. "I guess we go home."

IT WAS LONG AFTER DARK by the time the agents' flight landed at Minneapolis–Saint Paul. Windermere followed Mathers off the small plane, and they walked together out to the parking garage. Windermere's car was closer, her daddy's prize Chevelle, and Mathers lingered beside it as she unlocked the door. "Grab a bite somewhere?"

Windermere stiffened. She looked back at Mathers, who watched her, a grin on his face. She felt something inside her like panic. "What'd you say?"

The junior agent shrugged. "Just asked if you were hungry," he said. "We could get eats. Talk this thing over."

Windermere stared at him over the car. He was cute, definitely. Tall and slender and handsome, and there was a pleasing hint of muscle beneath his baby blue shirt. It had been more than two years since Mark had walked out, and Windermere had caught herself eyeing Mathers across the office a couple of times. She wasn't averse to the idea. Still, something made her hesitate, and she was pretty sure she knew what it was.

Stevens. She didn't even *like* Stevens that way—she'd better not, anyway, not with Nancy around—but they'd always had chemistry. Never acted on it, either of them, but it still somehow felt weird to Windermere, picking up with somebody new. Another cop, especially, after all the bullshit she and Stevens had been through.

It felt, she realized, a little bit like cheating.

Absurd. Still, she shook her head. Gave Mathers an apologetic smile. "I'm pretty beat, partner," she said. "I'd better just go home."

Mathers's smile didn't waver. "No problem," he said. "Guess I'll see you tomorrow."

He shot her a wave and ambled off across the parking garage.

Windermere watched him go, and when he was gone, she opened the Chevelle's door and slid in behind the wheel. She sighed and sat there, unmoving, for a minute or two, examining her reflection in the mirror. *What's wrong with you?* she thought. *The kid's harmless. It's just dinner.*

She let the question hang there for a moment. Then she started the engine. *Nothing's wrong. You're just tired.* She backed out of the parking stall and peeled out of the garage.

36

Stevens met Windermere and Mathers at the FBI office the next morning. He'd driven back from Fergus Falls the night before, arriving home in Saint Paul well after dark, dinner already cleared from the table and the kids in bed. He'd reheated some meat loaf and watched TV with Nancy, though they'd both been too tired to say much more than good night.

He'd mulled Paige Pyatt's words all two hundred miles home. Still couldn't decide what he thought of it all. Eli Cody had loved her; that much was certain. Somewhere, deep inside, she'd felt something in return. She'd kept all his letters; hell, it could have been love.

The easy answer, the answer that Stevens kept circling back to, would have been obvious if Cody himself hadn't been murdered. The hitch in Paige Pyatt's voice when she'd talked of Cody's hate for her husband—it didn't take much to jump to conclusions. Cody was a recluse with a hateful obsession. Not a huge stretch to picture him a killer. But why *now*? Why wait so long?

You don't have the whole puzzle, Stevens thought as he stepped off the elevator into CID. *Maybe Windermere has a few more pieces.*

But Windermere didn't have much. She sat Stevens down and told him all about her day with Alex Kent—"And Agent Davis, remember him?"—and when she came to the end, she had less than Stevens, just some history teacher with a stolen identity.

"So I let him go," said Windermere. "Davis didn't like it, but whatever. Kent isn't going anywhere."

"Means Salazar's probably clean, too."

Windermere shrugged. "Yeah," she said. "I mean, yeah. He doesn't know anything. Has a decent alibi and he sure as hell didn't look guilty. Anyway, our guy murdered Cody with Salazar behind bars. There's no connection between Salazar and Kent. How many accomplices could our shooter have?"

"So our shooter's stealing identities," said Stevens. "Using them for the killings and then disappearing again."

"That's what I'm thinking."

"Still doesn't explain *why* he's killing people," said Mathers.

Windermere rolled her eyes. "Ask Stevens what I think about motive."

"Mathers has a point," said Stevens. "Paige Pyatt said Cody had loved her for years. Said he was jealous of Spenser Pyatt. Hated him. Perfect motive, except—"

"Cody's dead, too," said Windermere. "And by the same hand as killed Pyatt, assuming the Liberty agent in Duluth gave a good description. Doesn't really fit the spurned-lover scenario." She paused. "Any other connections between Cody and Pyatt? Anything concrete?"

"Money," said Mathers.

Stevens shook his head. "Cody was nearly broke. Nobody stood to gain from his death."

"Family," said Windermere. "You said Mickey Pyatt is afraid someone's targeting his relatives."

"He is," said Stevens. "I had Fergus Falls Police post a guard outside the Pyatt's lake house. I'll talk to Mickey Pyatt and find out if there are any other family members we should watch."

"Good. What else?"

"Spenser Pyatt was one of the richest men in the country and he was straight-up assassinated," said Mathers. "There's gotta be a lead somewhere."

Stevens nodded. "Do we know what he was doing at the hotel that day?"

"Meeting friends for lunch," said Windermere. "Guess it was a weekly tradition, the good old boys' club. Pyatt's death seemed to shock the lot of them. No obvious connection to the murder there, either, but we're running full backgrounds on everybody at the table anyway."

"I'll take a closer look at Cody's situation, too," Stevens said. "Just to round things out. Maybe I'll ask Duluth PD to snoop around his place a little more, see what else they can dig up."

"You're from there, right?" said Windermere. "Call in some favors." She clapped her hands. "Okay," she said. "Let's get back to work."

37

Stevens called Duluth PD and left word for Donna McNaughton. McNaughton called back a half hour later. "What's up, Kirk?"

"I need Eli Cody's last will and testament," Stevens told her. "His finances, too. If you can find a willing judge, I'll fax through the paperwork."

"I know a guy," said McNaughton. "But what's the point?"

"Chasing our tails down here. Kind of hoping Cody's hiding something that'll spark some inspiration. Speaking of which, you mind combing through the old house one more time?"

"You gonna tell me what I'm looking for?"

"Anything that looks suspicious, Donna. Anything at all. Personal correspondence. Receipts. Maybe Cody was less of a recluse than we thought."

"I don't get it, Kirk. He's the victim."

"More to the point, he was a target," said Stevens. "And people don't just become targets without a reason. I want to know who wanted him dead."

"Got it," said McNaughton. "I'll head over there now. You owe me for this, though. Especially if I find something."

"Dinner's on me next time I'm in town." Stevens hung up the phone and found Windermere watching him, one eyebrow raised. "Old friend," he said.

Windermere nodded. "Uh-huh."

STEVENS SPENT THE DAY putting together the paperwork for Donna McNaughton. Faxed it up to Duluth and went home to Nancy and the kids. Friday morning, he went to see Mickey Pyatt.

Pyatt was a handsome fifty-something with an easy smile and a firm grip. Stevens warmed to him quickly. Unfortunately, the man had no answers when it came to his father's murder.

"I'm afraid I don't know," he told Stevens. "My dad had competitors, sure, business rivals. But enemies?" Pyatt shook his head. "He was a good man."

"He was rich," said Stevens. "Could money be the motive?"

"You mean his estate," said Pyatt. "Someone in the family. It's not out of the question—though, like we told the FBI, anyone who would have gained from Dad's death was already pretty well taken care of. He looked after his loved ones."

"What about Eli Cody?"

Pyatt's face darkened. "Yeah," he said. "Kind of weird, huh? He was family, I guess, but just barely. He kept to himself, as I'm sure you're aware."

"He was broke."

"He wasn't in the will, if that's what you're asking. He wouldn't have gained from Dad's death any more than you would have."

"Except he was in love with your mother."

Pyatt nodded. "I take it you don't consider Eli to be merely a victim in this case. Do you think he had some involvement in my father's death?"

"I don't know," Stevens told him. "Frankly, we don't know much at this point. Your mother implied that Cody held a long grudge, but I can't figure any reason he'd have wanted your father dead now in particular."

"As opposed to when my father married my mother, say?"

"Exactly."

Pyatt hesitated. "There is one thing." He glanced at Stevens. "This year—this spring, in fact—would mark fifty years that my father had known my mother. Not their wedding anniversary, but the anniversary of their actual meeting. I only remember because Dad always talked about meeting Mom on the night Wilt Chamberlain scored his hundred points. March second, 1962, remember?"

"Your mother told me that Cody'd known her first."

"Indeed he had," Pyatt said. "In fact, he was apparently on a date with my mother when my dad stole her away. A particularly disastrous date, to hear my mother tell it."

"Fifty years," Stevens said.

"It's a long time to hold a grudge," said Pyatt. "And in any case, Eli Cody is dead. So maybe the whole point is moot."

Stevens nodded. "Cody's death is a strange development, that's for sure."

"The whole situation is strange, Agent Stevens. I've seen the sketches of my dad's killer. He's nobody I've ever seen before, I know that."

"I saw him in person," Stevens said, standing. "You'd remember."

STEVENS LEFT PYATT and drove back to Brooklyn Center. Just as he arrived at the FBI building, his cell phone started to ring. Stevens parked the Cherokee quickly and answered it. It was Donna McNaughton.

"Processing your paperwork now," the cop told him. "Give it a day on the outside. Took a spin through Cody's house while I waited, didn't find much but an old desktop computer. We're bringing it in for the techs to have a look."

"Good thinking. Who knows what Cody had kicking around on that thing."

"Yeah, exactly. Anyway, I got something else for you."

"Shoot."

"Had to make a run out to the airport just now. Pick up my brother and his family. Anyway, while I'm waiting, the Liberty woman flags me down. Said she thought of something that might help us out."

Stevens frowned. "Yeah?"

"Said she was thinking about the guy who'd rented that little blue Kia, how weird it was that he came up on the computer as Alex Kent, since she was pretty damn sure his first name was Richard."

"Richard." Stevens fumbled in his glove box for a pen. "She get a last name?"

"Couldn't remember. All she knew was his first name was Richard and he was flying to Minneapolis. So, you know, maybe that helps."

"Sure does. We can use it."

"Good. I'll keep you posted on Cody's computer. And his bank statements, when they come in."

"Thanks, Donna." Stevens ended the call. Sat in the Cherokee, staring out the front windshield. *Richard something,* he thought, *out of Minneapolis.*

38

The pretty girl wasn't working at the Delta counter when Lind checked in for his flight on Friday morning. The man behind the desk smiled and handed Lind his ticket—"Enjoy your flight, Richard"—and Lind walked away, relieved.

He passed through security and sat in the lounge beside a Japanese family, a father, a mother, and two very young girls. They smiled at Lind when he sat down beside them. Lind smiled stiffly back and then looked away.

The oldest girl must have been three or four. She rolled a little toy truck along the carpet toward Lind. Reached his boot and paused. Looked up at Lind, a mischievous smile on her face. Then she rolled the truck over his boot.

Lind stiffened. He had to stifle every urge in his body to keep from kicking out at the girl. He gripped the armrest beside him. Planted his boots on the floor. The little girl giggled and drove the truck over his foot again.

"*Yumi.*" The girl's mother smiled at Lind. "I'm so sorry."

Lind steadied his breathing and forced another smile. "It's okay," he told her. "It's okay."

The woman's smile faded as she studied Lind's face. She snapped her fingers and said something in Japanese to her daughter, who giggled and ran to her mother, steadying herself on Lind's knee as she passed. The woman gathered up her daughters and said something fast and sharp to her husband, who glanced at Lind and nodded and reached for his suitcase.

Lind watched the family relocate a couple of rows down. Pretended not to notice the little girl's parents stealing concerned glances in his direction. The little girl playing happily on the carpet. He stared straight ahead and tried not to think about them, tried to ignore everything around him and relax.

THE FLIGHT TO MIAMI took just over two hours. Lind sat in his seat and drank coffee. The visions had returned last night, just before the phone rang. Showtime again, and Hang Ten, the strangled man and the chained-up young soldier. The visions had been worse than before, visceral, almost real. Lind had fought against them. Fought to wake up. He'd thought he might die if he stayed under any longer.

He woke up sweaty, a scream on his lips. The phone was ringing. It was the man, his seductive words promising relief. Salvation. He had another job for Lind. Another task to accomplish. Just a few more little errands, he said, and then he'd make the visions disappear.

Lind touched down in Miami and rented a little Chevy from the Liberty desk in the rental car terminal. He took a map from the counter and studied it in the parking lot, and then drove east through the city and across the MacArthur Causeway into Miami Beach. He checked in to a Marriott overlooking the ocean, turned on every light in his room, blasted the air-conditioning, and pumped the volume on the TV set. Then he brewed a big pot of coffee and sat on the edge of the bed, watching music videos and reality TV, anything to stave off the fatigue.

Around six in the evening, there was a knock at the door. Lind answered and found a bellman in the hallway. He held a package about the size of a cake box. "You're Richard O'Brien, right?" he said. "This came for you this morning. Overnight express."

Lind took the package back into his room and opened it on the bed. There was a picture inside, and a rifle, slick steel, in component parts.

Lind studied the picture until he'd memorized the face. Then he burned the papers in the wastebasket in the bathroom. Sat back on the bed and drank more coffee and watched more TV, assembling and disassembling the rifle and waiting for the hours to pass.

39

Richard O'Brien." Windermere looked up from her computer. "That's our guy."

Stevens peered over her shoulder. Mathers hurried over from his own cubicle. "O'Brien," said Stevens. "How do you figure?"

Windermere gestured to her screen. "Delta flies from Duluth to Minneapolis four times a day," she said. "Assuming the Liberty computer isn't totally screwed, our shooter brought his rental back just after four o'clock Monday afternoon. That puts him on the last Minneapolis flight of the day, the 5:20 departure."

"Sure," said Stevens. "Makes sense."

"According to Delta's passenger manifest, there were two men named Richard on the 5:20 flight, a Richard Michnek and a Richard O'Brien. Michnek's a Duluth local. He flew home this morning. Not our guy."

"And O'Brien?"

"Yeah," said Windermere. "O'Brien flew from Minneapolis to Duluth Monday morning. Arrived at 2:07 and left at 5:20. Just enough time to murder Eli Cody."

"So who is he?" said Mathers. "He's a Twin Cities guy?"

Windermere punched a few keys. "Guess not," she said. "Says he came all the way from Philadelphia that day. Long way to fly just to strangle a guy."

Stevens leaned forward. "He flew a Philly-to-Duluth round-trip on

Monday?" He peered at Windermere's screen. "What about Saturday? We need to know this guy's whereabouts when Spenser Pyatt was murdered."

"My next move, Stevens." Windermere grinned at him and reached for her phone. "I know a guy at the FAA. Let me make some calls."

STEVENS AND MATHERS WAITED, lingering behind Windermere as she attempted to connect with her FAA pal. Mathers raised an eyebrow at Stevens. "Hope this works," he said. "It'll be a huge pain in the ass if we have to do things official."

Stevens shrugged. "Worked before."

"The Pender case?"

"Caught up with the guy's girlfriend this way. Chased her out to Seattle."

"No shit?" Mathers grinned at Stevens. "Must have been a blast, man."

Stevens started to shake his head. Then he caught himself. "It was," he said, matching the junior agent's grin. "It really was."

"Mathers. Stevens."

The two men turned to find Windermere watching them, a funny smile on her face. "You boys want to reminisce on the good old days, or you want to do some police work?"

Stevens and Mathers hurried back to her cubicle. "You get something?"

"Richard O'Brien flew from Philadelphia to Minneapolis on Friday afternoon," Windermere said. "He flew home on the evening flight Saturday night."

"Hot damn." Stevens started to pace, his insides electrified. "So he's Philadelphia-based. Can we dig him up there?"

"We might not have to." Windermere let it hang until Stevens stopped pacing and looked at her. "According to my FAA guy, Richard O'Brien flew into Miami this afternoon. He's scheduled to fly home tomorrow."

40

Parkerson shut down his computer, satisfied. The preparations were made. The asset had his instructions. All that remained was the kill itself. Still, something itched in his mind.

It wasn't a problem, exactly. As kills went, Miami was a straightforward job. No, it wasn't doubt, the niggle in Parkerson's brain. It was instinct, some kind of sixth sense. And where Killswitch was concerned, Parkerson trusted his instincts.

He turned on his computer again. Opened an Internet browser and started a couple searches. The Pyatt shooting in Minneapolis. And the Cody kill in Duluth.

He found nothing new on Spenser Pyatt. The FBI was involved, sure, and that was unusual. They'd tracked down Allen Bryce Salazar, had probably released him by now, and Parkerson knew the Feds would keep looking for the asset. It was a misstep, but hardly fatal. He'd already decided he could live with it.

The Cody case, though. Parkerson found an article on the *Duluth News Tribune*. A straightforward account of Cody's murder. A quote from a Duluth PD spokeswoman. And then a throwaway line, at the end: "Duluth PD are cooperating with Bureau of Criminal Apprehension agents as the investigation proceeds."

Parkerson read the sentence again. The BCA was the state police force. As far as he knew, their jurisdiction didn't cover homicides in centers as large as Duluth. Unless the Duluth PD had requested their involvement . . . or somebody up there suspected something bigger was at play.

There. There was the itch in Parkerson's mind. The FBI on the Pyatt case. The BCA on Cody. Two irregularities on back-to-back kills. It could be completely normal, but it could also be a sign that the asset had really screwed up.

Parkerson checked his watch. A quarter past six on a Friday evening. Miami lay more than seven hundred miles to the south, and the kill was set for Saturday at noon. He sat in his chair and stared at his blank computer screen, mulling it over, running the calculations. Then, abruptly, he stood and walked out of his office, pulling the door closed behind him. He hurried through the near-empty building to the parking lot, where he found his car and sat behind the wheel.

Am I really doing this?

It was a dangerous play, Parkerson knew. If anyone saw him in Miami, connected him to the job, it would jeopardize the whole operation. Still, he had to be sure the asset wasn't compromised. Killswitch was too lucrative to risk.

Parkerson turned the key in the ignition. The big engine fired up, and he idled the car out of the parking lot. Waved to the guard in the hut and pulled out to the street, hesitated a moment, and then aimed the car at Interstate 95.

He punched in a number on his cell phone as he drove. "Honey?" he said, when the other end picked up. "Something big came up at work, really sudden. Gotta duck out of town for the night."

41

Stevens called Mickey Pyatt. "You have family in Miami? Anyone in Florida at all?"

"My aunt Margaret," said Pyatt. "In Fort Lauderdale."

"Get a hold of her," Stevens told him. "And anyone else you can think of down there. Tell them to get out of their homes and checked into hotels somewhere safe until they hear back from you."

"Okay," said Pyatt. "But why?"

"Just a precaution," said Stevens. "Your family's probably not in any danger. We might have a lead on the shooter, though. Just trying to be safe."

Pyatt hesitated. "I understand," he said finally. "Thanks."

Stevens hung up the phone and turned back to Windermere and Mathers, who were hunched over Windermere's computer. Windermere hung up her own phone as Stevens approached. "Liberty says a Richard O'Brien rented a red Chevy Cruze from their desk at Miami International," she said. "One-day rental."

"He's in the Liberty system," said Stevens. "How do we know he's not a phony?"

"We don't," Windermere said, "but he used the same name to book flights for the Pyatt and Cody murders. Maybe he's just getting lazy."

"Careless," said Stevens. "Fair enough. So we have his car. Liberty has his plates. We know he's flying out tomorrow afternoon."

"Miami PD is looking for the car right now," said Mathers. "We passed along his description, and they have his plates. Maybe we'll get lucky and a patrol car will spot him. If not, they'll pick him up at the airport tomorrow."

Stevens and Windermere swapped glances. "Yeah, fine," Windermere said. "Except some poor bastard will be dead by tomorrow."

42

Parkerson drove through the night on Interstate 95, through South Carolina and Savannah, Georgia, the traffic thinning out around him as darkness settled in. He played Bach at low volume on the CD player and kept the Cadillac humming at a steady southbound clip.

It was just after two in the morning by the time he reached Jacksonville, and he stopped for a cup of coffee and a bad hamburger at an all-night diner off the highway. The waitress was middle-aged. Rings under her eyes. The diner was mostly empty; a couple truck drivers played poker by the door.

Parkerson sipped his coffee and studied his reflection in the window. He looked as tired as the waitress and twice as unkempt. His suit was wrinkled. There was grease on his shirt. His hair was mussed, and his eyes were bloodshot. He was sick of driving. Sick of being awake. He wanted to crawl into a warm bed somewhere and sleep it off.

He thought about his own bed, his home, and wondered what his wife was thinking. If she'd bought his hurried excuse. Rachel didn't ask many questions about his job, and he didn't tell her much. He surely didn't tell her about Killswitch.

Not that she had any right to be upset with him. He was simply a service provider, filling a vacuum in the market. Morality was an imperfection, a crutch for the weak. Money was the only absolute.

Parkerson looked out at the highway, a few cars speeding southbound, and he felt a little shiver run through him as he wondered what waited at the end of the road. He was nervous, he realized. It went with the territory.

There had been other close calls, with other assets. Murder was a natural attention-getter. Sometimes there were witnesses. It wasn't normally a big deal. The alibis were sound. The escape routes were well planned. So far, nobody had managed to trace the assets.

Not yet, anyway.

Parkerson pushed back from the table. Downed the rest of his coffee and splashed cold water on his face in the bathroom. Dried up with a piece of rough paper towel and bought a Red Bull from the tired waitress as he settled his tab. Then he walked back to his car and idled out to the highway again. Miami lay waiting, 350 miles distant.

43

Stevens lay awake through the night, staring at the ceiling and wrestling with the covers. By three in the morning, Nancy had had enough. "Go away," she said, groaning, kicking at him under the sheet. "Some of us actually want to be here."

Stevens rubbed her back until he heard her breathing slow again. Then he slipped out from the covers and crept downstairs to the basement—his man cave, Nancy called it—sat in his favorite chair, and watched basketball highlights on mute. Triceratops followed him down, lay at his feet, and fell promptly asleep. He whimpered and growled, chasing imaginary prey in his dreams.

Hope he's catching something, Stevens thought. *Even if I'm not.*

He'd left Windermere and Mathers in the FBI office once it became clear that Drew Harris, SAC of Criminal Investigations, wasn't about to authorize a flight to Miami, not after Salazar and Kent had come up blanks.

"We'll get Miami on it," he told Windermere, winking. "We didn't poach *all* of their best agents."

"Just the Supercop," said Mathers, and Windermere groaned and swung a fist at him.

"Just the Supercop," said Harris. "Brief the Miami office and let them know what to look for. You have Miami PD involved also, I expect."

Windermere nodded. "Yes, sir."

"Should be a piece of cake, then." Harris gave her a smile. "You can fly down when they catch him. We'll make sure it's your picture that gets in the papers."

"I don't care about pictures," said Windermere, but her boss's decision was final. She and Mathers hung around on the phone to Miami, and Stevens made plans to rejoin them in the morning.

Now, though, Stevens stared unseeing at the TV screen and wished desperately he and Windermere were on scene. It was torture sitting and waiting while someone else worked the case, and what if the guy got away? Defeat would be a lot easier to swallow if he himself screwed up. Not so much if he was forced to watch a failed takedown from thousands of miles away.

But Harris had spoken, and there was probably no way Tim Lesley would have approved Stevens's flight to Miami anyway. Unless Aunt Margaret really was in danger . . .

The Pyatt angle. Stevens couldn't figure it. Donna McNaughton had called from Duluth that evening with news about Eli Cody. "Got our geeks into Cody's old computer," she said. "What a fossil. Guy was still using Internet Explorer, for Christ's sake."

"A dead end, then?"

"Not on your life. They found a bunch of old text files. Get this, Kirk: half-written suicide notes. Blah, blah, blah, my life's so crummy, the usual. But a lot of 'Fuck you, Spenser Pyatt' and 'I love you, Paige Sinisalo' in there, too."

"Jesus. Really?"

"Oh, yeah. You know he dated her once? Nineteen sixty-two. Fifty years ago, Kirk. And still carrying the goddamn torch."

"Pyatt's son told me about it," Stevens said. "I heard it ended badly."

"Not for Spenser Pyatt." McNaughton chuckled, grim. "At least not right away."

Suicide notes. Unrequited love, fifty years strong. Two dead octogenarians and a jet-setting killer on his way to Miami. Stevens shifted his weight. Settled back in his chair and tried to focus on basketball. On sleep. On anything but Richard O'Brien. It was an impossible task. Stevens sat in his basement until dawn, replaying his fears again and again as the sun rose over Saint Paul—and Miami.

44

Parkerson arrived in Miami a little before nine, his head buzzing and his eyelids drooping. He drove through the city and across Biscayne Bay to Miami Beach, parked the Cadillac a block from the Atlantic, and closed his eyes for a while.

An hour passed. Parkerson woke with the sound of the surf in the distance. He walked down Ocean Drive until he found a coffee shop, bought the biggest coffee he could find, and retreated outside to drink it.

He sat at a table on the patio and took out his laptop and broke into the Liberty rental car reservation software through the coffee shop's WiFi. Then he brought up an FAA manifest for the day and chose a name at random. Swapped out Lind's information for the patsy's and couldn't help smiling. Somebody named Peter Cook was about to have a hell of a bad day.

A tourist shop nearby sold binoculars. Parkerson bought a pair and checked his watch. Time to go. He felt like a child on a predawn Christmas morning, jumpy from caffeine or the anticipation or both. He walked back to the Cadillac, forcing himself to stay calm. Circled around to the southwest side of the island, where he pulled onto a side road and parked at the edge of Biscayne Bay, angling the Cadillac to afford a good view of the yachts moored at the marina on the water. Then he settled back with his binoculars and waited.

» » »

IT WAS A BIG BOAT, the *Kyla Dawn*. A hundred feet, maybe. It gleamed white in the sunlight as it rested on its moorings, the bay's small chop barely disturbing its sleek, graceful lines.

Lind watched the yacht through the scope of his rifle. He sat low in the rear seat of the rental Chevy, surveying the marina from across the water. He was parked in a warehouse lot on Terminal Island, midway across the MacArthur Causeway between South Beach and Miami proper. The man had told him about the island when he'd phoned with the instructions. He'd told Lind to park here and wait for the target. Lind had followed his instructions. He'd been sitting in the car, not moving, since just after dawn.

It was almost time. So far, there had been very little movement aboard. A couple of stewards in white carried grocery bags from the dock. A man who must have been the captain surveyed the yacht's hull. None of them interested Lind. None of them was the target.

As Lind watched, a black Rolls-Royce limousine pulled to a stop at the head of the dock. The driver got out and quickly circled to the passenger side. A man climbed out before he could reach the door. He was slim, dressed in a well-cut white suit. Lind frowned. He wasn't the target, either.

The man left his driver at the car, walked down to the floats, and crossed quickly to the *Kyla Dawn*. Lind watched him talk to the captain. They glanced back at the Rolls-Royce. Then the man climbed aboard.

Lind checked his watch. It was five minutes past noon. The target should have been dead. He was five minutes late.

Lind felt the first stirrings of panic. He wondered what would happen if the target failed to show. If the assignment wasn't completed. It had never happened before.

For five agonizing minutes, he contemplated the possibilities. Then another car pulled up, a tan Lexus. A man climbed out from behind the wheel. He was heavyset. He had a black beard. Lind relaxed. This man was the target.

» » »

PARKERSON GAZED APPROVINGLY across the water at the *Kyla Dawn*. She was a beautiful vessel. Clean. Sleek. Dwarfed every other yacht in the marina. He wondered how much she cost. How many more jobs he would have to arrange before he could afford something like her.

Parkerson tore his eyes from the yacht and surveyed the harbor. Pointed the binoculars across the bay, toward Terminal Island, where he'd determined Lind should set up. It was an ugly little island—parking lots, mostly. Try as he might, Parkerson couldn't pick out Lind's car from the rest.

He didn't see any cops, either. No police cars anywhere, marked or unmarked. There were a couple security guards at the marina, but they looked bored, restless. They didn't look like they were anticipating a murder.

Maybe we're clean, Parkerson thought. *Maybe nobody realizes we're here.*

A big black Rolls-Royce pulled up to the dock. A man in a white suit climbed out and walked down to the *Kyla Dawn*. Parkerson didn't recognize him. Five minutes later, a tan Lexus arrived and another man appeared, a fat man with a beard. Parkerson felt his pulse start to quicken. The target. Parkerson watched him navigate the narrow ramp to the slips. He moved slowly, unsteadily. Parkerson waited, his whole body tense, straining to hear the shot.

45

Mathers stood up from his computer. "Whoa," he said. "Holy shit."

Stevens and Windermere hurried over. "What's up?"

"Richard O'Brien just disappeared from the Liberty system." Mathers pointed at his computer. "Like, literally just now."

Windermere peered at the screen. "Peter Cook," she read. "You're sure you have the right file?"

"Damn sure," said Mathers. "Same red Chevy Cruze. Same plates."

"Same credit card," said Stevens.

"Exactly. This is the same account. Just somebody switched out O'Brien's name."

Windermere looked at Stevens. Stevens shrugged. "Any word from Miami PD?" he said. "Or your guys on the ground? Anybody see anything?"

Windermere shook her head. "It's noon there," she said. "O'Brien's flight home leaves in just over two hours. If he's going to kill someone, it's now."

"Maybe he's not there to kill anyone," said Mathers. Then he shook his head. "Nah, that's bullshit. Maybe he's done it and nobody's found the body."

Stevens nodded. "He's down there to kill," he said, feeling frustration rise like a flood tide. "He's down there to kill, and we're too late to stop him."

46

Parkerson barely heard the shot. Didn't see the muzzle flare. Saw the target go down and still couldn't find Lind.

He was watching the target cross the slip to the *Kyla Dawn*. The big man paused at the gangway, said something to the captain, and glanced back at the Lexus. Then his gaze swept the pier. He looked straight at Parkerson in the big Cadillac and Parkerson ducked back, feeling his heart syncopate.

When Parkerson looked up again, the target was at the top of the gangway, stepping aboard the yacht. He stood on the deck a moment, catching his breath. Then he started across to where the man in the white suit stood, waiting.

There was a pop like a firecracker in the distance. The bearded man staggered backward, his shirt blossoming crimson. The captain stared. A steward hurried out to the deck. Someone screamed. Then the target's head exploded. Parkerson gasped. *"Holy shit."*

The target dropped to the deck. The steward rushed to his side, crouched low, head up, searching for the shooter. The captain drew a pistol. He, too, searched the dock. His eyes fell on Parkerson in the Cadillac. Then kept moving.

Parkerson stayed low. Watched the chaos grow on the *Kyla Dawn*. More people approaching from aboard other boats. The steward now, shouting something. Gesturing with his hands.

In the distance, on Terminal Island, a little red Chevy backed away from the shore.

» » »

LIND MISSED LOW with the first shot. Caught the target in the chest. His second shot put him to bed.

Lind watched the man fall. Kept the scope on him to make sure he stayed down. Then, satisfied, he lowered the rifle and clambered over to the front seat of the car.

He backed away from the shore. Drove out of the parking lot and up the island to the ramp where the road joined the MacArthur Causeway. He drove halfway up the ramp and then slowed and rolled down the driver's-side window. Glanced in the rearview mirror; the ramp was deserted. Lind took the rifle from the backseat and hurled it over the bridge. It arced far out, over the guardrails, and fell out of sight, just as a green sedan pulled onto the ramp behind him.

Lind rolled up the window and stepped on the gas. Drove up the ramp and onto the causeway and merged with the traffic speeding toward Miami.

47

Reports of a shooting." Mathers's voice was tight. "Miami Beach Marina. Some guy on a yacht just got capped."

Stevens felt his stomach drop. "Tell me someone made the shooter."

Mathers held the phone tight to his ear. "Long-range," he said, shaking his head. "Came from across the water. Nobody saw anything."

"Jesus Christ. Who's the victim?"

"Nobody knows. Boat's called the *Kyla Dawn*. Owned by some rich guy, an importer or something."

Stevens looked at Windermere. Windermere's mouth was tight, her eyes hard. "Well, it happened," she said. "Now for the big test."

"We have guys in position?"

She nodded. "Miami PD and FBI. Airport security. They're all inside the terminal, waiting on O'Brien."

"Christ." Stevens paced the floor. "Christ, I wish we were there."

Windermere nodded. "Me, too."

48

Something was definitely wrong.

Parkerson didn't see it at first. He'd tailed Lind back to the airport, admiring the asset's apparent calm behind the wheel of the Chevy. He blended in with the rest of the traffic, didn't attract attention. Drove past a couple of police cruisers and showed no signs of panic.

Parkerson felt his own nervousness dissipate as he drove. The asset was damn good. The job was done. Another hour, tops, and the show would be over.

As they approached the airport, however, Parkerson felt his internal alarm trigger. Everything was not normal. He could feel it.

There were more police cars on the road than there should be, unmarked sedans and patrol cars alike. They sat waiting on the sides of the highway, both directions, their drivers staring out into traffic, watching. Parkerson watched the asset cruise past a navy blue Crown Victoria on the side of the road. The cop inside spoke into his radio, his eyes following the little Chevy as it passed him. He pulled out, slow, and merged into traffic. Fell in just behind. Shit.

Parkerson stood on the gas pedal. Pulled out to pass the cop and the asset just beyond, sped past them both toward the terminal in the distance. The asset was compromised, after all, and Parkerson was damned if he was going to sit around and watch.

» » »

LIND STARED after the gray sedan that had passed him, his foot wavering on the accelerator. The car looked familiar. It looked like the man's car. It looked like the car that had taken him away.

Lind watched the car speed toward the airport. The car had out-of-state plates. They didn't mean anything to Lind. He hadn't caught sight of the driver.

The car weaved in and out of traffic ahead. The driver didn't bother to signal. Lind watched until the car had disappeared into the mix. Then he stepped on the gas pedal again.

» » »

IN MINNEAPOLIS. Mathers dropped the phone from his ear.

"He's on his way to the airport," he told Stevens and Windermere. "Miami PD's got him tailed. We'll move on him as soon as he pulls into the rental car lot."

Stevens nodded, pacing, the adrenaline pumping. The bullpen around him was silent. Everyone in the office seemed to be watching. Even Harris, Windermere's boss, had come to the doorway. He caught Stevens's eye, his expression inscrutable.

Windermere paced a parallel track to Stevens. "Come on," she muttered. "Don't fuck this up."

49

There were police everywhere. Plainclothes and uniform, in cruisers and on foot. Parkerson drove into the airport complex, followed the signs toward the rental car return lots. Slowed the Caddy and waited on the shoulder for the asset to appear in the little red Chevy.

The asset drove slow, drove the speed limit, like he didn't see the tail behind him. Like he didn't realize the whole Miami police force was waiting to pounce. Parkerson waited until the Chevy was a few car lengths back. Then he pulled out into traffic ahead of it. Paced the asset into the vast rental car return structure. The cop in the Crown Vic followed, a few cars behind.

Wish I had a gun, Parkerson thought. *The kid's going to need help.*

Ahead of the Cadillac, the roadway curved and narrowed into a single lane. Concrete barriers on both sides. Parkerson stopped the Cadillac and climbed out, the engine still running. Behind him, the asset stopped the Chevy. The driver behind him leaned on his horn. So did the next driver. Soon the whole structure was filled with an angry chorus of horns and impatient shouting. Parkerson ignored the cacophony and hurried back to the Chevy. Stared past at the angry drivers beyond. The road curved out and away from the parking structure. The cop was stuck somewhere in the lineup, out of sight. He'd figure something was up soon enough. Time to hurry.

Parkerson opened the Chevy's door and peered in at the asset. The kid's eyes were devoid of emotion, his face slack. He stared up at Parkerson like he was sleepwalking. Parkerson shivered. "Killswitch," he said.

The asset blinked. "Change of plans," Parkerson told him. "Come on."

The asset let Parkerson unbuckle his seat belt and pull him out of the Chevy. Followed him back to the Cadillac and into the passenger seat. Parkerson buckled the kid in and circled around to the driver's side. Slid behind the wheel of the big sedan, his heart pounding sixteenth notes. Shifted the car into drive and stepped on the gas. The Caddy squealed away through the garage, leaving the little red Chevy marooned, the cop somewhere behind.

» » »

MATHERS FROWNED. "Still waiting," he said. "No sign of O'Brien."

Windermere checked her watch. "Should have happened by now," she said. "You're sure they didn't miss him?"

"They didn't miss him. O'Brien hasn't shown up at the Liberty desk."

"What about his tail?" said Stevens.

"The tail followed him into the rental car return center," said Mathers. "So we know he's in there, somewhere. Radio reception isn't great—all that concrete—so nobody's really sure what the holdup is."

"Any sign of Cook?"

"Cook's about fifty years old and he's got a family with him," said Mathers. "He cleared security, and he's waiting at his gate. Should I tell our guys to take him?"

Stevens glanced at Windermere. Windermere shook her head. "Wait on O'Brien," she said. "Damn it, make sure they're combing that Liberty lot. We can't lose this guy, Mathers. Make sure they know it."

"Roger."

"Jesus Christ." Windermere looked at Stevens. "What the hell's taking so long?"

50

The asset sat in silence as Parkerson drove away from the airport. Barely moved. Just stared out the window and watched the city fly by.

Parkerson glanced at him. "You know what happened?" The asset looked at him, blank-faced. "They were waiting for you," Parkerson said. "You know why?"

The asset shifted. "I don't know."

"You were careless in Minneapolis. They picked you up."

The asset said nothing.

"Duluth, too. Someone saw you, maybe. Called in your description, your car. You were careless and they followed you down here. Now you're fucked."

The asset stared out the window and didn't say anything. Parkerson searched the rearview mirror, his hands beating a staccato rhythm on the steering wheel. Saw no police cars behind him. The cops hadn't followed. The asset was safe. Killswitch was safe—for the moment.

Parkerson kept driving. No destination in mind. Just away.

51

Windermere dropped her hands. "It's over," she said. "He made us somehow."

Mathers listened into the phone. "They found O'Brien's rental car abandoned a couple hundred yards from the Liberty kiosk. Left his tail stranded in a big snarl of traffic."

Stevens swore. "We need Miami PD on every road out of the airport. Transit, too. Buses, taxis, trams, everything. Tell them to keep their goddamn eyes open."

"Nobody in the state has a clue what he looks like," said Windermere. "*We* saw him, Stevens. If we were there, we could have made him. Now he's gone."

Stevens looked around the bullpen, helpless, frustrated. The other agents who'd been watching now couldn't meet his gaze. They ducked down, turned away. Even Harris had disappeared from his doorway.

This is like trying to change a tire on a Mars rover, Stevens thought, *from down here on earth. How the hell do we catch this guy now?*

52

The asset sat in the diner and didn't say anything. Didn't make eye contact with Parkerson. Barely ate anything, just picked at his hamburger and drank a shitload of coffee. Frankly, it was a little unsettling.

Parkerson had driven them out of Miami and north along I-95 toward Daytona Beach. He'd driven because he couldn't think of anything else to do. Because the police were looking for the asset, and he figured it was safer to get the hell out of town. Nobody would look for them here. Not in this diner. Not yet. Parkerson stared across at the asset and tried to figure out what to do.

There was a TV in the diner, behind the long counter. It was playing the news on an endless cycle. Parkerson had watched coverage of the Miami Beach shooting four times since they'd walked through the door. He'd watched a breathless reporter at the Miami Beach Marina, standing alongside the *Kyla Dawn*. He'd watched the target's body as it was wheeled from the yacht. Heard eyewitness accounts of the shooting, none of which mentioned the asset or his little red car. Just as Parkerson figured they were safe, though, decided he'd overreacted just a tad, he heard the pretty blond reporter tell the camera that police and the FBI were looking for someone named Richard O'Brien.

So that settled it, then. The asset was compromised. The O'Brien alias was blown. Parkerson cut into his pork chop. What to do?

The smartest move would be to drive the kid to some woebegone swamp and put him out of his misery. End the chapter. It was going to happen soon enough anyway. Maybe this whole thing was a sign.

Parkerson eyed the kid across the booth. The kid stared down at the table. Clutched his cup of coffee. Drained it and asked for another. There wasn't an ounce of feeling inside him, Parkerson realized. The kid was the ultimate drone.

Parkerson finished his dinner and called for the check. Waited for the asset to finish his cup of coffee. Then he led the kid back out to the Cadillac. Buckled him up and set out into the sunset, searching for a back road and a swamp.

53

Mathers put down the phone. "No sign of this guy anywhere," he said. "Miami PD swept the whole airport. Canines, roadblocks, you name it. He straight-up disappeared."

"Damn it." Windermere sat heavy in her seat. "So where the hell did he go?"

"He abandoned the car at the entry to the rental car return building," said Stevens. "Left a traffic jam behind him. Stranded the tail. So what did the other drivers see?"

"Didn't see much," said Mathers. "The guy right behind O'Brien's Chevy is a Filipino national, doesn't speak much English. We're working on an interpreter, but it sounds like he's scared pretty damn shitless of the cops."

"Of course he is," said Windermere. "What about the other drivers?"

Mathers shook his head. "I guess there was a curve in the ramp," he said. "Bad visibility. Somebody said they saw another guy with O'Brien, but nobody's been able to get a decent description. For all we know, it's bogus."

Windermere and Stevens swapped glances. "Another guy?" said Stevens. "What, in the Chevy?"

"Like I said, it's chaos down there. Nobody's entirely sure." Mathers reached for the phone. "I'll call Miami back," he said. "Get some answers."

"Bullshit." Windermere stood. "I'm through with this armchair quarterbacking routine. O'Brien's still in Miami. We're going down there, and we're going to find him."

Mathers frowned. "I thought Harris said—"

"Things done changed, Mathers." She fixed her eyes on him. "I'll clear our travel with Harris. You go pack a bag."

54

Stevens watched from an empty cubicle as his FBI colleagues bustled around him, all excitement and nerves as they prepared for Miami.

This was FBI stuff. This was real hotshot policing. Stevens had tasted it once, when he'd chased down Arthur Pender, and it had been the most fun he'd ever had as a cop. Now Windermere was off to do it again, except this time she was bringing Mathers instead. Stevens watched them get ready, feeling extraneous and, if he were honest with himself, more than a little jealous.

You're a BCA agent, he thought. *This is how you wanted it. No cowboy stuff. No heroics. This is how you wanted your life, for you and Nancy both.*

Windermere came hustling past. Grinned at Stevens. Slapped him on the shoulder. "We're going to nail this bastard, Stevens," she said. "I can feel it."

"Damn right." Stevens cleared his throat. "Guess I'll step back and let you guys earn your paychecks," he said. "Not much use for me around here anymore."

Windermere stopped. "Bullshit. You're coming to Miami."

"This is FBI territory," he said. "What do you need with an old BCA agent?"

"Can't be the Lone Ranger without Tonto. Batman without Robin."

"Han Solo without Chewbacca," said Mathers.

Stevens laughed. "Anyone's the sidekick around here, it's you."

"Uh-huh." Windermere grinned at him. "We'll discuss it on the flight, Stevens. Unless you're too busy puking your guts out."

"Very funny. My boss would eat me for lunch."

"You're working the Pyatt angle, right? How do we know today's victim isn't Spenser Pyatt's long-lost cousin or something?"

"We don't," Stevens said, "but I can't just go bombing down to South Beach on a hunch, Carla."

"I'll clear it with Lesley." This wasn't Windermere. Stevens turned to find Drew Harris standing at Windermere's cubicle.

"Thank you, sir," Stevens said, "but I don't think you guys need me. Windermere and Agent Mathers are both more than capable."

"No doubt about that," Harris said, "but I need Mathers here."

Mathers blinked. "What?"

"I can't afford to send two of my agents on this manhunt, not the way this office is staffed. We're short manpower in CID as is, thanks to Homeland Security."

"So you're going to send the state cop to Miami," Mathers said slowly. "And keep me behind a desk in Minnesota?"

"I know you don't like it, son, but I'm short good agents. I can't afford to lose you and Windermere both." Harris turned to Stevens. "You're a part of this case, Agent Stevens," he said. "I know you work well with Agent Windermere. Don't you want to see this thing through?"

Stevens glanced at Mathers, who stared back, goggle-eyed. "I do," he said.

"Then pack a bag. I'll clear it with Tim Lesley."

Stevens nodded. "Yes, sir," he said. *But who's going to clear it with my wife?*

55

If the asset knew he was going to die, he didn't show it.

Parkerson drove blindly until the road beneath the Cadillac turned to dirt. The sun had set; it was dark beyond his headlights. Fog swirled up and across the road. The Cadillac was suddenly stifling hot.

Parkerson flipped on the AC and drove in silence, trying to keep his breathing steady. He was afraid, he realized. And sickened, nauseated by the messiness that was sure to come.

The asset sat beside him and didn't move. Didn't say anything. Just stared out the window and waited.

The road petered out ahead. So did the trees. Parkerson killed the engine and cut off the headlights. Climbed out of the Cadillac and stood in the gloom. There was water ahead; Parkerson could hear it. Hell, he was practically swimming already, the air was so humid. The night seemed to close in around him.

Parkerson walked ahead of the Cadillac to the edge of the road. Looked down and saw water, brackish and swampy. The fog swirled around him. There was no one around. This was as good a spot as any.

He walked back to the Cadillac, every nerve in his body tingling. He'd left his door slightly open, and the dome light burned through the gloom, the only light for miles. The night around the car was dead dark.

Parkerson studied the asset through the windshield of the Cadillac. He'd trained assets for nearly five years now. The assets had killed nearly forty people. Parkerson figured the twenty years he'd put in at his straight job had resulted, indirectly, in the deaths of thousands more. But he still hadn't grown comfortable taking lives himself. Not yet. Death was easy in the abstract. When it was numbers and figures, clean and absolute. Killing itself, though, was always messy. Parkerson looked at the kid and wished he had a gun. Something quick and efficient, at least.

There was rope in the trunk of the car. A tire iron. Parkerson popped the trunk and picked up the tire iron. Tested its weight. His stomach churned. His pulse roared in his ears. Was he doing this?

The asset still hadn't moved. Didn't he know what was coming, somewhere in that fucked-up brain of his? Did he care?

Parkerson swung the tire iron experimentally. Wondered how it would feel when it struck flesh and bone. How much blood it would draw. How long the kid would take to die. He felt suddenly nauseous. Tried to spit, found his mouth dry. He swore. Shook out his arms. The asset watched him.

Something in the car was chiming, electronic. Parkerson realized he'd left the keys in the ignition. The car had been chiming the whole time. Parkerson hadn't noticed. Either the asset hadn't, either, or he just didn't care.

It just seemed like such a waste. The other assets had earned their deaths. They had failed, each of them, had grown soft, developed defects. This asset here was still perfectly good. He could still follow orders. He could still kill at will.

Parkerson tapped the tire iron against his palm. So the Richard O'Brien alias was shot. So what? The apartment in Philadelphia was registered corporate. Another shell company, untraceable. Even if the police knew the asset came from Philly, they didn't have an address. The kid could grow a beard if he needed to. Wear a disguise.

A new alias. That's all the asset needed. The rental car scam was shot, too, but Parkerson could work around that. The asset was still valid. He was still fundamentally intact. He still had at least a couple kills left.

Parkerson looked back at the car. The asset hadn't moved. Parkerson swore and threw the tire iron in the backseat. Slid behind the wheel and sat there a moment, feeling the sweat drip down the back of his shirt, feeling his heart slow to normal pace. He took a long breath and turned the key in the ignition. "Fuck it," he said, shifting into reverse. "Let's get out of here."

56

Tim Lesley didn't need much convincing. "You want to do this?" he asked Stevens. "You think you can contribute?"

Stevens looked around the FBI bullpen, the phone to his ear. Windermere watched him. Met his eyes and smiled, encouraging. "I do," Stevens told his boss. "I want this."

"You're my best man," said Lesley. "I don't blame Harris for poaching you, especially not with that firecracker Windermere involved."

"Yes, sir," said Stevens. "Thank you."

"Catch the bastard, Stevens. And when you do, tell him the BCA sent you."

"Yes, sir, will do. Thank you, sir." Stevens hung up the phone. Threw a thumbs-up at Windermere. *Okay,* he thought, exhaling. *So the easy part's done.*

"MIAMI." Nancy Stevens stared across the kitchen at him. "Windermere."

Stevens nodded. He'd driven home from Brooklyn Center. Needed to pack a bag. Anyway, he figured Nancy deserved to hear it in person. "I know this is sudden," he said, "but it sounds like the FBI could really use me."

His wife sucked her teeth. Looked around the room. She'd been swamped with paperwork when he'd come through the door, barricaded behind piles of briefs and motions. There were dark circles under her eyes. "I don't know why they can't solve their own cases," she said.

Stevens sighed. "Yeah," he said. "Honey, I'm sorry."

"Sorry?" Nancy looked at him. "You didn't see this coming, Kirk? You didn't think you'd get mixed up in this one like you did with the kidnappers and Carter Tomlin?"

"Nancy—"

"This *isn't* sudden, Kirk. I saw this coming the moment you told me Windermere had a case. I knew you'd walk in here one night with that goofy look on your face and tell me you were going off to be a hero again."

"I won't risk my life," he said. "I'll let the FBI guys be the cowboys."

"Look," Nancy said, "I don't want to be the bad guy here. I don't want to be the naggy wife who keeps you from doing what you want."

"You're not the bad guy, Nancy. That's not it at all."

"It is, though. If it wasn't for me, you'd be right out the door."

"That's not true."

She looked at him. "Isn't it?"

Stevens didn't say anything. After a moment, Nancy shook her head. "I guess you have to get going."

Stevens nodded. "Pretty quick."

"You packed?"

"Not yet."

"You should pack." She looked at him. "I guess we'll talk this thing out when you get back. Assuming you do get back, Agent Stevens, and some psycho killer doesn't put you in a box first."

Stevens wanted to laugh. His wife looked so small at the kitchen table, though, tired and sad and alone. His heart ached for her. "I'll come back, Nancy," he said. "Soon. I promise."

She didn't look at him. "You'd better," she said. "Now get out of here."

57

Parkerson drove the asset to the old Atlantic Coast Line depot in Palatka, Florida. He bought a ticket from the Amtrak agent inside, and then walked back out to the parking lot to sit in the Cadillac and wait for the train.

The asset still hadn't said anything. He'd sat in silence as Parkerson reversed the big Cadillac down that godforsaken dirt road, unaware of how close he'd been to death. He'd sat and said nothing as Parkerson drove north, and he said nothing now, in the Amtrak parking lot.

The train station was nearly deserted. An older couple waited on the platform, surrounded by suitcases and overstuffed plastic bags. They were the only other people Parkerson could see. He checked the time and stared out the window down the tracks, searching for the train's headlight in the darkness.

He handed the asset the train ticket. "This will get you to Philadelphia," he said. "Get you home. Go back to your apartment and stay there. Understand?"

The kid nodded. "Yes."

"You're no longer Richard O'Brien." Parkerson held out his hand. "As soon as they take your ticket, you throw out whatever ID you have with that name on it. Everything. Give me your wallet."

Wordless, the kid produced his wallet. Parkerson took it, removed the

Triple A Industries credit card. Thought for a moment, and then dug in his own pocket and handed the kid a hundred dollars in twenties. "In case you need to eat."

The kid folded the money into his wallet. Didn't speak.

"Stay in the apartment," Parkerson told him. "Don't leave. Wait for my instructions. I'll have your new name and ID ready in a couple of days."

The kid put his wallet away. Parkerson studied his face. "What did I just say?"

The kid repeated his instructions, word for word. No hesitation. Like a robot. When he'd finished, he paused. Shifted his weight and looked at Parkerson like a first-grader with a full bladder.

"What?" Parkerson said. "What's the matter?"

The asset hesitated. Opened his mouth and couldn't seem to form words. "The visions," he said at last. "You—"

"I'll deal with the visions," Parkerson told him. "I have a few more jobs I need you to do for me. Then I'll make everything better. Understand?"

The kid looked at him, a glimmer of hope in his eyes. It was the first sign of life Parkerson had seen all day.

THE TRAIN SHOWED UP at a quarter to ten. Parkerson walked the asset onto the platform. Stood him in line beside the gleaming coach cars and watched the asset climb aboard and pick out a seat. The kid didn't look at him. He stared straight ahead, at the seat back in front of him. Didn't move, barely blinked, and then the train pulled away.

Parkerson watched the train inch away from the platform. He kept his eyes on the asset as long as he could. Then the coach car was gone and the train picked up speed, the diner flashing by, then the sleeping cars, until all that was left were the red marker lights on the end of the last car, disappearing into the night.

Parkerson stood on the platform for a few minutes, listening as the big diesel engine's throb slowly faded away. When he turned from the tracks, the platform was empty. He walked back to the Cadillac and slid behind the wheel. Closed his eyes and rested there for a moment. Then he straightened and fired up the engine. He still had a long way to go.

58

"Mathers hates you." Windermere grinned at Stevens as he settled beside her. "Poor bastard had his heart set on South Beach."

Stevens forced a laugh. "Miami's nothing special in the springtime, anyway."

"It's freaking *perfect*, Stevens. And manning the fort while we run off and have an adventure is hardly going to turn Mathers on."

"Yeah, well." The plane jolted back from the gate. Stevens gripped the armrests. "Right now, I'm not exactly concerned with what turns Mathers on."

"Maybe you should be," said Windermere. "The big dummy asked me out."

Stevens looked at her. "Really?"

"The other night, yeah. He tried to play it cool, but I could see what he was aiming for."

"You turned him down."

"I did." Windermere picked up her magazine. "Don't know why, though. It might have been fun."

She paged through the magazine and said nothing else, leaving Stevens to clutch the armrests and stare out the window, his stomach churning and his mind working like a hamster in a wheel as the plane shuddered its way down the runway.

IT WAS JUST AFTER MIDNIGHT when they landed in Miami. There was a federal agent waiting for them at the arrivals gate. He looked fresh, despite the hour, and he grinned wide when he saw Windermere. "There she is," he said, wrapping her in a hug. "You figure your old friends couldn't cut it down here, or what?"

"Roman." Windermere hugged him back. Then she gestured to Stevens. "This is Kirk Stevens, Minnesota BCA. We're working this thing together."

The agent studied Stevens. "A state cop, too," he said, deadpan. "You must really think we're weak down here, Carla." Then he grinned at Stevens. Held out his hand. "I'm just playing, brother. Roman Ojeda. Pleased to meet you."

Ojeda's energy was infectious, even after the flight, and Stevens smiled as he shook the man's hand. "Likewise," he said. "See if I can't teach the FBI a thing or two."

Ojeda grinned at Windermere. "A gamer. I like him already."

Stevens and Windermere followed Ojeda to his waiting Crown Vic. They piled in, and Ojeda drove away from the terminal. "Got a couple of rooms at the Golden Glades Hotel, couple blocks from the office." Ojeda glanced at Windermere. "Kind of shady digs, but we didn't know where else to put you."

Windermere nodded. "It's cool. We'll be close to home base, anyway."

"Get you your own ride if you want it. Weapons, whatever you need."

"Car would be nice. Guns, too. This guy's not exactly an amateur."

"Who is this cat, anyway? What's the story?"

"Wish I knew," she said. "We're still scrambling."

She gave Ojeda the rundown. The whole story, from Saint Paul to Duluth to Miami. In the backseat, Stevens leaned against the window and stared out at the night. He listened to Windermere for a while, tried to keep his eyes open. Within a few minutes, though, he'd drifted off.

When he woke, they were parked outside a hotel. Ojeda climbed from the car and walked them to the front doors. "Reservation's in your name," he told Windermere. "See you tomorrow."

Stevens stretched, yawning. "Christ," he said, following Windermere into the lobby. "I'm ready for bed."

"Yeah?" Windermere turned and grinned back at him. "Get your sleep when you can, partner. As of tomorrow, we're twenty-four seven."

59

Lind rode Amtrak's *Silver Star* through the night. He stared out the window, watching his reflection slowly fade as dawn broke over the Carolinas. The train trundled north through Raleigh and Richmond, Washington, D.C., and Wilmington, Delaware, and Lind watched the scenery pass and didn't move much, drank bad coffee and tried not to sleep.

Something had gone wrong in Florida. Lind could tell. He felt an emptiness gnaw in his stomach, a worry. He was counting on the man's help to make the visions go away. The man had promised he would help. It was a promise Lind clung to. It was the only thing that kept Lind from blowing his own head off.

The train pulled into Philadelphia's 30th Street Station early in the evening. Lind stood, stretched, and filed off the train with the rest of the passengers. Rode the elevator up to the concourse and walked outside to the street.

It was raining again. It was always raining lately. Lind ducked his head and walked into the city. He was soaked before he made it two blocks, but he hardly noticed. He walked back to his apartment, rode the elevator to his floor. Turned on the TV and every light in the place, brewed another pot of coffee, and sat down on the couch to wait for the man to tell him what to do.

60

"Cameron Ansbacher," Windermere announced. "That's our dead yachtsman. Owns a shipping company."

Stevens caught her eye across the boardroom in the FBI's Miami office. They'd commandeered the location for a temporary base of operations first thing in the morning. Now, with Roman Ojeda's help, they'd set to work hunting down their shooter. "A shipping company," he said. "And the boat's owner is an importer."

"Coffee." Windermere sat. "The guy imports coffee. Or that's what he claims."

"So we've got a shipper meeting with a coffee importer on a mega-yacht in Miami Beach. How does this tie in with Spenser Pyatt and Eli Cody?"

"I had Mathers go through our files on Pyatt this morning. He couldn't find any connection. Ditto for Cody."

"How's the kid doing up there in the cold?"

"Mathers?" Windermere shrugged. "He ain't happy, Stevens."

"Shit."

"Thought you didn't care what turned him on, partner." She grinned at him. "He's a junior agent. You know how many times I got stuck shoveling shit in this office while everyone else got to run off and play cowboy? It's a fact of life around here. Gotta put in your time."

Stevens shook his head. "Still robbed the kid of his trip to the beach."

"Still nothing, you big softie. Focus on the case." She picked up a stack of paper, examined it idly. "Mathers couldn't find anything linking Pyatt, Cody, and Cameron Ansbacher."

"Besides the fact that they were killed by the same shooter."

"Yeah," said Windermere. "The shooter's the same, but maybe that's the only connection."

"That's a pretty damn big connection, Carla."

"No doubt," Windermere said. "I'm just thinking maybe we get further if we treat Ansbacher and Pyatt like two distinct crimes. Add up all the facts and look for similarities."

Stevens mulled it over. "Okay," he said. "So what do we know about Cameron Ansbacher?"

ACCORDING TO MIAMI PD. Ansbacher was a fifty-six-year-old American expatriate living on the island of St. Kitts. He owned a small shipping firm, as advertised: a couple of old cargo ships used mainly, it appeared, to transport goods from Miami around the West Indies. He'd been in Miami to negotiate a contract with one Hugo Peralta for the import of coffee beans from Colombia into the United States. From what the police department could gather, the deal was almost done.

"And then Ansbacher stepped aboard Peralta's yacht and caught a bullet in his brain," said Windermere. "No deal."

"No deal." Stevens stared out the window to the highway beyond. "Huh. So maybe someone didn't want Ansbacher importing that coffee."

"Like a competitor? Like our shooter's some kind of murderous shipping magnate?"

"Who knows? The timing is suspicious, is all I'm saying."

"Ansbacher was scheduled to fly back to St. Kitts on Monday morning," said Windermere. "Maybe it's a coincidence he was murdered on

Peralta's yacht. Like it was the only time our guy could get to him before he flew home."

Stevens threw up his hands. "Shit. We're just guessing at this point."

Ojeda poked his head into the boardroom. "Hey, guys," he said. "Got a present for you."

"Is it security footage?" said Windermere.

Ojeda shook his head. "TSA's still being a bastard. But I have someone I want you to meet." He ducked back from the door. Ushered in a companion, a heavyset woman with dark eyes and a set jaw. She held Stevens's gaze like a challenge.

"This is Officer Oneida Ware," said Ojeda. "She thinks she saw our shooter."

Ware glared at Ojeda. "Don't *think* anything. I *saw* him. I saw them both."

Stevens and Windermere swapped glances. "Both?"

Ojeda laughed from the doorway. "I'll get Officer Ware a coffee. I think you're going to like what she has to say."

61

Stevens watched Oneida Ware sip her coffee across the boardroom table. The airport traffic cop stared back at him over her cup.

"We shut down O'Brien's alias," said Stevens. "Put a hold on his corporate credit card, too. No way he should have been able to skate undetected."

Ware put down her cup. "Wasn't skating alone," she said. "Like I said, he had help."

"Who?"

"Middle-aged white guy. Real clean. Nice suit. Blocked the rental car ramp in his Cadillac. I heard the commotion, a bunch of horns and whatnot, came out of the garage, and saw the Caddy was abandoned. Was about to call for a tow truck when the driver came back with your boy. Piled him in the car and drove off."

"He intercepted O'Brien," said Stevens. "Then they bolted."

"You remember the guy's face?" said Windermere. "Maybe we can get a sketch out. Put his face on the street."

"I can try," said Ware. "Don't know how much good it would do you. Guy was your everyday old white man, like I said."

"You remember anything else about him?" said Stevens. "About the car?"

"The car, yeah. Was a gray Cadillac. Four doors. Plates from out of state."

"What kind of out of state?"

Ware shrugged. "North Carolina, maybe? I didn't get a clean look."

Stevens made a note. "Anything else?"

"Nah. It was fast."

"But you're sure he's the guy."

"Yeah." Ware frowned. "I seen the drawings you all passed around. It's the same kid. Spooky eyes, like he was sleepwalking."

"That's our guy," said Windermere. She looked at Stevens. "Let's get Officer Ware to a sketch artist. Try and get a read on this mystery accomplice. If the TSA's not going to help us, this might be our only shot."

62

Parkerson drove north up Interstate 95 until he hit Savannah, Georgia. Then he made a detour.

He'd spent the night thinking about the asset, about the Miami job. He kept seeing the target's head explode, the asset's blank eyes. The kid was a genuine killer. A credit to the Killswitch program, and he'd gotten out of state clean. There were still too many new applications, though, for one asset to handle. It was time to expand the program.

He turned east onto Interstate 16, bombed across Georgia through Macon to Atlanta, where he found a cheap roadside motel with a vacancy sign, and parked the Cadillac for a few hours' rest. It was nearly five in the morning; the eastern horizon was just starting to show light. Parkerson had been surviving on Red Bull and adrenaline for the better part of two days.

He slept until nearly noon, and when he woke up he showered and drove to a shopping mall, where he bought fresh clothes and a toothbrush and changed in the mall bathroom, splashed cold water on his face, and examined himself in the mirror. His eyes were bloodshot and sunken, his hair unkempt; he needed a shave. He was starting to look like one of the assets himself.

Parkerson dried his face and walked out of the bathroom. On the way out of the mall, he bought a pair of cheap sunglasses and a Braves hat—a ready-made disguise. He drove the Cadillac into a leafy suburb in the northeast part of town, found a back road office complex, a couple of restaurants, and a sketchy talent agency. He parked across from a nondescript commercial low-rise and watched the building's front doors from inside the car.

It was a busy day, and Parkerson watched people walk in and walk out for a couple of hours, listening to more Bach and fighting the exhaustion and adrenaline that seemed to come at him in waves.

THEY BEGAN TO ARRIVE a little before three. Men, mostly, a couple of women. Most of them were still young, in their mid-twenties or so. Veterans, all of them, come for counseling or medication or simply a place of refuge. All of them potential new assets.

Parkerson knew that the average American citizen would find his actions reprehensible. The patriots would froth at his exploitation of traumatized veterans. Frankly, he didn't care. These soldiers were his best workers. They trained better, they killed better, and they didn't make mistakes.

As far as Parkerson was concerned, this was capitalism. This was no different than the railroads' employing Chinese laborers because they worked harder, or Andrew Carnegie's fighting the unions in his steel mills because they wanted unfair concessions. This was the pursuit of productivity, the American way. Soldiers made the best assets, morality be damned.

Parkerson watched the veterans arrive. Some came with friends and family; they were dropped at the doors out of minivans and midsize sedans, the drivers waiting until they'd disappeared inside the building before they idled slowly away. Parkerson ignored these candidates. He didn't need nosy relatives asking questions, pushy mothers, fathers, wives. He waited, and focused on the young men and women who came alone.

It was five minutes past three when Parkerson saw him. As young as the rest, and solitary. He walked across the parking lot, slow, from the road. Like he didn't realize he was late.

He had long, greasy hair and a peach-fuzz chin. Circles under his eyes, as though he hadn't slept in weeks. Just looking at him made Parkerson feel tired again. The kid crossed the lot, glanced in the Cadillac as he passed it. Parkerson met his eyes and knew in a split second that this was the one. He wore the same blank expression as Lind.

The kid walked to the low-rise and paused at the doors. Stood there for a moment, not looking at anything. Then someone opened the door and came out of the building. The kid hesitated, and then slipped in through the open door.

Parkerson stared after the kid and saw dollar signs. *That's the guy,* he thought, his adrenaline ramping up again. *That's my next asset.*

63

Ware said North Carolina plates." Stevens stared at his computer screen. "Virginia plates aren't much different, if you don't get a clean look."

Windermere circled around the table and peered over Stevens's shoulder. "Triple A Industries has a Richmond P.O. box," she said. "That's where you're going with this?"

Stevens nodded. "Maybe this guy's Triple A Industries."

"And, what, the shooter's his partner? They make these hits together?"

"I don't know," said Stevens. "Where was this guy when Spenser Pyatt was murdered?"

Windermere stared at the screen for a moment. "We'll get the sketch to Richmond police," she said, straightening. "Have 'em look out for gray Cadillacs. Who knows? Maybe our man checks his mail."

"If he hasn't gone underground yet," said Stevens. "We definitely spooked him. Could be they turned tail and ran for the border."

"It's a lot tougher to disappear than people think," said Windermere. "If we can find a loose thread to pull, we can unravel this case, Stevens. We just need a lead on these guys."

"Mathers making any progress?"

Windermere shook her head. "Not yet. He's pretty much stonewalled on Spenser Pyatt, though. As far as he can figure, there's no connection to the Ansbacher killing whatsoever. I have him trying to chase down Philadelphia O'Briens right now, maybe pick up the trail from that end, but I still think we have a better chance chasing our killer down here."

"Yeah," said Stevens. "But how?"

Windermere walked around the table to the wall of windows. Stared out at the bleak landscape: low-rise office buildings, the highway. They'd been over this all morning and half of the afternoon. The shooter was gone. And nobody had any answers.

Stevens's cell phone began to ring. He answered. "Kirk Stevens."

"Stevens, it's McNaughton." Even eighteen hundred miles away, Stevens could sense the excitement in his old colleague's voice. "You got time to chat?"

Stevens sat up. "Always."

"You'll notice I'm working on the weekend," said McNaughton. "All for you. Feel free to thank me with cash."

"I'll send flowers. What's up?"

"Couple of things I figured you maybe could use. First, I found a Post-it note in Eli Cody's desk. Just a word and a series of numbers. Didn't make sense, but I stored it away. Figured I'd check on it later."

"Sure," said Stevens. "I bet it's later now."

"Correct. We got into Cody's bank accounts this morning. He was pretty much broke, like we figured. At least relatively speaking."

"Relatively speaking."

"I mean, he comes from a family of multimillionaires," said McNaughton. "At the time of his death, Cody had exactly fifty-four thousand, one hundred and twelve dollars and eighty-eight cents to his name."

"Not exactly a fortune."

"Exactly. Here's the weird part. In the week before he was murdered, Cody made two hundred-thousand-dollar payments to a numbered bank account on the Isle of Man. First payment a week before his death. Second payment was initiated on Saturday afternoon, completed Sunday morning."

Stevens straightened. "Just after Spenser Pyatt was murdered," he said.

"I guess so. I mean, yeah. That's more your area of expertise. Point is, the numbered bank account matched the numbers I found on Cody's Post-it note."

Stevens frowned. "You said there was a word on that Post-it note, too," he said. "What was it?"

McNaughton paused. "Killswitch," she said. "The word was Killswitch."

64

The minivans began to return at ten minutes to four. Parkerson watched them from the Cadillac. At five minutes past four, the office doors opened and the veterans started to emerge.

Some of them came out in pairs, some in groups. Some talked to one another, even laughed, though not many. They shook hands or waved good-bye, or walked alone to the cars and minivans at the curb. The minivans pulled away. The veterans dissipated. Parkerson waited.

Finally, the shaggy-haired kid came out of the building. There was a woman beside him, a brunette, middle-aged. The kid towered over her, even slouched as he was. He stared down at her as she talked to him. Didn't say a thing. Finally, the woman stopped talking. She looked at the kid. They looked at each other. Then she seemed to sigh. Her shoulders deflated. She patted the kid on the arm and went back inside the building.

The kid felt around in his pockets and came out with a cigarette. Lit it and started across the lot. He passed the Cadillac again, and if he recognized it he didn't show it. He just walked, empty-eyed, out to the street.

Parkerson idled the Cadillac after the kid. Followed him down the block to a bus stop and waited in an adjacent lot. The kid stood at the shelter for ten minutes. Then the bus came and he climbed aboard.

Parkerson followed the bus until it stopped in front of a vast concrete apartment tower. The doors opened and the kid stepped down to the curb. He walked toward the tower. Parkerson followed. Parked the Cadillac outside the front doors and watched the kid walk into the lobby. There was a bank of mailboxes along the wall. The kid took out a key and opened a mailbox, stared inside a moment, and then closed it again. Then he walked to the elevators.

Parkerson climbed out of the Cadillac as the elevator doors shut. He walked into the lobby and checked the number on the kid's mailbox. Then he called another elevator and waited.

Parkerson rode the elevator to the eighth floor. He walked down the hall until he found the kid's apartment number, and he stood in the hall for a minute or two, straining to hear through the flimsy wooden door. He heard a TV but no voices. Finally, he knocked on the door.

There was no answer. Parkerson knocked again. Waited. Heard the lock disengage. The door swung open and the kid stared out at him, no recognition in his eyes. Parkerson looked past him into the apartment. It was a studio suite. An immaculate bed—looked like it had never been slept in. The TV on, loud. Bed aside, the place was a mess. There was nobody else in the room.

The kid stared at Parkerson, waiting. Parkerson grinned at him. "Hi there," he said. "Buy you a cup of coffee?"

65

"Killswitch," said Windermere. "What the hell is it?"

Stevens stared at his computer. "According to Google, it's an emergency shutdown trigger," he said. "Used when normal avenues fail."

Windermere cocked her head. "That doesn't help us. What else comes up?"

Stevens scrolled down the long list of search results. Shook his head. "Not much," he said. Then he leaned forward. "Wait."

"Yeah?"

Stevens clicked through. "It's an entry on a forum," he said, reading, "for gun enthusiasts. Guy says he's having problems at work. Hates his boss. His buddy says, 'Let Killswitch take care of it.'"

"And?"

"And the guy says, 'LMAO. Wish I could afford it.'" Stevens looked at Windermere. "What the hell's LMAO?"

"Laughing my ass off." Windermere arched an eyebrow. "It's Internet speak, Stevens. Thought you had a daughter."

"Guess I don't pay enough attention to her. Too busy solving the FBI's cases."

Windermere snorted. "Oh, is that what you're doing?"

"Trying to, anyway." He turned back to the computer. "'Let Killswitch take care of it,'" he read. "What does that mean?"

Windermere walked around behind him. He could feel her body close, her breath near his ear as she bent down and read over his shoulder. "He's a mercenary," she said. "Killswitch. A hired gun."

Her face was close to his, very close. Stevens moved back a little. "Go on."

"Cody paid two hundred thousand dollars to Killswitch the week Spenser Pyatt was murdered. You said yourself Cody had a hate-on for Pyatt."

"Yeah," said Stevens, "okay, but who in the hell paid to kill Eli Cody?"

"Mickey Pyatt. Or some other Pyatt. Revenge."

"No way. Mickey Pyatt called my boss himself. Anyway, he wouldn't use the same shooter that killed his dad. I think revenge is out."

Windermere picked up the phone. "I'm still telling Mathers to check out Mickey Pyatt. You BCA guys are a little too close to that family."

Stevens stared at her. "You're kidding me, Carla."

"Of course I am, partner. But I'm still going to need to see bank statements and alibis before I'm convinced they're the good guys." Windermere straightened and started to pace. "If this Killswitch angle is for real, Stevens, it means the Ansbacher murder is totally disconnected from Pyatt and Cody. It's a new job for O'Brien. Another assignment."

"Yeah, so who called it in?" said Stevens. "Who paid Killswitch to murder Cameron Ansbacher?"

Windermere stopped pacing. "I don't know, Stevens," she said, grinning, "but we're going to find out."

66

"Oh, my God. Are you insane?"

Lind looked up and found a girl staring at his shopping basket, openmouthed. Not just any girl. It was the girl from the Delta counter, the pretty, pale-faced girl who'd recognized him before his flight to Duluth. She was here, in the Super Fresh, and she was talking to him again.

"TV dinners and coffee." She was pawing through his groceries. "Oh, and Red Bull. Not a vegetable in sight. What are you, a long-distance trucker?"

Lind shifted his weight. Felt the first hint of panic, black and cold. He wondered how the girl had found him. "I'm not a long-distance trucker," he said.

The girl looked up at him with her big eyes. "You can't eat like this," she said. "So unhealthy. It's a miracle you're not three hundred pounds already."

Lind looked up and down the aisle. Wished the girl would go away. Wondered if he should just make a break for it.

He'd run out of coffee. He'd nearly fallen asleep, and he needed caffeine. Coffee. Red Bull. And maybe something to eat. The man had told him to stay in the apartment, but he couldn't expect him to starve, could he?

The girl was still looking at him. "You okay?"

Lind didn't answer. The panic was stronger now. His head started to buzz. He would attract undue attention, he knew, if he ran. People would stare. He would have to get through this. "Yes," he said. "I'm fine."

"I saw you by the coffee," she said. "Thought it was you. Do you live around here?"

The pressure was building in his skull. The buzzing inside his ears. Lind tried to keep his breathing steady. The girl frowned again. "You sure you're okay, man?"

"I'm fine," Lind said. "Really."

She studied his face for a moment, and Lind hoped she'd take the hint and just leave him alone. She sighed and straightened and started to turn away. Then she stopped. "I'm Caity," she said. "Sorry. I don't normally do this, I just . . . you know, I just wanted to say hi."

"Okay," Lind said. "Hi."

She looked down. Shifted her weight, like she was deciding something. The pressure was back now, just behind Lind's eyes. He watched her and waited and tried not to scream.

"Do you live around here?" she said again. "I mean, I guess you must if you're shopping here, right? I live down on Pine, like, a couple blocks that way?"

Lind nodded. "Okay."

"Where do you live?"

He shrugged. Thought of the man and wanted to pass out, to retch, to tear his face off. Anything to ease the pressure in his brain. "I live downtown," he said. "I have an apartment." He looked at her. "I need to go home now."

"Okay." The girl frowned. "Okay, yeah. I'm sorry."

Lind didn't say anything.

"I didn't mean to bug you," she said. "I just thought, you know, it was cool. Running into you and everything. I'm doing this thing where I'm trying to push my limits, you know? Get out of my comfort zone. I thought, what the hell, just say something to him. I didn't mean to make fun of your dinner."

Lind waited. She still wasn't moving. "It's okay," he said finally.

"Yeah," she said. "Okay. Guess I'll see you."

She turned and walked away. He watched her go, feeling the pressure ease as she drifted up the aisle. He'd upset her, he knew. That shouldn't matter. He should pay for his groceries and go back to the apartment and wait. He knew the man would want him there. He knew the man might be calling right now.

The girl stopped halfway up the aisle. Picked up a package of coffee and looked at it. Then she glanced back at him and frowned. "What?"

Lind shook his head. It was time to go. He should just turn around and walk out of the store. Now, before the panic came back.

He didn't move.

"I'm sorry," he said.

The girl furrowed her brow, but she relaxed a little. "What for?"

Lind looked at her. He opened his mouth to say something, and then closed it. He didn't know what to tell her. He wanted to disappear.

She stared at him, waiting for his answer. The panic was beginning again. Soon it would overwhelm him. He knew it. But the girl was still waiting.

Lind shook his head. "I don't know," he said. "I'm sorry."

67

"Cameron Ansbacher."

Windermere dropped a thick file folder on the table. It landed with a thud. Echoed around the boardroom. It was dusk outside the window. The highway was headlights and stop-and-go traffic, and inside, the FBI office was mostly deserted. Even Ojeda had begged off for the day.

Stevens picked up the folder. "This is everything?"

"Ansbacher's life. Everything I could pull up from the National Crime

Information Center database, plus a bunch of Google searches." Windermere sat beside him. "It's mostly Google searches. Apart from a couple minor flings with the law a couple decades back, Ansbacher's pretty well clean."

"He have family?"

"Goes through girlfriends like water, apparently. Nobody closer."

"Known enemies?"

"Guess we're going to find out."

Stevens studied the folder. It was thick. "You know my first thought," he said. "This guy's in shipping. Dealing with a quote-unquote importer."

"Drugs?" Windermere shook her head. "My first thought, too. But the DEA tells me he's clean, so far as they know."

"What about Peralta?"

"Straight coffee, no sugar." She looked at him. "Again, as far as they know."

"Sure. Can we trust their intelligence?"

Windermere made a face. "Who knows? Let's say yes, for the short term. See if any other stories present themselves. If not, we'll circle back to the drug angle."

"Right."

WINDERMERE HAD BEEN DILIGENT. Every hit on Ansbacher's name was printed and collated in the folder. And at first glance, the man's life looked unique. Lots of pictures from Miami Beach parties. Lots of young women, a few celebrity snapshots. Articles in the local newspapers, trade journals. Shipping magazines. Stevens scanned them. Kept looking. Then he stopped. "Anyone talk to Peralta?"

"Miami PD," said Windermere, "and then Ojeda did. Why?"

Stevens glanced back at the shipping magazines. "This guy was on Peralta's yacht to close a deal," he said. "Is it crazy that I want to know a little more about it?"

"About the deal."

Stevens nodded. "Spenser Pyatt was murdered because Eli Cody held a grudge. Ansbacher was closing a pretty big deal. I'm still wondering if maybe—"

"There isn't another spurned lover in the background?"

"Exactly."

Windermere stood. "So let's talk to Peralta," she said. "See if you're right."

68

The kid could hold his coffee. Not so much his liquor.

His name was Wendell Gray, he told Parkerson. He'd finished his last tour in 2011.

"Came home," he said, staring into his beer. "Everything was cool for a while. The dreams, though. They got worse."

"Visions," said Parkerson.

"Nightmares. Couldn't sleep." He looked at Parkerson with those dead eyes of his. "Still can't sleep."

"You did the right thing, though. You got help."

Gray scoffed. "What, the Vet Center? They can't help me. Nobody ain't been there can help me."

Parkerson caught the bartender's eye. Motioned at the kid's glass. Another round. Another couple of shots. The bartender nodded.

"You got family, Wendell?" Parkerson said. "Friends, a girlfriend? Anybody could help you?"

Gray shook his head. His eyes watered. "Got nobody," he said. "I just got myself."

The bartender slid down another beer. Two shots of tequila. Parkerson placed them in front of Gray. Patted his hand. "You got me, kid."

IT DIDN'T TAKE MUCH before Wendell Gray was blackout drunk, head lolling. Parkerson paid the tab and carried the kid back to the Cadillac. Stuck him in the passenger seat and opened the window.

He slid behind the wheel and studied his face in the rearview mirror. Tired eyes. He slapped himself awake and leaned forward and turned the key in the ignition, feeling the car rumble as the big engine fired up.

Wendell Gray was leaned up against the door, snoring softly. Parkerson idled out of the lot, praying the kid stayed unconscious for the next 250 miles. Thinking it would be nice if he didn't puke on the leather.

69

oly cow." Caity Sherman stood in the doorway, staring in at Richard O'Brien's apartment. "You have an amazing place, Richard."

Truth be told, she still wasn't quite sure what she was doing here. She'd struck up a conversation with the guy in the Super Fresh because, hell, why not? She'd seen him at the airport a few times now, and he was cute, even though he always looked kind of tired and mopey.

Anyway, it wasn't like she had many friends here. Might as well take a chance, right? The guy was a frequent flier, so he couldn't be too dangerous.

And then he'd kind of blown her off, and she'd figured, okay, another asshole in the world, and she'd walked away, no harm done. But then he'd called out to her, and the way he looked at her wasn't tired or mopey, it was desperate, almost pleading. And she'd melted, okay, a doormat as always, but something told her maybe he was just as lonely as she was. Maybe he needed a friend.

And now she was here, walking into his apartment, carrying two bags full of the groceries she'd helped him pick out, and she still wasn't sure exactly what she was doing. It wasn't like the guy was much of a talker— hell, he was *awkward*, and sometimes he got this spooky look in his eye, like he was somewhere else entirely. But she'd walked him through the supermarket anyway, replacing the TV dinners in the frozen-food aisle and clinging to that brief glimpse of life she'd seen in his eyes, telling herself she was doing her good deed for the day, totally altruistic, and it wasn't just the prospect of her own sad little empty apartment that was keeping her by this guy's side.

She'd walked him into the produce section. Picked out fresh vegetables—peppers and spinach and broccoli and tomatoes. Found pasta and sauce and extra-lean ground beef. "Normally, I wouldn't advocate eating meat," she said. "Humans don't need it. But you don't look like you want to be a vegetarian yet."

He'd blinked. "I'm not a vegetarian."

Caity grinned at him. "Not yet."

He hadn't complained. Not until she'd tried to get him to replace the Red Bull. Then he put his hand on her arm. "I need it," he said.

She paused. His touch was firm, but not threatening. More like clumsy, like he didn't know his own strength. Like he wasn't exactly experienced in the physical contact department. "It's so unhealthy," she said.

"I just need it," he said again.

"Okay," she said. "Keep it, then. If you eat right, though, you won't need it as much as you think. Trust me."

She'd filled up his basket with good stuff, kale and quinoa and even a little tofu, and after they'd both paid for their groceries, they walked out onto the sidewalk together. He looked down at his grocery bags. Then he looked at her. "Yeah?" she said. "Everything cool?"

He hesitated. "I don't know what to do with this."

He looked small. Small and helpless, and Caity wondered how he managed to do anything on his own, anything at all. She felt her maternal instincts kick in, and she sighed. "You have a kitchen?"

He nodded.

"Come on." She reached for his hand. "I'll teach you."

» » »

HE'D MADE A TERRIBLE MISTAKE. He'd talked to the girl, and now she was here. Lind stood in the front foyer and felt the panic squeeze his brain, paralyzing him. The girl was in his apartment now, and he didn't know what to do.

She'd set the grocery bags in the kitchen and wandered out into the living area, staring out the windows and up to the ceiling. "My God," she said. "What a place. Do you rent it?"

Lind shook his head, and she gasped. "You *own*. Oh, my God. Look at those ceilings. Is this a penthouse?"

Lind looked at her. "I don't know," he said. He watched her explore the apartment and wondered what the man would say if he found out she was here.

Kick her out.

That's what the man would say. Kick her out, or kill her. Lind looked at the girl. She was very small, five feet if she was lucky. He could kill her easily if he needed to.

Caity spun around to look at him, her eyes wide. "What do you *do*, Richard?"

She kept calling him Richard. She'd asked him his name in the store. Waited as he searched his brain, fighting off the headache that threatened to overwhelm him. Then she'd answered herself—"It's Richard, right? Richard O'Brien?"—and he'd felt the panic get worse. He wasn't Richard. He knew that much, at least. He knew he was no longer Richard O'Brien.

No connections. No friends. That's what the man said. *You're alone in this world but for me.*

The man would expect him to kill her.

Caity crossed the living area to him. "What a place," she said. "What kind of insurance are you in? You must be very successful."

Lind didn't answer. Caity waited. After a moment, she frowned. "You don't have to tell me," she said. "I get it. You don't want to talk." She turned toward the kitchen. "Let's get started on dinner."

He didn't want to kill her. He knew the man would expect it, knew the panic wouldn't disappear as long as the girl was around. Knew the man wouldn't make the visions go away if he found out about her. He knew he was supposed to kill her.

He couldn't. Not yet.

Caity poked her head out of the kitchen. "What, you think I'm just going to cook for you?" She laughed. "Get in here."

Lind looked around the apartment. Then he looked at her. She stood there, one hand on her hip, smiling at him. He closed his eyes and tried to chase off the panic. Then he followed her into the kitchen.

70

Peralta knew exactly what they were looking for.

"Phillip Comm," he said, between puffs from a fat cigar. "Trans-Caribbean. He bid just a little too high."

Stevens looked around the penthouse. The lights of the city twinkled far below. "How'd he take losing?"

Peralta sucked on the cigar. "Not well."

COMM LIVED IN a handsome Spanish Colonial home in Coral Way, half a mile from the ocean. Ojeda was waiting in his Crown Vic when Stevens and Windermere pulled up out front. He had another agent with him, a hard-edged young woman in a tactical vest. "Stevens," he said, "this is Foster."

Foster gave him a nod. Gave Windermere the same treatment. Windermere nodded back, tight-lipped. Then she turned to look up at the house. The whole place was dark. The driveway was empty. Windermere looked at Ojeda. "Go around back," she told him. "We'll try the front."

Ojeda disappeared into the backyard with Foster. Windermere looked at Stevens in the streetlight. "Got your sidearm?"

Stevens nodded. Ojeda had kitted them both out with FBI standard-issue Glock 22s. Stevens drew his from his holster and felt his heart rate automatically increase. He looked around the dark neighborhood. Then he met Windermere's eyes. "Let's do this."

Windermere drew her own sidearm. They crept up the path to the front door, low and fast. Reached the stoop and Windermere knocked. The door swung open. There was nobody behind it. Windermere glanced at Stevens. "Left in a hurry."

"Or someone broke in."

They crept into the house. Windermere called out Comm's name. There was no answer. The place was dark. Nothing moved. It was empty.

TWENTY MINUTES LATER and they knew it for certain. Comm was gone. There was nobody home.

He'd disappeared quickly. Thrown a pile of shirts on his bed and hadn't bothered to rehang them. His dresser drawers hung half open, bikini briefs and undershirts dangling. The light was still on in the master bathroom.

Stevens wandered down the second-floor hallway. Poked his head into doorways. He could hear Windermere looking around the bedroom, Ojeda and Foster downstairs. The adrenaline still pumped in his veins; he bounced on the balls of his feet, wondering if Comm had made it out on his own. If the killer had found him in time to tie up loose ends.

Stevens looked into another room. Comm's office. A laptop computer on a cherrywood desk. A model ship, a freighter. A stack of papers. Stevens leafed through them. Shipping invoices. Contracts. Paperwork.

Stevens surveyed the room. Books. Hardcover, blue. Ancient. The room was impeccably neat. Stevens looked under the desk, found the wastebasket and shook it a little, studying the contents. Then he smiled. Bingo.

Comm had tried to burn through the evidence. He had failed. He'd left ashes, a scrap of paper unburned. It was a bank account statement, a transfer confirmation. One hundred thousand dollars to a numbered account.

"Windermere!"

Stevens fumbled in his pocket. He'd made note of Cody's payment information earlier. Now he took out his notebook and compared Cody's Killswitch account numbers with those in Comm's wastebasket. Comm's paper was torn, and burned. The first four numbers were missing. The rest of the account, however, matched up perfectly.

Bingo.

Windermere came into the room, Ojeda and Foster behind. "What's up?"

Stevens showed them the trash. "The numbers match Cody's Killswitch transfer," he told them. "Comm's our guy."

"So where is he?" said Windermere.

"Guy's got a place in Houston," said Ojeda. He glanced at the model ship on Comm's desk. "Or . . ."

Windermere arched an eyebrow. "Or?"

"He has a ship, left Miami for Port-au-Prince tonight. Kind of a sudden departure, apparently."

Windermere looked at the model ship on Comm's desk. "Call somebody in Houston," she said. "Have them check out Comm's place." Then she grinned at Stevens. "How about a boat ride, partner?"

71

Parkerson drove Wendell Gray to the lake house.

He'd fallen in love with the lake as a kid, when the shorefront was still farmland and forest. It had been a peaceful place, an escape from the city and its noise and oppressive heat. Even his parents seemed to calm when they came out here; for blissful weekends, Parkerson could almost imagine that his mom and dad loved each other, that they could see past the relentless onslaught of bills and invoices and too-skimpy paychecks. His dad had sold his plot by the lake one desperate winter, and Parkerson could still remember the long, torturous summer that followed, endless days spent sweating in his room, wishing for the cool relief of the lake, longing for silence instead of his parents' unceasing crescendo of harsh words and slammed doors.

The lake was developed now, dangerous. Cottages and big summer homes crammed almost every inch of waterfront, and come summer the whole region would be crawling with families in monstrous sport-utility vehicles and powerful ski boats. For now, though, in early April, the lake was quiet.

They arrived at the lake just before dawn. Turned down the shore road and followed it to a stubby end. There was a dirt trail leading into the trees beyond. Parkerson slowed the Cadillac and turned down the trail. Crept over the bumps until he reached the house, a run-down little cabin in a clearing in the woods, the lake a few hundred feet distant. He'd purchased the place, secretly, shortly after he'd dreamt up Killswitch. Registered it to a dummy corporation and told no one he owned it, his own private bastion of calm. His Killswitch sanctuary.

Gray was still passed out in the passenger seat. He'd stirred a couple times on the drive. Parkerson had hushed him. Soothed him back to sleep. Now he circled around to the passenger door, hefted the kid up, and dragged him into the yard. Gray muttered a protest but didn't resist.

The house was musty. There was a layer of dust over everything. A steady drip from the tap in the kitchen. Parkerson frowned. The damn thing would have been dripping since midwinter.

He half dragged, half coaxed Wendell Gray through the door. Helped him across the scuffed kitchen linoleum and down a narrow set of stairs to the basement. The basement was damp and earthy. The ceiling was low. Parkerson had to duck as he dragged Gray along. Gray groaned. Struggled a little. "Hush," Parkerson told him. "Almost there."

This was the unfortunate part of the process. Training a new asset was a dirty occupation. There were no absolutes. There was only Parkerson and Wendell Gray, a scared, traumatized man, and the grim process of molding him into a workable asset.

Parkerson had built a room in the basement, walled in and sound-proof, after he'd purchased the cabin. He'd done some research on post-traumatic stress and advanced torture techniques. Gradually he'd honed the training process into an efficient regimen of reeducation and discipline. Broken men went into the room. Assets came out.

Parkerson unlocked the padlocked door and helped Gray inside. Sat him down on the thin iron bed and stood above him. Gray wavered, unsteady as a punch-drunk boxer. Parkerson lifted the kid's legs and helped him lie down. Made sure he was comfortable and then turned to check the projector.

Satisfied, he walked out. Closed the door behind him and relocked the padlock. Crossed the basement to a recliner, tilted all the way back, and picked up a remote.

The remote controlled the DVD player that would feed images to the projector inside the new asset's room. Parkerson pressed play, and then sat back to listen. The room was pretty well soundproofed, but sometimes, if he listened closely, he could still hear the screams.

72

The Coast Guard MH-65 Dolphin rocked and shook as the wind tossed it about. Stevens gripped Windermere's hand, tight, and stared down into the night. Far below them, the cutter *Vigilant* was a tiny cluster of lights on an otherwise coal-black sea.

Windermere peered across Stevens at the vessel beneath them. Then she grinned at him. "You get seasick, too?"

Stevens grimaced as the helicopter descended. The *Vigilant* looked impossibly small down there. "Guess we'll find out," he said.

The helicopter dropped down to a hover just above the cutter's stern. A crew member slid open the side door, and immediately the wind roared into the cabin, buffeting Stevens and pushing him back from the void. He stared out the yawning door and fought to keep his stomach under control.

The crew member yelled something. Gestured at Windermere. She listened, nodding. Then she turned to Stevens. "They're going to drop us on the stern," she said. "Don't think about it, just do it, okay?"

Stevens nodded. "Okay."

Windermere grinned at him again, her face close, her eyes bright. "This is FBI living, Stevens," she said. "Welcome to the big show."

The helicopter descended until it was just a few feet above the *Vigilant's* roiling deck. The boat looked bigger up close—it was probably a couple hundred feet long—but the black night seemed to dwarf it, and it rolled with the ocean's swell. Windermere glanced back at Stevens in the doorway. Flashed him a thumbs-up, then dropped out of sight.

The crew member turned to Stevens. "Your turn, sir."

Stevens closed his eyes and edged toward the open door. He could see Windermere on the deck below, hustling away from the helicopter's spinning rotors. A seaman stood on deck, arms outstretched, waiting for him. Stevens closed his eyes, thought of Nancy, and dropped.

A split second of gut-wrenching free fall. Then he hit the deck. The seaman grabbed him and hurried him away from the helicopter. The chopper's engine roared as it lifted off again. Within seconds, it was hundreds of feet above.

The ship was strangely quiet without the helicopter's screaming engine. Stevens let the seaman usher him to where Windermere waited at an open doorway. He looked around the vessel, his legs unsteady as the ship rocked beneath him. Then he looked up into the sky, found the helicopter's tiny lights as it raced back to shore. He leaned against the bulkhead and tried to calm his racing heart. "Holy shit," he said. "God damn the FBI."

73

Lind sat on his couch and stared at the television. The TV was playing infomercials. Lind wasn't watching. He was thinking about the girl, Caity Sherman.

She'd cooked him spaghetti for dinner. Meatballs and everything. "Totally simple," she said, "but it's comfort food. You don't quite look ready for quinoa."

Lind had watched her make it. He'd pretended to pay attention. Mostly, though, he was still thinking about what a mistake he was making. He was trying to keep the panic from overwhelming him again.

Mistake or no, the dinner was good. It was the first meal in a long time he'd enjoyed, maybe the first meal ever. He told Caity and she laughed. "Of course it is, silly," she said. "You only eat TV dinners. That stuff tastes like cardboard."

That wasn't the reason, Lind knew. Whatever he ate, no matter what it was, it all seemed to taste the same. It had been that way for as long as he could remember. Since he'd come back, anyway. Since he'd met the man.

The man.

The man would be angered by this development. Lind had tried to mitigate the damage. He'd eaten his dinner, and then when the dinner was over and they were sitting at the table and she was staring at him, he hadn't looked at her and he hadn't said anything. He'd wanted to look at her, but he didn't. He knew the man would be displeased if he did.

No connections. No friends.

They sat at the table in silence for a while. Lind stared down at his plate. The girl looked at him. Met his eyes, and looked away quickly. She stood and began to clear the table. Lind stood up, too. Tried to help. She smiled shyly at him—"Thanks"—and he felt a lurching sickness in his stomach.

The man wouldn't approve.

The girl talked as she washed the dishes. Handed him a dish towel and told him to dry. He dried, and she talked. Mostly about herself. She seemed to know that he wouldn't fill the silence.

Her name was Caity Sherman. She was twenty-five years old. She'd come to Philadelphia to study piano at UArts. Then she'd dropped out. "No money," she said. "I wasn't good enough anyway."

She'd worked a few jobs before landing at Delta. "I like it," she said. "In the short term, anyway." She paused, then laughed a little. "Just don't ask about the long term, because I have no idea."

She'd paused, waiting for a response. Glanced at him and he looked away. "What about piano?" he said finally.

She looked at him. "As a job? I don't think so." She paused. "I mean, I love it, but it's *hard*. It's really damn hard."

He dried a plate. "Yeah."

"Yeah." She sighed. "Yeah."

AFTER THE PLATES WERE DRIED and the kitchen was cleaned, she'd looked around and looked at him and kind of shifted her weight, smiling shyly. "I should go."

Lind nodded. "Okay."

"Okay." She took a pen from her purse and bent over the kitchen counter. Scribbled something on a scrap of paper and pressed it into his hand. "You won't call," she said, smiling, "but if you get lonely or whatever."

He took the paper from her and watched as she walked to the door. She waved good-bye and then disappeared into the hall, and he heard the elevator doors ding open just before his own door slammed closed. He stood in the kitchen for a long time, thinking about his mistake.

He would have to kill her, he knew. She knew too much about him. The man would be angry. The man would demand that she die. And Lind needed the man happy. He needed the man to make the visions disappear.

He didn't want to kill the girl, though. He wished he didn't have to.

74

The *Vigilant*'s skipper pointed through the wheelhouse windows at a line of lights on the horizon. "That's her," he told Stevens and Windermere. "The *Island Joy*."

"Comm's ship," said Stevens.

"Roger. We've just hailed her, and she's slowing, thank God." He turned to a seaman lingering close by. "Petty Officer Briggs will get you ready to board."

They followed Briggs aft through the cutter to the stern of the ship, where a team in black tactical gear was readying a rigid-hulled Zodiac intercept boat for launch. Stevens studied the men. They didn't say much. They wore grim expressions and carried compact machine guns.

You're a long way from Saint Paul, Stevens thought, feeling the cutter roll across another wave. *No way in hell Nancy ever finds out about this.*

Briggs came back with an armload of bright orange neoprene survival gear. "In case you fall overboard," she told Stevens. "Kind of rocky out there."

Stevens took the suit from her and pulled it on. Windermere dressed beside him, her eyes on the *Island Joy* on the horizon. Her jaw was set, her eyes narrowed. She looked like she was ready to kick somebody's ass.

The *Vigilant* slowed and the assault team launched the Zodiac, struggling to keep it close to the larger vessel in the swell. Windermere grinned at Stevens, and then climbed down the hull of the cutter to the little boat. Stevens hesitated a moment. Then he followed.

THE LITTLE ZODIAC skipped like a pebble over the waves, lurching and jiving as it sped toward the freighter. Stevens crawled up to the bow, where Windermere crouched, gazing forward, taking spray in her face with every new swell.

"Comm had better be on that ship," she yelled across at Stevens. "This is a hell of an adventure to have to explain if he isn't."

"Harbormaster said the ship left in a hurry," said Stevens. "Wasn't scheduled to depart for a week. This is suspicious, whatever it is."

"You got that right," said Windermere. "Maybe we get unlucky and it's just a mountain of drugs."

The Zodiac sped up alongside the freighter. The ship looked vast from up close, a featureless black hull topped with yellow sodium light. There was movement on board, faces at the rail. The Zodiac slowed, and the crew dropped a pilot ladder forty feet to the swell. Stevens watched as the team around him climbed up, one by one. Then Windermere shoved him forward. "Go for it."

Stevens felt his heart racing. Whatever his fears, this was kind of cool. He crawled back along the Zodiac to the swinging ladder. Watched as the pilot brought the small boat alongside. The hull stretched high above him, almost to the sky. The boat rocked in the swell. A chasm of roiling water appeared. Then the pilot gunned the engine and the ladder was there. Windermere slapped his back. *"Jump."*

Stevens jumped. His arms found the ladder and he pulled himself upward, feet kicking off against the slick hull. Then he was climbing, the ladder rocking against the side of the freighter. Stevens climbed and didn't look down.

The climb took forever. His arms ached at the top. He clambered over the hull and stood beside the assault team, his limbs screaming, his lungs begging for air. A minute or so later, Windermere appeared. She stretched. Shook her head. "Holy shit," she said. "That was cool."

She surveyed the deck of the freighter. The assault team had their machine guns drawn on the crew. The crew waited, eyes wide, their hands in the air. Windermere turned to Stevens. "Okay," she said. "Let's find Comm."

75

It took less than ten minutes for the new asset to start screaming. Parkerson left him alone for an hour.

The kid was curled up on his thin mattress when Parkerson finally walked in with breakfast. He'd puked on the floor. "Poor guy." Parkerson sat on the bed beside the kid. Rubbed his shoulder. "You just had a bad dream, is all."

The kid hugged his knees to his chest. Looked at Parkerson with wide eyes. "What the hell is this?"

"You're having nightmares," Parkerson told him. "Those visions you get. You're safe now. I'm with you."

The kid stared at him, shivering. Parkerson held up a plate. "I brought breakfast."

Gray closed his eyes tight. Rubbed his head and groaned. "Where am I?"

"You're safe," said Parkerson. "You just had a vision. Eat your breakfast."

"I feel like shit."

Parkerson nodded. "You had a lot to drink last night," he said. "You got crazy. You won't be drinking like that again."

The kid leaned his head back against the concrete wall. "No, I won't."

"No, you won't." Parkerson pushed the plate forward. "Now, eat up."

Gray looked at the food and grimaced. Looked at Parkerson. Parkerson held his gaze. The kid closed his eyes. Then he reached for the plate.

He ate, slowly at first. Then he found his appetite. He cleared the plate. Wiped it clean with his last piece of toast. Then he sat back and grinned weakly at Parkerson. "That was good shit, man."

Parkerson matched his smile. "I'm here for you," he told him. "Here to help. Whatever you need. You're safe now."

The kid frowned. "You got a pisser?"

Parkerson stood and picked up the kid's empty plate. Motioned to a bucket that sat in a corner of the room. "Right there," he said. "Use it."

"For real?"

"For real." Parkerson walked to the door. Turned back and tossed him a rag. "And clean up that puke while you're at it."

The kid started to complain. Parkerson ignored him. Walked out of the room and closed the door behind him. Locked the padlock. After ten minutes, he unlocked it again.

The bucket was beside the bed. The kid had used it. He hadn't cleaned up his puke. Parkerson sighed. "I said clean up that puke, soldier."

The kid rubbed his eyes. "I want to go home."

"Clean up the puke and we'll talk about it." Parkerson closed the door and locked it again. Waited another ten minutes. When he opened the door, the rag was filthy and the puke was gone.

"Good work," Parkerson told him. "I'm pleased with you."

"Can I go home?"

"You are home," Parkerson told him. He closed the door again. Locked it again. Walked back to the recliner and turned on the DVD player. Then he took the kid's empty plate and walked back upstairs. It was morning now; the sun shone through the trees. Parkerson rinsed the plate and left it out to dry. He locked up the cabin and walked out to the Cadillac. Stood beside the car for a moment, savoring the stillness of the grove. Then he slid behind the wheel and drove back to the city. It was nearly six-thirty. Time to go to work.

76

Comm didn't make it easy on himself.

The captain of the *Island Joy* swore innocence. The crew, Bahamian mostly, shrugged and held up their hands and said nothing. Windermere swore at them. Threatened, cajoled. Finally, she shook her head and turned to Stevens. "Let's tear this boat apart."

First they searched the house, the thirty-foot-tall superstructure that contained the bridge, the accommodations, the galley. They left a couple Coast Guard men to watch over the crew, and took the rest with them to scour the ship. The house yielded nothing. Comm wasn't there.

The ship was an old tramp steamer, the wheelhouse situated midway between bow and stern. Windermere and Stevens left the assault team to tear through the engine room. They walked up the deck together toward the bow, guns drawn.

"So where is he?" said Windermere. "Is this bastard on board or what?"

Stevens looked down the length of the ship. The house loomed white in the night sky. "He's here," he told Windermere. "He's here somewhere."

They reached the bow of the ship. A stairway led up to the mast and the anchor winches. Beneath it was an iron door to the ship's forecastle. Windermere walked to it. "What's in here?"

She turned the heavy wheel and it groaned in her hands. Stevens watched her, tensed. She turned the wheel hard over. Then the door was flung open. It swung inward, too fast. Windermere stumbled back. *"Shit."*

"You goddamn bastards." A desperate voice from inside the forecastle, action-movie heroic. *"You want me, you're coming with me."* Then gunshots, three of them, like a snare drum. Windermere dived for cover. Stevens ducked behind a bulkhead, his head down. Another three shots. Then Phillip Comm stepped out on deck, screaming, incoherent, waving a pistol in the air.

Shouts from the house. The assault team ran forward, machine guns at the ready. "Don't shoot him," Stevens called back. "Take him alive, but *be careful.*"

"You fuckers," Comm screamed. *"You'll never take me."*

Comm advanced from the doorway, staggering now, unsteady. His eyes were wide and wild, his pupils huge. He waved the gun at the advancing assault team, fired again. *If they kill this guy,* Stevens thought, *we lose Killswitch.* He watched Comm behind the bulkhead and searched for Windermere in the shadows, hoping she had the same notion.

As Comm advanced, Windermere crept around behind him, keeping low and to the shadows. Comm kept screaming at the assault team. Kept waving that gun.

He's hysterical. High on something. Or terrified. Or both.

Comm steadied his pistol again. Aimed across the deck and squeezed off another three shots.

Windermere tackled him. Leapt out from behind and took him down to the deck. Comm dropped the pistol. The assault team swarmed. Stevens picked himself up from the bulkhead and hurried over to where Windermere had Comm pinned. Comm struggled against her. She held him. He looked around at the assault team, at Windermere and Stevens, and seemed to deflate. "Who are you?" he said, wheezing for breath. "You're not *him*."

"FBI," said Windermere. "Coast Guard. Minnesota Bureau of Criminal Apprehension."

"You were expecting someone else?" said Stevens.

Comm nodded, still gasping.

Windermere elbowed him. *"Who?"*

Comm didn't answer for a moment. Then he laid his head back on the deck and stared skyward. "Killswitch," he said.

77

It was the strangest interrogation Stevens had ever conducted.

They brought Comm back to the *Vigilant* on the Zodiac, after they'd finished searching his little hideaway in the *Island Joy*'s forecastle. It was a hell of a cubbyhole: between the crates of bread, onions, and dehydrated milk that took up most of the room, Comm had built himself an ugly little nest for the voyage to Port-au-Prince.

"Gross," said Windermere, kicking a sodden sleeping bag aside. "He really moved in."

Stevens nodded. "Quite the little bachelor pad, huh?"

Apart from necessities such as the sleeping bag, pillow, and case of bottled water, Comm had packed with him the week's *Time* magazine, the month's *Penthouse*, another pistol and ammunition, and enough cocaine to kill a horse. Stevens figured he'd been nose-deep in the stuff when Windermere barged in on him.

The Coast Guard left a few men aboard the *Island Joy* to turn the ship around and supervise its return to the Port of Miami. Meanwhile, Stevens and Windermere rode with Comm to the cutter, where Petty Officer Briggs found them a spare room in which to hold their prisoner.

Now Comm sipped coffee and stared down at his mug. Avoided Windermere's eyes, and Stevens's. "I didn't know," he said. "I swear I didn't know you were cops."

"Just figured you'd come out shooting, huh?" said Windermere. "Better safe than sorry?"

"I thought you were Killswitch," said Comm. "I thought I was next."

Stevens cut in. "Before we go any further," he said, "you have the right to an attorney, Mr. Comm. You don't have to talk to us. You're well within your rights to say nothing at all until we hit Miami and you have a lawyer present."

Comm waved him away. "I don't care about that."

"You know anything you say can be used against you in a court of law."

"I know," he said. "I watch TV. Look, I don't care. Book me for whatever you want. Just fucking find Killswitch before he comes after me."

Stevens glanced at Windermere. Windermere grinned. "Be right back."

She was gone fifteen minutes. When she returned, she was holding a flimsy sheet of paper and a ballpoint pen. She slid the paper at Comm. "Sign here," she said. "This indicates that we've informed you of your rights and you've waived the right to an attorney."

Stevens frowned at Windermere as Comm signed and dated the form. "Where the hell'd you get that?"

She grinned at him. "Ojeda faxed it in."

"It's two in the morning."

"He loves me," she said, shrugging. "Tell me you wouldn't do the same."

Comm tapped the pen on the tabletop. Looked from Stevens to Windermere and back again. Stevens cleared his throat. "So you thought we were Killswitch," he said. "Why would Killswitch come for you? You paid him, didn't you?"

Comm sipped his coffee. Didn't look up. He nodded.

"So?"

Comm was silent some more. The cutter rocked in the swell. Its big diesel engines throbbed somewhere far below. Windermere sat across from him. Ducked down until she could see his eyes. "What's the deal, Comm?" she said. "What are you afraid of?"

Comm looked at her. Whether from fear or from shock, he'd seemed to calm. Now he stared into Windermere's eyes with a chilling intensity. "I went down to watch," he said. "I wanted to see for myself. Don't know why. I guess I just wanted to make sure I got my money's worth."

"You mean you watched Killswitch shoot Ansbacher."

Comm nodded. "I drove to Terminal Island. Parked across from the marina. I had a pair of binoculars, and I watched Peralta's yacht. I saw Peralta come aboard. Then I saw Ansbacher." He shook his head. "I guess I didn't think it would actually happen."

"You bought and paid for a murder," said Windermere. "Two hundred grand. You thought there was a chance it was bogus?"

"I was angry," he said. "I was desperate. I wasn't myself. I didn't think that anyone . . ." He looked at Windermere again. "I didn't think anyone could be so cold."

"The shooter was on Terminal Island," said Stevens. "Did you see him?"

Comm laughed. "Oh, yeah," he said. "Yeah, I saw him."

"And?"

"And he was a fucking weirdo, man. He was parked a couple stalls over. I didn't notice him until right before it happened. There was this truck parked between us. It moved just as Ansbacher came down the ramp. I glanced over and saw the guy's rifle. That's when I knew it was real."

"But you didn't stop him."

"I was scared shitless. The fucking guy had a rifle." Comm looked down again. "And I guess a part of me really did want Ansbacher dead."

"So you watched Killswitch shoot him."

Comm nodded. "Shot him twice. First time in the chest. Second time in the head. I couldn't believe it. I wanted to puke."

"Then what happened?"

"I looked at the kid. Couldn't take my eyes off him. I knew he'd kill me if he knew I'd seen him, but I couldn't look away. He was just a fucking young kid, man, in his twenties, but his eyes . . ." Comm shivered.

"We know," said Windermere. "We've seen him."

"Christ, I wanted to shit myself. He put away his rifle and climbed across to the driver's seat and took off. I followed—" Comm rubbed his eyes. "I didn't think he'd seen me, but then, just as I pulled onto the ramp up to the causeway, he'd stopped the car. Blocked the whole lane. I swear he stared straight at me in the rearview. I thought, This is it, I'm going down. This kid's going to kill me."

"But he didn't."

"He didn't," said Comm. "He just drove off."

"So why'd you think he would come back for you?"

Comm shivered again. "I just *knew*, man. Once he figured out who I was, I was gonzo."

Comm put his head down. Closed his eyes. "Shit," he mumbled into his arms. "What the fuck am I doing?"

Windermere studied him a moment. Then she stood up from the table. Looked at Stevens. "Got three or four hours until we're back in Miami," she said. "Come on. Let's get some rest."

78

Parkerson showered at home, changed clothes, and drove to his office. Waved his security badge at the guard at the gate and parked the Cadillac in the lot beyond. Turned off the ignition and sat in the car and felt himself drifting away.

He was tired, Christ. He'd slept maybe seven hours since Friday. He wanted to crawl into the Caddy's capacious backseat and just close his eyes for a while, but he didn't. He couldn't. He had real work to do.

He forced himself out of the car, across the parking lot, and into the low building. He made himself the biggest cup of coffee he could manage, and dragged ass into his office. Jamie was already at her desk. "Morning, Mr. Parkerson," she said. "How was your weekend?"

"Good," he replied, forcing a smile. "Busy."

She cocked her head. "Looks like it."

"Yeah. Really busy." He forced another grin at her as he entered his office. "Married life."

Parkerson collapsed into his leather executive chair and stared at his blank computer screen and let his head swim. The coffee wasn't helping. Maybe he needed drugs. There was so much to do.

There was work, first of all. As in high-paying, taxable, government-sanctioned work. He'd meant to take the files home that weekend, work on them in front of the television. He hadn't intended to drive down to Miami to witness a murder. To rescue the asset. To kidnap an army veteran from Atlanta, Georgia. He'd put in a long weekend, and he'd fallen behind. He would have to bust ass to catch up.

Then there was the program itself. Wendell Gray would need training, and Lind needed a new identity. Parkerson sat back in his chair and sighed. Wondered if he could afford to take a vacation somewhere when the new asset was ready. A beach, maybe. A resort, somewhere out of the country, but clean. Somewhere he could sleep, and not worry for a change.

Parkerson leaned his head back and stared at the ceiling. Closed his eyes and pictured a king-size bed and room service. The sound of the ocean. Felt himself drifting away. Then Jamie rapped on the door. "You have that nine-thirty," she said. "With the board. You okay?"

Parkerson sat up. "Just reviewing my notes."

"Oka-ay." Jamie stared in at him. "You really did have a weekend, huh?"

"Burst a pipe in my basement. Really screwed up my Sunday."

Jamie clucked. "Ouch. Anyway, the board's ready when you are."

Parkerson took a long drink of coffee. Turned on his computer and waited for it to load. Felt the buzzing in his head ramp up a notch, and wondered how he was going to make it through the week.

Then he thought of Wendell Gray in the lake house. Imagined the money his new asset would bring in someday soon, when the training regimen was complete. Enough money for a big yacht like the *Kyla Dawn*, maybe, or, better yet, his own private lake. An island in the middle, cool and calm. No traffic jams. No Jet Skis. No teeming masses to spoil his mood. The thought energized him, and he stood, grinning at the image, and strode from the room to meet the board.

79

Stevens grabbed a few hours' sleep in his suite at the Golden Glades. Then he woke up and called Nancy. "Hey," he said, "you have time to chat?"

His wife sighed. "I'm headed into the office, Kirk. It's a hell of a week." She paused. "I guess I have a couple minutes."

"How's your weekend?" said Stevens. "How are the kids?"

"Kids are good. Sounds like they miss you. Andrea's been all over me to tell her what you're up to."

Stevens frowned. Since she'd met Carla Windermere in the middle of the Carter Tomlin case, his daughter had become an FBI junkie. Stevens had to admit it pleased him, just a little, that she'd taken such an interest in the family business, but both he and Nancy still harbored concerns that their daughter's ordeal with Tomlin had left her with some yet-undiscovered psychological trauma.

"I told her I didn't know," Nancy said. "Just that it had to do with Spenser Pyatt. Why that means you're in Miami, I couldn't begin to guess."

"It's a contract killer," Stevens told her. "The same guy who killed Pyatt killed another man here. Both hits bought and paid for. We ran down another client last night."

"A contract killer. Well, I can't very well tell Andrea that, can I? After the whole thing with Carter Tomlin, I'm amazed the poor girl can still sleep at night."

"She's tough, Nance," Stevens said.

"Yeah, Kirk, I know she's tough. An experience like that, though. And her dad running around like Sylvester Stallone . . ." She was silent a moment. "Look, just be careful, all right?"

"Always, Nancy."

"Seriously. Don't get yourself killed." She sighed. "I'm going to tell the kids you're on vacation or something. Deep-sea fishing. Partying with supermodels. Whatever won't give them nightmares."

"Supermodels give me nightmares," Stevens said. "I'll come home as soon as I can." He told her good-bye, and that he missed her, and then he hung up the phone and leaned against the headboard and pictured Nancy at home and wondered why he'd even come to Miami.

But he knew why. He thought about chasing Comm on the *Island Joy*. The shoot-out. The interrogation. Comm was waiting now in the FBI's Miami office. He would doubtless have more to tell them.

Stevens thought about Killswitch. About the zombie shooter and the anonymous accomplice in the gray Cadillac. All of it a mystery, but Comm would have information. Sooner or later, the truth would be revealed.

The thought propelled Stevens out of bed. He showered quickly and went down to the hotel lobby, where he ate a fast breakfast and waited for Windermere.

80

Comm unwrapped the Sausage McMuffin. Scarfed it down, drained his coffee, and polished off the hash browns. Then he looked across the table at Stevens and Windermere. "Okay," he said. "What do you want to know?"

He was clear-eyed this morning. He seemed to have slept. There were shadows under his eyes, and he smelled like diesel fuel, sweat, and a night in a holding cell, but he held Stevens's gaze and set his jaw and sat at the table, lucid and ready to talk.

"Killswitch," said Windermere. "How did you find him?"

Comm looked around the interview room. Exhaled. "First things first. I don't want this bastard coming back for me."

Windermere nodded. "Of course."

"I'm no snitch. I'm no rat. I'm just—" He looked at Stevens. "You had to see this guy, man."

"You're safe," Stevens told him. "We're here to protect you."

"My mother, too. She's the only family I have. I want someone watching her until you guys catch this psycho. Understood?"

"He's not coming for your mother," said Windermere.

"How do you know?"

"He's a contract killer," said Stevens. "He probably wasn't coming back for you, even if he did make the connection. You paid him. The contract was done."

Comm shook his head. "My mother gets protection or I'm not talking."

Windermere swapped a glance with Stevens. "Fine," she said, sighing. "What's the address?"

Comm recited the address. Windermere wrote it down. Ducked out of the room and handed it to Ojeda. Comm watched her. When she was back inside the room, he nodded. "Okay," he said. "You guys have a computer?"

OJEDA BROUGHT IN A LAPTOP. Logged in to the CID wireless signal and opened an Internet window. Then he turned the computer toward Comm.

Comm typed in a Web address. "Killswitch-dot-com," he said. "Easy."

It was a generic-looking website. A stock image at the top, a soldier with a rifle. A couple of articles beneath, a long row of links. It didn't look like much more than a collection of news clippings, all of them related to guns. There wasn't anything to suggest it was a front for a hired killer. Windermere frowned. "This is how you found him?"

Comm nodded. "Looks pretty simple, right? It's not, though." He clicked on a link that said CONTACT and a pop-up form appeared. There were entry fields for name, e-mail address, questions. There was a drop-down menu. Comm clicked on it and scrolled.

"Contracting," he said. "That's what you select. And you have to be pretty damn crafty with your request. There's a code."

"A code," said Windermere. "How the hell do you know the code?"

Comm laughed at her. "Same way I know about Killswitch," he said. "It's not hard, if you know what to look for."

"And what do you look for?" said Stevens.

"People." Comm shook his head. "You look for people. Listen, I'm not exactly a choirboy. You saw the cocaine. I know people who have bad connections. Maybe I told my dealer I was looking to put out a hit. Maybe my dealer gave me Killswitch."

"Your dealer," said Windermere. "Who is he?"

"Nice try. I told you I'm no snitch."

"You're giving us Killswitch."

"I'm trying," said Comm. "You guys keep asking questions. Who my dealer is doesn't matter. Killswitch is out there. People just know about it."

Stevens cleared his throat. "So you typed in the code. You asked for contracting help. Then this guy got in touch and asked who you wanted killed?"

Comm shook his head. "It's not like that. First the guy has to vet you. Make sure you're clean."

"How?"

"The hell if I know. Wasn't like he came to my house." Comm picked up his empty cup of coffee. Glanced inside, and set it back down. "Not that I know of. Anyway, I guess he liked what he saw, because a week after I got in touch, he invited me in."

"Invited you where?" said Windermere.

Comm smiled to himself. Punched in another URL. "Killswitch-dot-com," he said, "slash special projects." He pressed ENTER and a gray page loaded up. There was a user name field and a password prompt. The rest of the page was blank.

"Special projects," said Stevens. "The murders."

Comm grinned wider. "Exactly."

Windermere glanced at Stevens. "Well, what are you waiting for?" she asked Comm. "Get us in."

81

Parkerson was in the middle of his presentation when his cell phone buzzed in his pocket. He ignored it for a minute or two. Then he froze.

His BlackBerry was on the long boardroom table with a stack of files and his coffee. That meant the buzzing in his pocket wasn't work calling, or his wife. The phone in his pocket was the Killswitch phone.

Parkerson stumbled through the rest of the presentation. The board stared at him, impassive. He rushed through his conclusion and sat down quickly. Drank his coffee and fought the urge to look down at the phone. Sat on his hands for ten minutes, wanting to burst.

There was a pause in the action. The lights came on, and Parkerson stood. "Excuse me," he said, gesturing sheepishly to his coffee cup. "Drank a little too much java. Be right back."

He hurried out into the hall and down to the men's room. Found a stall and took out the Killswitch phone. A text message. Someone had logged in to the Killswitch database. Parkerson scrolled through. Then he stopped. Comm.

Comm had returned to Killswitch. He'd logged in twenty minutes ago, was still in the database now, but he hadn't done anything. Hadn't written a message. He was just lurking inside.

Parkerson studied his phone. The job was done. The target was eliminated, and the fees had been paid. There was no reason for Comm to return. *Comm,* he thought, frowning. *What the hell are you doing?*

82

Comm scratched his head. "I don't get it," he said. "Everything was right here."

Windermere glanced at Stevens. Then back at the Killswitch database. Comm had entered his password and logged in to the Special Projects page. But the page had come back empty. There was nothing in the database.

"What were you expecting?" she said.

Comm looked at her. "Everything," he said. "My correspondence with Killswitch. My application."

"Job was finished," said Windermere. "No sense leaving the evidence kicking around. Especially if he figured there's a chance you'd tell the cops."

Stevens stared at the blank screen. "So what do we do?"

"Guess we try and trace the website." Windermere walked to the door. Poked her head out. "Hey," she called. *"Ojeda."*

» » »

PARKERSON RUSHED BACK to his office, board meeting be damned. Jamie stood up as he passed. "Mr. Parkerson?"

"Just a minute." He hurried past her and closed the door behind him.

Logged on to his computer and turned on the virtual network. Booted up the IP cloaker for good measure. Then he brought up the Killswitch database.

This was dangerous. He'd never used Killswitch during work hours. He'd certainly never ditched on a board meeting to tend to the project. This was panic behavior, irrational. This would attract attention from the chairman, from Jamie. But Parkerson had to know.

He waited as the database loaded, drumming his fingers on the desk. When the page was fully loaded, he searched through until he found Comm. Still online. Parkerson clicked on his name.

Logged in from Miami, the database told him. Spat out an IP address. Parkerson copied it down and ran a trace. Felt his heart stop as he read the results. Comm was logged on through a federal government server in Miami. Parkerson checked the address, knowing already what the search would find. A moment later, his fears were confirmed. Someone in the FBI's Miami office was inside the Killswitch database. Somehow, they'd logged in as Comm.

83

Ojeda shook his head. "Can't get a fix on him," he said. "His location keeps moving. Boston. Houston. Moscow. Beirut. He won't stay in one place."

Stevens peered at the screen. "How can he do that?"

"IP blocker," said Ojeda. "It keeps moving his IP address. Hiding it. He's not in those places, but we can't break through and find him."

Windermere looked at Ojeda. "Is there a way to beat this?"

Ojeda shook his head. "Not quickly," he said. "We give it to a techie for a few hours and he'll crack it, probably. Depends how good our guy on the other end is."

"This cybercrime stuff," said Stevens. "I feel like a goddamn barnacle."

Windermere grinned at him. "It's not your fault you're old, Stevens. And computer illiterate."

Ojeda grinned at them. Then he looked back at the laptop and his grin disappeared. "Oh," he said. "Oh, shit."

Windermere looked over his shoulder. "What's the deal?"

Ojeda clicked the mouse. Pressed a couple of buttons. "We're out of the database," he said. "Killswitch just kicked us out."

"He can do that?"

"Why would he boot us?" said Windermere.

"Must have figured out it's the FBI and not Comm," Ojeda replied.

"Well, shit."

Stevens studied the screen. "Can your tech guys still trace this guy's IP address?" he said.

Ojeda frowned down at the laptop. "I don't know."

84

The tech was a young guy named Kam. He copied the Killswitch IP address into his own tracer. Pressed a button and studied the screen. "Shouldn't be a problem," he said. "I've dealt with this program before."

Windermere grinned at Stevens. "Finally," she said. "Something's going right."

"What's your bet?" said Stevens. "Where do you think our guy's located?"

"Who, Killswitch?"

Stevens nodded. "I figure O'Brien's a Philadelphia local. That's the kid. But what about our mystery accomplice?"

Windermere thought about it. "His plates looked like Virginia," she said. "And Triple A Industries has a P.O. box in Richmond. Guess that makes sense to me."

"Sure," Stevens said. "As long as we're guessing, I'm saying San Diego."

"San Diego?" Windermere frowned. "We have no evidence whatsoever that Killswitch has ever *seen* San Diego."

"I know, I just figure this guy's unpredictable. I'll give you whatever odds you want we don't find him in Richmond."

"You're on. What are we betting?"

"Dinner."

"If he turns up in Richmond, you buy me dinner?"

"That's right. Anywhere else, and you're buying."

"I thought you said San Diego."

"Just a wild guess," Stevens said, grinning. "He turns up in San Diego, you're buying me the whole restaurant."

Kam swore behind them. Stevens and Windermere turned to find him staring at his computer screen, shaking his head. "What's the deal?" said Windermere. "Where's our IP address now?"

Kam held up his hands, palms skyward. "I beat the IP cloaker," he said. "Traced the address to a virtual private network. Beat the VPN no problem, but now this." He gestured at the screen. "I don't think I can beat this."

Windermere looked at the screen. Found a very angry-looking message from the Department of Defense. *Confidential*, it read. *Password protected. Access denied.* Windermere frowned. "What the hell is this?"

"Defense Department," said Kam. "Either your guy's an elite hacker or this IP address is originating from somewhere inside the DoD network."

"Shit." Stevens rubbed his face. "Can you beat it?"

Kam snorted. "If I could, I wouldn't be working here," he said. "I'd be on a beach somewhere or in jail." He paused. "Probably in jail."

Windermere looked up and met Stevens's eyes. "Nothing's ever easy," she said. "Not with this case."

"So, what?" said Stevens. "We get in touch with the Defense Department. See if they'll let us look around."

"And if not?"

He shrugged. "We turn off the computers," he said. "Find this guy the old-fashioned way."

85

Parkerson sat back in his chair. "There," he said. "That'll teach you."

He studied his computer screen, trying to make sense of what had happened. The FBI had found its way into Killswitch. And they'd done it from Miami, through Comm. How?

Parkerson opened another Internet window. Did a Google search for the Cameron Ansbacher murder. Found what he was looking for on the *Miami Herald*'s home page: "FBI Questions Suspect in Marina Shooting."

No names. But it had to be Comm. The Feds had caught up to him somehow, and he'd told them everything. Even logged them in to the Killswitch database. So the FBI knew. What did that mean?

They wouldn't be able to trace Killswitch to this office. He'd made damn sure of that. No way they could connect him to the project at all. They'd accessed the database, but he'd made sure to wipe out every one of Comm's records immediately after he'd received final payment. The FBI agents would have found themselves staring at a blank screen.

Security was compromised. It was a scary notion. But ultimately the

FBI couldn't have gained much from Comm's little bird act. They knew about Killswitch. Knew that it existed. But they wouldn't know where it came from, or who it planned to target next.

Jamie knocked and looked into the office. "Hey," she said, frowning, "the board's looking for you. Everything cool?"

Parkerson logged out of the database. Disabled the VPN and turned off his screen. He smiled at Jamie. "Everything's fine. Just a little emergency. Kid stuff."

Jamie's frown softened. "Oh," she said. "Is everything okay?"

"Is now." He grinned at her and stood. "I'd better get back to that meeting."

86

"You picked up Killswitch from your dealer," said Stevens. "We're going to need his name."

Comm stared across the table at him. "You know what they do to snitches in prison?" He shook his head. "Hell no. I'm not talking."

"You're already talking," said Windermere. "You're already a snitch. The question is whether you're going to talk enough to convince us to protect you, or clam up until we throw you in a cell with the baddest *ese* in D block and let him make you his girlfriend."

Stevens leaned across the table. "Look," he said, "you lead us to Killswitch, hell, that's a serial killer you're helping us catch. Nobody's going to let you get hurt, Phillip."

Comm shook his head again. "I'm not talking," he said. "I gave you all I could give you."

"What about Spenser Pyatt? What do you know about him?"

Comm stared at Stevens, blank-faced. "I'm supposed to know something?"

"What about Mickey Pyatt?"

"I never heard of the guy." Comm looked at Windermere. "Look, whatever your boyfriend's on about, I have no idea. I paid an Internet zombie to kill Cameron Ansbacher. That's all I got for you. I don't know shit about anybody named Pyatt."

Stevens swapped glances with Windermere. Windermere rolled her eyes. It had not been a very productive afternoon. The Department of Defense had categorically refused to allow Stevens and Windermere access to the Killswitch IP address. Then Derek Mathers had called Windermere from Minneapolis, his investigation into Mickey Pyatt both exhaustive and fruitless.

"Nothing," he told Windermere. "He showed me everything I wanted to see. Bank statements, financial records. For the rest of the family, too. No strange six-figure payments. No extra life insurance policies. I asked him about Killswitch and he just stared at me. He doesn't know, Carla. I think he's clean."

"Damn it." Windermere sighed. "I was kind of getting that feeling myself."

Now she followed Stevens out of the tiny interview room. Comm wasn't talking. Mathers had hit nothing but dead ends. Killswitch was slipping through their fingers.

"What the hell do we do now?" she asked Stevens when they were out in the hall. "How do we find this guy?"

Stevens rubbed his eyes. "We break Comm, we can follow his dealer back to someone who knows Killswitch."

"We're not breaking Comm, Stevens. You saw him."

"So we work around him. Talk to his friends. They give us his dealer, and we move from there."

Windermere sighed. "That's a lot of pounding the goddamn pavement."

"What if we trace the main Killswitch website?" said Stevens. "Not the special projects database. Just the front page."

Windermere shook her head and looked out the window. "It's the same IP address," she said. "The same DoD firewall."

"What about the credit card? Triple A Industries? O'Brien's used it for three jobs now. Rented Liberty every time. We follow it backward, find more leads."

"Mathers had the same idea." Windermere shrugged. "Liberty has no sign of anyone with a Triple A Industries card before Saint Paul. I figure he's too smart to use the same card for long. Different shell companies, and all of them leading to the same place." She paused. "How the hell do we catch up to these guys, Stevens?"

Stevens shook his head. Gestured into the interview room. "I guess we keep working on Comm."

AS IT TURNED OUT. Comm didn't provide the answer. Roman Ojeda did. The Miami agent poked his head into the interview room about an hour later, grinning wide.

"Amtrak," he told the agents, out in the hall. "Figured I'd check out the bus stations, train stations, charter aircraft companies. Maybe our boys ditched the Cadillac somewhere."

"Amtrak," said Stevens. "They took the train?"

"Just O'Brien. The kid bought a one-way ticket from Palatka, Florida, to Philadelphia the night of the shooting. Would have made it home the next evening. Guess he didn't bolt after all."

Windermere looked at Stevens. "Where the heck is Palatka?"

"Don't look at me. You used to live in this state."

"Palatka, Florida," said Ojeda. "Just south of Jacksonville. Just east of Gainesville. Home of the Florida Azalea Festival."

Windermere shook her head. "I'm not even going to ask, Roman. It's a hell of a drive from Miami, isn't it?"

"Train came in around ten," said Ojeda. "The kid had time."

"Drove all that way to climb on a train? They don't have Amtrak in Miami?"

"Doesn't matter," said Stevens. "What matters is he got on that train, and he rode it back home. He's in Philadelphia, that's the point."

Windermere grinned. "Well, shit, Stevens. If O'Brien's in Philadelphia, I'd say we should be, too."

87

Parkerson wanted nothing more than to go home and sleep. Right now, though, sleep wasn't an option.

He endured the board meeting. Slogged through the rest of the day. Waited for Jamie to leave, and then set to work establishing new identities for the assets. For Lind and Gray both.

There would have to be changes in procedure. The Liberty trick was over. That loophole was closed. Even if the rental company didn't realize what had happened, it was too risky to assume the FBI wasn't watching. Parkerson would have to establish a new protocol for ground transportation. He would need a new credit card, too. Another pain in the ass. He'd hoped to use the Triple A backdrop for more than just a handful of scores.

Hell, he'd have to review every aspect of the jobs. The FBI would be looking. They no doubt had a handle on the Killswitch MO. They'd be looking for patterns and waiting for recurrences.

Parkerson reopened the Killswitch database and typed messages to the two clients he'd already screened, informing them of the need for advanced security measures. Reassuring them their jobs would still be completed as scheduled. Asking them to kindly change their database passwords, for good measure.

Satisfied, he logged out of the database and left the office. Drove out of the complex and headed north on the interstate for a half hour and pulled off near the lake. There was a McDonald's near the off-ramp; he picked up a bag of hamburgers and a couple of Cokes at the drive-through and brought them with him to the lake house.

Wendell Gray had torn his room apart. He'd hurled the bed at the door. Clawed at the walls. Upturned his waste bucket. The room stank like shit. Parkerson looked in at him. Set his jaw. "This place is a mess," he said. "Clean it."

Gray stared at him. Wide, terrified eyes. Quick, shallow breaths. He sat on the floor, arms hugging his knees. His whole body shook. "Clean it," Parkerson told him. Then he closed the door again.

He turned on the projections and waited ten minutes. The asset hadn't moved when he opened the door. Parkerson sighed and left him again. Went into the locker where he stored the guns and ammunition and came back with a sap. The asset still hadn't moved.

Parkerson hit him. Hit him hard. The asset gasped and fell back. "Clean it," Parkerson told him. "Clean this damn room or you won't eat, understand?" He walked to the door. "Clean it," he said, "or the visions come back."

This time, the asset listened. When Parkerson opened the door again, ten minutes later, the bed was remade and moved back to its corner. The floor was scrubbed clean. The bucket was upright.

The room still smelled like shit.

Parkerson smiled at the asset. "Good work," he said. "Great job. You had another nightmare. It's okay."

The asset sat huddled at the edge of the bed. He was still shaking. He favored his right shoulder, where Parkerson had hit him. Parkerson sat down beside him with the McDonald's bag. "You're okay," he said. "Everything's fine. You just had a nightmare. I'm here now."

The asset stared at the floor, his breathing slowly calming. He didn't say anything. Parkerson brought out a burger. Lifted a Coke. "I brought food. Are you hungry?"

The asset nodded. "Yeah."

"Eat up," Parkerson told him. "Eat your burger before it gets cold."

The asset looked up from the floor. Stared at the bag of food. Then he reached in and took out a burger in wax paper. Parkerson watched the kid eat. Watched his shoulders straighten, his spirits start to lift. There was life in his eyes again. A shame. It wasn't going to last.

Parkerson stood and walked to the doorway. "Good work," he said. "Great job. Great first day."

The asset looked at him. Chewed his burger.

"Tomorrow, try not to spill your waste bucket. This place reeks."

The asset didn't say anything. Parkerson looked back at him. "I'll see you tomorrow," he said. "Be good." Then he closed the door again and locked it. Turned on the nightmares and walked out of the house.

88

The plane shuddered, some minor turbulence. Stevens barely noticed. He was too wired. He hadn't slept much the previous night, had had Ojeda dig him up a stack of unsolved assassination-type murders from around the country over the last year or so. Had the junior agent pare down the obvious drug killings, the gang shootings. Focused on victims who looked like they associated with people who could drop two hundred grand on a murder.

He'd flipped through the file all night. Hadn't gotten far. No reports of zombie-eyed killers. No gray Cadillacs. Just bodies, lots of them, and no answers.

He'd tried calling Nancy, too. Got Andrea. "You catch the killer yet, Dad?"

Stevens caught himself grinning at the sound of his daughter's voice. "Not yet, kiddo," he told her. "In fact, we might need you for this one."

"Really?"

"Sure," Stevens nodded. "It's all computers and websites and the like. Too complicated for your old dad."

"What about Windermere? She's younger than you."

"Smarter, too."

Andrea laughed. "*I* didn't say it."

"This stuff is too tough even for Windermere," Stevens said. "We need someone whip smart. Of the new generation."

"Fly me down," Andrea told him. "I'll solve your case in the morning and spend the rest of the day at the beach."

Stevens grinned. "Not much of a beach in Philadelphia, I'm afraid."

"Mom said you were in Miami."

"Heading north in the morning."

"Oh." Andrea paused. "Never mind, then. Solve the case yourself."

Stevens laughed. "Tell your mother I called, would you?"

"Sure, Dad."

"Love you, kiddo."

"You, too." She paused. "Be careful, Daddy. I mean it." Then she hung up the phone. Stevens sat in the hotel room for a while, thinking about his daughter. His son. His wife. He wondered if people got used to the absences, the cops who did this full-time, and their families. Or maybe, he thought, glancing at Windermere now, maybe they just stayed alone.

Windermere shook her head and looked longingly out the plane's window. "Didn't even get to take you for ceviche," she said. "Best thing about Miami."

Stevens smiled. "Best thing?"

"That and the nightlife," she said. "Salsa dancing. You dance?"

"Not since prom."

Windermere clucked. "Your poor wife." She exhaled and stared up at the ceiling. "Mathers is going to meet us in Philly. We'll get half the goddamn Eastern Seaboard looking for this guy, Stevens. Full statewide manhunt. New Jersey, too, and Delaware. FBI, state police, the works."

Stevens nodded. "Good stuff."

"Yeah," she said. "Just tell me we catch him."

"We'll catch him," said Stevens. "We'd better. Something tells me Killswitch isn't packing it in yet."

89

Lind watched TV in his apartment and waited for the man to call with instructions. Stayed hidden and tried to fend off the visions. It was what he'd always done between assignments. This time, though, something was different.

The visions still came. Lind woke up every few hours on his couch, sweating, screaming, heart pounding. He closed his eyes and saw Showtime and Hang Ten and the targets, the man in Miami reeling from the gunshot. Saw blood and bone. Heard the screams.

He couldn't escape them. They followed him everywhere, every night. He thought about what the man had said before he boarded the train, what the man had promised. Just a few more assignments. Then the man would save him.

Lind ate what remained of Caity Sherman's dinner. He stared out his vast picture windows to the street and wondered what she was doing. He'd kept her phone number. He tried to imagine what it would be like to call her. He couldn't. Every time he looked at the phone he felt the panic.

He knew he should call the man and tell him about the girl. He knew that the man would be angry, and that he'd tell him to kill the girl. So he didn't tell the man. Somewhere inside him, for some reason, he didn't want the girl to have to die.

He sat in his apartment and tried to fend off the visions, and he waited for the man to call with new instructions.

90

Mathers was waiting when Windermere and Stevens stepped off the plane. He wore a cocky grin and a raincoat. "April showers," he said, leading them out of the airport and into the parking garages. "You guys get sick of Miami?"

Windermere shook her head. "We're headed back to the beach the minute we find O'Brien," she said. "Harris finally let you off-leash, huh?"

"Figured you all could use a little assistance." Mathers stopped in front of an unmarked Crown Victoria sedan. "Forgot to tell me to pack my umbrella, though."

Windermere climbed in the front seat. "Wasn't any rain in Miami." She grinned wickedly back at Stevens. "You dance, Mathers?"

Mathers shrugged. "I could learn."

Windermere laughed. "Good answer," she said. "Guess we should have brought you along, after all."

THE FBI'S PHILADELPHIA OFFICES were housed in the monolithic William J. Green Jr. Federal Building downtown. Mathers led them up to the eighth floor, where he'd found himself an office and promptly filled it with every phone book and telephone registry in the Delaware Valley. "Here it is," he said, gesturing through the door. "Home sweet home."

Windermere turned up her nose. "Looks like a dorm room," she said. "Smells like one, too. Your mother still picking up after you, Mathers?"

"Ha ha." Mathers shook his head. "You sent me on a paper chase, Supercop."

Stevens looked around. "Looks like you caught it."

"Don't *you* start." Mathers ducked out of the office and came back with a couple of rolling chairs. Shoved them into the room and cleared a spot on the desk. "Welcome to my world," he said, settling behind a precipitous stack. "Come on in."

Stevens and Windermere swapped glances. Stood at the doorway and looked in at the mess. Then Windermere waded in and sat down. "We gotta solve this case, Stevens," she said. "I can't stay here for long."

Stevens laughed. "We'll find O'Brien."

"Might be tough," said Mathers. "I've pretty much cleared through metro Philadelphia. There are fifteen Richard O'Briens in the metro area. Five or six Ricks, and forty O'Brien, Rs. None of them have ever heard of our guy."

"I've got O'Brien's sketch out to local law enforcement," said Windermere. "We'll start working outside the city. Cover as much ground as we can. Maybe this kid has a brother or something, a grandmother."

Mathers nodded. "And if not?"

Stevens rummaged in his briefcase. Found Ojeda's folder, the thick stack of unsolved murders. "Assassinations," he told Mathers. "The whole country, the last year or so."

Mathers's eyes goggled. "That's a lot of murders."

"We can cross-reference them," said Windermere. "Get a list of the days O'Brien flew, the destinations. I'll call the FAA."

"Every Richard O'Brien over the last year? We'd get about a million hits."

"Narrow it down to Philadelphia departures," said Stevens. "Quick trips. If we know where this guy flew, I can start paring down murders in the destination cities. Maybe we find something that gives him away."

Windermere nodded. "Good thinking, Stevens," she said, looking out at the rain. "I just wish you'd thought of this in Miami."

91

Parkerson spent the week in constant motion. He had projects at the office to maintain. He had to create new identities for the assets. Order new weapons, take delivery, file off the serial numbers, and hide them at the lake house. He had to check on the asset morning and night, feed him, and continue his training. He stayed late at work, monitoring the Killswitch database, double-checking that the FBI hadn't somehow found its way inside. He spent his evenings in his office at home, poring over paperwork for his day job and vetting new applications for Killswitch.

He hurried Gray's training, pushed him hard. There were too many assignments in the pipeline for Lind alone. Parkerson itched for Gray to be ready. Itched to set him loose into the world. Itched to count the money the kid was going to earn.

So far, the asset's training was progressing smoothly, at least. Gray kept his room clean. He obeyed simple commands. Parkerson had used the sap only a couple times since that first troublesome day. He could almost *see* the asset's will breaking, watched as he became more and more dependent on Parkerson's daily visits to maintain his thinning veneer of sanity. The fire was dying in the kid's eyes. He was losing his grip. He didn't know where he was, or what happened to him when Parkerson left the room. All he knew was that Parkerson's presence meant relief. Soon he would be ready for his first real test. Another week, maybe.

So far, there was no sign the FBI had made further inroads into Kill-switch. Parkerson spent the week worrying, nonetheless. He'd labored for years on the database, struggling to get the business off the ground. It was a delicate undertaking; you couldn't just put an ad in *Guns & Ammo* touting your services as a killer for hire. You had to be subtle. You had to put the word out and hope that it spread.

You also had to work for cheap, at first. It was like dealing drugs; the first hit was free, or close to it. Parkerson hadn't made enough on the first scores to recoup his expenses. It had been a tough slog. A huge undertaking. Parkerson's head swam at the prospect of having to tear it down. The project was too lucrative now to quit.

Parkerson trained the asset. He managed the database and supervised his own projects at work. When he was lucky, he caught a few hours' sleep. Then, midway through the week, the pressure compounded.

One of the two pending clients logged in to the Killswitch database. Sent Parkerson an urgent message, wanting the kill he'd already partially paid for moved up on the calendar. A hundred-thousand-dollar bonus if completed this weekend. Time-sensitive. ASAP. Parkerson mulled it over that night. "Fine," he replied finally. "But you pay me up front."

The client accepted quickly. Within an hour, the money was transferred. Parkerson stayed late that night at the office. Left Wendell Gray starving and scared catatonic in the lake house basement as he worked overtime. He had flight arrangements to make. Hotel reservations. A weapon to put in the mail. Killswitch was back in business and humming. It was time to get the Philly asset on line.

92

They chased paper for days. Made a long list of O'Briens who'd flown from Philadelphia. Narrowed it down to a handful of likely candidates and took the list to Stevens's stack of murders. After a couple late nights and far too much fast food, they hit something.

"New York City," said Stevens. "Manhattan. February. Maria Nadeau and Johnny Thorsson, her lover. Found shot to death in a suite at the Carlyle. No trace of the killer."

"O'Brien was in New York that night," said Mathers. "Took a shuttle to La Guardia that evening. Left in the morning."

"Here's another," said Windermere. "Los Angeles. Benjamin Arnaud, the movie producer. January, you remember? O'Brien was there, too."

"New York," said Stevens. "And L.A. Which do we check out first?"

"I can take Carla to L.A.," said Mathers. "Hit up the LAPD and take a look at Arnaud's case. That'd leave Stevens to check out Manhattan. Sound good?"

Stevens studied the file. "Sure," he said, "except I'm not sure my BCA badge will open any doors in New York City."

"Shit." Mathers glanced at Windermere. "Can we get him a badge?"

Windermere shook her head. "Doubtful."

"I could take Carla with me," said Stevens. "Probably easier than trying to deputize me. God knows what I'd do with FBI power."

"Wouldn't fly anywhere, that's for sure."

Mathers frowned. "Okay," he said. "So you want to take Windermere?"

Windermere looked at Stevens, a twinkle in her eye. "Or you could take Mathers."

Stevens looked away. "Whatever works."

He could feel Windermere's eyes on him and wondered if she'd push it. Finally, she nodded. "You've suffered enough, Mathers," she said. "Check out Los Angeles. Stevens and I, we'll take New York."

"YOU'RE JEALOUS," she said later, as she and Stevens walked down Arch Street toward their hotel.

Stevens looked at her. "Pardon?"

"Of Mathers. You're jealous, aren't you?" Windermere grinned at him. "It's because he asked me out, isn't it?"

"Heck." Stevens frowned. "I'm not jealous. It's a valid point. Nobody's even going to give me directions if I show them a BCA badge."

"Uh-huh. You have a terrible poker face, partner."

They walked a block and a half as Stevens tried to figure out a rebuttal. The downtown streets were crowded; businesspeople and tourists. Finally, Stevens looked across at her. "Isn't that what you wanted?"

Windermere cocked her head. "What, Stevens? For you to be jealous?"

"You wouldn't have told me he asked you out if you didn't want me to feel something," he said. "Right?"

Windermere looked away. She didn't say anything until they reached the hotel, a Sheraton Four Points across from the convention center. Then she stopped on the sidewalk and looked out into traffic, her expression unreadable. "You're a married man, Kirk," she said slowly. "Why would I want to make you jealous?"

Stevens took a breath. "Am I wrong?"

"We're friends," she said. "You tell me about Nancy, I tell you about Mathers. No big deal."

"It feels like a big deal," he said.

"I've met your wife, Stevens. I like her. You think I want to ruin your marriage?"

"No. Jesus, no. Of course not."

"Do you want to ruin your marriage?"

Stevens shook his head. "Carla, I was making a joke. You told me I was jealous; I was pushing back." He paused. "I'm not one of those assholes who cheats on his wife."

Windermere looked away down the street. "Good," she said. "Then don't do it."

She turned and walked to the hotel doors. Disappeared inside. Stevens stared after her, his heart pounding. He waited until he was sure she'd cleared the lobby. Then he went inside. Rode the elevator to his room and called Nancy.

93

Windermere rode the elevator to her room, cursing herself. *You're a goddamn fool*, she thought. *What the hell were you doing back there?*

She *had* been trying to make Stevens jealous. Of course she had. Couldn't explain why, but there you go. Infuriating.

Stevens wasn't even her type. Hell, even if he wasn't already married to a beautiful woman. Even if he didn't have two wonderful kids. He was a middle-aged white guy. He didn't dance. Why the hell was she getting so moony?

The elevator doors opened, and Windermere walked out to the hall.

Found her room and unlocked it. The room was dark, cool, serene. She walked to the bed and lay down.

It was proximity. That's all it was. Emotions were bound to run rampant when you spent so much time with someone else. You weren't human unless you felt something.

And the history. Pender. Tomlin. Stakeouts and shoot-outs. You built chemistry with a person, especially someone like Stevens. He was a good cop. A decent guy, besides. He was calm and decisive. Smarter than he looked. He—

Enough about Stevens.

It was a temporary thing. Brought on by proximity and the excitement of the case. Maybe Stevens was right not to want to work with her. Maybe he'd figured out the same thing. Maybe he realized he couldn't trust himself around her. She'd seen something in his eyes down there on the street. He'd always looked at her like she was more than a partner.

"Christ." Windermere groaned. "Shut the hell up about him already."

Even if she was a bit moony, what the hell could she do? He was married. Had kids. She sure wasn't going to put that in danger. She'd met Nancy Stevens, and Andrea and JJ. The whole family was smart and funny and perfect. No way she was going to wreck that.

The whole thing was an illusion, this thing with Stevens. They would solve the case with Killswitch and then it would go away. Soon as they landed in Minneapolis. Hell, maybe she would take Mathers for a night out somewhere. Maybe teach the kid how to dance.

Windermere lay on her bed in the darkness. *Just work the damn case,* she thought, staring up at the ceiling. *Don't do anything stupid, you hear?*

94

The next morning, Stevens found Derek Mathers waiting for him in the hotel lobby with two cups of coffee and a sheepish smile. "Howdy, partner."

Stevens looked around. "Windermere?"

"Gone." Mathers shrugged. "Called me this morning, said she was hopping the early flight to Hollywood. Left us Manhattan and more goddamn rain."

"Sure." Stevens hoped his disappointment didn't show. "The Big Apple. Let's do it."

Mathers smiled and handed Stevens a cup of coffee. "Consolation prizes," he said. "For both of us."

MATHERS DROVE the Crown Vic up Interstate 95 and into New Jersey. Stevens sipped his coffee and stared out the window. Figured he was a fool to feel so surprised. He'd crossed a line last night.

What would you have done? he wondered. *How far would you have pushed it?*

I love Nancy. I'm not just some asshole who cheats.

Fine, but there was something there with Windermere. Or maybe there wasn't. Maybe he was an asshole like the rest of the men who hit on her, delusional, and he'd proved it last night. He'd chased her away.

"Guess Windermere heard from the state cops in Jersey," said Mathers. "Delaware, too. Nobody knows anything about this O'Brien character. We're going to have to find him the hard way."

"Sure," Stevens nodded.

Mathers was silent. Then he glanced over. "You really like her, huh?"

"What?" Stevens turned. "Windermere?"

"Yeah, Supercop. You guys are damn tight."

"Just partners," said Stevens. "Professional stuff. We work well to-gether."

"She's hot, though."

Stevens held up his left hand. "So's my wife."

Mathers glanced at him again. "Uh-huh," he said, nodding. "Uh-huh."

95

Windermere took a cab to the airport and caught an early-morning flight to Los Angeles. Spent the whole flight steadfastly refusing to think about Stevens. When the plane touched down at LAX, she was exhausted. Bamboozled. Hardly ready to work a cold case.

An LAPD detective, MacLean, met her at the terminal. He was a young-looking guy, trim. Grinned when he saw her. "Agent Windermere," he said, shaking her hand. "Welcome to Hollywood."

MacLean walked her out to his car, a silver BMW. "My day off," he said. "Kind of a last-minute thing."

Windermere climbed in. "Sorry," she said. "This your case?"

"Arnaud? Sure." MacLean climbed in beside her and drove away from the airport. "Biggest case I ever worked on, bar none."

"You been in homicide long?"

"Eight years," he said. He grinned at her again. "I look younger, right? Something in the air out here."

He slowed for a stoplight. Pressed a button on the dashboard and the

BMW's roof folded back. MacLean grinned at her again. "Hollywood," he said.

MACLEAN TOOK HER across town to Arnaud's house on Mulholland. Rather, what was left of the house. "Tore it down," MacLean told her. "The new owners, as soon as they bought it. Didn't want the bad vibes, I figure."

Windermere stared out at the remains: a flimsy steel fence and a mile of blue tarp, the sound of a band saw from beyond. Through the trees to either side, she could see the skyline in the distance. Whatever his house looked like, Benjamin Arnaud would have had a hell of a view.

"How'd it play?" she asked MacLean. "The murder. What happened?"

"Hard to say for certain," MacLean said. "No witnesses. Arnaud's girlfriend found him shot dead by the pool. One shot, to the back of the head. Spattered his brains all over the film script he was reading."

"Nobody heard the shot?"

MacLean gestured around the car. "Everything's kind of private out here," he said. "People like it that way. They leave each other be."

"So your killer walked up, found Arnaud by the pool, killed him, and disappeared."

"That's right," MacLean nodded. "Chucked the pistol in the pool before he left. Was a Beretta, nine-millimeter. Serial numbers shaved off."

"No trace."

"No trace. Not much for forensics, either. Shooter came in, took the shot, disappeared. Like a ghost."

Like a ghost. Windermere looked around. The road was mostly deserted, the houses hidden in the trees. "Anyone have a motive?"

MacLean shook his head. "None that stuck. Had a few suspects, but all of them checked out. Alibis, every one."

Windermere looked at him. "Who was your strongest?"

"Suspect?" He shrugged. "Like I said, they all had airtight stories."

"Yeah, but who was the one? If you had to figure one person had motive, who would it be?"

MacLean dug around in his pocket. Took out a pack of cigarettes and lit one. Offered the pack to Windermere. Windermere shook her head. "Hate these things," said MacLean. "But I gotta have something keeping me sane."

He took a long drag and exhaled. Watched the smoke drift lazily out of the car. "One guy?" he said. "Probably Roy O'Connell. You know, the director? I guess Arnaud slept with his daughter. O'Connell didn't like it."

Windermere nodded. "Who would?"

"Yeah, but listen: O'Connell was at some dinner in the valley. Accepting a humanitarian award, of all things. A hundred people swear they saw him. He's clean."

Windermere looked out at the empty road again. "Not necessarily," she said. "Let's go see him."

96

The detective looked like she'd walked in from central casting. Jaded New York policewoman. Took no shit. Would kick your ass in a heartbeat. Then she smiled.

She had the kind of smile that would brighten even the worst murder scene, Stevens decided. It dominated the lobby of the Carlyle. "Erin Nordin," she said, shaking Stevens's hand. "A long way from home, aren't you?"

Stevens introduced Mathers. "Seems to be my MO these days," he said, matching the detective's smile. "Not enough crimes in Minnesota or something."

"So you thought you'd come to Manhattan and start solving ours."

"Already been through Miami and Philadelphia. Hoping it gets easier the farther north I go."

Nordin laughed, sharp, unself-conscious. It echoed around the room, drawing glances from the bellhops and a frown from the concierge. "You picked a bad place to start," she said. "This Nadeau case isn't exactly a slam dunk."

"Tough, huh?"

"As they come. Nadeau's having a fling with some Swedish boy toy in a thousand-dollar-a-night suite. Somebody walks in, shoots them both. Disappears."

"Like a ghost."

"No witnesses anywhere. According to the security footage, guy wore a Yankees cap and sunglasses with the tags on 'em. Walked in and walked out and vanished in the streets."

Stevens looked around the lobby. Met Mathers's eyes. Mathers shrugged. "You said Nadeau was having a fling," Stevens said. "You check out the husband?"

Nordin shook her head. "Nothing doing there. He was the first guy on my list. Figured he was jealous, he wanted her dead."

"She was cheating," said Mathers. "Of course he'd be mad."

"He was heartbroken," said Nordin. "He wept like a baby. Swore he'd known for years and he just didn't care. Loved her anyway. Crazy."

"Crazy," said Mathers. "He have an alibi, though?"

"Checked that out, too. He was in Paris. Actually, about the time Nadeau was killed, he was on an Air France jumbo jet somewhere over the Atlantic. Wasn't him."

"We're dealing with a contract killer," said Stevens. "Even if Nadeau's husband didn't pull the trigger, he still could have arranged the kill."

"He could have," said Nordin, "but I'd be damn surprised if he did.

Marc Nadeau was as forthcoming as we could ask for. Opened his house to us, whatever we needed. And, like I said, he knew she was cheating."

Stevens paced a couple of steps. "And no trace of the killer."

"None."

"Find the weapon?" said Mathers.

Nordin shook her head. "No, sir. Probably in the East River somewhere with the rest of the guns."

"Damn it." Mathers looked at Stevens. "This guy's like a damn ninja."

"Or a robot," said Stevens.

Nordin watched them a moment. Then she gestured to the elevators. "You guys want to see the room?"

97

The package arrived midway through the day. Lind signed for it and took it into his apartment. Sat on the couch and slit the envelope open.

It was a delivery from the man, a whole new identity: counterfeit driver's license, Social Security card, a couple hundred dollars cash. Lind set the envelope on the coffee table. Then he studied the driver's license again.

Andrew Kessler. That was the name on the license. That was what the man had decided his name should be.

Lind memorized the information on the card. His name. Birthday. Address. Just like the man taught him. He made sure he memorized everything. Then he looked at the picture.

It was an old picture. Lind couldn't remember where it had been taken, or when. He had longer hair and he was trying not to smile, and failing at it. Lind stared at the picture and tried to remember ever wanting to smile. He couldn't.

He wanted to remember, he realized. He tried. He stared at the picture until he felt the panic start to well up inside him. Then he threw the ID card aside, out of sight. Turned on the television and tried not to think anymore. He sat on the couch and ignored the package. Watched TV and drank coffee and fought off the visions. A couple days later, the phone rang again.

98

It was a fantastic room. It told Stevens nothing.

Nordin gestured to the king-size bed in the middle of the room. "Here's where we found them." She looked at Stevens. "They were, you know, *in flagrante* when the deed was done."

Mathers stifled a laugh from the doorway. Stevens shook his head. Walked to the window, peered out. Saw nothing but New York beyond. "When'd they make the reservation?" he said. "For the room."

Nordin frowned. "Good question," she said. "I'm not sure."

"Nadeau made it?"

"I assume so," said Nordin. "I didn't ask that either, though. Does it matter?"

Stevens walked back across the room. Looked into the bathroom. It was bigger than most New York apartments. "Our killer knew Nadeau would be here," he said. "How?"

Nordin pulled out her cell phone and punched in a number. Wandered over to the window, her phone in her ear. She muttered something into the handset and waited. Mathers looked at Stevens. "You feeling something?"

"Not sure," Stevens said. "Getting nowhere with the why. Might as well try the how."

Nordin hung up her phone. "Front desk says the reservation was made a couple nights before the murder." She paused. "And Nadeau didn't make it. Thorsson did."

"JOHNNY THORSSON was a twenty-three-year-old party boy," Nordin told them. They were outside the Carlyle now, waiting for the valet to bring up Mathers's commandeered Crown Vic. "Lived in a loft in the Meatpacking District. I guess he was some kind of tennis sensation for a while. Sounded like that all went to shit when he met Maria Nadeau."

Stevens looked out into traffic, the street choked with yellow cabs and black town cars, angry horns everywhere and exhaust. He frowned. "How do you mean?"

"Well, he wasn't playing much tennis," Nordin said. "Kind of fell into a fast-moving crowd."

"And Nadeau was the catalyst."

"One of." Nordin glanced at him. "Thorsson had lots of friends."

The valet arrived with the Crown Vic. Mathers took the keys and climbed behind the wheel. The valet lingered until Stevens shoved a couple dollars in his hand. Then he disappeared. Stevens and Nordin climbed in the car.

Mathers pulled away from the curb. Was boxed in immediately by a stretch limousine and a bread van. He swore and looked at Stevens. "Where the heck am I going?"

Stevens didn't answer. He stared out at the limousine, black and sleek and anonymous. "A loft in the Meatpacking District," he said. "I don't know much about Manhattan real estate, but I'm guessing his digs weren't cheap."

"You'd be correct," said Nordin. "Seven figures, easy."

"So how does a twenty-three-year-old party boy afford a place like that? Who's paying for it?"

Nordin frowned. Picked up her cell phone. "I'm not sure."

Stevens watched the limousine glide away down the street. "Huh," he said. "Let's find out."

99

If Roy O'Connell knew anything about Killswitch, he wasn't talking.

Windermere and MacLean found the director at his Malibu beach house, doing laps in his infinity pool. Windermere stood at the end of the pool. Waited until he'd finished a lap. Until he looked up, breathing heavy, squinting in the light.

"Killswitch," she said.

O'Connell frowned. "I don't get it," he said. "Is this some kind of hidden-camera trick?"

"No trick," said Windermere. "No cameras. I just want to know what you thought of Benjamin Arnaud."

O'Connell's face clouded. He looked at Windermere again, then at MacLean behind her. "I get the feeling I should be calling my lawyer."

Windermere tossed him a towel. "Suit yourself."

FORTY-FIVE MINUTES LATER. O'Connell sat, fully dressed, in his expansive living room, a postcard view of the ocean behind him and a bulldog lawyer in a five-thousand-dollar suit in front.

"I don't know what to tell you, Agent Windermere," the director told her. "I didn't like Arnaud. Of course I didn't. My daughter was barely eighteen when he . . ." He shook his head. "Anyway. I didn't like the man. Maybe I was happy to hear he'd got what was coming to him—"

The lawyer stiffened. *"Roy."*

O'Connell shrugged. "I didn't kill him, Jerry. I was at a function that night. A hundred people saw me."

"Sure they did," said Windermere. "For the purposes of my case, though, where you were at the time of the killing doesn't matter. What do you know about Killswitch?"

"Killswitch." O'Connell frowned. "It was a movie, right? Steven Seagal."

Windermere didn't say anything. Waited, hoping her silence would convince the director to keep talking. After a moment, he shook his head.

"Look," he said. "I don't know any Killswitch. I don't know what you're talking about. If you're alleging I killed Benjy Arnaud, you're wrong. I'm a goddamn movie director."

"You're a father," said Windermere. "Maybe you didn't like the thought of Arnaud's hands on your daughter. Maybe you decided to do something about it."

"I did do something about it. I severed all ties with Arnaud's production company. I told him I'd never do business with him again, and if I saw him in public I'd probably punch him out. I didn't kill him, though. That's a fact."

Windermere looked around. "You'd be willing to show me your computers, your phone records, here and at your office? Your financial records, all of that?"

"Not without a warrant," the lawyer said.

"Relax, Jerry." O'Connell smiled at Windermere. "Whatever you need, Agent. I have nothing to hide."

IOO

Eight hours of fruitless searching later, Windermere was forced to conclude that either Roy O'Connell was a very good liar or he really did have nothing to hide.

She'd managed to talk her way into a glorified broom closet down the hall from the Criminal Investigative Division at the FBI's West L.A. offices, had commandeered a couple of Bureau techs to comb through O'Connell's hard drives, and in the meantime had plugged away at a fossilized computer and a labyrinthine phone system, looking for someone or something that would point the finger at Benjamin Arnaud's killer.

MacLean hung around until early evening, talking her through his own investigative process, pointing her toward questions he'd been unable to answer the first time around. For all of his Hollywood pretense, Windermere decided, the detective was a pretty good cop. Windermere wasn't finding many holes as she reviewed his work, and after Roy O'Connell's records came back clean, the FBI agent was forced to conclude that she didn't have the slightest clue who'd paid for Benjamin Arnaud's murder. Killswitch, in this case, had been remarkably fastidious.

How many others? Windermere thought. *How many more murders has Killswitch committed, murders we just don't know about because the guy's too goddamn good?*

MacLean begged off around the time the sun finally set. He'd made a play at her, had run one hand through his perfect hair and fixed her with a movie star smile. "Feel like a drink, Agent Windermere? Sometimes it takes a bit of social lubrication to make the pieces fall into place."

Horrible line notwithstanding, Windermere had been tempted. Mac-

Lean was a decent-looking guy, and after that debacle with Stevens, she could use some distraction. In the end, though, she couldn't do it. She shook Mac-Lean's hand and told him she'd probably see him tomorrow, watched him walk off and then settled back into her work.

Now, with darkness settled in outside, she sat back from her ancient computer and surveyed the tiny workspace. *My own office. Hardly all it's cracked up to be.*

She thought about Stevens and wondered if he and Mathers were making any progress. Wished she hadn't bolted on Stevens so quickly. She wondered what he'd thought when he found Mathers waiting for him in the hotel lobby that morning. Whether he'd been surprised or upset. If he'd missed her.

Knock it off, dummy. Who cares if he missed you?

Windermere stared out of her tiny office to the dark sky in the windows beyond. Thought about Stevens some more, and then pushed the BCA agent from her mind. Turned back to her computer and brought up a gossip website, figuring maybe a spurned movie star would dish on Roy O'Connell.

She waded through tripe for an hour, got nothing but paparazzi pictures and pregnancy rumors. Felt her eyelids getting heavy and stood and walked out to search for the coffee machine. Then she felt her phone buzzing. Stevens's number.

She answered. "Stevens?"

"Mathers." A pause. "I borrowed his phone."

Windermere swallowed. "Oh," she said. "Okay, Mathers. What's up?"

"Doing the New York thing." Mathers sounded tired, but cheerful. "Anyway, we figured we should tell you: We got ourselves a guy here. Says he paid Killswitch to murder Maria Nadeau."

101

He wasn't supposed to die, I swear."

Stevens leaned forward and studied the man across the table. It had been a long night, and he hadn't slept any. Now, as morning broke over Manhattan, he found himself crowded into a 24th Precinct interview room with Mathers and Detective Erin Nordin—and this man, one Sebastian Morgan, a plump, aging socialite who'd spent most of the last hour in tears.

They'd found Morgan at his West End Avenue townhouse, had roused him out of bed around five in the morning. It had been a long night already by that point; Stevens, Mathers, and Nordin had turned Manhattan upside down looking for the money behind Johnny Thorsson's loft, leaving Stevens exhausted and half-deaf from a succession of nightclubs and loft parties and drugged-up friends of Thorsson's, one of whom had finally pointed the finger at Morgan.

Morgan knew the score as soon as he opened the door. He stared out at Nordin, then Mathers and Stevens, and he sighed, his eyes welling with tears. "Let me get dressed," he told them. "Then I'll talk."

Now the big man sat across from Stevens and struggled to keep his composure as he told the story. "He wasn't supposed to die," he said. "I swear."

Stevens leaned forward. "Johnny, you mean."

Morgan nodded. "He didn't even like that woman. He was with her for the money. Everyone knew."

"He liked you, though."

"Liked me?" Morgan shook his head. "We were in love. I told him I could take care of him. He didn't need to sleep with that slut anymore. He didn't listen."

Stevens sat back. "So you killed her. And Johnny, too."

"He wasn't supposed to die," Morgan said. "I didn't think the killer would shoot him, too. I just wanted to scare him. Show him he needed me."

Mathers stepped forward. "Did you pay him?"

Morgan nodded.

"After the killing, I mean." Mathers looked at Stevens. "You said they paid in installments, right? So did you pay the second installment, or what?"

Morgan looked down at the table. He didn't say anything. Stevens leaned forward again. "Mr. Morgan, we'll be looking at your bank statements," he said. "We're going to find out, one way or the other."

Morgan still didn't answer. He didn't look up, just sat there in silence, his breath growing ragged, more labored. Finally, he looked up, his eyes wet with tears. "Why couldn't he have loved me?" he said, stifling a sob. "We could have been so happy together."

AN HOUR LATER. Stevens stood in an observation room adjoining Sebastian Morgan's little corner of hell. He drank strong precinct coffee and ate a breakfast sandwich and stared in through the two-way mirror at Morgan as Derek Mathers pressed him for information.

Morgan was guilty. He'd waived the right to an attorney and signed a full confession. Had admitted, tearfully, that he'd paid for both murders. That he'd wanted to punish Johnny Thorsson for spurning him.

He'd found Killswitch, he said, through a musician friend, though everyone knew about it. He had seen Thorsson with Nadeau at a party one night, had tried, one more time, to seduce the young tennis pro. Thorsson had rebuffed him. That night, drunk on champagne and high on cocaine, he'd filed an application with Killswitch. A few weeks later, Johnny Thorsson and Maria Nadeau were dead.

Morgan was guilty. He'd confessed to it all. But he didn't know a damn thing about Killswitch. He'd found the website easy, had filed the application and transferred the payments, provided Killswitch with the details of Johnny Thorsson's hotel reservation, but for all of that, he knew less about the program than Comm had, and Comm didn't know much. In essence, he was no help at all.

Stevens stared through the window. Mathers sat at the table across from Morgan. Detective Nordin stood in a corner, barely able to contain her excitement. She'd close her homicide case; she had reason to be thrilled. For Stevens and Mathers, though, Sebastian Morgan was just another dead end.

Stevens watched Mathers. He hadn't hated working with the kid. In fact, he'd kind of enjoyed it. The kid was a smart-ass, but sharp. Had a good sense of humor and could talk basketball all day. Didn't even seem to hold a grudge after the whole Miami fiasco. The kid was a Bulls fan, but nobody was perfect.

Still, though, he wondered about Windermere. She'd spoken to Mathers this morning from Los Angeles, and from what Mathers was saying, she wasn't having any luck, either. Mathers seemed to think they'd be heading back to Philadelphia pretty quick, joining up with the state cops and canvassing the countryside for Richard O'Brien. Working the phone book. Chasing needles in haystacks.

Philadelphia. Stevens couldn't help feeling like a third wheel now that Mathers and Windermere were going to be back working together. Certainly they wouldn't need his help running the manhunt, and with the Pyatt family pretty much removed from the equation, Stevens figured Tim Lesley would want him back on BCA turf. Besides, Nancy was getting impatient back home. She was swamped with work, had been stuck by herself with the kids for nearly a week now. And who knew how Windermere would react when she saw him; he'd pretty much alienated her the last time they'd spoken. Maybe it was time to go home.

Hell, Stevens thought, *give Mathers and Windermere a chance to get to know each other. They don't need me hanging around.*

In the interview room, Sebastian Morgan was crying again. Stevens stared through the window and watched the man sob, thinking about Windermere and Killswitch and home.

102

The phone rang in the morning. That evening, Lind drove to the airport.

It was Friday. So the man told him, when he gave Lind his flight information. When he outlined his instructions for the job.

Friday. Lind was surprised, though he didn't know why. The girl had come over on Sunday. Since then, he'd been alone in his apartment.

Sunday to Friday. Five days.

Lind locked up his apartment and drove to the airport. Left his car in the overnight lot and walked into the terminal. Stopped before he reached the Delta counter and surveyed the long row of desks.

She was there. Caity Sherman. She was working at the priority counter. Lind smiled a little. He started toward her. Then he stopped.

The identification in his pocket said Andrew Kessler. Caity Sherman thought his name was Richard O'Brien. She would want to know why his ID said different. She would ask questions that he wouldn't be able to answer.

Lind turned and walked to the other end of the Delta counter and checked in on a computer screen. He kept his back to the priority lane and didn't look back at Caity Sherman. The machine spat out his ticket and he took it and walked toward security. Was nearly at the entrance when she called out behind him. "Richard."

Lind turned around. She'd left the Delta counter and was standing in the middle of the terminal. "You didn't like my cooking," she said, grinning. "Is that it?"

Lind hesitated a moment. Then he walked back toward her, keeping the Andrew Kessler ticket hidden. "I liked your cooking," he said.

She pretended to pout. "You just didn't want to talk to me? I'm all alone at the frequent-flier desk."

"I'm sorry," he said.

"Uh-huh." She paused. Then she grinned again. "I'm just teasing. Where are you headed?"

"I'm headed . . ." He couldn't think. He knew the man would expect him to lie. "I don't know."

She frowned. "You don't know where you're going? Let's see your ticket."

"No." He snatched it away from her. Glanced quickly at the departures screen above her head. "Houston," he said. "I'm going to Houston."

"Houston." She studied his face. Then she shrugged. "Well, you'd better hurry. They're about to board."

"Thank you," he said.

She shook her head and turned back to the counter. "Don't mention it."

Lind watched her go. He'd extricated himself. He'd lied and she'd believed him, and now she was leaving. Disaster averted. He'd won.

"Hey," he called out. Felt a sudden spasm of panic when she turned around. He looked down at the ground and tried to steady his breathing. "It was . . . it was good to see you."

She snorted. "I bet."

Lind watched her walk back to the ticket counter. He still felt the panic. Hell, he was terrified, shaking. He knew the man wouldn't approve. Still, he wanted to see her again. To hell with the man.

103

Windermere stared at Stevens. "Home," she said.

Stevens nodded. "For the weekend. Maybe longer. Gotta check in with Lesley at headquarters." He gestured around Mathers's cramped little office. "You guys can spread out a little. You don't need me here."

Windermere studied Stevens's face. The BCA agent looked worn out. Discouraged. He'd announced his plans shortly after they'd met back in the FBI office in Philadelphia, after taking down Johnny Thorsson's spurned lover in Manhattan.

He's right, she thought, *probably.* She and Mathers could handle the paperwork and whatever other half-cocked leads came through the pipeline. Still, it seemed sacrilege to walk away in the middle of the case.

"What about a trap?" she said. "We'll use the code Comm gave us and ask Killswitch to set up a hit. Worm our way inside that way."

"Too soon," Stevens said. "He'll be suspicious after Comm broke into the system. Especially if he finds out Morgan went down."

"The DoD lead, then. Maybe we get lucky and they come through with the access."

Stevens shook his head. "It's Friday night, Carla," he said. "They're not going to let us into their computers before Monday at the earliest. And even then it's not likely they'll give us anything."

Right again, Windermere thought. The DoD hadn't exactly been positive when she'd outlined the situation. A department spokesman had given her a stern lecture about Homeland Security and threat levels for fifteen minutes before she'd hung up on him. They probably weren't about to call back with the keys to the kingdom.

"So you're just going to go," she said. "Leave us behind."

Stevens sighed. "My wife needs a break," he said. "She's swamped with work. It's been a week. I owe her a weekend, at least."

Windermere looked at him. "Fine," she said.

"There's a flight out tomorrow morning. I'll spend the night here and take off first thing."

Windermere glanced at Mathers. Her young colleague was snoozing into a stack of addresses. "This is about the other night, huh?"

Stevens stiffened. Looked at Mathers. Then pulled her out into the hall. "No," he said when they were alone. "I don't know. Maybe it is. Even if it's not, I'm sorry."

"You're sorry?" She looked at him. "For what?"

"I don't want to be the asshole," he said. "I thought we were joking around, flirting a little. I wasn't trying to, you know, make a move or anything."

She felt her heart soften. "I know you weren't, Stevens. You don't need to be sorry."

"Sure feels like it."

"Well, it shouldn't." She took a deep breath. "I wasn't angry with you, Kirk. I was mad at myself for flirting with you. It's not right."

Stevens stared at her. She felt like he must be reading her mind. "I love my wife," he said finally.

"I know you do," she replied. "This is just—"

"Infatuation. It's transient."

"An illusion."

He looked at her. "You believe that?"

She shook her head. "I don't fucking know, Stevens."

Stevens said nothing. He was close to her in that tiny hallway. She could sense his body near hers. Feel his warmth. For a brief, panicked moment, she half believed he was going to kiss her. She caught herself hoping he did.

Instead, he shook his head and stepped away. "I'm going home," he told her. "Call me if anything turns up."

104

The asset stared at Parkerson with that slack expression of his. "Go on," Parkerson told him. "Do it."

Friday night. The asset had been at the lake house for five days. He'd responded well to the training so far. It was time to advance the regimen.

"Do it," Parkerson told him. "You don't want the visions to continue, do you?"

The asset looked exhausted. He'd been locked in the room with the visions for five days and four nights. Probably hadn't slept more than twenty minutes at a stretch.

He'd stopped trashing the room, though. The bed remained fully made. The waste bucket stayed upright. He seemed to calm down when Parkerson came in the room. He seemed to trust Parkerson, seemed grateful for the food, for the reprieve.

"Do it," Parkerson told him. "Do it for me."

Slowly, the asset turned to the cardboard box beside the bed. Parkerson had picked it up on his way to the lake house. A gift for the asset. A test.

The asset reached inside the box and pulled out an orange cat. The cat purred and nuzzled the asset. The asset held it. Looked at it.

"Do it now," Parkerson told him.

The asset gripped the cat tighter. The cat struggled. Yowled and clawed at the asset. The asset clenched hard and twisted the cat's neck. Bones snapped and the cat spasmed once. Then it dropped, lifeless, into the cardboard box.

Parkerson nodded. "Good work," he said. The asset seemed to relax a little. Parkerson kicked the box away. Held up the McDonald's bag. "Let's eat."

105

It was nearly midnight when the plane landed in Las Vegas. Lind spent the flight alongside a rowdy bachelorette party. They drank, swore, and laughed so much there was no danger he'd fall asleep.

He walked off the plane and through McCarran International Airport, dodging slot machines and more wild crowds of partiers. The airport was a zoo, even so late at night. He waited forty-five minutes in a stifling taxi line before it was finally his turn to leave.

No more rental cars. Lind hardly registered the change in procedure. He'd listened to the man's instructions, and now he followed them. That was that.

The taxi driver was an old man with a patchy beard and a smoker's cough. He studied Lind in the rearview. "Where you headed, man?"

"The Flamingo," Lind told him. "The Strip."

THE HOTEL WAS EVEN LOUDER than the airport. There was a twenty-minute wait at the check-in desks. Lind watched the crowds mill around him, everyone smiling, squealing, hysterical, drunk. He suddenly felt very tired.

The desk clerk was young, his face pockmarked with acne scars. He checked Lind in and then squinted at his computer. "Says here we have a couple packages for you." He grinned at Lind. "You forget your bathing suit?"

Lind shook his head. "No."

The man shrugged. He disappeared through a swinging door and came out with the packages: a parcel, shipped by courier, and an envelope with Andrew Kessler's name on it. Handed them to Lind, then glanced around the lobby and leaned in. "You need anything, brother?" he said. "Looking to party tonight? Want a girl?"

Lind thought about Caity Sherman and shook his head. Picked up the packages and his room key and rode up to his room in an elevator jampacked with German tourists. Found his suite and walked in and sat on the bed. He wanted so badly to sleep. He couldn't. As soon as he closed his eyes, he was back in that desert Humvee.

He switched on the TV and turned up the volume. Turned on all the lights and pumped up the air-conditioning. Walked to the window and stared out at the Strip, the vast crowds, the chaos. He stood at the window for a while, and then picked up the parcel and tore it open.

Another weapon. Another photograph. Inside the envelope was a Bellagio room key. Lind put the handgun and the key card in a drawer. He memorized the photograph and burned it in the bathroom wastebasket. Then he walked back to the window and stared down at the Strip, watching the partiers come and go until dawn.

106

Stevens caught the morning flight direct from Philadelphia to Minneapolis. Arrived at eleven and made it home five minutes before noon. He paid the cabbie and stood outside and surveyed his house for a moment, enjoying the sunshine, breathing the fresh air. Then he walked up the front stairs to the door.

Andrea was in the kitchen when he walked in from the hall. She looked up from her sandwich and blinked. "You're home," she said, chewing. "You catch the bad guys?"

"Not yet," he said. "Where's your mother?"

"Work." Andrea frowned. Paged through her magazine. "You didn't solve the case? How come you're home?"

"Guess I needed a break," he said. "Couldn't leave your mom high and dry for too long. Anyway, I missed you guys."

He mussed her hair. Andrea swatted him away. *"Dad."* She looked up at him. "So you just took a break? Is Agent Windermere still working?"

Stevens nodded. "She has a partner. This kid Mathers."

"So she doesn't need you. That's why you came home."

"We're kind of stuck," he said, sighing. "We reached a dead end. I figured maybe I should step back for a while."

Andrea shook her head. "I don't get it. The bad guy's still out there?"

Stevens nodded. "Uh-huh."

"So why aren't you chasing him?"

"I told you, Andrea. Your mom—"

"Who cares about Mom?" Her eyes flashed. "This guy's a killer, isn't he?"

Stevens stepped back. "Andrea—"

"Well?" She looked at him. "There's a murderer out there, Dad. You and Windermere need to catch him. You need to catch him before he comes after *us*."

"Honey, he's not going to come after us."

"Coach Tomlin did." Andrea was breathing shallow now, fast. She looked down at her magazine and bit her lip. "What if it happens again?"

Stevens looked at his daughter and felt his heart melt. "It won't, honey. This guy doesn't even know who we are."

"Do you know who he is? Maybe he lives next door, Daddy. Maybe you work with him." Andrea stood. "Catch him, Daddy," she said. "Don't just give up."

She hurried out of the room, leaving Stevens alone in the kitchen. He lingered there, listening to his daughter stalk through the hall and upstairs. Heard her door slam, and sighed. "Damn it, kiddo," he said. "I'm trying."

107

ind woke up breathless, on top of the bed. The TV blared beside him. Harsh sunlight glared in through the dusty window. It was daytime, midmorning. He'd been dreaming again.

He sat up and breathed deep, trying to calm his racing heart. Stared down at the carpet until the panic disappeared. Until he could hear the sounds of the TV over the roar of his pulse in his ears.

He brewed a pot of coffee and drank it all. Showered in ice-cold water. Didn't look at himself in the mirror as he dressed. When he was ready, he stuffed the pistol in the back of his pants. Pulled his shirt over top and slipped the Bellagio room key in his pocket as he walked from the room.

The lobby was quieter this morning. The partiers were gone. It was still early for Las Vegas. There was plenty of time left to kill.

Lind found a Denny's and ate a greasy breakfast. Then he walked, aimless, up and down the long boulevard. Wandered in and out of casinos until a few hours had passed. Then he turned and headed north, toward the Bellagio. Passed its majestic fountains without stopping to look, walked up the long driveway and into the lobby. He lingered there a moment, anonymous in the crowd, and then followed a sign toward the hotel elevators. The gun pressed into his back; the crowd ebbed and flowed, and the slot machines clamored. Lind pictured the man's face. Imagined a life without the visions. He hurried his pace. It was time to complete the assignment.

108

Windermere spent the day cooped up in that tiny office with Mathers. Despite the stall in their case, Mathers was in good spirits; he laughed and teased Windermere, attempting to prod her out of her funk.

It was Stevens's fault. The BCA agent had turned tail and ditched her, headed back to his family and left her with a case that suddenly seemed unsolvable. Not that she could blame him. Rats off a sinking ship. Or maybe he just missed his wife.

Yeah, or maybe she'd scared him away. He'd scared himself away. They'd come close to something, she knew, closer than they'd ever come before. On the street outside the hotel, earlier in the week, she'd nearly . . . what, kissed him? Expressed her true love? Who the hell knew what she was doing. Or what he was doing, for that matter. That was why he'd recused himself. He was scared he'd do something wrong. And, really, who could blame him? It was good he was gone.

Except Windermere missed him. That was a fact, annoying as it was. She was a goddamn FBI agent, and a good one. No way she should be pinning her emotional well-being on any man, least of all Stevens, god damn him.

Windermere struggled to push Stevens from her mind. It would have been easier if the damn case was going anywhere. If they had any momentum whatsoever. Right now, they had a name and a city and a hired killer's website. They had cops watching a P.O. box in Richmond, Virginia, though apparently Killswitch never, ever checked his mail. They had a string of shell companies and Internet IP addresses hidden behind a Department of Defense security wall that, from what Windermere could ascertain, they could never breach.

This whole case hinges on what the DoD's hiding, she thought. *Give me ten minutes of server access and we put our killer away.*

It wasn't happening. So, what, she and Mathers were just going to keep working through phone books, trying to find O'Brien? That was what passed for police work these days?

Fuck it.

Windermere looked up from her laptop. Stared across the cluttered desk at Mathers. The kid was hunched over his own computer, comically oversized for his tiny chair. Windermere stifled a smile. "Mathers," she said, "I'm dying over here."

Mathers looked up at her. "Thank God," he said, stretching. "Thought I was the only one."

"We can't keep doing this," she said. "We're treading water. Somewhere, our guy's out there, probably ready to kill again, and this bullshit is driving me insane."

"So what do you want to do?"

Windermere looked around the tiny office. The reams of paperwork, the maps, the names crossed off lists. One giant haystack with one tiny needle. A goddamn treadmill of monotony. She ran her hands through her hair. Rubbed her eyes.

"Toss me Sebastian Morgan's statement," she told Mathers. "Let me have a look through it one more time."

Mathers searched through a mound of papers and came out with a file. Slid it across the desk. "What are you thinking?"

"Not thinking, Mathers," Windermere said. "Fishing." She paged through the file. Then she looked up. "I guess they never found the murder weapon, huh?"

"Nope. NYPD figured our guy ditched it somewhere."

Windermere thought for a moment. "What about the bullets?" she said. "They run any ballistic analysis?"

"Not sure," Mathers said. "You want I should check?"

Windermere settled back in her chair. If the FBI, by some miracle, had the murder weapon fingerprinted in its ballistics database, it might be possible to trace the gun to another crime. And maybe that crime would produce the loose thread that would unravel Killswitch, once and for all.

"Please," Windermere told Mathers. "Give New York a call. Maybe this time our Hail Mary works."

109

He found the target's room without a problem. Followed the signs to the bank of elevators, showed the room key to the security guard, and joined a group of young people in a crowded car. They piled off on the fourteenth floor. Lind rode alone to the thirty-fifth.

He had memorized the target's room number. Now he walked down the long corridor, reaching back for his pistol and disengaging the safety.

He gripped the gun tight in one hand and knocked on the target's door with the other.

There was no answer from within. No movement behind the pinprick peephole. The light behind it stayed constant. Lind gave it a minute before he knocked again. Still no answer. He slid his key in the lock and felt the lock disengage.

Slowly he pushed the door open and crept into the room. The gun was heavy in his hand, the steel slick. Behind the door was a long hallway, dark, save for a thin beam of light coming through the curtains in the room at the end.

The hallway opened up into a spacious living area. There was nobody waiting, no movement. There were no lights on anywhere. Lind checked the whole suite: the kitchenette, both bedrooms. The sheets were tangled and lived in; there were clothes on the floor. Bottles in the living room, half-empty glasses. Thin lines of white powder and a baggie of pills, but no people. The target was gone.

Lind stood in the dark living area and waited. Gripped the gun tight and hoped the target would return quickly. He realized he was nervous.

It was a new kind of nervous. It wasn't the sensation he normally felt as he waited to complete an assignment, the sick fear that he would fail, that the target wouldn't show, that he would disappoint the man. Lind knew the target was coming. The target always came. The man was never wrong. No, there was something else unsettling Lind. He felt a hint of panic when he tried to explore it.

Caity Sherman. He kept thinking about the girl. He'd thought about her on the flight out, on the cab ride to the hotel. He'd thought about her all morning as he wandered the Strip. He'd thought about her, he realized, while he dreamed.

He knew he should have killed her. He knew the man would be angry. He shouldn't be thinking of her now, in this hotel room, on assignment. He should be focused on the target. On pleasing the man. He should be focused on making the visions go away. But he couldn't.

He couldn't stop thinking about Caity Sherman. The way she'd smiled at him. The way she'd laughed and teased him. The way her face had fallen when he'd tried to brush her aside. Lind caught himself hoping he hadn't hurt her feelings. He hoped he would see her again.

This was bad. Lind knew it was bad. He felt the panic behind his eyes whenever he saw her. The buzzing like a million hornets inside his skull. He felt like he wanted to claw his brain out through his ears.

Still, he couldn't escape her. He stood in the target's dark room and thought about Caity Sherman, fighting the waves of panic and trying to stay calm. He stood there for a long time. He started to feel worried. He started to wonder if the target wouldn't come.

Then he heard voices, and a key in the door. Laughter from the hallway, and a fresh beam of light. The target was here. Lind gripped his pistol tighter and tried to push Caity Sherman from his mind.

110

A man and two women. They came into the room, laughing, dressed for the pool. The man went for the cocaine on the table. Dragged a woman with him. The second woman fumbled with the light switch. Then she saw Lind and screamed.

Lind stepped out of the shadows. Leveled the gun at the man as the women shrank back. He was a big guy, the target, slick hair, middle-aged. He wore a towel around his waist and a gold chain on his neck, and he glared at Lind, masking confusion with anger. "What the fuck, man?" he said. "Who the fuck are you?"

The woman screamed again, from the corner. Lind knew he would have to kill them, too. Collateral damage. They'd seen his face. The man would expect them to die.

The target stood, his palms up. "What do you want, man? Who are you?"

It was an easy assignment. He would shoot the target, and then he would shoot the women. Then he would leave. Quick and clean. An easy assignment.

The target took a step toward Lind. Lind took a step with the gun. The target drew back. The women gasped from the corner. The target's anger was gone now. "What do you want, man?" he said, his voice high-pitched and frantic. "You want money? Whatever you need, man, it's yours."

Lind didn't reply. He brought the gun up to the target's face. Reached out and grabbed him by his gold chain. Twisted it, dragging the man closer. The target gasped for air, begged, the gun to his temple.

Pull the trigger. Pullthetriggerpullthetriggerpullthetrigger.

Lind saw the man in Duluth. Saw the man in Miami. Saw the blood. It seemed to fill the hotel room, and it belonged to the Miami target, the Saint Paul target, the Hollywood executive, and the New York adulterers. It was the blood of the terrified soldier, chained to that brick wall.

Lind tried to shake his head clear as the target begged for his life. Gritted his teeth and felt that awful panic rising, pounding in his ears like a drumbeat. His world shook and shattered. He closed his eyes and saw Caity Sherman. Saw blood. Heard the gun roar and realized he'd pulled the trigger.

The target screamed. The women screamed. Lind opened his eyes, expecting carnage. Instead, he saw gun smoke. A bullet hole in the ceiling. The target clutched at his ear. Lind had missed him.

The target struggled. Gasped. Swore. He'd dropped his towel; he fought in a blue Speedo for his life, his body fat and unremarkable and pathetic. He clawed at the chain around his neck. The women screamed again, a chorus, never ceasing. The panic roared in Lind's ears. The whole world was one narrow tunnel, his ears staticky noise. He knew he had to kill the target.

He couldn't.

Lind let go of the target's chain. The man wrenched free, scrabbled backward, across the room. Lind fought more waves of panic. He lowered the gun. Somewhere in the chaos, he realized he should run.

▌▌▌

Lind hurried to the elevators. Pressed the call button three times and glanced down the long hallway. Nobody was coming. Somewhere in the distance an alarm was sounding. Lind pressed the call button again.

The elevator doors opened. Lind stuffed the gun in his waistband and climbed aboard, his heart still pounding, the panic at his throat. He leaned against the elevator wall and waited as the car plunged to earth.

He sleepwalked across the gaming floor. Passed an army of uniformed security guards headed up into the tower and felt a wave of panic so strong, it forced him off his feet. He sat at an electronic slot machine and tried to clear his head. He'd failed to complete the assignment. The man was going to be angry.

Lind steadied himself on the back of his chair and then walked across the casino and out the front doors. He started down the curving driveway toward Las Vegas Boulevard, stopped halfway down, and walked to the shore of the vast lake that fronted the casino. Took out his cell phone and dialed the man's number. After a moment, the man picked up. "You good?"

"No good," Lind told him. "I failed the assignment."

The man swore. "What the hell do you mean?"

"The assignment wasn't completed. I failed to complete it."

"Jesus Christ." The man paused. "What the hell happened? Don't answer that. Where are you now?"

"Outside the casino. I found the target, but I couldn't complete the assignment."

"You found him. He *saw* you?"

Lind looked around. "Yes."

"God damn it. You have to get out of there." The man paused again. "Your flight's in, what, ninety minutes? Get to the airport and get the hell out of town."

Lind nodded. "Okay."

"We'll talk about this later. *Go.*" The man ended the call. Lind pocketed the cell phone. Took the gun from his waistband and threw it in the lake. Then he walked to the Strip. Pushed through the crowd on the sidewalk. Hesitated a moment, and then walked off the curb and out onto the boulevard.

Horns honked. Brakes squealed. Lind walked to a marooned cab. Opened the door and slid in the backseat. "Airport," he said.

The cabbie spun in his seat. "Shit, man, you crazy? I can't pick you up here."

"Airport." Lind pulled out his wallet. "A hundred dollars, cash."

The cabbie stared at him. More horns blared outside. Finally, the cabbie shook his head. "Shit," he said. "Fucking tourists." Then he stepped on the gas.

112

Someone knocked on the door. "One second," Parkerson called, struggling to keep his voice calm. "I'll be out in one second."

"Dad?"

"Sweetheart, I just need one second." Parkerson turned back to his computer. Stared at it a moment, blankly, and then reached for his scotch. The asset had failed his assignment. Who the hell knew why?

The kid had been compromised in Miami. That was the problem. He should have been terminated. Should have died that night by the swamp. Parkerson hadn't killed him, and now the Vegas job was shot. Now the whole program was at risk.

Someone knocked on the door again. "Dinner's getting cold, Daddy."

Parkerson spun. *"One goddamn second,"* he said. *"Just give me one goddamn second of peace."*

There was a pause. Then a wail from outside. Fast footsteps away from the door. Parkerson exhaled, shaking his head. Turned back to his computer. Tried to figure out a plan. He picked up the Killswitch phone. Dialed the Las Vegas client. "There's been a problem," he said. "The target wasn't destroyed."

There was a long pause on the other end of the line. Then, "Fuck you."

"We had unexpected difficulties. I'll refund the money. No problem."

The client swore again. "Fucking right it's a problem. I need that man dead."

"My asset ran into a situation," Parkerson said. "Look, I'll get the job done. I'm just going to need a little more time."

"Bullshit," said the client. "I need him gone this weekend. You're saying you can't finish the job?"

Parkerson stared at his computer screen. Had a bad idea. A risky idea. "I might have somebody else," he said. "Let me get back to you."

113

Mathers sat up. "Bull's-eye," he said. "You're a genius, Carla."

Windermere hurried over. "That's what I've been telling you, Mathers. What'd I do now?"

"Ballistics." Mathers grinned at her. "You were right."

Windermere frowned. "You're shitting me," she said, peering over Mathers's shoulder. "The Nadeau piece is in the system?"

If it was true, it was a lottery-ticket break in the case. The FBI's ballistics database held unique fingerprints for over 500,000 weapons, data that could allow law enforcement officers to link crimes that had been committed using the same guns. Trouble was, there were over 220 million firearms in the country. The odds of hitting a match were pretty damn slim.

"It's not the weapon," Mathers said. "It's the bullets." He gestured at the screen, his smile growing. "The killer left shell casings on the floor of the Carlyle. According to the NYPD, they're a particular brand of nine-millimeter rounds, custom stuff. Only available direct from the manufacturer, somebody called OneShot, out of Galveston, Texas."

Windermere stared at the screen. "Custom rounds," she said, straightening. "Anyone from the NYPD talk to these OneShot people?"

"They didn't get anywhere," Mathers said. "Too many people buying up these bullets. But they had no idea the Nadeau murder was anything more than a stand-alone case."

"But if Killswitch used these bullets for more than one killing . . ." Windermere clapped her hands. "Hot damn, Mathers. Told you I was a genius. Stevens is going to flip when he hears this."

Mathers looked at her. "Assuming he cares."

"Of course he'll care, Mathers. It's his case, too."

"Except he bailed on us."

"He didn't—" Windermere sighed. "Yeah," she said. "I guess he did."

Mathers glanced at his computer again. "Anyway," he said. "Probably have to wait until Monday to get ahold of the OneShot people. And that search is going to take some time, too."

"So what do we do until we get the results back?"

Mathers grinned at her again. "How about dinner?"

THEY ATE AT A FONDUE JOINT a few blocks from the hotel. Three courses: cheese, meat, and dessert, the whole works. Mathers gave her his all-American smile. "It's Saturday night in the City of Brotherly Love," he said. "Might as well live it up."

They drank beer instead of wine, at Windermere's insistence. A couple bottles in and she started to forget about Stevens. She looked across the table at Mathers. "All right, you goof," she said. "What's your story, anyway?"

Mathers grinned wider. "Grew up in Wisconsin," he said. "Studied law at Marquette. Graduated, joined the Bureau. Hilarity ensued."

"Why?" she said.

"Why what?" He laughed. "Hilarity didn't actually ensue, Carla. It's—"

She shook her head. "Why'd you join the Feds, dummy? What's so great about law enforcement?"

Mathers chewed for a moment. "You want the truth?"

"Hell no." She drank. "I want the lie you tell the pretty girls at the bar. Of course I want the truth."

"All right." Mathers grinned at her again. "You ever see that movie *Point Break*? Keanu Reeves, Patrick Swayze?"

"The bank robbers in the Richard Nixon masks. Yeah, I saw it."

"The surfers. Keanu's Johnny Utah. Has to infiltrate that gang of surfers, only Swayze figures him out."

"I remember," said Windermere. "They go skydiving."

"And the end, he tracks Swayze to that one beach. Monster waves. Swayze convinces Keanu to let him go out and surf, knowing full well he's going to die."

"Good times," said Windermere. "But what the hell does this have to do with you? You figured you'd join the FBI and it'd be all surfing and skydiving?"

Mathers nodded. "Something like that."

"Instead you're in Philadelphia. Working the damn phone book."

"I'm eating fondue with a beautiful woman," said Mathers. "I'd say I'm pretty comfortable with my career choice right now."

Windermere might have laughed in his face some other time. Tonight, though, she couldn't meet his eyes. "Jesus," she said, looking down at her plate. "Easy, buddy."

Mathers looked at her. She could feel it, his eyes on her. Knew he was smiling that shit-eating grin. Thing was, she was starting to like it.

114

Windermere and Mathers walked back from the restaurant to the Sheraton Four Points after dinner. It was a cool night, and damp; Windermere shivered but refused Mathers's proffered coat.

"What are we, dating?" she asked the young agent.

Mathers just grinned that all-American grin of his. "Just wanted to prove chivalry isn't dead, Agent Windermere. No offense meant."

"Shit," she said. "I can take care of myself."

She was drunk, a little bit, though she wasn't sure why. She'd had three beers, maybe four. Normally, she'd be fine. But tonight, for some reason, she was tipsy. Giggly. She kept catching Mathers's eyes on her. Hated herself for how flushed his looks made her.

You're tired. Exhausted from this ridiculous case. You're pumped up because your idea worked, and that corn-fed goofball over there keeps giving you the eye.

Well, so she was drunk. So what? She was allowed to get drunk. She was an adult, wasn't she? She'd worked the case for a week plus, solid, no stops. She was allowed to relax a little. Unlike Stevens, she didn't get to go back to Minnesota. Had to take her breaks where she could.

And so what if she was maybe crushing on Mathers a little? The agent was pretty cute, and even if he wasn't the most intellectual guy in the world—really, what the hell was up with that *Point Break* stuff?—he was better-looking than Stevens.

Windermere let Mathers hold the door for her when they reached the hotel. Matched his grin and skipped into the lobby, light-headed and light on her feet. "Maybe you are a gentleman, after all," she told him. "Even if you hide it well."

Mathers pretended to pout. "When have I been anything but a gentleman?"

She punched his arm. "Man up, Wendy," she said, pressing the elevator call button. "Drop your purse and try to keep up with me."

The elevator doors opened. Windermere walked in, pressed the sixth-floor button. Then glanced at Mathers. "Eight," Mathers said. *"Please."*

She pressed eight. Curtsied. *"You're welcome."*

They rode up in silence. Mathers grinned at her. Windermere watched her reflection in the mirrored doors. Watched his reflection. The elevator stopped at floor six. The doors slid open. Then they slid closed. The elevator climbed toward eight. Mathers frowned. "Thought you were on six."

She turned to him. "Shut up," she said. She shoved him back until he hit the elevator wall. Then she leaned up and kissed him, hard. He went rigid for a minute. Then he relaxed, kissed her back, his tongue pressing against her lips, his hands wrapping around her and pulling her closer to him. She let herself melt into him, let his tongue spar with hers. She kissed him, and she thought, briefly, about Stevens. Then the doors opened and she pushed Stevens from her mind. Held Mathers's hand and led him down the hall to his room.

115

"You have yourself a very stubborn daughter, Agent Stevens." Nancy Stevens looked across the bed at her husband. "Girl latches onto an idea and she won't let go."

Stevens put down his paperback. Dared to give her a smile. "Takes after her mother," he said. "Whip smart and stubborn as hell."

Nancy shook her head. "Got her dad's brains, that one."

"Her dad's looks, you mean."

"Better take that back," Nancy said, frowning. "I'll march you down there to her room and you can apologize right now."

Stevens laughed. "Fine," he said. "She got her mother's looks, too. Beautiful, smart, and stubborn. Lord help the man she ends up with."

"What, like you have it bad?"

Stevens dog-eared his book and set it on the nightstand. "I have it just fine," he said. "I need a pretty girl to keep me honest. Keep me in line."

Nancy frowned. "A policeman," she said, sighing. "Or an anchor, holding you back. Kirk, that's not how I want you to see me."

"I know," he said. "And I don't, I swear it."

It had been a tense homecoming so far. Stevens had walked the dog around Lexington-Hamline, bought milk and a newspaper from the corner store. He'd lobbied his son unsuccessfully for a game of catch, and settled instead for a distracted conversation while JJ slayed dragons on his Xbox. Then Nancy had come home from work, and if she'd been surprised to see Stevens, she didn't show it.

"How long?" she said, hanging her coat. "When are you gone again?"

She looked worn-out, and Stevens's heart ached to see her. "I don't know," he told her. "It's up for debate."

But they hadn't debated, not really. He'd made his famous chicken Parmesan for dinner and they'd eaten, largely in silence. Andrea was still upset, from the looks of it, and Nancy was exhausted. His attempts to engage either of them in conversation were met mostly with one-word responses. Meanwhile, JJ spent most of the meal feeding scraps to his dog. They'd eaten, cleaned up, and gone to bed with nothing accomplished.

Now, though, they were talking. Nancy's expression had softened; she looked at Stevens, it seemed to him, with something closer to the old spark. "I don't want to hold you back, Kirk," she said. "Not from something you love."

Stevens snuck an arm around his wife's shoulders. Pulled her close. She leaned in readily, snuggled against his chest. "I don't have to go back," he told her. "Windermere and her partner have the basics covered just fine."

"What does Lesley say?"

Stevens sighed. He'd talked to his boss earlier in the day. "Lesley says it's up to me," he said. "The Pyatts are cleared, as victims and suspects, so there's no reason for the BCA to stay involved. I can be back in the office working cold cases on Monday, if I want."

"You don't want to abandon your case in midstream, do you?"

"I don't want to abandon you," he said, squeezing her tighter. "You need me at home more than Windermere does."

Nancy was silent awhile. Then she twisted in his arms and looked up at him. "Your daughter," she said. "I don't know how you got to her before I did, but she's square on your side."

"Didn't seem like it at dinner," Stevens said.

"Oh, believe me, she's firmly pro-Dad." Nancy laughed. "She ambushed me one night. Wednesday. Asked me what I thought would happen if you'd let Carter Tomlin get away with it. Asked me how many people I thought would have died before someone finally stopped him."

Stevens shook his head. "That's different," he said. "Her life was in danger. Of course I was going to chase Tomlin."

"That was my argument. She was ready for it. Asked me what made her so special, anyway? Why should she get special treatment when I didn't want you helping anybody else?"

"Jesus," Stevens said. "You think she's okay? I mean, after Tomlin . . ."

Nancy sighed. "I don't know, Kirk. I keep looking for cracks in her armor."

"She told me I should get back out there and solve the case," Stevens said. "Before the bad guy came after our family again."

"The doctor said she might experience flashbacks. PTSD. You think we should take her to see someone?"

"Counseling." Stevens shook his head. "She seems so damn invincible most of the time," he said. "Like her mother."

Nancy snuggled closer. "I'm not invincible. Not by a long shot." She looked up at him and sighed. "I don't know, Kirk. Maybe it's selfish, but I want you around."

"I miss you," he said. "God, I miss you when I'm gone."

"Bull." She grinned up at him. "You've got Windermere to keep you company."

Stevens leaned down and kissed her, long and slow. When their lips parted, he sighed. "I don't know what to do, Nance."

She grinned again, mischievous. "About Windermere?"

"No," he said. "About you. About us."

She laid her head on his chest and stared across the room. "I'll be here, Kirk," she said. "We'll be here. Just don't forget we're not invincible, either."

116

Late that night, the phone rang. Stevens rolled over in bed, checked the time: nearly midnight. He fumbled for the handset as Nancy groaned beside him. "Agent Stevens," he said.

"Agent, it's Drew Harris. I'm sorry if I woke you." The FBI's Special Agent in Charge of Criminal Investigations spoke softly, but there was an electricity to his voice. "I haven't been able to raise Mathers or Windermere."

Stevens reached for the light switch. "No problem, sir. What can I do for you?"

"I've been following your progress on the Killswitch case, Agent Stevens. It's a big one for my division. The Bureau's involvement in high-profile investigations like these is always under scrutiny, and this case in particular is not one we can afford to let slip through our fingers."

"Yes, sir." Stevens rubbed his eyes. "We feel we're making good progress, sir. This guy is slippery, but we'll get him."

"I know you will, Agent Stevens, and I'm not calling to light a fire under your ass. I just ducked into the office this evening and came across something I thought you and Agent Windermere should have a look at." He paused. "There've been reports of an attempted shooting in Las Vegas. An unidentified man broke into a suite at the Bellagio and fired on the occupants."

Stevens scratched his head. "You think it's related to Killswitch?"

"I've seen the police sketch, Agent Stevens. It's your guy."

"God damn it." Stevens looked around the room, helpless. "So he did it again."

"To a point," Harris said. "The shooter didn't kill anyone. Didn't even draw blood. Fired a shot through the ceiling and ran."

"Didn't kill anyone? The target's—"

"Still alive, Agent Stevens. And still in Las Vegas."

"I'll be damned." Stevens kicked off the covers. "Thanks for the heads-up, sir. This is huge."

"Try and wake up Windermere, would you? And get your asses down to Vegas and talk to that target." Harris ended the call. Stevens stared at the phone for a moment, his thoughts racing. If Harris was right, then O'Brien had bugged out. Somehow, Killswitch had failed.

Nancy rolled over beside him. Stevens turned to find her staring at him from underneath the covers. "They—"

"I heard," she said. She rolled over to stare at the ceiling. "Just don't get yourself killed, Kirk."

117

Windermere woke up in Mathers's bed with her phone ringing and the big lug snoring beside her. It was dead dark in the room. Her head hurt. The clock on the night table read half past one.

Windermere let the phone ring a minute. Lay back and stared into the darkness and tried to decide how she felt about what she'd done with Mathers.

They were both adults. Mathers was a good-looking guy, and she liked him. He didn't come off as a whack job, and he was pretty damn good in bed. She'd had fun with him, and now it was over, and in the morning they could go back to work.

This was the part of the whole ordeal where she was supposed to feel guilty, she knew. She was supposed to look over at Mathers, at the junior agent's broad expanse of back, and wonder what the hell she had done. Windermere sat up in bed and pulled the sheet around her. Looked at Mathers, listened to him snore. Didn't feel guilty at all, to be honest.

She wondered if Mathers would be weird in the morning. If he'd think of what had happened as anything more than a fun night in a strange town with a good-looking colleague. She hoped not. The last thing she needed right now was a boyfriend. After Mark, hell, she'd pretty much resigned herself to spending the rest of her life alone.

Mathers was a young kid. He was a good-looking cop. No doubt he had plenty of girls chasing him. He wouldn't jump to conclusions. He'd understand she wasn't looking for any repeat performances.

The phone was still ringing. Loud and insistent. Windermere chased Mathers from her mind and fumbled for the phone on the nightstand. Three missed calls. Shit. She answered. "Windermere."

"Carla." Windermere's stomach flipped. It was Stevens. "Guess I woke you."

"You know I don't sleep, Stevens." Windermere swung her feet over the bed and hurried into the bathroom. "What's up?"

"I got a call from Drew Harris just now. Said he heard something out of Vegas that might help our case."

Shit. "My boss called you?"

"Said he couldn't get ahold of you or Mathers. You guys hit the clubs or something?"

Windermere locked the door and turned on the light. Caught a glimpse of herself in the mirror and quickly turned away. She sat down on the toilet and ran her hands through her hair. "Turned in early," she said. "So?"

"So listen," he said. "Harris is keeping tabs on our case. Apparently the whole Bureau's watching."

Mathers knocked on the bathroom door. "Carla?"

Shit, shit, shit. Windermere covered her phone. "One second," she said. "Be right out."

"You on the phone?"

"Home base," she said. "Be out in a minute."

"Who was that?" Stevens asked her when she was back on the line. Windermere shook her head, rubbed her eyes, laughed at her predicament.

"Room service," she said. "I skipped dinner. You said something about Vegas."

"Yeah. Right. So according to Harris, some kid snuck into the Bellagio with a pistol today. Broke into a guest suite on the thirty-fifth floor. From the LVPD description, it sounds like O'Brien."

"Shit." Windermere stood. "Holy shit. He kill someone?"

Stevens paused. "No," he said. She could tell he was smiling. "That's the best part. He bugged out for some reason. Got away, but the target's still alive."

"Still alive," she said. "And we're sure it's Killswitch."

"Young kid, skinny, matches the description. LVPD's faxing you a sketch and some security cam stills, but on the surface it sounds pretty damn close."

Windermere looked at herself in the mirror again. Looked a hell of a lot less tired than she had five minutes ago. "Good stuff, Stevens," she said. "How soon can you meet us on-site?"

"Vegas? I figured you guys could—"

"Bull," she said. "This is your lead. You're working it with us. Don't act like you don't want to be here."

He paused. "You know I do."

"I'll get you a flight, Stevens. See you in Sin City."

She ended the call just as Mathers knocked on the door. "One second," she told him. Then she stared at her reflection. *Stevens,* she thought. *Mathers. Sin City.* Things were bound to get messy.

No time for that now. She had a lead to work. Windermere pushed away from the mirror and opened the bathroom door. Found Mathers waiting for her, wrapped in a bedsheet. He smiled at her, sleepy. "Everything cool?"

Windermere brushed past him. Looked around for her clothes. "Rise and shine, big guy," she said. "We're going to Vegas."

118

aint Paul, predawn. Nancy Stevens pulled her Taurus to the curb outside Holman Field, the Saint Paul downtown airport on the banks of the Mississippi. She looked across the car at her husband. "This is a new one. Minnesota BCA agent flies private FBI jet to Las Vegas. Why would you ever want to stay home?"

Stevens stared out the window at the airfield, where a chartered Cessna Citation waited on the tarmac. It looked flimsy and impossibly small. "I hate flying," he said.

"You say that," she said, "but you sure do enough of it."

Stevens turned away from the plane to look at his wife. He'd told her he didn't need a ride, would be just as easy in a cab, but she'd insisted. Now she sat bleary-eyed in a housecoat, staring out at the first hint of daylight. "I don't have to do this," he said. "I can stay."

Nancy snorted. "What, after the FBI's chartered you a jet? I don't think so, Kirk. You're going."

He looked at her. "We never finished our conversation."

"Yeah," she said. "I guess this pretty much finishes it."

"Nancy."

She sighed and sank back in her seat. "I'm upset, Kirk. I don't want you to go. The worst of it is, I can see Andrea's point."

He smiled, rueful. "Our little debate champ."

Nancy smiled, too. "And I'm supposed to be a lawyer. But she's right. You're good at what you do, whether it's Tomlin or Arthur Pender or whoever. Maybe I'm being selfish expecting you to stay home and work regular hours." She looked at him. "Maybe you're not meant for that."

Stevens stared out the window. "Selfish or not, Nancy," he said, "I want to do what's best for this family. If you need me—if Andrea needs me . . ."

Nancy laughed. "We both know what she'd say."

"If she needs help, Nancy, I don't want to leave her. Even if she thinks my sticking around will lead the bad guys to our door."

"She's fine when you're gone," Nancy said. "She gets excited when she hears about your cases. This weekend is the first time she's shown any signs of trauma."

Stevens stared out the window. "Still," he said.

"I'll make an appointment with the doctor. We'll see what he thinks. In the meantime, maybe it's better you're on the road if she's going to stress out when you're here." Nancy leaned across and kissed him. "Just catch this guy and get home again safe. We'll manage until you get back."

Stevens wrapped his arms around her. Held her tight and tried to think of an answer. "I won't go if you want me to stay," he said finally. "I'm perfectly happy working cold cases at BCA headquarters, if that's what it comes down to."

Nancy shook her head. "No, you're not, Kirk. You don't have to pretend just to please me. You're made for the blockbuster stuff, and I guess

I'll have to deal with it. Just think twice before you try and play the hero, okay?"

She kissed him one more time. Then released the brake and idled toward the airfield. "And keep your grubby paws to yourself around Windermere, understand?"

119

Parkerson woke early Sunday morning and drove out to the lake house. Turned off the projections and brought the asset breakfast. Coffee. "Drink up," he told the kid. "You're going to need it."

The asset obeyed him, wordless. The training was working. The kid's eyes were vacant. He looked tortured, shell-shocked. He looked ready for work.

It was too early in the training for this kind of maneuver. Far too risky. The asset could bug out and go catatonic, could revert to normal as soon as he hit the outside world. Looking at Wendell Gray, though, Parkerson didn't believe it. The asset looked compliant. He looked totally pliable.

Parkerson turned the hose on him. Sprayed the kid down until he was soaking wet and shivering. Then he tossed him a towel and a stack of fresh clothes. "Put them on," he told the kid. "Haul ass. Big day today."

Typically, Parkerson liked to ease the kids into killing. A couple small animals, then maybe a man. Sometimes the assets didn't make it that far. Sometimes they became training fodder for the next candidates. There was a symmetry there that appealed to Parkerson, a ruthless efficiency.

Never before had he trained an asset in the field. He'd been careful so far. This was a necessary risk, though, for Killswitch. Parkerson couldn't afford to disappoint a client. This would keep the program running smoothly.

The kid finished dressing. Parkerson led him out to the Cadillac. Drove away from the lake house and out onto the interstate, south toward the city and the airport. Parkerson parked in the economy lot. Then he turned to the asset. "This is field training," he said. "Your first assignment. Understand?"

The asset stared at him, blank-faced. Parkerson slapped him. "I asked you a question, soldier. Do you understand?"

The asset nodded once. "I understand."

"Better," said Parkerson. "We'll be traveling today. You and I are business colleagues, and friends. You will stay close beside me. You will engage me in conversation. If anyone else talks to us, you will be pleasant and civil, but you will allow me to carry the conversation. Understand?"

The asset nodded again. "Yes, sir."

"Any deviation from these boundaries will result in your immediate and dishonorable discharge from duty. You'll be returned to your room, and I'll leave you to your visions."

The asset flinched.

"If you complete this task, I'll make the visions disappear and return you to your normal life. Understand?"

The asset looked at him, for the first time with hope in his eyes. "Yes, sir," he said. "I understand, sir."

"Good." Parkerson reached for the door. "Let's get started."

120

Lind sat awake on the couch. He hadn't slept. Hadn't closed his eyes. Thing was, he barely felt tired.

He kept replaying the Las Vegas assignment in his head. The whole disastrous day. He kept seeing the target, his face, his wide eyes. Heard his desperate voice and his panicked gasps for air. Saw the gun pressed to the target's temple. Then . . . nothing.

Something had happened in that Bellagio suite. It was like he'd come out of the blackness for a moment—like, even through the panic, things were suddenly clear. Now, though, Lind couldn't remember. It was like chasing a dream. Every time he thought about what had happened in that suite, the truth seemed to slip further and further away.

He remembered breaking into the target's room. Remembered standing in the shadows and waiting. Remembered walking out of the casino afterward, dumping the gun in the lake. Anything in between, though, and his head hurt. He couldn't think for too long or he'd feel like he wanted to jump out a window.

The man had called him again, after he'd arrived home. Given new instructions. "Don't leave the apartment," he'd said. "Don't talk to anyone. Wait for my orders."

Something was wrong. Lind knew it somewhere deep inside. It had come to the surface during that botched assignment, a sick realization that he'd done terrible things. That he did them because the man told him he had to.

That was why he'd walked away. Because, beneath the panic and the awful fear, he'd recognized for a moment that something wasn't right.

He'd failed the man. He hadn't completed the assignment. But the assignment was wrong. He'd known it, briefly.

Caity Sherman's phone number sat on his coffee table. Lind had been staring at it all morning. There was something about her that felt different from the man and the assignment and the visions. There was something that made him realize he was wrong.

Except he couldn't think, not clearly. Every time he tried to think about Caity Sherman he felt the panic start to rise in him again. Felt his head start to pound like there was a demon inside. He couldn't think about Caity, and he couldn't think about Las Vegas. He couldn't think about anything for long.

Lind shook his head. He picked up Caity's phone number and walked to his phone. Pushed the panic as far down as he could and dialed the number. Waited as the phone rang. Then she picked up. "Hello?"

The blackness lurched up inside him again. Overwhelming. Lind reeled and steadied himself on his kitchen counter. Tried to keep his eyes open. Caity cleared her throat. "Hello? Who is this?"

Lind gritted his teeth. "I did something," he told her. "Something bad."

121

So we're cool, right?" Windermere looked at Mathers across the aisle as the plane banked on its final approach for Las Vegas. "I mean, about last night?"

Mathers looked out the window. "Yeah," he said. "I mean, I guess so."

"I just don't want things to be awkward," she said. "We're both adults."

Mathers had been quiet all morning. He'd tried to maneuver her back into bed once she'd come out of the bathroom, but she'd fended off his advances, fled for her own room and a hot shower, where she'd thought about Stevens and Mathers and what awaited in Vegas.

Then she'd met Mathers in the lobby, had spent the cab ride to the airport trying to finagle a couple seats on the first flight to the desert, and by the time she'd talked her way onto a packed US Airways 737, she was too tired to do more than tiptoe around the subject in between futile attempts at napping.

Now, though, as the plane approached Sin City—and Stevens, waiting on the ground—Windermere realized she was going to have to hit Mathers with a heavy dose of real talk.

"You're a lot of fun, Derek," she said. "I don't regret last night. But I'm not looking for much more than what already happened. I don't want this to impact our work."

Mathers looked around the plane, jammed full with rowdy bachelor parties and sorority girls. "Or your relationship with Stevens," he said.

Windermere blinked. "Pardon?"

"It's obvious you two have a thing going." Mathers shrugged. "I don't know, Carla. I think you're pretty cool. I think we get along."

"Yeah," she said. "We do."

"If last night was it, then that's fine, I guess. But I like you. I can see us going places. And to be honest, I wouldn't mind if we did."

He looked at her, his mouth turned up, but shy, nothing at all like the cocky smirk he'd flashed at her over fondue last night. Windermere tried to hold his gaze. Then she looked away.

Shit, she thought, staring out the window at the casinos on the Strip. *This is about to get real goddamn messy.*

122

The asset hung beside Parkerson like a scared dog. Lingered and kept his mouth shut and didn't bug out, behaved himself through security and onto the plane.

The flight passed uneventfully. The asset stared out the window and didn't say anything. Didn't move. Parkerson wondered what he was thinking. He wondered again if his plan wasn't risking too much.

The client had assured Parkerson that his target remained in the city. He'd changed hotels, and bolstered his security, but he'd stuck around as scheduled, until his flight late that afternoon. The client had promised to have a man on the ground, waiting with details. A clean weapon and access to the target. In return, Parkerson had offered a discount. Hated giving money back, but what could he do?

The plane's engines slowed and the aircraft started its descent, circling low over the desert so that those inside could sneak a peek at the spectacular casino resorts on the Strip down below.

Viva Las Vegas, Parkerson thought. *Viva Killswitch.*

123

tevens landed in Las Vegas early, the sunrise having paced the chartered FBI Citation over the Midwest. He climbed off the plane at
the private jet terminal, bummed a ride to McCarran International, and
settled in between the baggage claim and a bank of slot machines to wait
for Mathers and Windermere.

He hadn't slept much all week, and the cramped Cessna hadn't offered
much in the way of space to stretch out. He'd spent the flight staring out
the window, watching dawn overtake the small plane and thinking about
his daughter, hoping he was doing the right thing.

He should have been exhausted. He wasn't. He was wired. Somewhere
in this city, amid the cacophonous jangle of slot machines and the crush
of tourists, a man had faced down Richard O'Brien and lived. No way
Stevens was sleeping until he talked to the guy.

O'Brien had failed. He'd left his target alive. From what Stevens could
tell, there was no reason for it. He'd snuck into the target's room, apparently with a key card. He'd ambushed the guy. Waved the gun in his face
and shot a hole through the ceiling. Then he'd walked.

A scare tactic, maybe? A threat? Or maybe the gun jammed. Maybe
the kid's weapon misfired and he didn't have a backup. He couldn't kill
the target, so he ran. Either way, Stevens needed answers. And somewhere
in this city, there was a man who could give them.

Windermere and Mathers arrived just after nine. They walked through
the terminal, bleary-eyed, coffee cups in their hands. Windermere gave
him a half smile when she saw him. "Stevens," she said. "Hey."

Stevens hesitated. "Hey," he said. He grinned at her, awkward, for a second. Shook Mathers's hand.

Windermere and Mathers swapped glances, and then Windermere cleared her throat. "Been here long?"

"Couple hours. I hate it already."

"You ready to work?"

He nodded. "Just waiting on you."

"Good," she said. "Let's talk to this guy. Unless you'd rather hit the slots first."

Stevens glanced at the machines. "Already lost my whole stake. I got nothing better to do than chase Killswitch."

Windermere grinned at him. "Well, okay," she said. "Let's go get him."

124

Caity Sherman stared at Lind, her face a mask of concern. "What is it?" she said. "What did you do?"

Lind stepped back, allowing her into the apartment. She paused in the foyer, looked in at the living room, the sunlight streaming in through the windows. "This place looks even better in the daytime," she said.

Lind followed her gaze. It was impressive, the apartment, vast and open and stylish, though he'd never really noticed. It was far nicer than any home he'd lived in before the man—

Lind felt his throat constricting. He couldn't think about before. The panic suffocated him. He ran his hands over his eyes. Leaned against a wall. The girl—Caity, her name was Caity—put her hand on his shoulder. "What's going on?" she said. "Are you okay?"

Lind opened his eyes. "I'm okay," he said. "I'm just—fine."

Caity took his arm. Led him into the living room and sat him down on the couch. He heard her walk away, heard the tap running. Then she was back beside him, pressing a glass into his hand.

He drank. He was thirsty. Emptied the glass and she refilled it for him. Then she sat down beside him and studied his face. "What's going on, Richard?"

Lind set the glass down on the coffee table. The man wouldn't like this, he knew. The man was already displeased. He'd told Lind to wait for new instructions. He would be angry if he knew about the girl.

Except she kept calling him Richard, and that wasn't his name. Maybe she didn't know his real name. Maybe she didn't know who he was. Every time Lind thought about it, his head hurt even more.

He knew he didn't want to kill her. He didn't want her to leave, even. Every time he looked at her, he felt the panic again, but he felt something else, too. Something better. Something like the clarity he'd felt at the Bellagio.

"You said you did something bad," Caity said. "What was it?"

Lind hesitated. "I failed the assignment," he said, finally.

"Wait, what assignment? Like, for school or something? What did you fail?"

He shook his head. Couldn't tell her. If he told her, she would leave. He couldn't let her. Caity put her hand on his. Squeezed. "I'm sure everything's fine," she said. "Everybody makes mistakes, Richard."

Lind didn't say anything. Didn't bother to tell her his name wasn't Richard. He sat and let her hold his hand, felt the warmth of her body close to his, and he closed his eyes and tried not to think about anything. Tried to keep the panic at bay.

125

The client's contact waited at the bottom of the escalators. He was small and dark, with suspicious eyes. "FBI's here," he told Parkerson. "They're onto your hit."

Parkerson stared at the man and felt his throat tighten. The goddamn FBI. "Where is the target?" he said. "Where'd they take him?"

"Still at his hotel, last time I checked," the contact said. "He switched rooms last night. Moved across to the Rio, other side of the highway. FBI guys are talking to him there."

Parkerson tried to focus his thoughts. No way they'd get access to the target's room now, no matter which hotel he'd moved to. Not with the goddamn FBI on the scene. What the hell was he going to do?

The smart money said walk away. Cancel the hit and refund the client's money. Make it back later. There was no shortage of jobs. Parkerson glanced at the asset. The asset looked back at him, blank-faced. "Shit," Parkerson said. "I guess we're headed home."

The contact pursed his lips. "There is another option."

"What option?" Parkerson said. "I can't take the guy out if the FBI's watching."

"There's a parking garage at the Gold Coast," said the contact. "Across the street from the Rio. If your man here can shoot from long range, I can get you the equipment."

Parkerson frowned. "Like a sniper."

The contact nodded. "It's not a difficult shot."

"The target will be in transit later this afternoon," Parkerson said. He glanced at the asset again. Mulled it over and saw an opportunity. Then he pulled out his phone and dialed the client. Left the asset with the contact and walked behind a Starbucks kiosk. "I hear the FBI's got your man," he said. "You still want him dead?"

"Want him dead?" The client laughed, humorless. "Buddy, I *need* him dead. Before he gets on that plane."

"We'll do it," said Parkerson. "But the price just went up. A half million in my account before we pull the trigger."

"Christ." The client paused. "This is your fucking fault, you know that?"

"You want him dead or what?"

Another pause. Then, "Five hundred thousand. I'll get you the money."

Parkerson ended the call. Walked back to the contact. "Wouldn't be Vegas without a little gambling," he grinned. "Let's find us a rifle."

126

Julio Ramirez didn't want to talk.

"FBI?" he asked Windermere. "The fuck I need you for?"

They'd driven to the Rio in a rented Buick. Windermere drove. Stevens rode shotgun. Mathers sat silent in the back. There was something up with the kid, Stevens thought. He hadn't said much since he'd climbed off the plane. Tired, maybe. Worn-out from the case. Except this was a big break. He should be thrilled.

Julio Ramirez had moved from the Bellagio to the Rio immediately after Richard O'Brien's visit. It was something of a step down: the Bellagio sat plum in the center of the Strip, featured art galleries and high-roller tables and high-end shopping boutiques. The Rio stood a mile distant, gaudy in blue and red, a crummy consolation prize amid strip malls and fast-food joints and interstate on-ramps.

"Kind of a last-minute request," the Rio's head of security told Stevens. "Guess we were the only penthouse in town."

Stevens nodded. "How long's he booked?"

"Just one night. Heard he's flying home this afternoon."

Windermere glanced at Stevens. "Good thing we got him in time."

ALONG WITH HIS CHANGE in surroundings, Ramirez had picked up a couple new friends. They stood by the door, imposing and inscrutable, mountains of men with bad dispositions.

"Private security," Ramirez said. "Best in the business. Damned if I need any FBI with me."

Windermere tried to peer around a guard and into the room. The guard shifted slightly, blocking her path. "Even if you don't need the FBI, Mr. Ramirez, the FBI needs you. How about you tidy up in there and let us come in and talk?"

Ramirez scowled. "Talked to the cops already."

"The LVPD, yeah, and they appreciate it." Windermere stuck a hand on her hip. "We're the Feds, Julio. There's big things popping off. You're a target. We're trying to catch a killer."

Ramirez stared at her. Windermere held his gaze. Finally, the big man shook his head. *"Puta,"* he said. "Give me five minutes."

127

Fifteen minutes later, Julio Ramirez's door swung open again, and a security guard led them into the suite. It was vast and airy, overlooking the Strip. Stevens could see Caesars Palace in the distance and, to its right, the Bellagio. He stared at the sprawling structure and wondered again what had made O'Brien fail.

The security guard led Stevens and the two FBI agents into a large living area. The scent of marijuana lingered in the air. Two women decades Ramirez's junior lounged on the couch. There was a baggie of something hidden between the couch cushions.

Ramirez said something to the women in Spanish. They looked at Stevens and Windermere and disappeared into a bedroom, muttering as they went. Then Ramirez looked at Windermere. "So what the hell do you want?"

Windermere sat down opposite the big man. Stevens walked to the window. Mathers lurked by the hallway. "I want to know what happened," Windermere said. "Step by step, nice and slow. I want to know why he didn't kill you when he had you begging for your life."

Ramirez made eyes at a security guard. The guard raised an eyebrow. Then Ramirez looked back at Windermere. "You can't read a police report?"

Windermere shook her head. "I want to hear it from you, Julio. This kid found his way into your room. How?"

Ramirez shrugged. "Maybe he bribed a maid."

"Ambushed you. Held a gun to your face. What'd he say?"

"He said nothing. I asked him did he want my money, he didn't say nothing." Ramirez frowned, his veneer slipping a little. "He just stood there and looked at me with those eyes, man. Like a ghost or something."

"Yeah," she said. "Then what?"

"Then he pulled the trigger, man. Nearly blew out my ear and still didn't say nothing."

"Then he ran," said Stevens.

"Like a little bitch. Like he just figured out who he was fucking with."

Stevens looked at the big man. "You call security?"

"Fuck you, did I call security. Somebody somewhere must have heard the shot, though. The big guys came up in a hurry."

"You know anyone would want you dead, Julio?" said Windermere.

"I know a lot of people." Ramirez narrowed his eyes. "But that's my business, not yours."

Windermere looked at Stevens. Then she shook her head. "You know we can do this the hard way."

"Not without my lawyer. I got rights." Ramirez grinned a toothy grin. "Now, if that's all you got for me, you gotta scram, Feds. I got a plane to catch in about ninety-five minutes."

128

The contact gave Parkerson a car key and promised to return with the rifle. Parkerson took the asset to the parking garage at McCarran and found a dark blue Honda Civic in the long-term lot. There was a shopping bag in the back with a pistol and a couple pairs of sunglasses and twin "Viva Las Vegas" hats.

The asset let Parkerson maneuver him into the passenger seat. He still hadn't said much. Parkerson buckled him in and looked at him. "You ever done any sharpshooting?"

The kid nodded. "Little bit."

"You any good?"

"Killed everything I shot at."

Parkerson studied the kid's face. No emotion anywhere. Scary. He circled around the car and climbed in the driver's side. Drove out of the parking garage and along the highway to the casino.

The Gold Coast Casino was a sad-looking white building with a glitzy marquee advertising one-dollar Heinekens and good odds on craps. There was a low parking structure attached. Across from the garage was the Rio.

Parkerson drove the Civic to the top of the structure. Angled the car to get a good look at the Rio. Directly across the street was a long taxi queue and the valet line, uniformed bellmen keeping watch. Parkerson sat back in his seat and cranked up the AC. Settled in to wait for the contact.

THE CONTACT SHOWED UP a half hour later. He backed his Cadillac truck up to the Civic and climbed out with a package the size of a suitcase.

Parkerson gave the man an envelope in return and watched him drive away, leaving nothing but empty cars around them. Parkerson opened the package and unwrapped the rifle. It was a big gun, powerful, deadly. Looked like a movie prop. Parkerson cradled it in his hands. Imagined shooting the target himself, imagined what it would feel like.

Messy, is what it would feel like. Dirty. This is what the asset's here for.

He felt around in the backseat of the Civic for his briefcase. Took out a picture of the target, a description. Studied it and showed it to the asset. "This is your target," he said. "I want him eliminated."

The asset looked at the picture. "Memorize his face," Parkerson told him. "He's going to come out of the casino over there. You're going to shoot him. Then we're going to leave. Understand?"

The asset nodded. "I understand."

Parkerson slipped the pistol into his waistband. Gave the asset sunglasses and a Las Vegas hat. "Don't let anyone see you," he told him. "Don't tell anyone what we're doing. This is covert, you follow?"

"I follow."

Parkerson studied the asset, trying to gauge his level of obedience. This was it, he knew. The moment of truth. The smart money still said he should run. He knew it. Five hundred thousand dollars, though, said he should stay.

He pulled his own hat low, over his face. Slipped on the sunglasses and stared out at the Rio, waiting for the target to show.

129

Stevens and Windermere left Mathers to watch Ramirez's room at the Rio. Drove across to the Bellagio to check out the security footage.

"You believe that guy?" said Windermere as she pulled up to the valet stand. "Barely escapes with his life and still doesn't want to help catch the killer."

Stevens climbed out of the Buick. "From the look of it, I'd say he considers us a bigger threat than O'Brien."

"Yeah, well." Windermere shook her head. "The hell do I want with some gangbanger and his girlfriends? All I care about is taking down Killswitch."

They walked into the casino. Crossed the gaming floor to the hotel and found the director of security waiting. Gates was his name. He was a big guy, officious. Studied Windermere's badge hard, and then nodded and led them into the bowels of the building.

"What's up with Mathers, anyway?" Stevens asked as they walked. "You wear him out back in Philly? The kid's pretty damn quiet."

Windermere struggled to keep her face neutral. Felt her stomach do an unpleasant flip. "Guess he's tired," she said. "Long days. Tough case."

"Guess so," said Stevens. "He's usually so damn chipper."

Windermere said nothing. Hurried to catch up to Gates and prayed Stevens would drop the subject. Mercifully, the security director chose that moment to stop before a heavy door. "Security center," he said. "The Fed goes in. State cop, no way."

Stevens frowned. "Seriously?"

Gates looked at him, impassive. Then Windermere stepped up. "He's assisting a federal investigation," she said. "Has the same rights as I do. We both go."

Gates didn't say anything.

"You want I should call my boss first?" Windermere asked him. "Or yours?"

Gates exhaled. Shook his head once and stepped aside. Windermere smiled at Stevens. "After you, partner."

They walked into the Bellagio's massive security center. Machines hummed in all corners. There were screens everywhere, all of them cycling between views of the casino. Windermere turned to Gates. "Show us the kid."

HE WAS AS SCARY ON-SCREEN as he'd been in real life. Stevens watched O'Brien appear on the security footage, a sleepwalker amid the hotel lobby's chaos. He stood there, unmoving, as people ebbed and flowed around him. Bystanders glanced at him and hurried away.

"Too grainy to see his eyes," said Windermere. "But that's him."

"Sure is," said Stevens. "The guy gives me the creeps."

They watched as O'Brien seemed to jolt back to life. He looked up and then walked, steadily, out of the lobby and into the casino. The view on the screen changed. O'Brien walked down a long carpeted floor, past slot machines and roulette wheels. He didn't slow down. He didn't look around.

The screen changed again. A bank of elevators and a security guard. O'Brien walked on-screen. Showed the guard something. "A room key," said Gates. "We don't know how he got it."

Stevens glanced at Windermere. "Killswitch gave it to him."

"How'd Killswitch get it?"

Stevens shrugged. "Maybe the Defense Department hooked him up."

Windermere looked at him. Laughed a little. Then turned back to the screen. O'Brien was climbing onto an elevator with a group of tourists. The doors slid closed.

The screen changed to the thirty-fifth floor. O'Brien walked off the elevator and down a long hall. Paused in front of a door and took a pistol from his waistband. Knocked a couple times and used the key card to get in. The screen didn't change. Windermere looked at Gates. "Anything from the room?"

Gates shook his head. "Afraid not."

The elevator doors slid open again. Julio Ramirez stepped into the hall, trailed by his two girlfriends. They walked down the corridor to the room, jostling and laughing. Unlocked the door and walked in. "And then nothing," said Windermere. "Who the hell knows what happened."

Gates leaned forward and pressed a button. The tape fast-forwarded a ways. Then O'Brien appeared again, down the hall. Gates slowed the tape.

"This is where we got the call," he said. "Guest on the thirty-sixth floor caught a bullet in her couch. We sent security to investigate." He looked at Stevens and Windermere. "We take guest safety very seriously here."

Windermere looked at him. "I bet you do."

On the tape, O'Brien walked fast to the elevator and jammed the call button. Looked back. Pressed the button again. Stevens leaned forward, squinted at the screen. Then the screen changed.

"That's pretty much it," said Gates. "He rode the elevator down, dodged our guys headed up. Sat at a slot machine for a minute and then walked out of the casino. Hijacked a taxi and rode off into the sunset."

Windermere's phone was ringing. She picked up. "Mathers," she said. "What, right now? We'll head back." She hung up the phone. "Ramirez is leaving for the airport."

Stevens nodded. Stood up from the monitors. Then he stopped and looked at Gates. "Can you scroll back some?" he said. "To the thirty-fifth floor again?"

Gates pressed a button and the screen changed again. Now O'Brien was standing in front of the elevator. "Pause it," said Stevens. "Right there." He leaned forward. "Yeah," he said. "There."

Windermere frowned at him. "What do you see?"

Stevens pointed at O'Brien. "His eyes," he said. The footage was grainy, but there was something there. A look on the kid's face where there was nothing before.

Windermere stared at the screen. "Holy shit, Stevens," she said. "That kid's terrified."

130

Ramirez wasn't slowing down. "Out of my way, man," he told Windermere as he barreled through the lobby, his entourage hurrying to keep up. "Got a plane to catch."

Windermere stood her ground. "Your life's in danger, Julio. You walk out of here, we can't protect you."

"Got my boys with me. The fuck I need you for?"

He pushed past Windermere and toward the front doors. Beside

Windermere, Mathers shook his head. "Couldn't stop him," he said. "Told me I'd have to shoot him to keep him here."

"Should have," said Windermere. "Could have interrogated him from the hospital." She glared after Ramirez. "Guess we'll see you in Los Angeles, Julio," she called out. "If you make it that far."

The big man ignored her. Made the front doors with his entourage and kept going. Disappeared into the sunlight.

» » »

IN THE CIVIC. Wendell Gray straightened. "Target in sight."

Parkerson sat up. Looked over the asset's shoulder to the Rio below. Saw the target walking from the Rio's front doors, headed for the valet line. He had an entourage in tow, a couple security guards and two pretty girls. Parkerson watched the man walk, confident, impatient. Totally unaware that his life was almost over.

In the passenger seat, the asset chambered a round.

» » »

STEVENS STARED at the FBI agents. "Well?" he said. "What happens now?"

Windermere looked around the lobby. "Hell if I know, Stevens," she said. "I feel like we just let our only lead walk."

"Could follow him to Los Angeles," said Mathers.

Stevens shook his head. "What does he know, anyway? We keep chasing our tails. Nobody knows Killswitch." He looked at Windermere. "Brought you all the way out here, partner, and for nothing."

Windermere opened her mouth. There was a *bang* from outside the front door. Then screams. Mathers frowned. "Was that—"

Windermere drew her sidearm. "Sure was."

131

They ran out the front doors, sidearms drawn. Met a wave of people running the other way. "Valet stand," said Mathers. "To the right."

They ran right. Hugged the wall of the casino. Dodged terrified bystanders, a mob, all of them screaming. Rounded the corner to the valet stand and found Julio Ramirez facedown on the pavement, his security guards nowhere in sight.

There were more gunshots. Like firecracker pops. Stevens ducked behind a Corvette and Windermere crawled behind him. *"The parking garage,"* she said. *"Across the street. On the roof."*

Another *pop*. Mathers cried out and dropped, clutching his face. Stevens felt his stomach lurch, but the kid sprung up again. Hugged the wall, his face bloody. Caught a stone chip or something. Ricochet.

Stevens backed up tight against the Corvette. Peered across the hood and the casino lot. Across the roadway to the parking garage beyond. Scanned the roof, the parked cars. Then he saw the sniper.

» » »

THE ASSET KEPT SHOOTING. Long after the target was down. He had a look on his face, a sick smile. Parkerson reached for the weapon. The asset shrugged him away. Kept shooting. Lit up the driveway. Parkerson grabbed the kid's arm. *"Time to go, soldier."*

The kid kept shooting until he'd emptied the mag. Down below, there were bystanders injured. Dead, probably. A guy leaned against the casino wall, clutching his face. He was holding a pistol.

Parkerson slapped the asset. *"Wendell,"* he said. *"Time to go."*

"Time to go," the asset said. He grinned at Parkerson, breathing hard.

Parkerson took the rifle from the asset's hands. Wiped it down the best he could, then shifted into gear and drove across the garage. Halfway to the exit, someone stepped from between two cars. An older man, paunchy, a concerned look on his face.

Parkerson leaned on the horn. The man stood there, jaw set. Crossed his arms and glared at Parkerson, shaking his head. Parkerson swore. "Jesus Christ." He backed up the Civic. Shifted into drive and aimed straight at the man.

The man's eyes went wide as the Civic approached. He didn't move, though, didn't duck for cover. Went up and over the hood and bounced away to the pavement. Parkerson kept driving. Sped down through the garage and out onto the street. Sped away before the police appeared.

132

The airport," said Windermere. "Shut it down *now*."

The cop nodded and hurried off, shouting into his radio. Stevens watched him go. Then walked to the edge of the garage and looked down at the Rio.

They'd run for the Gold Coast as soon as they'd seen the sniper. Watched the little blue car peel off and disappear from sight. Heard it squeal down the ramps and out to Flamingo Road. But by the time they'd reached the garage it was gone.

Stevens turned back to Windermere. "Rental cars," he said. "We need men there, too. And O'Brien's picture in every LVPD cop's hands. How's our witness?"

Windermere glanced across the lot at the ambulance by the ramp. The shooter had run a man down on his way out of the lot. As far as anyone knew, he was the only person to get a good look at the car. And he was unconscious. She shook her head. "He's alive, anyway," she said. "Let's hope he stays that way."

Stevens followed her gaze. Watched the paramedics hoist the man onto a stretcher. The shooter was gone. Julio Ramirez was dead, as were both of his security guards and his girlfriends. One bystander was seriously injured, and the only man who'd seen the shooter's car was a coin flip for survival. Stevens looked around the grim scene. "God damn it," he said, "so what now?"

"If this is O'Brien, he's flying home," said Windermere. "Soon as we get that airport locked down we can start combing the place for him, hope he didn't decide to go Greyhound."

"Or a train," said Stevens.

"No Amtrak in Vegas, Stevens." Windermere started for the stairs. "I bet this sucker tries to fly."

133

Parkerson wrestled the Civic to the airport along a series of back roads. Parked in a far corner of the long-term lot and hustled the asset out of the car. Popped the trunk and left the rifle inside, with the pistol, the sunglasses, the cheap Las Vegas hats. Wiped down the car, quick as he could, and then grabbed the asset by the arm and hurried him into the terminal.

The asset went willingly. He'd lost the rebellious streak he'd displayed at the scene. The bloodlust. He was docile again, compliant. He followed Parkerson across the lot and into the terminal.

McCarran was chaos. There were police everywhere. Parkerson felt his heart skip like an old record. Forced himself to keep walking. Focused on blending in. Led the asset past a couple city cops, who scrutinized their faces. Smiled at them, polite, and kept walking. Made the US Airways desk and cocked his head at the agent. "What's all the fuss?"

The agent was a pretty, young woman. She grinned back at Parkerson. Leaned in, conspiratorial. "There was a shooting just now at one of the casinos," she said. "Cops are trying to shut down the airport."

"Holy crap," said Parkerson. "They get a look at the suspect?"

The girl nodded. "This guy," she said, holding up a photocopied police sketch. "Guess they're thinking he's on the Philadelphia flight."

Parkerson looked at the sketch. It was a drawing of Lind, no question. "Philadelphia," he said.

The girl grinned at him again. At the asset. "Just be thankful you're not on that flight," she said. "Those guys aren't going anywhere today."

134

Are you out of your mind?"

McCarran Airport's deputy director stood behind his desk, his face bright red, staring at Windermere like she'd asked if she could borrow a kidney.

Windermere cleared her throat. "Mr. Rawson, we're dealing with a serial killer here. This is a nationwide manhunt. If this guy's in your airport, we need to find him."

Rawson exhaled slowly. Gripped the edge of his desk and released it. "I understand your concern, Agent Windermere," he said. "Certainly, I respect your need to apprehend this fugitive. But you cannot—*cannot*—ask me to shut down my airport. The logistics involved. The lost revenue. For one man?" He shook his head. "Impossible."

Windermere stared at him. "If this guy gets away, my case evaporates, Rawson."

"I appreciate that, Agent Windermere." Rawson held her gaze. "All the same, the only way you're closing this airport is through the FAA."

WINDERMERE CALLED her guy at the FAA. Begged him not to hang up. "It's time-sensitive," she told him. "I lose this guy and I'm screwed."

"You have any evidence at all your guy's in the building?"

"Precedent. This matches his MO."

"What about the rental car situation? He drop off a car?"

Windermere shook her head. "Not yet," she said. "Nobody's seen him at Liberty or anywhere else."

"So you don't know he's there."

She sighed. "No, I don't."

"You have no evidence whatsoever that he came to McCarran. And you want to shut down one of the busiest airports in the country so you can play a hunch."

"It's more than a hunch," she said. "I know how this guy works. I can catch him. Just help me, damn it."

There was a long pause. Then a sigh. "Sorry, Carla," the man said. "I don't have that kind of power. And I don't think I have the evidence to sway anybody who does."

Windermere ended the call. Glanced back at Stevens and Mathers, who lingered in the doorway, Mathers now wearing a fresh bandage on his cheek. "Well, that's that," Windermere said. "On our own, boys."

135

Philadelphia," said Stevens as they hurried through the terminal. "Gate A12. Boards in ten minutes."

Windermere and Mathers followed Stevens through the crowded airport. The place was chaos: displaced travelers, crying babies, angry businessmen swearing into their cell phones, and police of all stripes wading through the mix, staring at printouts of the composite sketch of Richard O'Brien and scrutinizing faces in the crowd.

Stevens led them through the security checkpoint, flashing badges quickly at the harried TSA guards. Then they were through, and racing down the terminal concourse toward gate A12 and the Philadelphia flight.

"Better hope he's on this flight," Windermere muttered as she dodged tourists and slot machines on her way after Stevens. "There's about a hundred other flights leaving at the same time."

It was true. Rawson had categorically refused to shut down his airport, even for an hour, and Sunday afternoons were gong shows at Mc-Carran. If Richard O'Brien hadn't chosen a direct flight, he was going to get away clean.

There were two airport cops waiting at the gate. They'd commandeered the microphone and stood at the head of a long line of confused passengers. Stevens and Windermere showed them their badges. "Any luck?"

The cops shook their heads. "No O'Brien on the manifest," they said. "Nobody who looks like him at the gate yet, either."

Windermere surveyed the line of travelers. Young people, old people, fat and skinny, couples and families and groups. Confused people, angry people, tired and impatient people. No zombies. Nobody like O'Brien.

Behind them, the US Airways gate attendant cleared her throat. "Excuse me," she said. "We really need to start boarding if we're going to have an on-time departure."

Windermere looked at her. Then she looked back at the line. "Grab the manifest, Stevens," she said. "Work with me. Mathers, you guard the line."

Mathers nodded and wandered out into the crowd. Stevens took a copy of the manifest from the gate agent and stood beside Windermere. "We'll board," Windermere told the agent. "But we're doing it my way. One by one."

136

A cross the concourse at gate A13, Parkerson sat with the asset and watched the cops search the Philadelphia crowd.

There were three of them, a black woman and two men, one older and one young. The young guy had a bandage on his cheek, and they all wore the same look of grim determination. FBI, Parkerson figured. Maybe they were the same agents who'd tracked Comm. Maybe they'd even broken into Killswitch.

Parkerson shivered a little, watching them. They'd gone straight to the Philadelphia gate. That meant they knew where Lind was based. He was compromised. Parkerson cursed himself again for not killing the kid in Florida when he'd had the chance. *One moment of weakness,* he thought, *and this whole program's in jeopardy.*

Across the aisle, the FBI agents were boarding the Philadelphia flight. They stood at the front of the line and checked faces and ID cards against the passenger manifest. It was a slow process.

Parkerson checked his watch. Then he looked at the asset. The asset stared at the carpet. Looked like he was sleeping. "Don't move," Parkerson told him. "Don't talk to anyone. Don't even make eye contact, understand? I'll be back."

The asset didn't look up. "Okay," he said.

Parkerson stood and walked to the check-in desk. "Howdy," he told the gate agent. "What do you think? Are we leaving on time?"

The agent smiled back at him. "Pretty close," she said. "Sounds like they wanted to shut down the airport, but I don't think that's happening. Maybe they caught the guy. I don't know."

"Good stuff." Parkerson winked at her. "Wife'll kill me if I get home too late." He grinned at the gate agent again, and then hurried back to rejoin the asset. Sat beside him and stared across the aisle, watching the FBI agents and praying they didn't look in his direction.

137

God damn it," said Windermere. "He's not here."

They'd worked through the entire manifest. Boarded the whole flight. The gate agent stood at the top of the Jetway, eyebrow raised. "Everyone checked in," she said. "Can I go ahead and close the aircraft doors?"

Stevens and Windermere swapped glances. "Guess we have to," said Stevens. "If he's not here, he's not here."

"So where is he?" said Mathers.

"Maybe he took a connecting flight," said Windermere. "Or maybe he caught the bus."

"Or maybe he's hiding out in Las Vegas somewhere," said Stevens. "He had a later flight. Or he's afraid to come to the airport."

"In which case, what?" Windermere frowned. "We sit back and wait for him to turn up?" Her phone buzzed. She glanced at it. Answered. "Windermere." She listened. Frowned. Stevens watched her, hoping for good news but not seeing it on her face. Finally, she nodded. "Yeah," she said. "Appreciate it. Thanks for looking."

She ended the call and looked across the concourse. "That was my FAA pal," she said. "Figured since he couldn't shut down the airport, he'd do me a favor and check for O'Brien's name on any passenger manifests out of Philadelphia or Las Vegas this weekend."

Stevens studied her face. "And?"

"And if it was good news, Stevens, I'd be hauling ass somewhere." She looked at him. At Mathers. "No O'Brien, R, either airport, all weekend."

"So, what?" said Mathers. "He took a bus here?"

"Or he used another alias," said Stevens. "Killswitch knew we were onto him after the Miami job. He swapped out O'Brien's name for some other identity. Slipped him right under our radar."

Mathers scratched his head. "So what do we do?"

Windermere and Stevens looked at each other. "We comb passenger manifests," said Windermere. "Look for patterns. I'll call my FAA guy back. Ask him to hook me up with everything Philadelphia to Vegas this weekend."

"Back to square one," said Stevens. "God damn it." He surveyed the concourse. Across the aisle, another flight was boarding, another long line of passengers with a couple of city cops at the end, staring at their print-outs of O'Brien. He watched passengers file aboard the plane, and felt like he was seeing the case slip away.

138

There was no sign of O'Brien anywhere, no matter which alias he was using. Stevens worked the airport with Windermere and Mathers all afternoon and into the night. Divvied up the departures and worked every flight they could, assisting the airport cops and LVPD in screening departing passengers, slow-boarding the planes and studying faces, searching for the skinny kid who'd shot up Sin City.

Stevens looked at thousands of faces. Checked off hundreds of names on countless manifests. Endured complaints and half-muttered insults from worn-out gamblers and exhausted parents, his own nerves frayed to threads by the ever-present clamor of the slot machines in the terminal. He didn't find O'Brien.

Finally, as dusk settled over the airport and the twinkling lights of the distant Strip, Stevens ran into Windermere walking away from an Aeromexico flight. *"Aguas calientes,"* she said, rueful. "Figured maybe he made a run for the border."

Stevens glanced out at the plane. "No luck, though."

"No luck," she said, "anywhere."

"Heard from Mathers?"

Windermere shook her head. "Guess if he found something, we'd know it."

"What about your FAA guy?"

"Still collecting the manifests," she said. "He's going to fax them our way when he gets them." She looked at Stevens. "Kirk, this guy's gone. I can feel it."

"Maybe he's still in Vegas," said Stevens. "Hiding out somewhere. Takes a lot of guts to roll through an airport like this after you just killed a man."

Windermere shook her head. "You saw this guy, Stevens. Guts he has in spades. He's gone, and we lost him. We lost our best shot."

"Got the FAA manifests. We'll find him again."

"That's all catch-up," she said. "We're playing from behind. I want to get ahead of this guy for once. Preferably before more people die."

"Sure," he said. "But how?"

"I don't know," she said. "We need some goddamn luck, partner."

She looked exhausted, utterly depleted. Stevens surveyed the concourse again. Saw Mathers in the crowd, far off, hurrying their way. The kid looked excited about something. "Luck, huh?" he said. "Looks like Mathers might just have our share of it."

Windermere turned and they watched Mathers approach, as eager as a retriever with a tennis ball. "Youthful exuberance," said Stevens. "You find O'Brien?"

Mathers shook him off. Turned to Windermere, his eyes bright. "Not quite," he said. "But I did hear from LVPD. Sounds like our witness just woke."

139

The plane was quiet. Parkerson sat beside the asset and stared over his shoulder out into the night sky, trying to focus his thoughts.

They'd made it out of Las Vegas alive. Slipped out right under the FBI's nose. Parkerson had made eye contact with one of the agents, the older white man, just as he boarded the plane. Had felt an electric jolt of fear as he met the man's gaze. The man stared at him, though, without any recognition. Watched him board the plane and didn't move or react.

They were safe. Assuming there were no FBI agents waiting on the ground when the plane landed, the Las Vegas mission had been a success. More than a success. He'd earned half a million dollars for the job. And he'd broken in a new asset who'd proved he could kill.

Parkerson looked at the asset beside him. The kid stared out the window, docile as a lobotomy patient, no sign of the kill-happy psychopath he'd become at the Gold Coast. Parkerson nudged him. "Look at me."

The asset turned and looked at Parkerson. Looked through him, more like. No sign of comprehension. "You did good today," Parkerson told him. "You did really good. You completed your assignment, just as instructed."

The asset didn't say anything. Parkerson glanced around the plane, saw nobody watching. No one listening. He reached across the armrest and took the asset's hand in his own.

"However," he said, "when the mission was complete, you showed weakness. You disobeyed a direct order to cease fire and retreat."

The asset didn't speak. Parkerson took the kid's index finger. Bent it slowly back. Watched the kid's face. "Do you understand, soldier?"

The asset glanced at his finger. Parkerson had it bent back nearly to breaking point. He winced. "Yes, sir."

"Your primary task in all missions is to eliminate your target. Your secondary task is to remove yourself from the scene without being detected. I will provide you with the tools with which to extricate yourself. You simply have to maintain your focus and composure and walk away from the scene. Is that clear?"

The flight attendant appeared before the asset could answer. Parkerson released the asset's finger. The flight attendant smiled down. "Water, sir?"

Parkerson smiled at her. "No, thanks." He waited until she'd continued up the aisle. Then he took the asset's finger in his hand again. Bent it back. "Are we clear?"

The asset winced again. "Yes, sir."

"I can help you with the visions," Parkerson told him, "but I need you to obey me. Do you understand?"

"Yes, sir," the asset said, staring at him. "I understand."

Parkerson held the kid's gaze. Wrenched his finger back a little farther. Then he released it. "Good," he said. "Because I have another assignment for you."

140

Caity Sherman sat on the couch, watching reality TV and listening to Richard O'Brien sleep in the bedroom.

He was not a sound sleeper. In fact, she wondered how he slept at all. He seemed to cry out every four or five minutes. Woke up gasping. He'd tangled the sheets around his skinny legs before she'd even walked from the room.

Another charity case. Another dysfunctional creature. Caity could hear her mom already. "Pick a nice guy, for Christ's sake. A *man*. Stop adopting these losers. It's sad, Caitlin. It's *dangerous*."

She figured he could use a friend. That's why she'd left him her number. Mostly, she hadn't expected him to call, and when she'd seen him at the airport and he'd acted all weird, she'd written him off and figured she'd forget about him. But then he had called her, and sounded desperate and miserable, a couple steps from a breakdown. And, try as she might, she couldn't just ignore him.

Maybe it was a mistake to come over. He could be a killer, for all she knew. The way he looked at her sometimes, it was like he didn't even remember who she was. But she'd come anyway. Something told her the guy didn't have many friends.

He hadn't said much. She'd sat with him, tried to comfort him, convinced him to relax a little. She'd calmed him down some, she could tell. And he hadn't tried to kill her, or even pull a move.

She'd put him to bed. Tucked him in and sat with him until he seemed to drift off. Now he was sleeping, but it sure didn't sound peaceful. He needed help; that much was obvious. More help than Caity figured she could give him. Still, she couldn't just walk away now, could she?

I'll stay a little longer, she thought, turning back to the TV. *Just until he calms down. Then I'll go.*

141

The witness was an older man from Boise, Idaho. His name was Larry Klein. His wife met Stevens and the FBI agents outside his hospital room.

"We'd just come out of the casino," she told them. "We were headed to the Strip for the Wayne Newton show. We'd almost reached the car when we heard the gunshots. Screams. Larry figured he should investigate."

"Didn't think about calling security?" said Stevens.

Klein shook her head. "Not my husband." She gave Stevens a weak smile. "He was in the Navy, a long time ago. Figured that made him invincible."

"So he went to have a look," said Windermere. "You didn't."

"I waited by the car," she said. "I left the engine running in case the bad guys came for us. Larry got there just as they tried to drive away."

"You see the car?"

"It was blue," she said. "Dark blue. That's all I remember. I put my head down and prayed Larry wouldn't get shot."

"Then they ran him over," said Stevens. "You get a look at them?"

Klein shook her head. "I didn't," she said. "But Larry did."

Windermere looked at Stevens. "So let's talk to Larry."

LARRY KLEIN GAVE THEM a weak smile as they entered his room. He was a barrel-chested guy with thick white hair and jowls, and his breathing was labored as he lay on the hospital bed. "G-men," he said, "and G-woman. Nice to meet you."

"Pleasure's ours," said Stevens. "You feeling okay?"

"Nothing a little bed rest won't fix." Klein glanced at his wife. "Just a shame we have to miss Wayne Newton."

Mary Klein clucked. Stevens laughed. "I'm sure he'll stick around."

Windermere handled the introductions. Mathers, then Stevens. Klein's eyes narrowed. "BCA?" he said. "What's Minnesota want with me?"

"Long story," said Windermere. "We're hoping you saw something to-day, Mr. Klein."

Klein nodded. "It's a lot of it hazy," he said. "Had a couple of those dollar beers at the Gold Coast before we left the casino. Then with the car accident . . ." He shrugged at Windermere. "You know."

"Anything you remember," said Stevens. "Anything at all."

Klein thought. "Was a little blue car," he said. "One of those foreign jobs. Japscrap. Couple guys in it."

Stevens frowned at Windermere. "Two guys?"

"An older guy driving. Maybe forty or so. A weak chin. His partner was younger. Had hair past his shoulders, dark brown. He looked tall."

Windermere and Stevens swapped glances. Richard O'Brien had still had a buzz cut in the Bellagio's security footage. "Maybe he wore a wig," said Windermere.

"They both wore sunglasses," Klein said. "And baseball caps. It all happened so fast, like I said."

"So who's the second guy?" Stevens asked Windermere. "Killswitch?"

"Does that sound familiar?" Windermere asked Larry Klein. "Killswitch? Did you hear any mention of that word?"

Klein frowned. Shook his head. "It's all so hazy," he said. "I did hear some shouting, but I don't think I heard that word."

"What did you hear?" said Stevens. "Anything distinct?"

"The older man." Klein thought for a moment. "A kind of southern accent. He sounded like a drill sergeant. Like he was giving orders. I think he even said the word 'soldier.'"

Stevens glanced at Windermere. "Anything else?"

Klein thought some more. "A name," he said. "I couldn't quite make it out. It was loud, you see. I was a little bit tipsy. And it happened so fast."

"Try and remember," said Stevens. "What kind of name?"

"It all happened so fast." Klein stared up at the ceiling. "I'm trying to recall. I think the man called his friend—" He exhaled. "Wendy."

142

Parkerson was up and out of his seat as soon as the plane reached the gate. He hurried the asset through the terminal to the departures area and bought him a ticket on the last flight to Philadelphia. Then he walked the kid to the security line.

"It's a solo mission this time," he said. "I'll have a rental car waiting for you, and a hotel room downtown. Check into your hotel and await my instructions."

The asset nodded. "Yes, sir."

"This is an important job," Parkerson told him. "For you and me both. Don't screw it up."

The asset looked energized by the prospect of more killing. He grinned at Parkerson. "I won't screw it up."

It was a risky assignment. Another potential mess. But Parkerson knew he wouldn't sleep until there was absolutely no chance Lind could jeopardize the program. The Philadelphia asset needed to die, and fast.

"I believe in you," Parkerson told the asset. "Get this job done and I'll make the visions go away. I'll fix you, understand?"

The asset suddenly looked hopeful. "Yes, sir," he said. "I understand."

Parkerson nodded. Dug in his wallet and took out a handful of cash. "For food," he said. "And incidentals. Get going."

The asset pocketed the cash. Looked at Parkerson again, hesitated. *"Go,"* Parkerson told him. Slapped him on the back as he turned away. "Make me proud."

143

Wendy," said Windermere as they walked out into the hospital parking lot and climbed into her rented Buick. "What the hell does that mean?"

"Klein said his memory was hazy," Stevens said. "Who knows what he heard?"

"Wendy." Windermere started the engine and backed out of the lot. "Windy? Window? And 'soldier.' Like a goddamn fill-in-the-blanks."

"Julio Ramirez had girlfriends," said Stevens. "We know their names?"

"Not Wendy." Mathers, from the backseat. "One was Kristen Owens and the other was Alexa Polowski. Both died on scene."

Windermere shook her head. "Christ. What a bloodbath." She glanced at Stevens. "It's getting worse, partner. We have to get ahead of this guy."

Stevens stared out at the Las Vegas night. "Any word on the FAA stuff?"

"At the FBI office," said Mathers. "Came through while we were talking to Klein. Tied up the fax machines for a half hour, they said."

Windermere rolled her eyes. "Goody," she said. "More paperwork."

"We'll find something," said Stevens. "Maybe there's a Wendy aboard."

Windermere snorted. Drove a couple miles as the car fell silent. Then she shook her head. "Wendy," she said again. "Winslow? Wendig?"

144

The asset rode the plane north to Philadelphia, just as the man had instructed. He spent the flight staring out the window, fighting the fatigue that threatened to drag him into sleep. He drank coffee and waited for the plane to land.

Get this job done and I'll make the visions go away.

The asset replayed the man's words in his head like a mantra. He needed the words. He felt like he hadn't slept in months. Years, maybe. He couldn't remember ever sleeping. Couldn't remember much, anymore, but the man and his visions. He needed the man to make the visions disappear.

The plane landed in Philadelphia. The asset walked into the terminal and dialed the man's number on the cell phone he'd been given. "I'm here," he said.

"There's a rental car waiting for you at the Alamo desk," the man told him. "Use the credit card and ID I gave you. Drive to the Club Quarters hotel downtown and wait for further instructions. Understand?"

The asset nodded. "I understand."

He rented a car using the name the man had given him. The name was David Gilmour. The asset knew this wasn't his real name. He couldn't remember being called anything else, though. Anytime he tried to remember, his head hurt and his vision swam, and he felt the nightmares returning again.

The asset named David Gilmour drove into the city, as instructed. He checked into the hotel and watched television in his room until his phone rang. Then he answered. "Hello."

"There's an apartment complex on Arch Street," the man told him. "At North 19th Street. In unit 1604 there's a man waiting. Tomorrow you'll go to his apartment. You'll gain entry however you're able. Eliminate the target and extricate yourself without being detected. Do you understand?"

The asset nodded. Imagined a life without the visions. "Yes, sir," he said. "How will I eliminate this target?"

"This is a rush job," said the man. "I didn't have time to arrange any tools. Inside the apartment, you'll find a pistol in a cupboard under the sink. Should you have time to retrieve it, you may use it. Otherwise, I trust you can figure out some other option."

"Yes, sir," said the asset.

"The man is quite small. You should have no problem eliminating him."

"Yes, sir. Understood."

"Visit him in the morning. I'll have a flight home booked for early afternoon."

"Yes, sir," the asset said. "Understood."

"Good." The man paused. "Call me when you've completed the assignment."

"I will."

The man ended the call. The asset put down his phone. Walked back to the bed and sat and turned up the TV. Watched infomercials and waited for dawn.

145

"OneShot Custom Ammunition." Stevens read the cover sheet off the fax and then looked at Windermere. "What's this all about?"

It was Monday morning. They'd been working all night, save a brief couple of hours when they'd crawled into various corners of the FBI's Las Vegas office to sleep. There hadn't been time to book hotel rooms, and as far as Stevens was concerned, none of them could afford that kind of time off, anyway. Killswitch had come and gone. It was time to work, work, work until somebody caught a break.

Windermere swapped glances with Mathers. Mathers cleared his throat. "Carla had a brain wave in Philly," he said. "Figured we'd check the ballistics on Johnny Thorsson's murder weapon."

"FBI database didn't have the gun," said Windermere, "but apparently the ammunition used to kill Thorsson and Maria Nadeau was some kind of custom job."

"OneShot Ammunition," said Mathers. "Available only by special order through the manufacturer."

"We figured we'd try and get ahold of their sales records, see if any names jumped out at us. And maybe put together a list of other unsolved shootings featuring OneShot Ammunition." Windermere shrugged. "We thought at the very least it'd give us a few more threads to pull."

Stevens looked from Windermere to Mathers, and then down at the fax. "Well, all right," he said. "Let's check it out."

THE PEOPLE AT ONESHOT weren't exactly receptive to Stevens's inquiries.

"Gonna have to ask you to call back with a warrant," the guy on the phone told him, between bites of what sounded like a very large sandwich. "Can't just go giving out information on our customers willy-nilly."

"Willy-nilly," Stevens said. "I guess not."

"Wouldn't be much help to you anyway," the guy said, still chewing. "We sell thousands of custom rounds a month here. We're a major outfit."

"I can tell," Stevens told him.

"We're going to be one of the big boys pretty quick, you hear? Remington, Winchester; we'll be up there right quick, you wait."

"I get you," Stevens said. "So if a guy called up and wanted to order, say, a thousand rounds at a pop, you guys could pull it off, no sweat."

There was a pause. Stevens listened to the man chew. "Depends on the time frame," the guy said at last. "How soon would you need it?"

"You tell me. How long would it take?"

"Month, maybe longer." The guy swallowed. "Only a couple guys ever call in with orders that big, anyway. We don't normally deal with the volume buyers."

"Couple guys, you said?"

"Yeah, two or three. There's this guy Rollins in Wyoming, he likes to shoot. Another guy, Draper, in Colorado. And there was Gardham, too. He ordered a shit ton, once, but we never heard from him again."

"Gardham, huh?"

"Something like that." The man stifled a belch. "Anyway, you want any more information outta me, you're gonna have to call back with a warrant, understand?"

"I understand," Stevens told him, and hung up the phone.

146

Lind sat up in his bed, breathing hard. He looked around the bedroom. It was morning, he saw, or daytime, at least. He'd been sleeping.

He'd dreamed. He remembered dreaming. He hadn't slept well. His bed was damp with sweat and his heart was pounding, but he'd slept, regardless. The visions hadn't kept him awake.

Lind pulled himself out of bed. He was wearing yesterday's clothes; they were wrinkled and tangled and sweaty. He changed out of them, pulled on fresh jeans and a T-shirt, trying to ignore the buzzing in his head, the dim panic behind his eyes. He didn't know what it meant. There was no reason for it. He changed and walked out to the living room.

She was there.

The girl. Caity Sherman. She lay curled up on the couch, sleeping. Lind remembered he'd called her. She'd come over. He'd talked to her, and she'd put him to bed. Then she'd fallen asleep on his couch.

The panic intensified. What had he told her?

Caity shifted a little. Rolled over and blinked open her eyes. She rubbed her face and sat up. "Oh my God."

"You're still here," he said.

"I'm sorry." She stood, fixing her clothing. "I must have just— I was waiting for you to fall asleep. I didn't mean to—"

Lind shook his head. "I don't sleep much," he said.

Caity stopped and looked at him. "I heard you," she said. "You were having nightmares, it sounded like."

"They're not nightmares. They're visions."

"Visions?" Caity frowned. "Visions of what?"

Lind walked to the couch and sat down. Rubbed his eyes, trying to chase off the panic. The man wouldn't like this. The man had told him to stay in the apartment and wait for instructions. He wouldn't be happy that Caity Sherman had come over. He would be angry that she'd stayed the night.

Caity sat down beside him. "Richard," she said. "Visions of what?"

"My name isn't Richard," he said.

"Sure it is," she said, frowning. "I've seen your ID. I checked you in at the airport, remember?"

The panic was growing. A blackness behind his eyes. A buzzing in his ears. Lind shook his head, tried to chase it. "My name isn't Richard."

She sighed. "So what is it, then? Rick?"

"Andrew." He took his ID card from his wallet. "My name is Andrew Kessler."

Caity took the ID from him. She studied it. Looked at his face and then back to the picture. "Your name's Richard," she said, shaking her head. "I remember."

"No," he said. His vision tunneled. "My name is Andrew Kessler."

"That's a fake ID. It doesn't even have the right address." She stared at him. "You're creeping me out, man."

Lind rubbed his face again. Held his hands over his ears. The buzzing wouldn't disappear. The black panic. She couldn't be here. She shouldn't. "My name is Andrew Kessler," he said again.

The girl grabbed his face. Turned him to look at her. "Your name's Richard," she said, peering into his eyes. "What the heck is *wrong* with you, man?"

147

"W endell." Mathers looked up from his computer. "Wendell Gray, former U.S. Marine. He went missing from his home in Atlanta sometime last week."

Stevens circled around to the junior agent's computer. Looked over his shoulder at a picture of Wendell Gray, a good-looking twenty-something with an easy smile and a buzz cut. "Our guy has long hair," he said.

Mathers nodded. "This is before the war," he said. "They don't have a recent picture of him, but according to the missing person's report, he's since grown his hair out."

"Wendell Gray." Windermere frowned. "Where is this coming from, Derek?"

Mathers sighed. Rubbed his bandaged cheek absently. "Plugged 'Wendy' and 'soldier' into the computer, *Carla*," he said. "Started playing around with various other names. Didn't take long."

Stevens looked at Mathers. Then at Windermere. There was something happening between them, meaningful looks. Stevens cleared his throat. "He went missing sometime last week, you said?"

"Guy was kind of a loner, apparently," Mathers said. "Screwed up in the head from the war. Didn't show up for a psych evaluation on Wednesday, and the Vet Center asked Atlanta PD to have a look at his apartment. Found the place deserted."

"When's the last confirmed sighting?" said Windermere.

"Sunday. Gray had group counseling sessions at the Vet Center, bunch of soldiers with shell shock, PTSD, psych issues, whatever. He walked out of there, and that's the last anyone's seen of him."

"Family?"

"Broke contact. They haven't talked to him since he came back from Iraq. No work connections, either. He was living off disability checks."

Stevens studied the picture of Wendell Gray on Mathers's computer screen. "Well, okay," he said. "Let's see what Larry Klein thinks."

148

The man called David Gilmour found the target's apartment. It was a nice building, tall and clean. Gilmour waited outside the front doors until a woman came out with a little gray poodle. Then he ducked in and hurried through the lobby to the elevator.

He rode the elevator alone to the sixteenth floor. Walked out when the doors opened and surveyed the hallway. It was the top floor of the building. There were only four apartments this high. On one end of the hallway was a fire door. The asset walked to it and pushed it open. A stairwell. An escape route.

Eliminate the target and extricate yourself without being detected.

The asset walked back down the hallway to unit 1604. Hesitated in front of the door. He heard voices. A man's voice. Had to be the target. Then he paused. There was another voice. A woman's.

The asset looked up and down the hall. Replayed the phone conversation with the man in his head. Unit 1604, the man had instructed. *There is a man waiting.* Nothing had been said about any woman.

The asset lingered by the door. Felt a slick creeping blackness at the base of his skull as he wondered what he should do. The man wanted the target dead. He didn't say anything about a woman. Well, hell, the asset would kill the woman, too. A little bonus.

The asset straightened and turned to the door. Felt something like excitement, anticipation. He imagined the target dying in his hands. He hoped he wouldn't have to use the gun.

The asset raised his hand. Made a fist and knocked on the door.

149

Larry Klein squinted at the picture of Wendell Gray. "That could have been him," he said. "I don't know. He had long hair and sunglasses, though."

Stevens nodded. "It's an old picture."

"I was a little bit tipsy, see," Klein said. "From those one-dollar beers. And it all happened so fast."

"LET'S ASSUME WENDELL GRAY IS OUR GUY." Stevens told the FBI agents as they rode the hospital elevator down to the parking lot. "Let's just see where it takes us. Based on Miami and Minnesota, what do we know?"

"They probably flew into town the night before and flew out immediately after the fact," said Windermere. "There's no Wendell Gray on any FAA manifests—you're welcome, I checked—but that's hardly a surprise."

"Probably used an alias," said Stevens. "Gray and O'Brien both."

"And the third man, too, for that matter."

"Exactly," said Stevens. "So we check the FAA manifests for any suspicious trips into Vegas this weekend, likely from the Eastern Seaboard. O'Brien probably arrived Friday night. Gray and his partner on Saturday."

"And then what?" said Windermere. "O'Brien took off Saturday night with the job left unfinished? Why didn't he stick around and kill Ramirez himself?"

Stevens pictured the kid on the security footage at the Bellagio, the look on his face as he'd waited for the elevator after failing to kill Julio Ramirez. He'd been scared. Just for a moment, the fear had shown through.

"He bugged out," Stevens said. "Couldn't do it. Something clicked in him and he couldn't kill Ramirez."

Windermere stared at him. "So Killswitch brought a couple more killers—Gray, and whoever—out here to finish the job."

"Exactly," said Stevens. "Gray and his partner are O'Brien's replacements."

"Christ. How many more of these zombie bastards are there?"

"I don't know," Stevens said. "But Killswitch is controlling them all." He looked at Windermere. "We have to find this guy."

150

The girl stared at him. "Who are you, Richard?" she said. "Andrew. Whatever. What the hell is your deal?"

Lind didn't answer. Her questions made his head hurt. Made the black panic grow colder. The blood pounded in his ears, and he looked away. "I'm sorry," he said. "I'm sorry. *I'm sorry.*"

He could feel her eyes on him. "There's something wrong with you," she said. "I can't be here."

Lind heard her footsteps and didn't move to stop her. He knew he should let her leave. The man would want it that way. Pretty soon she'd be gone and everything would be fine.

Except it wouldn't. The visions would come back. The man would give him more assignments. Somewhere, deep down, he knew he needed her to stay. "Stop," he said, standing, unsteady. "Please."

Caity looked back at him from the edge of the living room. "You scare me," she said. "I'm sorry, Richard. I have to go."

"Please," he said. "Don't."

She studied his face, her brow furrowed. "You have some issues, man," she said. "Seriously. I mean—"

There was a knock at the door. One single knock, loud. Caity froze. "You expecting somebody?"

"No," Lind said. "Never."

There was another loud knock. Then the door splintered open with a sound like a gunshot. Sagged off its hinges and fell inward. Caity screamed.

There was a man on the other side of the door. Tall and long-haired and lanky. He stared in at Caity and Lind, his eyes cold and emotionless.

Caity screamed again. The man came for her, quickly. Grabbed her by the throat and threw her against the wall. She made a sound like a deflating basketball. Slumped, her eyes lidded. The man came for Lind.

Lind didn't think. He was trained for this. The attacker came at him, reached for him. Lind swatted him away. Backed up and regrouped. Threw a punch that caught the bigger man in the stomach. The man didn't flinch. He kept coming.

Lind swung again. The man blocked him. Countered with a punch of his own. Lind saw it coming, tried to duck away. The punch caught his left shoulder and sent him reeling across the room. His shoulder tingled, went dead. The attacker kept coming.

Lind fought with his right hand. Tried to dodge the man's punches.

The man was quick for his size. His punches packed power. Lind caught him once in the jaw. Froze him, momentarily. Then the man countered, an uppercut that knocked Lind off his feet.

The man loomed above him. Lind sat up, breathing heavily, searching for a way out. Across the room, Caity Sherman moaned. Struggled to stand up and collapsed in a heap. The attacker looked at Lind with the hint of a grin. He hadn't said anything. He'd just come in and destroyed.

He's going to kill you. He'll kill you and Caity unless you do something, fast.

There was a gun in the kitchen. The man had given Lind two pistols, SIG Sauer P220s, told him to hide one under the sink and the other in the car. Use only in emergencies. This was an emergency.

The attacker followed Lind's gaze. Grinned at him, a soulless, evil grin. "Go ahead," he said. "Get the gun."

Lind stared at him, his mind struggling to process. The attacker knew about the gun. He leered down at Lind, breathing hard. Leaned down with both hands open and reached for Lind's throat.

Lind rolled away from him. *"Caity."* Caity Sherman looked up at him, slow. Her eyes were dazed, unfocused. "There's a gun under the sink," he said. *"Get it."*

The attacker laughed in Lind's face. Crossed the living room toward the kitchen. Lind pushed himself to his feet. Had to move. Bolted across the living room just as the attacker opened the cupboard door and came out with the pistol.

"I was going to kill you slow," he said. "You had to ruin it."

Lind flung open a cupboard drawer. Came out with a carving knife. Flung himself at the man as the man turned around, plunged the knife deep into his shoulder. The man screamed. Dropped the gun. Swung at Lind with his free hand and caught him flat in the face, knocking him back across the kitchen floor.

Lind picked himself up. Watched the attacker pull the bloody knife from his shoulder. The gun was five or six feet away. The attacker was still closer. Lind looked at Caity, and then he looked at the door.

Time to go.

He ran to Caity. The attacker dove for the gun. Fumbled with it, his hands slick with fresh blood. Lind pulled Caity to her feet and hurried her out the doorway. *"Come on."*

Lind pulled Caity down the hall to the fire escape door and shoved her through. There was a noise behind him, and Lind turned back and saw the attacker in his open doorway, leaning against the ruined frame, clutching his shoulder. In his other hand, he held the gun.

Lind locked eyes with the attacker once more. Felt a chill run through his body. Then the man raised the gun. Lind spun through the doorway, hit the stairs. Heard the door slam shut above him just as the gun went off.

151

Lind half dragged, half carried Caity Sherman down the fire escape stairwell. *"Hurry,"* he told her. *"We gotta move."*

Caity was still dazed. She moved slowly, said nothing. Let Lind maneuver her down toward the parking garage.

There were no sounds from above. No doors slammed open. No gunshots. The only sounds in the stairwell were their own pounding footsteps and Caity Sherman's gasps for breath. Lind hurried her down as fast as he could go.

He didn't know who the attacker was. Couldn't imagine who wanted them dead. All he knew was that he needed to get away, and quickly. And he knew instinctively that he should save the girl.

They ran down the stairs, endless flights. Caity lagged behind him. Lind pulled her onward. They reached the parking level and he burst through the door, ran through the dim lot to his car. Shoved Caity into the passenger seat and slid behind the wheel.

He drove out of the garage and stepped on the gas. There were sirens in the air, police cars down the block. Lind searched the sidewalk, but didn't see the attacker. He kept his foot planted and sped away from the scene.

152

The man called David Gilmour listened to the target's footsteps recede in the stairwell. He leaned against the open doorframe and clutched his shoulder where the target had stabbed him. The wound hurt. It was deep. The pain wasn't entirely unpleasant.

The target was escaping. The asset knew this. He was already gone. The asset looked at the pistol in his hand. Its grip was smeared with blood. His blood. The bastard had stabbed him.

The target had escaped. He'd taken the girl with him. The asset stood in the doorway a moment. Then he straightened.

Extricate yourself without being detected.

He retreated into the target's apartment. Found a clean T-shirt in the bedroom and wrapped his wound as best he could. Then he walked back into the hallway. There was someone waiting.

A man. A young man in black-framed glasses. He peered out at the asset from his own doorway. Saw the blood. Saw the gun. His eyes widened. "Holy shit, man. What are you—"

The asset shot him. Once, in the chest. The man staggered backward into his apartment. The asset waited until his door had swung closed. Then he walked to the elevator and pressed the call button down.

153

Parkerson was in his office when the Killswitch phone rang. He checked that his door was closed and then answered. "Are we good?"

A pause. Then a long breath. "No."

"Jesus Christ." Parkerson felt every muscle in his body get tight. "What the hell happened?"

"The target escaped," the asset said. "He injured me with a knife. Then escaped before I could kill him."

"Shit." Parkerson ran his hand over his face. "*Shit*. Are you wounded? Were you seen?"

"I'm not wounded. Not seriously."

"But were you *seen*?"

The asset paused. "One person. I eliminated him."

"God *damn* it." One witness dead. And Lind still alive. Parkerson wondered if this was what a heart attack felt like.

"There was a woman with him also, sir. With the target."

"Impossible," said Parkerson. "The target doesn't know any women. You had the wrong unit."

"Negative. I entered unit 1604, as instructed. The target was waiting inside the apartment with the woman. I neutralized them and found the gun under the sink. Before I could eliminate either of them, however, the target attacked me. Then they both escaped."

"Jesus Christ." Parkerson sat back in his chair. "Where are you now?"

"I've returned to the hotel and am awaiting further instructions."

"Keep waiting," Parkerson told him. "I'll call you back shortly." He hung up the phone. Then he exhaled, long and slow. *Jesus Christ,* he thought. *How the hell am I going to fix this?*

154

"Holy *crap*." Caity Sherman shook her head and tried to focus her thoughts. "What the *hell* just happened?"

Richard—or Andrew, or whatever his name was—didn't answer. He was driving. They were out of the city now, headed south on the Delaware Expressway. Richard hadn't said anything since he'd thrown her in the car. Before that, she could barely remember.

"Where are we going?" she said. "Say something. Please."

Richard kept driving. Caity looked at his face and shivered. His eyes were blank. His face was expressionless. His apartment had just been invaded by a crazy psychopath and he should have been absolutely losing his shit. He wasn't even sweating.

Caity, meanwhile, was scared enough for the both of them, and by now they'd put a good fifteen miles between themselves and the attacker. Her head hurt. She was pretty sure she had a concussion. Somebody had just tried to kill her and she had no idea why. "Richard," she said. "Andrew. Where are we going?"

Richard blinked and looked at her. "I don't know."

"You don't know?" Caity looked out the sports car's side window. Saw industry, warehouses. She shivered again. "You're just driving."

"Yeah."

He was into something serious, she could tell. He was a part of this madness. Real people would have cornered the first cop they saw. Explained the situation and let the professionals handle things. Richard hadn't even looked for a cop. He just drove.

Now he pulled out a cell phone. Held it to his ear and waited. "Yes," he said. "There was a problem."

He listened. Caity listened. The man on the other end said something. "I had to leave the apartment," he said.

Shit, she thought. *That's putting it mildly.*

"Interstate 95. Southbound." Richard glanced at her. "A civilian. She was in danger." He looked at her. Bit his lip and shook his head. Suddenly, there was emotion in his eyes again. There was *fear*. "No," he said. "*No*. She was in danger."

Caity shivered and looked out the window. The highway was grim and featureless. It occurred to her that Richard might be taking her somewhere to kill her. She looked at him and tried to convince herself she was crazy. She couldn't.

"I understand," Richard said. He looked out the front windshield. "Exit 6. Just across the state line." Another pause. "I understand."

Richard ended the phone call. Signaled right and cut across two lanes of traffic to the Exit 6 off-ramp. "We're safe," he said. "My boss is coming to get us."

155

Parkerson stared at his cell phone. The target had escaped. He was safe. And he'd brought a woman with him.

A woman. Parkerson rubbed his eyes. What was the kid doing picking up girls? And why the hell had he lied about her?

He'd told Parkerson she was a civilian he'd protected. Had flat-out denied she'd been inside his apartment. The asset had sworn the girl was inside when he'd arrived. She was Lind's goddamn friend. And he'd lied about her.

The whole situation made Parkerson's head hurt. After Miami and Las Vegas and now the bullshit with this girl, it was clear that Lind was no longer the reliable drone he'd once been. He was a liability now, unpredictable. Altogether too human.

He had to be stopped.

» » »

THE ASSET CALLED DAVID GILMOUR answered his phone. "Sir?"

"The target has been located," the man told him. "He's parked off Interstate 95 just across the Delaware state line. Exit 6. Find them."

The asset stood up and walked to the door. "Interstate 95," he said. "Exit 6."

"He's driving a black Ford Mustang coupe. The woman's still with him. Terminate them both."

The asset nodded. "Yes, sir."

"Call me when you've completed your mission," said the man. "We'll bring you home. But treat the target with caution. He has a gun in that Mustang. And he's dangerous with a weapon."

The asset couldn't help grinning. "Yes, sir," he said. "I'll eliminate them both."

He rode the elevator down to street level. Found the rental car where he'd parked it and settled behind the wheel. Slipped the target's pistol between the driver's seat and the center console and pointed the car at the highway, feeling his wound throbbing and looking forward to settling the score.

156

"Andrew Kessler." Windermere put down the stack of manifests. "Flew in direct from Philadelphia Friday evening and left Saturday afternoon, right after things went sideways at Bellagio."

Mathers stood. "That's O'Brien," he said. "You want I should run through the Philadelphia phone book? Try and find him?"

"You can try," said Stevens, "but I don't think you'll find anything. Kessler is probably another alias."

"How can you be sure?"

Stevens looked across the conference room at the junior agent. "I don't think Killswitch is foolish enough to send his operative in under his real name," he said. "Especially after what happened in Miami."

Mathers typed something into his computer. "I have an Andrew Kessler at 1585 Euclid in Camden, New Jersey," he said. "We move on it tonight and bag this guy." He looked at Windermere. "Right?"

"An alias," said Stevens. "Just like Alex Kent and Allen Salazar. We move on Kessler, we'll find a terrified man with no connection to Killswitch."

"You don't know that," said Mathers. "Anyway, what else do we have?"

Stevens stared across at the kid. He'd been quiet all day. Had labored at his computer and hadn't said much. But once or twice Stevens had caught him staring in Windermere's direction when he thought nobody was looking.

What the hell's this about? Stevens wondered, though he figured he had a pretty good idea. The kid had a crush on Windermere. Well, didn't everyone?

Anyway, he was right. There wasn't much else to go on, as far as Killswitch was concerned. The guy manning the phones at OneShot hadn't given Stevens much to work with, and as far as unsolved shootings were concerned, few forensic techs in the country bothered to catalog the brand of bullet used in the murders they worked. Windermere had a stack of files trickling in, but it was short and, as of now, inconclusive.

The investigation in Vegas was moving just as slow. O'Brien—or Kessler—had waylaid a cab to take him to the airport. The cabbie didn't say much beyond what Stevens and Windermere already knew. The Bellagio's maintenance crew had found a pistol in the lake out front of the hotel, a 9mm Beretta with the serial numbers shaved. So far, Vegas PD had been unable to trace it.

That pretty much summed up O'Brien. Wendell Gray and his partner were similarly enigmatic. Airport police at McCarran had found a dark blue Honda Civic in long-term parking that matched the description of the car that had run down Larry Klein. In the trunk was a Remington with a scope, along with a pistol and a couple pairs of sunglasses and "Viva Las Vegas" hats. So were the hats, for that matter. And the car had been reported stolen Sunday morning and wiped clean for prints before the killers abandoned it.

Killswitch was good. He'd waltzed his men into Las Vegas right under their noses, murdered Julio Ramirez, and waltzed back out again. And nobody—nobody—had been able to get a decent read on him.

Mathers looked at Windermere. "We have to check Kessler out, right?"

Windermere was quiet a moment. Then she shook her head. "We'll get agents in Philadelphia to take a look at Kessler's address," she said. "No sense in our flying all the way back for nothing."

"Philly's where the action is," Mathers said. "There's nothing for us in Vegas. Not now that Ramirez is dead."

"Philly's where O'Brien is," said Stevens. "I don't think O'Brien's a factor anymore. We want to get ahead of Killswitch himself."

Mathers frowned at him. Then he turned to Windermere, who nodded. "Stevens is right," she said. "O'Brien flubbed the job. If Gray is really his replacement, it's him we're after."

Mathers snorted. "Of course you would say that."

"I beg your pardon?"

Mathers shook his head. "Don't worry about it."

"You mean of course I'd side with Stevens," said Windermere. "That's what you're talking about."

"Yeah," Mathers said. "Exactly."

"Because why, Derek? Because I like him better?"

Stevens stood up. "Okay," he said. "Let's take a step back a moment. This isn't about who likes who better."

Mathers shook his head. "You have no idea."

"Shut *up*, Derek."

Stevens looked at Windermere. "What am I missing here?"

"Nothing," Windermere said, glaring at Mathers. "You're right. This isn't about me, or either of you. This is about how we're going to find Killswitch. Okay?"

Mathers held her gaze for a moment. Then he shook his head. "Fine," he said. "So how do you suggest we do it?"

Stevens reached for the stack of manifests again. "Wendell Gray and his partner," he said. "We find them in here."

et's start with an easy one." Caity Sherman stared at Lind from the passenger seat of the Mustang. "What's your name?"

They were parked outside a deserted Jiffy Lube off the interstate. Traffic blew past in the distance; night was starting to fall. The air was noisy and unsettled outside. Lind shifted in his seat and looked out the window. "I need you to talk to me," Caity said. "I'm afraid, Andrew."

Lind couldn't look at her without the panic welling up. He shook his head. "My boss is coming," he said. "Everything will be fine."

"I don't care about your boss," Caity said. "If you don't talk to me right now, I'm going to get out of this car and flag somebody down and tell the police the whole story. Understand? You need to start talking to me, Andrew. Right now."

Lind felt his stomach churn. "No police," he said.

"No?" Caity looked at him. "Then you'd better start talking. You said you failed an assignment. Right?"

Lind looked at her. Tried to shake off the buzzing in his head. "Yeah," he said.

"Good. What kind of assignment?"

The buzzing intensified. Lind shook his head again. Couldn't clear his thoughts. *You can't tell her,* he thought. *The man won't approve. The man won't be happy if you tell her what you've done. He'll kill her. He'll kill her, and he'll kill you. He'll never make the visions go away.*

"I don't know," he said. "I don't remember."

Caity shook her head. "Come on. You fly all over the place. You were flying to Houston the last time I saw you. What did you do there?"

The blackness was starting, behind his eyes. Caity's voice was like razor blades to his eardrums. His brain swelled until his skull wanted to burst. Lind closed his eyes and squirmed in his seat.

"No?" Caity said. "What about Miami, then? I checked you in to that flight, remember? What did you do in Miami?"

Miami. Lind closed his eyes. Saw the target on the yacht. Felt the kick from the rifle as his finger pulled the trigger. Watched the man's head explode.

You had to do it, he thought. *The man promised he'd make the visions go away. You had to do what he told you.*

Lind heard the screams in his ears. The crack from the gun. He saw the target stagger backward and drop to the deck.

"What did you do in Miami?" the girl said.

Lind saw the man in Duluth, scrabbling and clawing. Saw the bottle of liquor tipping onto the floor. He saw the white-haired man in Saint Paul, the shouts and screams as he fell onto the cobblestoned driveway. He saw the adulteress in Manhattan and the movie executive in L.A. The terrified kid in the man's basement. He saw the blood, everywhere.

"What did you do, Andrew?" The girl wouldn't stop talking. "Who the hell are you?"

The man won't like this. The man will kill her. He'll kill you, too. You'll never be free from the visions. Never. The man will make sure you suffer forever.

The man was wrong, though.

Lind opened his eyes. Looked across the car and fought to keep his eyes on her face. Fought the blackness behind his eyes, the panic. The visions that threatened to engulf him. Caity. Caity Sherman. He focused every last ounce of strength on her eyes. "I can't do this anymore," he told her. "I just can't."

158

Mathers looked up from his computer. "I know we don't care about Philadelphia anymore," he said slowly, "but it sounds like shit just got real."

Windermere and Stevens swapped glances. "Define 'shit getting real,'" said Windermere.

"Nobody knows the whole story yet," Mathers said, reading from his computer, "but there was a shooting in a downtown apartment this afternoon. Somebody's penthouse got invaded."

"Deaths?"

Mathers nodded. "Next-door neighbor," he said. "Shot in the chest. Sounds like he was an innocent bystander, though. Police think the real target got away."

"How do they figure?"

"Penthouse 1604 was broken into. There were signs of a struggle. The man who lived in the penthouse escaped, as did the shooter."

Stevens caught Windermere's eye. She shrugged. "Who owns the condo?" he asked Mathers. "Who's the target?"

"Unknown target," said Mathers. "Condo's owned by a corporation called Kodiak Shore, but the neighbors say it was a young man living there." He turned to Windermere. "Description sounds a hell of a lot like O'Brien."

"Anybody see the shooter?"

Mathers shook his head. "No."

Windermere didn't say anything for a moment. Then she turned to Stevens. "O'Brien muffed the job. Killswitch came up there to fire him?"

"Could be," said Stevens. "Kind of a quick turnaround, though."

"Either way, we need to be over there," Mathers said, standing. "No way we sit around chasing needles in these manifests now that O'Brien's on the run." He looked at Windermere. "Right?"

Stevens surveyed the office. "I'm not so sure," he said.

"What the hell do you mean?"

Stevens looked up. Found Mathers glaring at him, fire in his eyes. "Listen," he said, "we get up to Philadelphia six hours from now if we're lucky. That puts us six hours behind O'Brien and Killswitch. We've spent this whole investigation playing catch-up. Only way we take them down is if we get ahead."

"So okay, Kirk," said Windermere, "how do you propose we get ahead?"

Stevens looked at the stack of passenger manifests. Sat back in his chair and stared at the ceiling, trying to work out a shortcut. "What other flights left around the same time as the Philadelphia flight Sunday afternoon?" he said.

"Hundreds," said Windermere. "You saw the airport."

"I mean within an hour or two, tops. Killswitch likes to get his assets out immediately after the kill. Ramirez died around two in the afternoon. That means the killers probably flew out between three-thirty and five, right?"

Windermere glanced at Mathers. Mathers sighed. "If you say so."

"So narrow it down," said Stevens. "What are we working with?"

Windermere picked up a printout. "Dallas, Los Angeles, Houston, Los Angeles, San Francisco, Philadelphia, Charlotte—"

"Charlotte," said Stevens. "Oneida Ware said Killswitch's Cadillac had North Carolina plates. Wendell Gray disappeared from Atlanta shortly after Killswitch was in Miami. He could have swung through and picked up Gray on the way home."

Mathers frowned. "Kind of tenuous, isn't it?"

"Maybe," said Stevens. "Let me see the Charlotte manifest."

Windermere handed over the stack of paper. Stevens read through it. Windermere's FAA buddy had included arrival information for every passenger on the list. Now Stevens scanned the page, looking for a pattern. Found what he was looking for near the bottom.

"Gardham," he said. "There it is."

Windermere looked at him. "You sure?"

"The OneShot guy mentioned somebody named Gardham had put in a major order for ammunition. Now here's a Gardham, Thomas, in the manifest. Flew in from Charlotte Sunday morning, accompanied by one David Gilmour. Both flew out on the afternoon flight. That's a hell of a quick turnaround."

"Few hours," said Windermere. "Just enough time to kill Julio Ramirez."

"I'm guessing Gardham is probably Killswitch himself," Stevens said. "He came to Vegas with Wendell Gray in person."

"And then flew back to Charlotte once Ramirez was dead. Just like he bailed out O'Brien in Miami."

Stevens grinned. "Exactly."

159

The asset drove the little rental car across the state line into Delaware. He picked up the cell phone and steered the car with his free hand as he called the man. "Approaching Exit 6," he said.

"Good," the man said. "They're in a black Ford Mustang parked outside a Jiffy Lube north of the highway. Don't let them get away."

The asset pulled onto the off-ramp. "Yes, sir," he said. "I'll call back when the job is done."

160

Caity Sherman stared across the car at the guy—Richard, Andrew, whoever—feeling a chill run through her body as she studied his anguished eyes. "Can't do *what* anymore?" she said. "What do you do, Richard?"

This was stupid. She should get out of here while she still had the chance. He was clearly unsettled. He was probably insane. Whatever he was into—drugs, gambling, murder—it was obviously dangerous as hell.

Except she couldn't just leave him. He looked so utterly miserable. Tortured. She wanted to comfort him. And a part of her, she admitted to herself, wanted to know just what the hell had screwed him up so good. "What is it?" she said. "What do you do?"

Richard/Andrew sat in the driver's seat and stared out the windshield into the dimming light. He didn't say anything—what else was new?

"Tell me," she said.

He turned, slowly, and looked at her. There was pain in his eyes, and fear. Vulnerability. "I kill people," he said. "For the man."

Okay. That was it. Time to get the hell away from this guy. Caity wrenched her door open. Unbuckled her seat belt and dashed from the car. Heard Richard/Andrew calling after her and ignored him.

Run, she thought. *Run for your life.*

She hurried across the empty parking lot. There was a gas station in the distance. Lights on. Traffic on the road. She was going to flag someone down and make them call the cops. She was going to get far away from Richard/Andrew/whoever and she was never going to flirt with strangers again.

She glanced back at the Mustang. Richard/Andrew wasn't chasing her. He was still behind the wheel, wasn't even looking at her. She slowed for a moment.

He just told you he kills people. You're not going back there.

She turned back toward the gas station lights just as a silver Nissan pulled in from the street, headlights bright in the twilight. Caity waved and ran to it as it slowed. "Oh, my God," she called to the driver. "Please help. There's a guy in that Mustang, and I think he's lost his mind."

The driver climbed slowly out of the car. He looked at Caity. Caity met his eyes and stopped. Stopped babbling at him. Stopped hurrying toward him. Stopped everything and just stood there.

It was the man from the apartment. He'd found them.

Every instinct in her body screamed at her to run. She couldn't. She stood, frozen, and looked at the man, those empty eyes and the bloody wound in his shoulder. The man studied her from across the car. Then he came around for her, slowly.

Caity screamed.

161

Lind watched Caity Sherman run from the Mustang. He heard her screaming outside. Heard a car door slam shut. It all came to him muffled, like he was underwater.

I need help.

His head hurt like never before. His vision was nearly black, and his ears buzzed like a million angry hornets. He wanted to puke out every organ, every ounce of life from his body.

He saw the targets again. Miami. Duluth. New York. Los Angeles. He heard the screams and the gunfire. Couldn't escape the blood. The last electric twitches before the targets expired.

You're a killer. You killed for the man. You killed so many people.

Lind screamed himself ragged. Shook the car on its tires. Nothing changed.

There was something going on across the parking lot. Lind could hear it. He'd heard Caity Sherman screaming, and he'd heard a car door slam. Caity screamed once more, desperate, then silence. Now there was only the muffled sound of the highway through the trees. Lind thought about the man and felt a chill like icicles on the back of his neck.

He knows, he thought. *He knows where we are.*

There was a silver Nissan sedan parked across the lot. In the dim light, Lind could just make out the driver on the pavement beside it. He was a tall man with shaggy hair. Lanky. He was the attacker from the apartment in Philadelphia. Lind recognized him. He'd followed them here, into Delaware.

And now he was outside, strangling Caity Sherman to death.

162

The asset called David Gilmour had the woman by the throat when he heard the big Mustang's engine rumble to life. She was sinking to her knees in front of him, clawing at his hands, gasping for breath. She was dying in front of him. In a minute or two, she'd be dead.

But the Mustang was coming. The asset gripped the girl tight and ignored her flailing hands. Looked up and heard the big engine roar.

The second target was coming.

The asset kept his left hand tight on the girl's throat. Fumbled with his right for the pistol. The girl redoubled her fight. Wrenched at his hand. Sent a bolt of burning pain through the wound in his shoulder. The asset screamed and dropped the girl. She scrambled away.

The Mustang was still coming. The asset pulled out the gun. Squeezed three shots that missed high. The Mustang kept coming.

The asset dove out of the way. The Mustang crumpled the little Nissan's front fender. Glass shattered. Steel screamed in protest. The asset rolled away from the car. Heard the Mustang's door open. Saw the target climb out.

The target came for him. No hesitation. Dodged the asset's kicks and fell on him, raining punches. The asset swung back with the pistol. Caught the target, hard, across the face. The target reeled back, fell away. The asset came up firing. Shattered the driver's-side window on the target's car.

The target ran. Ducked behind the Mustang and scrabbled away on the gravel. The asset gave chase. Circled the Mustang. Heard the passenger door open and saw the dome light flick on.

Then the target appeared again. Stood up from the passenger door, slow and steady. He was holding his own pistol now. Had it aimed square at the asset's chest.

163

Lind held the pistol on the attacker. Watched the triumph slowly fade from his face. The man held his own pistol at waist level, pointed down. Lind aimed the gun at the man's head.

There were sirens in the distance. For a long moment, nobody moved. Then Lind spoke. "Stop," he said. "This isn't what you want."

The attacker didn't move. Didn't blink. Lind looked him up and down. Looked into his eyes and flinched and stepped back.

There was no life in the attacker's eyes. *Just like mine,* Lind realized. *This guy's another one like me.*

The attacker started to inch toward Lind. Lind leveled the gun, his finger tight on the trigger. "This isn't you doing this," he told the attacker. "This is the man's fault. He brainwashed you, too. You see the same visions, don't you?"

The attacker blinked. Paused. Lind relaxed the gun. "He told you he'd make the visions go away," Lind said. "He's a liar. He's using us both."

The attacker studied Lind, frowning. Then his lips curled up in a cold sneer. "Maybe," he said. "But I kind of like it."

He started toward Lind again, evil in his eyes. Lind straightened the gun. Aimed it at the man's head. "Stay back," he warned him. "Stay back or I'll shoot."

The man didn't listen. He kept grinning. He kept coming for Lind.

164

Caity watched the man walk toward Richard/Andrew. She heard the sirens, knew the police wouldn't come soon enough. Richard/Andrew held the gun high. Leveled it at the man's face. *Shoot,* she thought. *Kill him. Then we all go home.*

But Richard wasn't shooting. The man was getting closer, and she could tell by the look on Richard's face that he wasn't going to do it. Was he a killer or wasn't he? Was it all talk? The man was almost on him now. He was laughing at Richard.

She stood. *"Shoot him, you moron."*

The attacker spun at her and fired. Caity ducked. Heard something hit the ground hard, an expulsion of breath. When she stood again, Richard was standing, his gun trained at the attacker. He'd knocked the man over, sent his pistol skittering off into the shadows. *"Shoot him,"* she said. *"For Christ's sake, just kill him."*

Richard looked across at her. "I can't," he said.

What the hell.

The attacker took off across the lot on his hands and knees, crawling for his weapon. In a couple seconds he'd be shooting again.

Caity slid behind the wheel of the Mustang. Shifted the big engine into reverse. Then she paused. She looked out at Richard. He was watching the man. He wasn't doing anything. He was going to get himself killed.

God damn it.

Caity shoved the passenger door open. *"Get your ass in the car."*

Richard looked at her. Blinked. Then, mercifully, he obeyed. She waited until he was halfway in his seat before she gunned it in reverse. Pulled clear of the Nissan and squealed across the lot. Dodged an oncoming police cruiser, slid across the intersection, and aimed the Mustang at the highway.

165

The asset watched the Mustang squeal out of the lot. Watched the police cruiser squeal in. He fumbled in the dark for the pistol, came up with it. Stayed hidden in the shadows as the cruiser pulled to a stop alongside the Nissan.

The cop sat in his cruiser a moment. The asset watched him. Gripped the pistol in his hands and tried to figure his options.

His adrenaline was running. He wanted to kill the cop. He wanted to walk out, gun blazing, and put five or six holes in the man's body. He wanted to kill, the target's words be damned. Maybe the man had done this to him, maybe not. He liked it. He wanted to kill again.

The cop was shining a spotlight on the Nissan. Easy prey. The asset massaged the trigger. Pictured the blood. Somewhere inside him, though, he heard the man's voice. He remembered his training.

Extricate yourself without being detected.

That cop was talking on the radio. He was telling his dispatcher he'd responded to a report of shots fired. Happened upon this Nissan. He was phoning in the plates. Every outfit in the country would look for the asset if he murdered a cop.

Too much attention.

The asset slunk into the shadows. Circled around the dark Jiffy Lube building and into the trees behind. Made his way through the forest until he came to another road. It was a quiet road, not as busy. The asset waited in the shadows until he saw headlights approach. Then he stepped onto the pavement and waved the car down.

It was a truck, an old Chevy, two men inside. The asset kept the pistol hidden until he was right close. The driver rolled down his window. "What's the problem?"

The asset stuck the gun in the man's face. "Out," he said. "Both of you."

The men complied, their eyes wide. "No trouble, man," the passenger said. "Take the truck if you need it. Not worth spit anyway."

"Fuck you," said the driver. "That's my truck."

"It's my *life*."

The asset brought the men around to the shoulder. Stood them in a ditch and watched them go pale. They wore checkered shirts and blue jeans. Looked something like farmers. The passenger wore a knife on his belt. "Hey, listen, man," the driver said. "Don't shoot us, okay?"

The asset leveled the gun at him. "Deal," he said. "Let me see that knife."

166

Mathers's phone beeped. He caught Windermere's eye across the lounge. "County police in northeast Delaware got a call about shots fired just south of the state line," he read. "Couple cars in a Jiffy Lube parking lot, screaming and the like. Cruiser checked it out, found an abandoned Nissan, some spent shell casings, nobody around."

Windermere and Stevens looked at each other. They were sitting in an empty corner of McCarran Airport, waiting to board a late flight to Charlotte. Outside the windows, the sun was just disappearing behind the Spring Mountains, rendering the casinos on the Strip a dramatic silhouette. Windermere frowned. "Okay," she said. "So what does this have to do with us, Derek?"

Mathers scrolled down on his BlackBerry. "The Nissan was a rental," he said. "Checked out from the Alamo desk at Philadelphia International this morning. Registered to one David Gilmour."

Stevens felt his stomach flip. "Shit."

"Guy called it in from an Exxon across the street. Said he heard a woman screaming, sounded like she was dying. Saw another car peel out, a muscle car, black." Mathers looked at Windermere. "Word from Philadelphia is O'Brien kept a late-model Ford Mustang parked at his apartment, a—"

"Black Mustang." Windermere swore. "I get it, Derek. Gilmour broke into O'Brien's pad. O'Brien escaped, and Gilmour chased him down. Caught up off the interstate just across the state line to much shooting and gnashing of teeth."

"The woman," said Stevens. "Who is she?"

Mathers shrugged. "Could be an innocent bystander. Maybe another Killswitch killer. Or maybe one of the boys just got lonely."

Windermere stood. Walked to the window and stared out at the planes on the tarmac. "Christ," she said.

"You still thinking we should be headed for Charlotte?"

Windermere turned back from the window. Didn't answer. She looked at Stevens for a long time. Then she looked at Mathers and sighed. "Switch your ticket," she said. "Head to Philly. I'll take Stevens to North Carolina."

Mathers stood. "Damn right."

Windermere watched him hurry away. Then she turned to Stevens. "I really hope you're right, partner."

167

The Mustang was fast. Caity drove it as hard as she dared, the big engine roaring and the wind howling through the ruined driver's-side window as the car ate up miles on the interstate. Her head pounded and her throat was raw. Probably bruised to hell, too, from the attacker's big hands. And meanwhile, Richard/Andrew seemed dead fucking calm in the passenger seat. Was sitting there staring out the window like they both hadn't just cheated death—again.

"Why didn't you shoot him?" she said finally. "You had your gun right in his face. Could have killed him and saved us a shitload of trouble. Why'd you cop out?"

Richard said nothing. The wind buffeted the car, and Caity shivered and turned up the heater. Wondered where she was supposed to be going. She looked at Richard. "Come on, talk to me. Why'd you flake?"

Richard pursed his lips. He shifted in his seat. "That guy back there," he said finally, "the attacker. He works for the same man that I worked for. The man sent him to kill me, because I failed the assignment."

"I figured as much," Caity said. "So?"

"The man, he brainwashes people. With these nightmares." He looked at her. Caught her expression. "It sounds crazy, I know. I don't know how it works. But it does. He brainwashed that guy like he brainwashed me."

Caity stared out at the marks on the highway. Watched them disappear like Morse code beneath the car, every dash like a snare drum beating behind her eyes. She rubbed her face and looked away. "You realize you sound completely insane."

"I know," he said.

"How did he find you? He just took you off the street?"

Richard paused again. Caity watched him stare out the window. She wanted to shake him until he gave her some answers. "I was a soldier," he said, "in Iraq. I was in a convoy and an IED got us, an explosive device." He sucked in a breath. "Blew up my Humvee. Killed a bunch of my friends. It fucked me up good."

He'd pressed himself back in the seat. Screwed his eyes closed. Every word sounded like a thousand-pound weight. "They brought me back to America," he said. "Some veterans' hospital in I-don't-know-where. They kept me in a bed for a while and then checked me out. I had to come back every week for, like, a psych test. That's where I first saw this guy, the man. He was waiting for me outside the clinic one day."

She waited. "Yeah?" she said. "And then?"

"And then, I don't know," he said, shaking his head. "Every time I try to remember, I feel like my head is going to explode. Like I want to claw out my own eyeballs. I can't take it."

"You can't remember," she said. "But somehow he brainwashed you. Turned you into a killer. And this other guy, too."

O'Brien nodded. "And more, maybe. Who knows?"

"So this guy who attacked us, he was a brainwashed killer. And you still couldn't pull the trigger."

He was quiet for a while, a couple miles. Then he looked at her. "I've killed people," he said. "I didn't want to, but I did. The man made me think I didn't have a choice. He made that guy back there believe the same thing."

Caity shook her head. "No," she said. "No way. That guy was evil."

"If he's evil, then I'm evil, too," Richard said. He was staring out the window again, out into the night. She turned back to the road and just drove and said nothing.

Finally, she shook her head. "We have to go to the police, Richard."

He looked up. "No."

"Did you hear what you told me? There's a murderer on the loose. We have to tell someone."

"I'm a murderer, too," he said. "By the time anyone gets around to listening to my story, the man will have found out they got me. He'll have time to escape."

"So, what?" she said. "What are you proposing we do?"

He looked at her. "I want to find him," he said. "I want to find him and shut him down myself."

Caity didn't say anything for a moment. She drove in silence. "God damn it," she said finally. "Just once, I want to meet a normal guy."

168

The asset called David Gilmour drove south on Interstate 95 in the old Chevy pickup. He drove until he'd put a few miles between the truck and the Jiffy Lube. Then he pulled out his cell phone and dialed the man's number. The man answered quickly. "Tell me you got them."

"The targets are gone," the asset told him. "They escaped."

For a long moment, there was no answer. Then the man swore, and the asset could hear something breaking on the other end of the line. When the man came back, he was breathing heavily. "Where are you?"

"On Interstate 95. Approaching Wilmington."

"And you let them get away."

"I intercepted the woman in the parking lot. Before I could eliminate her, the man attacked me. He was armed, as expected. I was unable to overpower him."

"You were armed, too, god damn it. What happened?"

The asset paused. "I didn't sufficiently disable the woman, sir. She rejoined the fight. The targets managed to stall me until law enforcement arrived."

"Police?" The man swore again. "You got away, though?"

"Yes, sir. I abandoned the rental car and escaped into the woods. Found another vehicle and neutralized the occupants."

"Neutralized them." The man paused. "Exactly how did you neutralize them?"

The asset glanced at the bloody knife on the passenger seat. "Completely."

169

Parkerson put down the phone. Looked around the den and slammed his fist on the table. *"God damn it."*

On the other end of the line, the asset waited. Let him wait. This was a whole new pile of bullshit to wade through. A big knot to untie. It had been a mistake to send Gray to Philadelphia alone. He'd fucked up two killings, and now Lind and his mystery girlfriend were on the run, headed who knows where. Plus the collateral damage. One dead in Lind's building. Two more "neutralized" somewhere in goddamn Delaware. A big fucking mess. Bigger than a mess. An unmitigated disaster.

Someone knocked, softly, at the door. Parkerson turned to see his wife peering in at him. "You say something, honey?"

Parkerson glanced at the Killswitch phone in his hand. He shook his head. "Just talking to myself."

"Everything okay?"

"Work stuff." He shrugged. "Tight deadline. High pressure, as always."

"Oh, no." Rachel walked into the room and put her hands on his shoulders. Squeezed. "You're so tense."

"Gonna be this way for a while, I'm afraid."

"Anything I can do?"

Parkerson leaned into her hands. Closed his eyes and enjoyed her touch. Then he shook his head. "I just have to work through it. Pray it ends soon."

Rachel leaned down and kissed the top of his head. "Don't work too hard," she said. "It's only life and death."

Parkerson forced himself to smile. It was a little joke she was always telling him, though this time his wife had no idea just how right she was. He leaned up and kissed her briefly, and gave a little wave as she slipped back out of the den. Then he picked up the Killswitch phone and stared at it.

The girl could drag Lind to the cops. Maybe Lind would remember his training and run; maybe he would kill the girl, or she'd flake out and get scared and they'd both disappear. It was a nice fantasy, but Parkerson knew he should plan for the worst.

He leaned back in his chair and stared up at the ceiling. What could the girl know? What could Lind know, for that matter? The kid had been brainwashed pretty good. He'd forgotten his own goddamn name, for Christ's sake. What did either of them know about Killswitch?

Wendell Gray was still out there, though. Someone, somewhere, would have seen him. Somebody would find the bodies of the poor bastards he'd "neutralized" and report their car missing. Wilmington wasn't big enough to hide out in for long.

Parkerson checked his watch. It was late. Too late to think about flying to Delaware. Something had to be done, though. Wendell Gray was a failure. Too risky to keep him around any longer.

Parkerson picked up the Killswitch phone. "You there?"

The asset coughed. "Yes, sir."

"Good." Parkerson stared up at the ceiling and let out a long breath. "Drive south," he said. "Don't stop. Come on home."

170

tevens glanced at Windermere across the aisle. The cabin was dim; outside the windows, night had set in. Most of the plane was asleep. Windermere, though, was awake. She sat ramrod straight in her seat, flipping through a copy of the week's *Time* magazine. Stevens watched her and wondered if she ever slept.

"You think he finds anything in Philly?" he asked her. "Mathers, I mean. Think this Charlotte thing's a mistake?"

Windermere looked up. Cocked her head. "You having second thoughts, Stevens?"

"I'm just sick of coming in second," he said. "I want to be waiting for these guys at the finish line for once."

"And you're sure the finish line's in North Carolina."

"No," he said. "But I'm damn sure it's not in Philadelphia."

"So what's with all the second-guessing?"

Stevens sighed. "I'm just not sure what the heck's our next move. We're back in needle-haystack territory down here. At least Mathers's got some rubble to poke through."

Windermere nodded. "Yeah," she said. "Right."

"What's up with you two, anyway?" Stevens said, frowning. "Mathers was weird the whole trip to Vegas. Did I miss something back in Philly or what?"

Windermere made a face. "Nothing, Stevens," she said. "Don't even worry about it. You didn't miss a thing."

"Come on." He grinned at her. "There's definitely some tension there,

Carla. Don't deny it. What happened? You shut him down again? Put him in his place?"

Windermere sighed and sat back in her seat. "Don't worry about it, Stevens. Okay?"

Stevens studied Windermere for a beat. Then he reached for his in-flight magazine. "Huh," he said. "Sorry I asked."

171

They checked into a motel in Newport, Delaware. Caity paid with her credit card and parked outside the room. Lind followed her inside.

He wasn't sure what he was doing. He wasn't sure of anything at the moment. Hadn't really been sure of much since he'd returned from Vegas. Longer, even. Since he'd met the man.

He was a killer. Somehow, the man had brainwashed him. Had turned the visions on him until he was nothing—a hollow, murderous shell. A killer.

Lind pushed past Caity Sherman to the motel room's bathroom. He stood over the toilet in flickering fluorescent light and retched, violent, until he puked. It didn't take long.

He was a killer. He remembered every kill. He didn't remember his name, or his birthday, or what his mother looked like, but he remembered the bodies. He remembered the man.

Lind puked again. He puked until his stomach was empty and he could only retch, dry, into the bowl. Until Caity Sherman came to the doorway and sighed and wet a washcloth and wiped his face clean. She flushed the toilet and helped him to his feet, led him out to the bed, and eased him down on it.

"You really didn't know," she said, "did you?"

Lind stared up at her. He was shaking. He felt feverish. "I knew," he said. "Somewhere inside, I knew."

"You're different now." She swabbed his forehead with the washcloth. "You're a human again. You're not brainwashed anymore, I can tell."

Lind closed his eyes. Felt the cool, wet cloth on his skin. "That doesn't make it any better."

Caity stared down at him. He could see the fear in her eyes, the uncertainty. He knew she didn't trust him, either. Finally, she looked away. "So what are you going to do?"

Lind closed his eyes and saw the faces again, in Miami and Duluth, in Saint Paul and New York and Los Angeles. He saw the face of the scared kid in the dark little room, and he saw the man pressing the revolver into his hands. He saw the man smile, heard his voice, and he shivered and opened his eyes.

"I'm going to give in to the visions," he said. "I'm going to let them drag me back in and hope he brainwashed me well enough to find him."

Caity stared at him. "Holy shit."

Lind nodded. "Yeah," he said. "I'm not thrilled about it, either."

172

The flight landed in Charlotte a few minutes before midnight. Windermere rented a Camry from a half-conscious Avis clerk and headed into the city with Stevens.

She didn't say anything as she drove. Neither of them had really spoken since she'd brushed off Stevens on the plane. She knew Stevens would have more questions about Mathers, and she wasn't so sure she wanted to face them.

She drove from the airport east into downtown Charlotte. Pulled into a Marriott in the city center and parked and turned off the ignition. She sat there in the quiet for a moment. Then she sighed and rubbed her eyes.

"I'll hook us up with the locals in the morning," she said. "Work out a plan of attack. If Gilmour flies home, the FAA's going to call me. With any luck we can pick him up at the airport."

"Or tail him to Thomas Gardham," said Stevens.

"Even better." Windermere paused. "I'll call Mathers in the morning, too. See if he's finding anything useful up there."

"Sure." Stevens looked at her again. "Look, Carla, whatever happened—"

Windermere shook her head. "I know, Stevens."

"I didn't mean to touch a nerve. Really none of my business."

"I *know*, Stevens. Let's just drop it, okay?"

Stevens held up his hands. "Yeah," he said. "Sure, Carla. Whatever you want."

Windermere rubbed her eyes again. "Great," she said. "Sorry." She reached for the door handle. "Let's just get some rest."

173

Lind closed his eyes and tried to focus, conscious of every sound in the room. He could hear Caity breathing from where she sat, facing him, on a chair by the TV set. He could hear the toilet running in the bathroom, and trucks speeding past on the highway outside.

The motel room was dark. The bed was soft and comfortable. The whole place was as quiet as could be. He'd fallen asleep in louder situations than this. Brighter. He'd slept practically standing up in an ice-cold shower with a full pot of coffee running through him. This should be easy.

But it wasn't. Lind kept seeing the attacker. The look on his face as he'd strangled Caity Sherman. The bruises on her neck. The ragged sound she'd made when he'd thrown her against the wall. When he'd turned to come after Lind.

Lind tried to steady his breathing. Listened to the rush of traffic and tried to clear his mind. He waited. Nothing happened. "It's not working," he said, opening his eyes. "I can't fall asleep."

Caity frowned in the dim light. "It's a bad idea," she said. "I told you we should go to the cops."

Lind shook his head and lay back again. "No cops."

Caity didn't say anything. He heard her stand up, felt her weight on the bed as she lay down beside him. She hesitated a moment, and then wrapped her arm around him. Lind stiffened. "What are you doing?"

"Hush," she said. "Close your eyes."

Lind started to protest. She shushed him. He forced himself to close his eyes and felt her warmth close to his body, her hand tracing paths on his arm. He listened to her breathing and the sound was hypnotic. He felt himself slipping away.

Then he was under.

HE WAS IN THE DESERT. Riding in the Humvee, headed out on patrol. Showtime in the driver's seat. Mini-Me and Slowpoke in the back. Hang Ten in the turret. Everyone laughing, Showtime saying something about Hang Ten's Hawaiian girlfriend. It was loud in the Humvee. It was bright and hot outside. The big truck jostled over the bumpy terrain. Lind sat in the shotgun seat and stared out the window at the desert. Let the truck carry him along.

This isn't the right vision. This isn't where you need to be. You need to keep moving. You need to get out of here.

The convoy slowed to enter the city. Lind stared out the window at the suspicious-eyed men who watched the Humvee pass. Soon, he knew, one of them would push down on a detonator button. Soon the whole world would explode. He didn't want to be here when it did.

Lind forced himself to close his eyes. Steadied his breathing and tried to drown out the noise of the truck. Tried to picture the hotel room and Caity, and gradually the rumble of the Humvee's engine faded away.

Lind opened his eyes again. Heard screaming. The drone of more engines. He looked around and found he was lying down. Realized he was aboard the army transport plane. *Still not right.*

Someone screamed again. The plane jostled with turbulence, and the screaming intensified. The engines roared. Lind closed his eyes. *Get me out of here.*

"Hello there."

Lind opened his eyes. Quickly closed them again as his heart jolted up-tempo. The man was there, smiling down at him under that blue baseball cap. He saw Lind's expression and laughed.

"Don't be scared," he said. "I'm a friend of yours, soldier."

Lind looked around. Saw blue sky, heard traffic in the distance, the whir of automatic doors sliding open and closed behind him. He was outside a hospital. The veterans' hospital.

"It's a big day for you," the man told him. "We're taking you home. What do you think of that?"

Lind stared at the man. *Who are you?* his mind screamed. *Tell me who you are.* His body wouldn't respond. He couldn't make himself speak.

Lind followed the man down the sidewalk toward a waiting Cadillac. The man helped him into the passenger seat and buckled his seat belt, grinning at him the whole time. Then he circled around to the driver's-side door.

This was where the vision usually ended. Lind had climbed into this Cadillac a thousand times in his dreams. He'd never before seen where the Cadillac took him. Today had to be different.

Lind forced his eyes to stay open. He fought off the blackness that encroached like a blanket, the panic that lurked just beyond. Every moment he stayed in the dream, the panic got worse, the blackness more inviting. Lind fought it off, desperate. He gripped the armrests and made himself focus. He thought about the people he'd killed, and the man who'd made him do it. He thought of Caity Sherman, waiting for him in the motel room. He gritted his teeth and forced himself to stay conscious. The blackness came for him. The panic clawed at his mind like a wave.

Then, all at once, it receded. The blackness disappeared. The panic was gone. Lind sat in the passenger seat of the Cadillac as the man pulled away from the curb. He watched the road. Watched the man. Looked for any sign, any clue. He clung to the vision and searched its edges for something, anything that could help him.

Then he saw.

174

Stevens was awake, barely, when the knock came on his door. He was lying in bed watching *SportsCenter*, waiting for the Timberwolves highlights and missing Nancy and the kids. He'd called home as soon as he checked into the room, woke Nancy to ask about Andrea.

"She's fine, Kirk," his wife had replied, in between yawns. "Soon as I told her you'd gone back to work, she lit up like a Christmas tree. I took her in to the doctor today anyway, just to be safe. He's going to set her up with a counselor, but he doesn't think we have any reason to be worried."

"You tell him I was out of town on a case?"

Nancy yawned again. "No," she said. "Why would I tell him that?"

"I don't know." Stevens sighed. "I just want to know that I'm not doing Andrea any damage being out here, I guess. I worry about it."

"She'll be fine, Kirk. Just hurry up and come home."

Stevens told her he would, and he told her he loved her. Then he hung up the phone and turned on the TV and watched it and thought about home. Now, at nearly two in the morning, he was ready for sleep. Or he had been, until he heard the knock at his door.

The knock came again, insistent, and Stevens cursed softly and swung his legs to the floor. He walked to the door and stared out through the peephole. Then he stepped back. "Shit," he said. "One second."

He hurried back into the room and pulled on yesterday's pants. Fixed his hair in the mirror and turned on another light. Then he unlocked the door and let Windermere into the room.

"Hey," she said. She walked past him and sat in an overstuffed easy chair. Eyed the bed. "You asleep?"

Stevens followed her into the room. Leaned against the wall and gestured at the TV. "Not quite. Waiting for the Timberwolves' score."

Windermere glanced at the TV. "Beat the Grizzlies 92 to 86," she said. "Love had a double-double."

Stevens frowned. "You hate basketball."

"Yeah, well." She made a face. Looked around the room, anywhere but his eyes. Then she laughed, a humorless staccato. "So, I slept with Mathers."

Stevens laughed, too, more out of shock than anything. Then he caught the look on her face. "Jesus," he said. "That's why you came over?"

"No." Windermere sighed. "Yeah."

"In Philadelphia. While I was away."

"I was, I dunno, lonely," she said. "He was there. We got drunk. You were off with your wife. I figured, why the hell not?"

Stevens stared at her across the room. She sat in the armchair and held his gaze, about as beautiful as he'd ever seen her. He leaned against the wall and tried to think up a response. "So, what?" he said finally. "Why tell me this, Carla?"

She shrugged. "I swore I wouldn't. Then I figured you'd find out eventually. I wanted you to hear it from me."

"How thoughtful."

She looked away suddenly. "Yeah, well."

"That's why Mathers was so weird in Vegas, huh?"

She nodded. "We're not together. It was a one-night thing, and before you ask, it's not something I normally do. I don't sleep around, Stevens, but it's damn well within my rights if I want to."

Stevens didn't say anything. *Why does this feel like a fight between two married people? Why should I give a damn who Carla sleeps with?*

Except, of course, he did. It was irrational—didn't make any sense at all—but there you go. He felt jealous of Mathers, and angry, just as if Windermere were his cheating wife.

You're the cheater. Just by feeling this way, you're unfaithful to Nancy.

Stevens let out a long breath. "Sure," he said. "Of course. It's none of my business, anyway."

"No," Windermere said, after a moment. "It's not."

"Exactly."

Windermere didn't say anything else. They stared at each other. Then Windermere looked away, and Stevens wondered what she was thinking.

Who cares what she's thinking? She's not your damn problem.

"This is why you came over?" he said finally. "To tell me about you and Mathers, at two in the morning?"

She shook her head. "Actually, no." She reached into her pocket and pulled out her cell phone. "Got a text from Mathers in Delaware. I guess he made it down to that crime scene pretty quick."

"And?"

"And it's a murder scene, Stevens." She looked at him. "Police found two bodies in a ditch a half mile from the scene. Two guys—as far as anyone can tell, they're just innocent bystanders. Cut up pretty bad, and their IDs are missing."

Stevens pushed himself off the wall. "Can't be a coincidence," he said.

"No way," said Windermere. "Local cops are working on names for our victims, but in the meantime it's more bodies for O'Brien or Gray. And they're still at large, Stevens, up there in Delaware."

"And we flew to Charlotte." Stevens leaned against the wall and ran his hands through his hair. "God damn it all, Carla."

175

Early the next morning, Lind parked the Mustang outside a little police station along the highway in Newport, Delaware. He turned off the ignition and looked at Caity Sherman. "Okay," he said, "this is it."

She was bruised, he saw: her cheek and her throat, where the killer had strangled her. Her clothes were torn and dirty, her hair unkempt and her eyes tired. She looked deflated, and Lind felt something like shame when he looked at her. He'd dragged her into this mess. The man had been right to warn him not to make friends.

Caity stared out the window and sighed. "You're going to be okay?"

"I'll be fine once I find him," he said.

"You don't have to find him." She reached across and touched his hand. "You don't have to go after him, Richard. I'll talk to the police. You stay hidden. We'll let them solve the problem."

A uniformed police officer had come out of the station house. He walked slowly across the lot to a patrol car. Noticed the Mustang and studied it for a moment. Lind watched him, anxious. It was time to go. "Give me a head start," he told Caity. "Like we agreed, okay? Don't tell them everything right away."

Caity snorted. "What would I tell them?" she said. "I don't *know* anything. You won't tell me where you're going."

"The lake house," said Lind. "That's where he took me."

"Yeah, and where's that? You don't even know."

"I'll find it," he told her. "If I can find the hospital, I can retrace his steps. I just have to remember the way."

Caity looked at him. "This is a bad idea."

"Just give me a head start, okay?"

"Even if I told them everything I know," she said, sighing, "there's a thousand hospitals and a million lake houses. I don't even know your real name."

Lind looked at her. "Malcolm," he said. "That's my first name. I don't know my last. The man in the dream called me Malcolm. That's my name."

"You're sure?"

He nodded. "It feels right."

Caity studied his face for a long time. Then she exhaled. "Well, okay, Malcolm," she said. "I guess this is good-bye."

"Yeah," he said.

"I'm sorry I can't come with you."

"No you're not." He squeezed her hand. "Thank you, Caity."

She gave him a smile. "With a *C*," she said. Then she reached for the door. Climbed halfway out of the car before she stopped and leaned back inside. Fixed him with a look. "Take care of yourself," she said. "Be careful, okay?"

Lind nodded, and she leaned across and kissed him once, quickly, on the cheek. Then she ducked out of the car and slammed the door closed behind her. Lind watched her as she crossed the parking lot. When she'd reached the police station, he turned the key in the ignition and the big Mustang rumbled to life. Slowly, he idled out of the lot and headed back toward the interstate.

176

Wilmington, Delaware, Stevens thought. *Derek Mathers.*

It was morning. The bedsheets lay in tangles around him. He hadn't slept much through the night, and he wasn't sure whether it was Andrea and Nancy or Mathers and Windermere or Gilmour and Gardham that had kept him awake.

One thing was for certain: Richard O'Brien and David Gilmour had been in Wilmington, Delaware. And two more men were dead.

Gilmour's doing, probably. O'Brien's Mustang was missing. Gilmour's rental car was abandoned. The two murdered men had been discovered on the side of a lonely road. Gilmour had probably hijacked their car.

So he was mobile. So was O'Brien. They were both up in Delaware. And meanwhile, Stevens had dragged Windermere to North Carolina. They still had no leads. And Windermere had slept with Mathers.

Stevens rolled over in bed. Kicked the sheets off his legs. Who the hell cared who she slept with? She was young and beautiful, and he was married. She'd had a boyfriend when they'd met, and he hadn't cared then. Why the hell did he care so much now?

They'd come close in Philadelphia. That was why he cared. They'd

shared something, briefly, and at the last moment, they'd flinched. He'd
gone home to Nancy, and she'd gone straight to Mathers.

Stevens stared up at the ceiling. It was stupid to feel this way. It was
practically cheating. He was never going to leave Nancy, not in a million
years. So why did it matter who Windermere slept with?

Stevens didn't have an answer. He had a jealousy problem and a labyrinthine case. Sighing, he swung his legs off the bed and stood stretching
in the hotel room, trying to push Windermere from his mind.

177

Lind drove south on Interstate 95, the wind whipping through the ruined driver's-side window and shaking the car. He stopped at a roadside gas station outside Baltimore and filled the tank. Bought a McDonald's
hamburger and a large Coke and sat in the restaurant and ate and stared
at the cars headed southbound.

Somewhere down that road was a hospital. Lind could picture it—a
sprawling brick high-rise complex, modern and clean-looking—in his
mind. He could trace the path the man drove in his Cadillac from the
hospital parking lot to the highway, down miles and miles of highway, to
the little house in the trees by the lake. He could trace the path farther,
too, if he wanted, could follow the man out of the Cadillac and through
the trees and into the musty old house, down the creaking narrow staircase and into the basement. Into that stinking little room where the
nightmares began.

He could follow the man now. He remembered. Soon enough he
would walk down those stairs again, but not yet.

Lind pushed the thought from his head. Pushed away the panic and the buzzing in his ears, the insidious black behind his eyes. He ate his hamburger and stared out at the cars and trucks on the highway and thought about how he would find the man.

He wondered what Caity Sherman was telling the police. Looked out at the big Mustang in the parking lot and wondered how much time he had. It wouldn't take long to find the lake house, he knew, just a couple days. He hoped Caity would give him that long.

Lind finished his hamburger and walked out to the car. Just as he reached it, the cell phone in his pocket started to ring. Lind stiffened as he felt it. It was the man's phone.

You always answer the phone. When I call, you always answer, understand?

The phone buzzed and chirped in Lind's hand. He held it at arm's length, fighting panic that threatened to envelop him. He knew he had to answer. The man had trained him that way.

The man had tried to kill him. He'd sent another asset to the apartment. The man wanted him dead.

Lind slipped behind the wheel of the Mustang and reached for the pistol beneath the passenger seat. Took it out and studied it. The phone went silent in his other hand. He looked at the pistol some more, and then slid it between the driver's seat and the console. Dropped the phone out the empty window and drove back to the highway.

178

Windermere was waiting in the lobby when Stevens came out of the elevator. She sat in a patch of sunlight, a stack of papers in one hand and a cup of coffee in the other, a breathtaking still life.

She looked up when Stevens approached. Took a sip of coffee and brandished the papers. "Courtesy of the North Carolina Department of Transportation," she said. "Gray Cadillacs. Every one in the state."

Stevens studied the stack of papers. "That's a lot of Cadillacs."

"I also called ahead to the local FBI office. They promised to hook us up with a phone book and a computer that does Google. We're in great shape, Stevens. You want the phone book or the Cadillacs?"

Stevens looked at the stack of papers. Then at Windermere's face. He couldn't chase the feeling of hopelessness from his mind. "Jesus," he said, "when's the next flight to Delaware?"

Windermere frowned. "You want to cut and run, partner?"

"What are we doing here, Carla? We're back to the needle-in-a-haystack stuff. You saw how far that got us in Philadelphia."

"So you're thinking we should just give up on Charlotte. Run up to Delaware and fall in behind these chumps again."

Stevens shrugged. "What else do we have?"

She leaned forward. "We have plenty, Stevens. I think you're dead on the ball with this Charlotte stuff. Thomas Gardham is somewhere in this city, and we're going to find him. We don't need to hold Mathers's hand up in Delaware, either of us. We need a better strategy here."

"Sure." Stevens eyed the NCDOT files. "Maybe the Cadillac angle pans out."

"Forget the Cadillacs." Windermere fixed him with her eyes, fierce. "I want something better. Something unique. I want the old-school Kirk Stevens. Give me some of that voodoo you pulled when you figured out Arthur Pender. That's what I'm looking for here, partner."

Stevens laughed, despite himself. "What am I, a witch doctor?"

Windermere's phone beeped. "You can be anything if you put your mind to it." She held up a finger and peered down at her iPhone's tiny screen. Typed something, and waited. Started to type something else and then shook her head.

"Forget texting," she said, punching in a number. "I'm too old for this crap." She waited, the phone to her ear. "This is Windermere," she said finally. "What's up?"

Mathers? Stevens felt another pang of jealousy. Quashed it. *She works well with the kid. They'll make a good team.*

"That's all she got?" said Windermere. "Nothing else. She doesn't know the where or when?" She waited. "Yeah, okay, but how many freaking lake houses are there in the world?"

She caught Stevens's gaze. Rolled her eyes. "Yeah," she said. "Okay, fine. Call me back if she says anything else, okay?"

She put down her phone. Grinned at Stevens, eyes bright. "A woman named Caity Sherman just showed up at a police station outside Wilmington," she said. "She claims to have spent the last two days with Richard O'Brien."

Stevens stared at her. "Holy shit," he said. "What else did she say?"

"She said a man burst into O'Brien's home and attacked them. Chased them into Delaware and attacked them again. They got away last night." She frowned. "Just who this woman is and why she rolls with O'Brien, nobody's quite sure yet. Anyway."

"Anyway," said Stevens. "What's this about lake houses?"

"Yeah." Windermere grinned. "It's a damn good thing we didn't pack it in and head north, partner. O'Brien's headed south. Sounds like he's looking for Killswitch. This woman claims a man kidnapped O'Brien and made him into a killer. Brainwashed him. Did the same thing to Wendell Gray."

"Brainwashed," said Stevens. "Like an old sci-fi movie."

"Yeah, or something," she said. "Point is, O'Brien's headed our way and he's looking for the lake house where Killswitch trains his killers."

"Which lake house?"

"Has no idea. Plans to drive around until he finds it, I guess."

"Jesus," said Stevens. "That's a needle in a haystack itself."

"Except maybe he knows more than he told Caity Sherman."

"In which case we're stuck with the haystack and he's already got the needle." Stevens shook his head. "God damn this case, Carla."

"Caity Sherman did say one more thing, though," Windermere said. "According to her statement, O'Brien's real name is Malcolm."

"Malcolm." Stevens waited. "Malcolm what?"

"Malcolm she doesn't know. But it's better than nothing."

"Christ." Stevens looked around the hotel lobby. The stack of NC-DOT Cadillacs on the table. "Malcolm," he said. "A mystery lake house. That's a couple bullshit excuses for breaks."

Windermere grinned at him. "So use your voodoo, Stevens. Solve this thing."

Stevens looked at her. Then he sighed. "All right," he said. "Let's get to work."

179

Parkerson stared at his cell phone. Lind wasn't answering. Either he'd broken training or he'd been captured, and, frankly, Parkerson would have preferred the latter at this point.

If Lind was in jail, he would break down and talk. That was almost a certainty; Parkerson didn't train his assets to resist interrogation. It didn't matter. What did the kid know, besides a couple of fragments?

Anyway, if Lind was in jail, it would be on the news soon enough. Then Parkerson would know what to do. He would know if the kid had given the police anything they could work with. If there was even the slightest chance law enforcement was headed his way.

So far, though, none of the major news sources had reported anything about Lind turning up anywhere. His girlfriend was alive and in custody—she was a pretty, young Delta Airlines employee, said she'd befriended Richard O'Brien after seeing him at the priority check-in counter a few too many times. Parkerson shook his head. Lesson learned. No frequent-flier status for the next asset.

Caitlin Sherman was her name. She'd shown up at a police station in some pissant town south of Wilmington. The reports on the news didn't have much except her picture and a police sketch of Lind. A description of the Mustang and a phone number to call. If they knew where he was going, they weren't saying.

Parkerson stared at the kid's picture on TV until it went away. Wondered where he would go. Parkerson hadn't trained him for this kind of endgame eventuality. He'd always told the assets to get out and avoid detection. Get back to base. So maybe the kid was headed to Philadelphia, the apartment. Maybe he was too brain-dead to remember it was compromised.

Or maybe he was headed to home base. Maybe he was coming back to the lake house. Parkerson mulled the thought over for a few minutes. Couldn't shake the sudden chill. He picked up the Killswitch phone and dialed Wendell Gray's number.

"It's me," he said when the asset came on the line. "How far away are you?"

180

The asset called David Gilmour set down the cell phone and kept driving. He had driven through the night, stopping twice for gas and Red Bull and coffee. Now it was midmorning and he'd put five hundred miles behind him. Now he was almost all the way home.

The asset was tired. His shoulder throbbed where the target had stabbed him. Blood had seeped through the shirt he'd wrapped around his wound. The asset hurt. He was sick of driving. He was more than a little afraid.

He'd failed to complete two assignments. Both of the targets had escaped. The man would be angry, he knew. The man would want to punish him. The man would make him endure the visions. He wouldn't make them go away.

The asset shivered and kept driving, favoring his wounded shoulder. He glanced at the pistol on the passenger seat and pressed harder on the gas pedal. The old truck sped up. Soon he'd be back at the lake house. The man would be angry. But the asset would be safe.

Soon he would be safe.

181

Windermere sat up straight. "Here he is," she told Stevens. "Here's O'Brien."

They were sitting in a conference room at the FBI's Charlotte office, papers spread everywhere, computers open and coffee mugs thrice refilled. Sun streamed through the windows. Morning had come and gone without any action, but now Windermere was excited.

Stevens hurried around to the FBI agent's side of the table. Looked over her shoulder at her laptop computer. A face on the screen, a missing person report. A twenty-five-year-old kid with a shaved head and a wide smile. Malcolm Lind.

"Disappeared from the Army Vet Center in Durham almost a year ago," said Windermere. "Fought in Iraq, caught an IED that killed a bunch of his buddies. Came home with psych trauma and fell off the map."

Stevens stared at the screen. If he blocked out the kid's smile, the light in his eyes, he could see the resemblance. Malcolm Lind was healthier than the man they'd chased through downtown Saint Paul weeks ago. His skin was better; he wasn't so skinny. He looked vibrant and alive, and his smile was infectious. In Minnesota, he'd looked like a corpse.

It was the same guy, though. No question.

"Malcolm Lind," said Stevens. "He have family?"

Windermere scrolled down the page. "Elizabeth City," she said, nodding. "Wherever that is. Mom cleans motel rooms and stepdad's a house-painter. Looks like they gave up the search a long time ago."

"They're in for a heck of a surprise."

"Long-lost son found a year later, only he's a brainwashed contract killer? I'd say they've got a shock or two coming. You think he goes home?"

"What, back to Mom and Dad?" Stevens shook his head. "No, I don't."

"Why not?"

"He's been gone a year. If he's really brainwashed, I don't think he cares about family anymore. I think he goes back to Killswitch."

"So we're back where we started," said Windermere. "We know this guy's name, but we don't know where he's headed. Some lake house somewhere."

"Probably around here, if that helps."

"Only marginally." Windermere shook her head. "You looked at a map? There's lakes everywhere. A hundred houses to a lake. We don't have the time or the manpower."

"What about Gardham? The OneShot stuff. He'd have to have an address to pick up the ammo they were sending him."

"And a purchase permit if he was buying guns," said Windermere. "Except there's no record of a Thomas Gardham applying for any such permit in the entire state. And nobody seems to have an address for him, either."

"OneShot will. If we come back with a warrant."

"Yeah," said Windermere. "But what are the odds they give us anything useful? I doubt Killswitch leaves his real address out in the open."

Stevens walked to the end of the long table and stared out the window beyond. "How the hell did Malcolm Lind just disappear, anyway?" he asked Windermere. "Nobody saw anything?"

"Took a while before anyone realized he was missing," said Windermere. "Aside from his weekly meeting with the psychiatrist, he didn't leave his house, apparently. His parents didn't have the time or the money to come to Durham more than once a month. Time their next visit rolled around, Lind was a ghost."

"Or a zombie." Stevens looked across the table. The phone book lay open in front of him, and he paged through it idly. Pizza delivery menus and car mechanics and a message from the chamber of commerce. Stevens stopped. He flipped back a page. "Wait a second."

Windermere looked up from her computer. "Give me something good."

Stevens stared down at the page. He'd made it to the front of the phone book. There was an information section, a little mini-guide to the region. The message from the chamber of commerce and a couple of maps. A list of major industries in the region, important employers. One industry in particular stood out.

"What?" said Windermere. "You got something or what?"

Stevens looked at her. "Every time we try to get an angle on Killswitch we get stonewalled by the Department of Defense," he said. "We never figured out why."

Windermere frowned. "And?"

"Fort Bragg is a hundred thirty-five miles from here," Stevens said, reading. "That's a monster army base. A hundred fifty thousand people. Houses the U.S. Army command, the reserve command, special ops, and the 82nd Airborne."

"So you think this guy's military? He's some kind of soldier himself?"

Stevens shook his head. "I don't think so. Our guy couldn't run Killswitch on a base without attracting attention. He wouldn't be free to dash off to Vegas and Miami as he pleased."

"So, what?" Windermere stared at him. "Enlighten me, Stevens, please."

Stevens showed her the phone book. "Defense contractors," he said. "Outside the base. There are hundreds of them in the region, big and small. Four of the top ten contractors in the country are based in Charlotte. If our guy's a big enough fish in one of these contractors' ponds, he'll have Defense Department clearance and the freedom and resources to move."

Windermere thought about it. "He'd have money. Enough for a Cadillac and a lake house."

"And a brainwashing habit. That can't be cheap."

"Freedom, too, like you said." She paused. "Except, why does he have to live here in Charlotte? Looks like there's a hundred more contractors out by the base."

"Close to the airport. Thomas Gardham flew into Vegas and out in the same day. That means he was at the airport here in Charlotte early in the morning and late at night. No way he drives over two hundred fifty miles on top of that."

"If he lived near the base, he could fly into Fayetteville," said Windermere. "Or Raleigh. I see your point."

"So we assume he's local," said Stevens. "That narrows our field of candidates considerably."

Windermere grinned at him. "Nice work," she said. "Now let's see how many defense contractors drive Cadillacs."

182

Lind drove south through the morning and into the afternoon. He drove the speed limit with the wind in his ears; he didn't listen to the radio or look out at the scenery. He stared straight ahead through the windshield and tried to remember.

It was early afternoon when the first memories started to stir. He'd driven through Richmond, Virginia, and the highway branched out. Interstate 95 continued south toward Fayetteville and, miles distant, Savannah, Georgia. To the southwest, Interstate 85 forked off toward Raleigh-Durham.

Durham. Lind turned onto I-85 without thinking. Followed the highway to the middle of the city, where he stopped at a gas station and bought a Red Bull and a map. "I'm looking for a hospital," he told the man at the counter. "For soldiers."

The man nodded. "The Veterans Center," he said, reaching for a pen. "Lemme see that map."

Twenty minutes later, Lind parked the Mustang outside the hospital doors. It looked just like it had in the visions: tall, square, and clean, eleven stories of modern brick centered in a vast medical complex. Lind stared in at the building and remembered walking to the curb, unsteady, leaning on the man to guide him. He remembered climbing into the Cadillac and letting the man buckle his seat belt, remembered everything before and everything after.

Lind shivered and turned up the heater. He didn't get out of the car. He didn't look around the hospital grounds. He'd found what he'd come for. He shifted back into gear and pulled out of the lot. Closed his eyes at the stop sign and tried to empty his mind. Then he opened his eyes and kept driving. He didn't know where he was going, but he followed the visions.

183

Windermere dropped another stack of printouts on the conference table. "Damn it," she said. "This guy couldn't drive a Porsche?"

Stevens eyed the stack. "Lot of Cadillacs in this town?"

"Tons." Windermere flopped in to her seat. "And most of them gray. This is every Cadillac in Charlotte cross-referenced with a list of known employees for the four major defense contractors in the city. As you can see, we're still in needle-and-haystack territory, Stevens."

Stevens nodded. "Sure," he said, "if we're relying on the North Carolina Department of Transportation to do our detective work for us."

Windermere frowned. "What do you mean?"

"Check this out." Stevens circled the table and spun Windermere's
laptop to face them. "While you were killing trees, I was doing some research of my own." He typed in a few keystrokes. Then gestured to the
screen. "Who's that?"

A man, middle-aged. Receding hairline and a weak chin. Bore more
than a passing resemblance to the sketches Oneida Ware and Larry Klein
had produced. Windermere frowned. "Thomas Gardham?"

"Looks familiar, right? His real name's Michael Parkerson. Senior vice
president at Magnusson Aerospace. I'm hoping you're going to tell me he
drives a gray Cadillac."

Windermere studied the man's face. "And you found him how?"

"Google," Stevens said. "Searched out the websites for each of our four
major contractors. They all had lists of their top executives. Magnusson
had pictures and a bio."

"Lives outside Charlotte with his wife and two kids," Windermere
read. "Played ball for the Tar Heels. He's one of yours, Stevens."

"A middle-aged white man. The root of all evil."

"I meant a ballplayer," she said, grinning, "but yours works, too. Great
computer work, by the way. Maybe you're not as out of touch as you
look."

"Took a while to figure out, I won't lie. First thing, I had to Google
what the Internet is."

Windermere slapped his arm. "Funny. This guy drive a Caddy or
what?"

Stevens reached for the printouts. "Let's find out."

184

The asset called David Gilmour pulled the old truck off the interstate around China Grove, North Carolina, just as he'd been instructed. He followed Highway 152 west through forest and patchy farmland, the afternoon sun dipping low in the sky and glaring harsh through the Chevy's front windshield.

The asset drove through Mooresville to Interstate 77, where he pulled into a gas station parking lot and unfolded a map. When he'd figured out his location he pulled out again, crossed the interstate, and continued west.

The man's instructions were good. The asset found the lake house with no problem. It sat on one skinny arm of a much larger lake, the shore crowded with mobile home trailers and boat sheds and new, monstrous mansions. The lake house itself sat in a grove of trees, hidden from the neighbors and the narrow access road. The asset pulled the pickup into the trees and parked alongside the house, killed the ignition, and sat in the stillness, letting his muscles relax and testing the wound in his shoulder.

The wound throbbed. The T-shirt was saturated with blood, dried and crusted. The asset unwrapped the shirt, slowly, and examined the wound. It gaped at him, ragged and raw. It smelled bad. The asset looked at the wound and hoped the man arrived soon. The man would be able to help him.

The asset climbed out of the truck and into the stillness of the grove. It was early spring, and the lake was still largely deserted. The house sat dark amid the trees, seeming to sag from the weight of the shadows. The asset suddenly felt afraid. It was a new fear, quite different from the panic that came with the visions. He realized the house made him nervous.

The asset stood beside the truck for a long time, studying the house. There were no other cars in the grove. The man hadn't arrived yet. The asset wrapped his good arm around himself and shivered a little. He stood there, indecisive. Then he pulled out the cell phone and called the man. The man picked up. "Yeah?"

"I'm here," the asset told him. "At the lake house."

There was a pause. "I'm just about to have dinner," the man said. "You're going to have to wait for me."

The asset looked around. "I can wait."

"Let yourself into the house. Stay out of sight. There's a spare key in a little cup under the deck. Go inside and wait for me. Just sit there and wait, understand?"

"I understand," the asset told him.

"Don't touch anything. Don't go wandering off. I'll be there when I can."

"I understand."

The man ended the call. The asset put the phone away and looked at the house again. Something gnawed at his insides, and he realized he didn't want to go in. Something scared him in there, though he didn't know what. He looked back at the road and felt his head start to buzz. Felt the panic creep in as he thought about leaving.

He couldn't leave. The man wanted him here. His orders were to go inside and wait. He would wait.

Quickly, before he could stop himself, the asset reached in the truck and came out with the pistol and the knife. He stuffed the pistol in his waistband and circled the house to the deck and bent down to the dirt, scratching in the shadows for the cup and the key.

185

Stevens called home from the passenger seat of Windermere's rented Camry. Got the answering machine, of course; it was the middle of the day. Nancy would be working, Andrea and JJ at school. Stevens ended the call and looked out the window, watched the outskirts of Charlotte pass by.

Windermere watched him from the driver's seat. "Everything cool?"

Stevens turned away from the window and sighed. "My daughter," he said. "I think the whole Tomlin thing affected her more than we realized."

"She okay?"

"I don't know," Stevens said. "Half the time she's the happiest girl in the world. I came home from Philly, though, and she seemed to think I was putting the whole family in danger. She thought I was leading the killer straight to our house."

Windermere exhaled. "Yikes."

"Nancy says she's okay. She talked to a counselor." Stevens stared out the window some more. "Still doesn't feel right to be out here."

He picked up his cell phone again. Scrolled through to Andrea's cell phone and pressed CALL. Waited as the phone rang in his ear.

"Daddy?" Andrea answered, half whispering. "Daddy, I'm at *school*."

Stevens felt his body relax. "I know, honey," he said. "I just wanted to check on you. See how you're doing."

"I'm *fine*, Daddy." Andrea sighed. "This is about that fight we had, isn't it? You told Mom, and now she thinks I'm screwed up in the head."

"Nobody thinks you're screwed up in the head, honey. We just worry about you. After what happened last year."

"I'm fine," Andrea said. "I get scared sometimes, that's all. We don't have to make a big deal about it."

"So you're okay," Stevens said. "You're not scared right now?"

"I'm scared I'm going to get a detention for talking on my cell phone." Stevens could hear her rolling her eyes. "Are you almost done with your case?"

Stevens glanced down at the picture of Michael Parkerson in his lap. "Just about," he said. "Just about caught up to the bad guy."

"Catch him, Daddy. Hurry up and come home."

"Will do, sweetheart," Stevens told her. "I love you."

"I love you, too, Daddy. Bye."

Andrea ended the call. Stevens looked at his cell phone for a minute. Then he put it away. Beside him, Windermere kept driving, saying nothing. Somewhere in the outskirts of Charlotte, Michael Parkerson waited.

186

It took a couple hours before Lind picked up the trail. He drove around Durham in the Mustang, stopping every few minutes to rack his brain for the memory that would lead him down the right path.

Finally, he broke through. Found himself on Interstate 85 again, headed toward Greensboro. He remembered this drive. It had been a bright, sunny day. Warm. The air-conditioning blasted, giving Lind chills. The man sat in the driver's seat, humming along to classical music on the radio. He smiled at Lind. "Bach," he said. "The Brandenburg Concertos. My very favorite. You know them?"

Lind had shaken his head. "No."

"Six of them, written for the margrave of Brandenburg in the early 1700s. A margrave was a kind of governor." The man paused. Listened. "My favorite's the third," he said. "Three violins, three violas, three cellos. It's marvelous stuff."

Lind stared out the window. "Where are you taking me?"

"I'm taking you home, Malcolm." The man was smiling. "You're safe now."

NOW LIND DROVE WEST in silence, the only sound the unceasing roar of the wind through the empty driver's-side window. It was early evening by the time he reached Greensboro. His stomach rumbled a complaint, but still he pressed on, unwilling to risk losing the trail for the sake of a cheap hamburger. He followed the interstate as it curved southwest toward Charlotte, the sun sinking lower in the sky.

Soon it would be dark. He would have no way to follow the vision once the sun set completely. He wouldn't remember the terrain. Then what? He would be lost, hungry, and cold, marooned until morning— assuming he could pick up the trail again.

Lind pressed harder on the gas pedal, and the big Mustang accelerated. The miles began to blur past. Lind stared out at the road, searching for signs, racing the setting sun to the horizon. There was no time to waste.

187

The lake house was musty inside, and very still. Light filtered in through grimy windows. There were no sounds. The asset sat in a moldy armchair and looked at the gun in his lap.

He didn't know why the house made him afraid. There was nothing strange about the place. It was a crummy old shack in some trees by the water. There was dusty furniture and a broken TV and a couple ugly paintings on the walls. It wasn't a scary house. But it scared the asset nonetheless.

He sat in the armchair for a long time and looked down at the pistol and wondered what to do. He hoped the man would come soon. Except the man scared him, too. The man scared him as much as the house did.

The target in Delaware claimed the man had brainwashed him. Said he was using the visions as tools. The asset hadn't listened. He enjoyed killing. And, anyway, the man had promised to help.

The asset shifted in his seat. He hadn't completed his assignment. He'd failed the man, twice. And now he was here, in this lake house, and he was afraid.

The asset stood and walked to the window. The old Chevy sat alone in the trees. The man still hadn't arrived. There was nobody around. He surveyed the cabin. The old furniture. The back door to the deck. The cramped kitchen.

In a corner of the kitchen was a wooden door. The asset walked to the door and swung it open. There was a stairway down, into blackness. The asset stood at the top, wishing he could close the door and go back to that moldy armchair and wait for the man. Instead, he gripped the pistol tighter and descended the stairs. Reached the bottom and fumbled for the light switch.

The fear was even worse here. The basement stank of shit. The asset stood at the base of the stairs and looked around the low room. He recognized his cell, the door yawning open. He understood now why he was so afraid.

The asset shivered and turned away from the cell. He crossed the basement to a recliner in the corner. There was a remote control there, a DVD player, and a small TV. The asset turned on the power and a harsh sound blared from inside the cell. Lights and grating noise. The asset quickly turned off the DVD player, feeling the panic thudding in his skull. He put the remote down and tried to catch his breath.

He left the remote alone. He continued to explore. There were drawers beneath the DVD player. The asset opened the top one. Found paperwork, ID cards, wallets. He recognized his own wallet. Picked it up and examined it.

The wallet was slim. There was an old video store membership. An expired credit card. A Georgia driver's license with the name Wendell Gray. The asset looked at the picture. The name, the address. Wendell Gray. That was his name.

He felt a faint twinge of recognition. A shudder of panic. He pushed the memories back, and the panic disappeared with it.

The asset started to replace the wallet when something fell out of a pocket. A picture. The asset stooped and picked it up. A tiny picture, cut out, a woman's face. She had graying curly hair, a flowered dress, concerned eyes. The asset's eyes narrowed. He remembered this woman.

He put the wallet away. He kept the picture. He tightened his grip on the gun.

188

Windermere pulled the Camry over to the curb. Pointed up the road to a pristine white two-story Colonial perched across from a park at the top of a small hill. "That's the place," she said. "Parkerson's home base."

Stevens nodded. "And there's the gray Cadillac."

They'd followed Michael Parkerson's trail to a quiet suburban street in Cornelius, an outlying community twenty miles north of Charlotte along Interstate 77. It was close to Magnusson Aerospace, and just as important, it was close to Lake Norman, the vast man-made inland sea that provided hydroelectric power and recreation to metropolitan Charlotte's more than two million residents.

Malcolm Lind told Caity Sherman he was headed for a lake house, Windermere thought. *Plenty of those on Lake Norman.*

She glanced across the Camry at Stevens. "Everything cool on the home front, partner?"

Stevens nodded. "Sounds like it."

"Andrea's okay? Nothing to worry about?"

"She's mortified that her dad's such a sap," Stevens said. "That's about it."

"Good," she said. "Then let's get our game faces on."

Stevens nodded. "I'm ready." Reached into the backseat and dug out a Kevlar vest. Windermere watched him, marveling at the voodoo he'd done to get them here. Parkerson drove a big gray Cadillac. He had Defense Department clearance. And, hell, he even looked like Thomas Gardham. He was Killswitch, no doubt, and Stevens had found him.

He's made for this stuff, she thought. She studied her colleague across the Camry and suddenly thought of Mathers. Felt a quick pang of guilt and chased it from her mind.

Stevens is your partner, not your boyfriend. Get your head in the game.

Windermere straightened and pushed Mathers away. Pushed Stevens away, too. Behind the Camry, a Cornelius PD cruiser pulled to a stop. Windermere studied it and knew there was another patrol car up the block, ready to guard Parkerson's house from the rear and ensure their suspect didn't get far if he ran. She watched in the rearview as a uniformed police officer climbed out of the cruiser and stood stretching on the pavement, his movements measured and deliberate. Then she reached for her Glock, checked it. "Ready?"

Stevens checked his own sidearm. "Always."

Windermere squared her shoulders and climbed from the car, the adrenaline pumping electric through her body. "Killswitch, partner," she said. "Let's do this."

189

Parkerson was finishing the last of his lasagna when the doorbell rang. Before he could put down his fork, Krista was up and out of her seat, running for the front door. Parkerson glanced at his wife. "We expecting anyone?"

Rachel stood. "I don't think so," she said, frowning, and followed her daughter from the room. Parkerson heard the front door swing open, the low murmur of voices. Beside him, his son played with his food, shifting in his seat. Parkerson grinned at him. "Probably that neighbor girl from down the block," he said. "Guess she has her eye on you."

His son's eyes snapped up and his cheeks flushed bright red. "Come on, Dad."

"Hard to blame her," said Parkerson. "You're practically a grown man now." He bent down to his lasagna again. Then Krista came running back into the room.

"They want you, Daddy," she said.

There was something in her tone. "Who wants me, honey?"

"A man and a woman. They don't want Mommy, they want you."

"They didn't say who they were?"

She shook her head. "They showed Mommy badges."

Parkerson felt his heart syncopate. He stood, forcing a grin at his son. "Guess they finally caught me," he said, walking to the kitchen doorway and peering down the hall.

There were two of them, a man and a woman, just as Krista had described. The man was middle-aged and slightly paunchy. The woman was taller and beautiful. They were talking to Rachel. They were in plain clothes, but they had guns on their hips. Parkerson recognized them. They were the Feds from the airport in Las Vegas.

Shit.

Parkerson ducked back from the doorway. He leaned against the wall and looked across the kitchen, trying to focus his thoughts. "Dad?" His son frowned at him. "What's going on?"

"Nothing," Parkerson told him. "Give me a minute, Stevie, okay?"

"Michael?" Rachel called from the hallway. "Somebody wants to talk to you, honey."

Parkerson looked around. Through the kitchen window he saw movement, a shadow. Then another cop appeared at the window, this one in uniform, his hand at his holster. Parkerson looked away quickly.

If the police had tracked him here, it was over. They knew who he was. They could figure out the rest. As soon as they attached him to Killswitch, he was done for, and that wouldn't take long. The data was right there on his computer.

It was over. There was no bullshitting to be done now, no fancy cloaking devices. If the police had tracked him here, the whole game was over. "Honey?"

Parkerson pushed himself off the wall and walked across the kitchen toward the closet by the back stairs. Smiled at the cop through the window and kept his movements deliberate. Behind him, Stevie stood up, confused. "Dad?"

Parkerson ignored him. Slipped on a pair of his old runners, nice and easy, and walked across to the back door. Grinned at the cop as he pulled the door open. "Evening."

The cop frowned at him. "Mr. Parkerson—"

Parkerson made a fist and hit him as hard as he could. The cop reeled back. Parkerson pushed past him and ran. Behind him, someone shouted, but Parkerson didn't look back. He crossed the backyard and jumped the small fence at the end of his lot. Cut through the neighbors' backyard and kept running.

190

Windermere ducked past Rachel Parkerson and ran through the house, dodging two confused kids and a stunned city cop on her way out the back door. *God damn it,* she thought. *I guess that settles that.*

They'd barely shown Parkerson's wife their badges when the bastard started running. He'd known what they were there for. Hadn't even bothered with pretense.

Ahead of her, Parkerson had hopped the fence into his neighbor's lot and was slipping around the side of the next house. Windermere gripped her Glock tight and ran. *"Stop,"* she yelled. *"FBI!"*

Parkerson ignored her. Disappeared around the side of the house. Windermere ducked her head and ran.

» » »

PARKERSON BURST OUT into the neighbors' driveway, one street over. The street was quiet, peaceful. A couple kids played basketball a few houses down. Someone was watering his lawn. Another night in the suburbs.

A blue Ford Explorer pulled around the corner and started up the block. Parkerson recognized it. Gulped some air and hurried toward it, met it as it turned up a driveway. "Jerry," Parkerson said, a sheepish smile on his face. "Man, glad you're here."

His neighbor stepped out of the car, a concerned look on his face. "Everything okay, Mike?"

"Rachel needs milk," he said. "My car's in the shop. Do you mind?"

Jerry frowned. "Mike—"

Parkerson heard voices behind him. The Feds burst from between two houses, guns drawn. Parkerson turned back to his neighbor. Ripped the keys from his hand and slid behind the wheel. Slammed the door closed and fired up the engine as Jerry banged on the hood, shouting something, chasing him back down the driveway.

Parkerson shifted into drive just as the cops approached. Stood on the gas and heard the big engine roar. The Ford surged down the street, leaving the cops sucking exhaust. He reached the corner and turned and just drove.

» » »

"*SHIT.*" Windermere watched the big SUV disappear. "God *damn* it."

Beside her, Parkerson's neighbor was losing his mind. Windermere tuned him out. Stevens appeared beside her, panting for breath. "Jesus Christ," he said. "This bastard is slippery."

Windermere holstered her Glock. "We need backup," she said. "Whoever we can get. Every eye on the road looking for blue Ford Explorers."

Stevens nodded. "We'll get him," he said. "He won't get far."

"We'd better goddamn get him," she said. "We've come too far to watch him flee the freaking coop, Stevens."

She stood in the center of the road, staring down at the empty intersection. Watched a Cornelius PD cruiser speed past, lights blazing, siren loud. She waited until it had disappeared, then turned around and hurried back to Parkerson's house.

191

Parkerson watched the rearview mirror and hardly dared to breathe. The street was empty behind him. The cops were gone. He kept driving.

They'd be calling in his plates, he knew. There'd be police on his tail, locals and state troopers and FBI alike. He had to get out of Jerry's Explorer. Hide out somewhere and figure a plan.

His heart wouldn't stop racing. Fifteen minutes ago, he'd been eating lasagna with his kids. Now he was running for his life. How the hell had they found him? Didn't matter; they'd done it. The only important thing now was escape.

Escape.

The asset was at the lake house. He'd driven down from Delaware in a dead man's car. Maybe they were lucky and the police hadn't ID'd the victims yet. Maybe the car wasn't made. They could swap the plates, anyway. And the asset was armed. There were guns at the lake house. And nobody but Parkerson and the asset even knew the place existed. They'd be safe there, for a while. At least until dark.

Parkerson drove north, avoiding the interstate. He circled the lake and took side roads until he reached Mooresville, where he risked a heart-stopping five minutes on busy Highway 150 before ducking off onto rural roads again. He kept his eyes glued to the rearview mirror, searching for cops. Didn't see a one. He was close to the lake house now. Almost in the clear.

The lake road was deserted. Parkerson waited at the intersection until he was sure nobody had followed him. Then he turned and followed the shore to a little grove of trees at the end of the road. Drove into the grove and parked beside an old Chevy truck next to the cabin. Killed the engine and sat in the driver's seat, waiting for his heart to slow. The lake twinkled through the forest, a late-evening show. Soon the sun would be down. Night would fall, and he could escape undetected.

Parkerson looked out at the old truck alongside. The house was dark behind it. There was no sign of life, but Parkerson knew the asset was inside, waiting for instruction. Waiting, though he didn't know it yet, to die.

Wendell Gray would have to be disposed of. He was an anchor now, a liability, even if he'd shown potential. It would be messy. It would be violent and difficult and altogether unclean. Parkerson felt slightly sick as he thought about it.

Still, it was a necessity. Gray had to die, and so he would. Parkerson straightened and reached for the door handle, steeling himself to the task. The sun was setting. It would be nighttime soon. In a few hours, he could escape.

192

Windermere and Stevens circled back to Michael Parkerson's house in time to meet a cavalry of assorted police vehicles—state patrol cruisers, local radio cars from the Cornelius PD, a couple unmarked sedans and SUVs from the FBI detachment in Charlotte. As they walked up to the house, another FBI agent emerged from the front door.

"Wife doesn't know shit about any lake house," he told Windermere. "Claims she has no idea where her husband might have gone."

Windermere looked down the driveway at the chaos in the street. "I'll handle the circus," she told Stevens. "You talk to Parkerson's wife."

Stevens watched Windermere wade into the mess of law enforcement, her hands raised, her presence commanding. Watched the cops swarm to her like iron filings to a magnet. *Better her than me,* he thought, turning toward the house. He walked up to the porch and pushed open the front door.

Rachel Parkerson sat in the kitchen, dinner half-eaten around her. She looked up as he walked into the room. "You catch him?"

Stevens shook his head. "Not yet."

"I don't get it," she said. "Where did he go? The last guy said something about a lake house?"

Stevens sat down opposite Rachel at the kitchen table. A couple kids watched from the doorway, a teenage boy and a young girl. "Right now, we're not sure where your husband went," he said. "We're hoping you can help us."

Rachel shook her head. "I don't know anything," she said. "What's this about, anyway?"

"We think your husband was using his position at Magnusson to run an online crime website." Stevens glanced at the kids in the doorway. "Effectively, he killed people for money."

Rachel Parkerson looked up. "You're not serious."

"It's not the worst of it," he said. "If our suspicions are correct, he kidnapped two young men—and potentially more—to kill for him. Soldiers, both of them, war veterans with psychological issues. He trained them to carry out his murders."

"I don't believe it." Rachel shook her head. "Are you hearing yourself? Michael is a good husband. A father. He would never do anything like that."

"Sure," Stevens said. "You're as shocked as anyone right now. We'll figure it out together, okay?"

"There's nothing to figure out, Officer. You have the wrong guy."

Stevens glanced at the kids again. They were listening, rapt. He sighed and turned back to Rachel Parkerson. "We put your husband at a contract killing in Miami two Saturdays ago. A witness saw a gray Cadillac at the scene. Was your husband at home that weekend?"

Rachel closed her eyes. Leaned back and didn't say anything. "He drove to Miami that weekend," she said finally.

"What about this weekend? Was he in town the whole time?"

Her shoulders slumped. "He had to fly somewhere. For business."

"On Sunday."

"Sunday, yeah."

"He flew to Las Vegas," Stevens told her. "He brought one of the soldiers he'd kidnapped. Together, they murdered five people at the Rio Casino and ran over an innocent bystander. The bystander lived. He gave us a description that matches your husband."

Rachel Parkerson stared up at the ceiling. Exhaled, slow.

"Your husband is a very dangerous man," Stevens said. "We need to know how to find him."

Rachel stayed silent a beat longer. "I thought he was just stressed from work," she said finally. "You know, he handles these big defense contracts. I figured it must be the pressure setting him off. I never knew."

"How could you?" said Stevens.

"He's my *husband*."

"He's a skilled liar. A manipulator."

"He's the man I married," she said. "He isn't some psychopath. He's a nice guy and a good father. He's a good human being."

"We need to find him," said Stevens. "He's a dangerous man. We think he keeps the men he's kidnapped in a lake house somewhere, but I checked your family records, and you don't own any lake property."

Rachel nodded. "That's right."

"He probably purchased it using a shell corporation. Did he ever mention anything like that to you? Ever talk about a lake house anywhere?"

"No." Rachel rubbed her eyes. "God damn it, *yes*. I don't know if he owned anything or not. He was sure obsessed with that lake, though."

"What lake?" Stevens said. "Lake Norman?"

"He said his family used to have a patch of land somewhere, a trailer. Bought it right after they dammed the river in the sixties. He took us out one time, right to the spot. Said he used to love it out there."

"You think he might have gone back?"

"How should I know?" Rachel sighed. "You tell me."

"Sure," said Stevens. "Fine. You said he took you there once."

"That's right. Me and the kids."

Stevens looked her in the eye. "Can you find your way back?"

193

Parkerson swung open the cabin door and peered into the darkness. "Hello?"

There was no answer, only stillness. The whole house was dark. Parkerson fumbled against the wall for the light switch. Flipped it on and surveyed the small room.

The asset wasn't inside. The living room was empty. So was the tiny kitchen. Parkerson stepped through the doorway, frustration mixing with the first tinges of fear. It was creepy out here in the quiet. Where the hell was the asset? This was no time for games.

Parkerson checked the bathroom and the two tiny bedrooms. Both were empty. Tried the back door; it was stuck. He tugged it until it opened, sending a winter's worth of dust billowing into the room. The asset hadn't used the back door, anyway. Parkerson walked back into the kitchen. The basement door was ajar. There was a dim light from downstairs.

"David?"

Parkerson stood at the top of the stairs and peered down. Listened. Heard nothing. Damn it, now he really was creeped out. All the guns were in the basement. The ammunition. Locked up, but still. He stepped back into the kitchen. There was a hunting knife on the counter. It was crusted with dried blood. Parkerson took it and walked back to the stairs.

"David?" he called. "Soldier?"

Still no answer. Shaking his head, Parkerson gripped the railing and started down. The whole house was silent. Crickets chirped outside. The low buzz of the forest at twilight. And nothing but eerie silence from inside the house.

A stair creaked beneath Parkerson's feet. He stiffened, half jumped, laughed at himself. *Calm the heck down,* he thought. *Nothing to be afraid of. The asset's probably bugged out, is all.*

Parkerson reached the bottom of the staircase. The basement was lit by a single dim bulb. Shadows everywhere. The door to the asset's cell was open. The asset wasn't inside.

He was standing by the projection equipment. He was watching the nightmares on the small TV screen. The sound was muted. The images on-screen sent light flickering up onto the asset's face. His eyes weren't empty anymore. They were dark. The asset turned to look at Parkerson. "You did this to me," he said, his voice low and menacing. "You made me this way."

Parkerson hid the knife behind him. Held up his free hand. "The war made you this way, David," he said. "I'm just trying to help."

The asset raised his own hand. *"Shut the fuck up."* His whole body was shaking. Parkerson stared at the kid's hand. He was holding a pistol, sleek and shiny and black. The pistol was shaking, too. It was shaking bad.

194

"Drop the gun, soldier."

Parkerson tried to keep his voice steady as he stared at Wendell Gray's gun. The asset's whole body was shaking, his face a dark mess. He looked about a half second away from murder, and Parkerson didn't want to be standing in front of the kid's gun when he finally set off. "Let's just calm down a minute," he said. "Let's think this thing through."

Wendell Gray's eyes went darker. He was injured, Parkerson saw. There was a big gash in his shoulder, all dried black and bloody. "I'm not your soldier," Gray said. "Don't you call me your soldier. My name is . . . my name is . . ." He brought the gun to his face. Scratched his cheek with the back of his hand. "My name—"

"Your name is David Gilmour," Parkerson told him. "You're a friend of mine. You're my friend."

"David Gilmour." Wendell Gray relaxed a moment. Then he frowned. *"No."*

"David. It's true."

"No." Gray scratched his forehead with the barrel of the gun. He was still shaking. He was sweating. "You're lying to me. You showed me the visions, and you made me kill for you."

"I was trying to help you, David. I—"

"Drop the knife."

Parkerson glanced at the big knife in his hand. Then at Wendell Gray again, at the gun Gray had aimed square at his forehead. It kept bouncing around. One slip on the trigger and that would be the end. "David—"

"Drop. The. Knife."

Parkerson let the knife slip from his hand. Gray relaxed a little. He stared at Parkerson over the gun. "You did this," he said. "Now I'm going to do it to you." He motioned toward the open cell door. "Get in there."

Parkerson frowned. "David, please—"

"My name is not David." Gray's voice tore. *"Quit calling me David and get in the room."*

Parkerson stared at the kid. At the gun. Then he turned and let the kid push him into the cell. The room stunk of shit and sweat and urine and puke. It was tiny. "What's your name, then?" Parkerson said, turning back to the asset. "What's your name, David?"

Gray stared at him. Sweat dripped off his forehead, and he wiped it away with the pistol. "Shut up," he whispered.

"What's your name, smart guy? Just tell me your name."

Gray screwed his eyes closed. "Shut up," he said. *"Shut up shut up shut up."*

Parkerson saw his chance. He leapt at the kid, knocked his gun arm away. Drove him into the cell door. Gray wasn't ready. He staggered, off-balance, as Parkerson clawed at the gun.

Gray held his grip tight. He regained his balance quickly. He was younger than Parkerson, and much stronger. He shoved Parkerson away, easy, and came after him. Smashed Parkerson's nose with the butt of the gun. The force was like an explosion. Parkerson hit the concrete, hard. Stared at Wendell Gray's shoes for a moment. Then he lay back and passed out.

195

Rachel Parkerson leaned forward between the two seats and pointed through the windshield. "There," she said. "There's the lake."

Stevens followed her gaze past the T-intersection and into the gloom. The sun had set fully on the ride out to the lake, and he could see nothing but blackness beyond a few modest cabins down a slight slope a hundred feet distant. "Guess I'll take your word for it," he said.

"It's there," she said. "Lake Norman—or part of it, anyway. This is where Michael took us, right here." She pointed through the windshield again. "Guess his daddy owned that plot of land there."

"So his lake house should be somewhere around here."

Rachel shrugged. "If you say so."

Stevens glanced at Windermere in the driver's seat. Then he ducked low and looked in his side mirror. Behind the rental Camry, a convoy of law enforcement sat waiting in their cruisers and SUVs and unmarked sedans, ready to hunt down Michael Parkerson, wherever he was. Stevens studied the long row of headlights for a moment. Then he straightened. Surveyed the intersection, the cabins and trees beyond. "Okay," he said, "let's start looking."

196

Music. Screaming. Chaos. Parkerson opened his eyes and quickly closed them again. Screwed them tight against the violent crazy assault from the projector on the wall. He was lying on the concrete floor of the cell. His head throbbed. The door was closed and the asset was gone.

Rather, Wendell Gray was gone. He wasn't much of an asset anymore.

The screaming continued. The music. The room flashed and shattered like the strobe in a nightclub. The walls were projector screens. Murder. Death. Torture. Misery in all forms. The screaming continued. Parkerson could feel his brain swelling against the side of his skull.

He sat up slowly. Covered his ears and tried to push the sounds from his mind. Tried to ignore the projections. Tried to think. He crawled to the heavy door and wrenched at it. The door didn't move. It was locked tight, secure. Wendell Gray had locked him inside.

Parkerson crawled to the bed and pulled himself onto the flimsy mattress. Held his head in his hands and tried to concentrate. Gray was misguided. The projections would never torture Parkerson the way they'd tortured the assets. The assets were damaged. Mentally weak. He, Parkerson, was strong.

Still, he could see how a few hours in this place would start to wear on a guy. Parkerson stood, unsteady. Brought his hand to his face and touched his nose, felt a sudden sharp pain. His hand came back bloody. The bastard had broken it.

Parkerson wrenched the bed from the wall. Dragged it into the middle of the room and stood atop the flimsy mattress. He could reach the ceiling easily. There was a panel, amid the soundproofing. Parkerson lifted it out. Above the panel was a hatch. A combination lock.

He'd designed the room this way. He hadn't been shortsighted enough to believe he'd never wind up in this room. The assets were too unpredictable. They were violent. In his work at Magnusson, he'd seen time and again the need for fail-safes. For escape clauses. For another way out.

Parkerson turned the combination lock. The lock clicked, and the hatch opened. He stood on the bed and looked up into darkness, grinning to himself despite the throbbing in his head. *Out we go,* he thought, hoisting himself up. *You just can't keep a good man down.*

197

It was dark outside, too dark to see much. The road dipped and curved beneath the big muscle car. Lind drove as fast as he dared, relying on instinct. Relying on the vision that kept slipping away.

He drove west, through China Grove toward Mooresville. Carried on north, circling the town and meeting up with the interstate on the other side. Nothing looked familiar, not in this darkness. Nothing made sense at all, but Lind had long ago shut down his mind. He'd stopped thinking. Let his hands on the wheel and his feet on the pedals make the decisions. He followed and tried to keep his mind empty. Tried not to think about what he'd have to do when he found the man.

He drove over the interstate and past a couple gas stations, a fast-food joint, and a big-box store. Then he saw a sign. Lake Norman, it read, with an arrow. Lind slowed the car.

Lake Norman. Lind searched his memories, chasing the vision through his subconscious. Then he remembered. The man had stopped the Cadillac at the McDonald's across the street. "Better get us some victuals," he'd said, grinning. "Wait here."

Lind had sat in the Cadillac and watched the man inside the restaurant. The man had looked out at Lind every couple of minutes, kept glancing back, like he was afraid Lind would run. Lind sat and watched the man until he came back with a paper sack and a couple of Cokes. "Dig in," the man said, handing the sack to Lind. "You must be starving."

Lind hesitated. Then he opened the bag. He unwrapped a chicken sandwich as the man piloted the Cadillac out of the parking lot. He was chewing the sandwich as the man pulled back out onto the road. As he passed the road sign and turned to follow the arrow.

Lake Norman, the sign said. Lind remembered. He drove the Mustang to the intersection and followed the sign.

198

Windermere picked up the radio. "Here's the deal," she said. "We're thinking Parkerson's in one of the houses along the shore. Look for a blue Ford Explorer SUV, but be careful. No light shows. We don't want to spook him."

The radio crackled. Six voices radioed back the affirmative, one by one. Windermere put down the handset and looked over at Stevens. "You feel lucky?"

Stevens stared out into the gloom. "He's out there."

"Good. So which way am I turning?"

"You're asking me?" Stevens paused. "Let's go left."

Windermere hit her blinker. "Left it is." Then she picked up the radio. "We're going left," she said. "I want a couple of cars with me. The rest of you guys head right."

She crept the Camry around the corner and idled slow down the empty road. To the left, a farmer's field climbed a slight slope. To the right, trees and cabins and the black water beyond. Most of the cabins were empty, no lights on inside and no cars in the yards. "Hope you're right, Stevens," she said. "We put enough damn time into this case. I want to close it ourselves."

Stevens stared out at the night. "Closed is closed."

"Not for me. Not after that needle-in-the-haystack bullshit."

"There's still Lind."

"Small fry," she said. "I want the big fish."

They passed more empty houses, bigger ones now. Still no sign of the Explorer. No signs of life anywhere. "He could have hid the truck," Stevens said. "Kept the lights off. We probably have to go house to house."

"Maybe he's not here at all." Windermere glanced at Rachel Parkerson in the backseat. "Maybe the lake house is on a whole other lake. Maybe we're in the wrong locale altogether."

"This is his lake," said Rachel. "If he has a lake house, this is where he'll be."

"So you say."

Rachel frowned. "What does that mean?"

"You're his wife," said Windermere. "No offense, but if it were my husband, I might be tempted to send the cops on a goose chase. Give him enough time to bolt."

Rachel Parkerson's eyes flashed. Then she sunk back into her seat. "I'm not smart enough for that," she said, staring out the window. "Maybe if I'd thought of it first."

Windermere glanced at Stevens. Stevens wasn't paying attention. He was staring out into the trees, stiff as a hound on a scent. "There's a light on out there," he said. "In the trees."

Windermere slowed the car. Followed his look. Sure enough, a dim light past the end of the road. A grove of trees. A dirt path. Windermere picked up the radio. "Got a light over here," she said. "Someone babysit wifey while we check it out."

She parked the Camry and turned off the ignition. Behind them, a Cornelius PD cruiser pulled in and stopped. A uniform stepped out and met them by the back of the Toyota. Windermere gestured in at Rachel Parkerson. "This is our man's wife," she said. "She's liable to get squirrelly. Lock her up in your squad car until we figure this out."

The uniform opened the rear door and helped Rachel Parkerson out of the backseat. She looked at Windermere and Stevens through hollow eyes and allowed herself to be led to the patrol car. Windermere waited until the woman was secured. Then she turned back to Stevens. "Got your gun, partner?"

Stevens nodded. "Girl's best friend."

"Good," she said. "Let's check this place out."

199

Parkerson pulled himself out of the cell and closed the hatch behind him. Straightened and looked around the gloom. He was standing in a tiny closet, he knew, in one of the cabin's small bedrooms. Except for the muffled noise from the projections, the whole house was still.

Parkerson waited in the darkness. If the asset was around, he would have heard the hatch open. He would have come into the bedroom to investigate. Did that mean he'd gone?

Nothing seemed to move. Nothing made any noise. Parkerson crept out of the closet and into the bedroom. Bumped into the bed and followed it to the doorway. The door was closed tight. There was light behind it.

Parkerson pulled the door open gingerly, slow as he could. Peered out into the living room. Saw nobody from his angle, and pushed the door wider. Then he ducked back quickly. Wendell Gray was still out there.

The kid was sitting in the living room, his back to the bedroom door. He'd set the pistol down beside him, and he wasn't moving. He was just sitting there, staring at something in his hands: a picture. He stared at it and didn't move.

Slowly, carefully, Parkerson pushed the bedroom door open. Prayed Gray wouldn't see his reflection in the dark windows. He crept into the living room and toward the asset and the gun. Then he stopped.

The big hunting knife sat on the kitchen table, discarded. Gray would have carried it upstairs after he'd locked Parkerson away. Parkerson looked at the kid and the gun sitting beside him. Felt the throbbing in his nose, imagined the FBI agents at his door. Gray had fucked up. Lind had fucked up. They'd cost him Killswitch and they deserved to die.

Gray still hadn't moved. He was staring at that picture. It was a woman, Parkerson saw, an older woman in a floral-print dress. Parkerson hesitated, relishing the moment, the anger coursing through him alongside something darker, something scarier.

Twenty years building missiles and bombs, he thought. *Five years running Killswitch. Hundreds of bodies with my fingerprints on them, and I've never wanted to kill anyone so bad as I do right now.*

Parkerson glanced at the gun again. Shook his head. Too clean. He crept to the kitchen table and picked up the knife.

200

tevens and Windermere crept through the trees, their guns drawn. The night was quiet around them, and very still. Save the dim light ahead, the grove was pitch-dark.

Except there was a noise, too, Stevens realized, a muffled, erratic throb. It wasn't music—there was no discernible rhythm—but it wasn't natural, either. Stevens gripped his pistol tighter and kept moving.

As they approached the light, Stevens could see it was coming from inside a small cabin, saggy and mossy and old. The windows were streaky and grime-stained, the light hardly much better. Stevens crouched beside Windermere and studied the place. "You see anybody?" Windermere whispered.

Stevens shook his head. Then he looked again. "Wait." A shadow moved on the wall, through one of the windows. After a moment, a man appeared, his back to the window. Stevens motioned toward him. "There."

"Parkerson?" said Windermere.

Stevens squinted. "Can't tell."

Windermere looked around the grove of trees. There were two trucks parked alongside the house, an old Chevy pickup and—she stiffened. "That's a Ford Explorer, Stevens."

Stevens pointed at the window. "Yeah," he said. "And that guy has a knife."

201

The knife felt good in his hand. Better than he'd expected. Parkerson gripped it tight and advanced on Wendell Gray. The kid still hadn't moved from the chair. Didn't know what was coming. He held on to that picture like it was his last grip on sanity.

Slowly, Parkerson reached for the gun on the table. Slid it out of Gray's reach. Then, before the kid could react, he twined his fingers in Gray's lank, greasy hair, dragging him to his feet. The kid struggled. Kicked and thrashed. Parkerson held the knife to his throat.

"Your name's whatever I say it is," he hissed. "You belong to me now."

The kid fought. Parkerson wrenched his head back. Held the blade to his windpipe and realized he enjoyed the sensation, the power.

Fuck it, he thought. *This is fun.*

Then something moved outside. Just a shadow, and just for an instant, but Parkerson saw it. He looked up through the window and saw headlights through the trees. Multiple headlights. More shadows. He knew, suddenly, what they meant.

Something thumped on the front stairs. Then the door. *"Michael Parkerson,"* a woman's voice shouted. *"FBI. Drop your weapon and surrender yourself."*

Shit.

Parkerson pressed the knife against Gray's throat and fumbled for the pistol with his free hand. Found it just as the Feds kicked down the door.

Two of them. The man and the woman. They'd interrupted his dinner and they'd chased him out here. God knew how they'd found him so fast. Parkerson kept Gray between himself and the doorway, a human shield. Raised the pistol and the Feds ducked away. Disappeared into the blackness.

"I'll kill him," Parkerson told them, his hand slick on the knife handle. "Try anything stupid and I'll slit this kid's throat."

The man spoke. "You don't need to do it, Michael," he said. "This is over already. Don't make it worse."

"Fuck you," said Parkerson. "I decide when it's over." He looked around quickly, from the doorway to the windows. Outside, the shadows moved. The headlights blurred. There were so many headlights. There were cops everywhere. Soon they'd have the whole place surrounded.

Parkerson inched Wendell Gray through the living room toward the back door. There wasn't much time. The woman cop peered in the doorway. Parkerson fired a shot, and she ducked away, quick. "Don't you fucking try it," he said, backing toward the door. "Don't you dare."

202

Windermere stared across the tiny cabin at Parkerson and his hostage. *Who the hell's this kid?* she thought. Then she knew.

David Gilmour. Wendell Gray. Somehow, he'd made it back down from Delaware in time to turn an arrest into a goddamn hostage scenario, though why Parkerson would take his own brainwashed killer hostage, Windermere didn't have time to consider.

Guess it's everybody for himself at this point.

Parkerson had a knife pressed tight to Wendell Gray's throat. He had a pistol pointed clear at the doorway, his eyes wide and his face flushed bright red. His nose was broken and bloody, his every wheezing breath frantic. He was panicking, clearly. He was a ticking time bomb.

Wendell Gray stood slack and uncomprehending. He stared at Windermere with Malcolm Lind's empty eyes as Parkerson manhandled him through the cabin toward the back door.

Windermere kept her eyes fixed on Parkerson. Called out to the backup in the trees. "He's headed out the back door. And he has a hostage. Somebody get over there *now*."

Parkerson shook his head. "I don't think so." He fumbled with the door with his gun hand, pulled it open, and stepped onto the threshold. Brought the gun up again and yanked Wendell Gray's head back. Pressed the knife to his windpipe.

Windermere leapt up. *"No."* Parkerson grinned at her, a sick, humorless smile. Then, in one motion, he slit Wendell Gray's throat.

Windermere squeezed the trigger as Wendell Gray slumped to the floor. Too late. Parkerson dropped out the doorway, laughing, maniacal. Her shots found only darkness. He was gone again.

203

He was close now.

He could smell the lake through the ruined driver's-side window, that same fresh smell from the first time he'd arrived. He remembered this intersection, could picture the view out over the water. The sun had been setting when they'd pulled up here. The lake was lit up with sunlight like diamonds. He'd stared out at it, at the holiday people on their docks and in their boats. He'd felt a sudden sense of peace. Then the man turned the wheel and drove into the trees. That sudden peace disappeared, as quick as it arrived.

Lind waited at the intersection. He was close now. The lake house lay to the left, in a thick grove of trees. The man would be there—if not now, then soon. Lind would be waiting for him.

Except there were lights down the road, headlights and confused shadows. Shouting. The sharp crack of a gunshot. Lind stiffened.

He spun the wheel over and idled out of the intersection. Drove down the lake road and pulled onto the shoulder. In the distance, he could see police cars. Lots of them. Well, good. Let the police catch the man. Let them bring him in. Lind had done enough killing for one lifetime.

Except the shouting wasn't stopping. More gunshots now, two of them, in quick succession. The shadows seemed to dance in the trees. No police in the world could slow down the man, Lind knew. Not the man who'd brainwashed him. That man was too powerful.

He glanced at the pistol on the passenger seat. People were still shouting. Somebody was shooting. Lind stared down at the grove. Knew the man was escaping. He killed the big Ford's ignition and picked up the pistol. Reached for the door handle and climbed out of the car.

204

Windermere ran to Wendell Gray. *"Help,"* she screamed. *"Someone call a damn ambulance."*

Gray lay on the floor, making burbling noises. There was blood everywhere. Windermere rolled him over. Put her hands on his throat and tried to cover the wound. Apply pressure. Do something.

It was no good. The wound was too deep. The kid was going to die, and there was nothing Windermere could do.

She looked up just in time to see Stevens blow past her, gun drawn. Heard shouting outside. More gunshots. She kept her hands on Wendell Gray's throat and watched Stevens disappear. Whatever she tried, the blood kept coming.

Still, she stayed with him. Kept pressure on his wound. Held him close and urged him to hang on, screamed again for the ambulance, for help, anything. Swore at the kid when she felt him slipping. *"Don't you fucking do it,"* she told him. *"Don't you die on me yet."*

Gray stared up at her with those zombie eyes. His pulse weakened. Windermere held him, tight as she could. She was too late. The wound was too deep. The kid died in her arms.

Windermere let him go. Looked down at her bloodstained hands and the pistol beside her. The dark night and the chaos beyond. Wendell Gray lay there, unmoving, dead on the dirty wood floor. Windermere wiped her eyes. Slammed her bloody fist down.

"Fuck," she said. *"Fuck."*

205

Parkerson fled through the woods, dodging dark trees and uneven ground as he ran from the grove. Behind him, spotlights flashed and men shouted. Parkerson turned back with the pistol and fired a couple shots, wild. He kept running.

He zagged through the forest, down the slope to the shore, running hard, his heart in his throat. Ahead of him was the lake, inky and black, and he slowed as he reached the water, hands on his knees, his fingers slick with Wendell Gray's blood. He stood there, out of breath and giddy, replaying the asset's last moments in his mind.

A real killer, at last.

The shadows moved behind him. The voices got closer. No time to waste. Parkerson straightened and ran again, parallel to the shore. The terrain was lumpy and uneven, the ground soft. He misjudged his footing and the shoreline gave way, nearly sending him splashing down into the water. He regained his balance and kept running. The cops were far behind him. They didn't know the lake like he did. He could disappear into the darkness.

Parkerson ran past a couple big houses, the new ones. Reached the old lots with their trailers. A dock jutted out to the lake. A path wound its way up to the road. Parkerson ducked into the trees. Started up the slope to the road. *I'll flag down a car,* he thought. *Anyone. Hijack the ride and maybe take a hostage. Get the hell away from here.*

He crept through the trees. The road lay just ahead. The cops still hadn't seen him. They were too far away. Parkerson felt a wave of triumph. No way they'd catch up. He was practically free.

206

Stevens burst out of the forest and found himself at the lakeshore. He stopped and stood still a moment, searching the night. He'd seen Parkerson cut this way as he ran from the cabin after he'd slashed Wendell Gray's throat. Now, though, he was gone.

It was dark as coal out. No moon. The forest was vast and labyrinthine and Parkerson knew the terrain. He'd be impossible to track if he made it away from the shore. They'd have to wait and pray they caught him come morning.

There, though, up the shoreline. Something splashed in the water, a rustle like a miniature avalanche. Stevens squinted along the bank. Thought he saw something in a shadowy copse of trees. A branch shaking. A hint of movement. *Maybe he doesn't want to hide out,* he thought. *The road back to town's that way. Maybe he wants to escape.*

Stevens glanced the other way, down the shoreline. Saw nothing but black forest. Turned back and stared across at the thin copse of trees again, stared hard. There was something in there, definitely. Something moving.

Stevens checked his pistol. Glanced back toward the grove, the lights of the police, the voices. Then he crouched down and crept forward, quiet as he could, down the shore.

207

There was something moving down there, Lind could hear it, a rustling in the bushes, hushed and furtive. Down the road the shouting had slowed. Now and then someone called out from the darkness, but the action had faltered. The urgency was gone. There'd been no more gunshots.

Lind stood by the Mustang and looked down toward the lake. It had been a picture-perfect postcard the first time he'd seen it. Now it was nothing but shadows and gloom.

The rustling stopped for a few seconds, and then started again. An animal in the woods, hiding from a predator. Gathering whatever courage it could find to make an escape.

Lind waited.

There were sirens in the distance. More police cars. More cops.

They'd called for backup. They hadn't arrested the man. The man had somehow broken free, and now he was in the woods somewhere, hiding in the blackness, trying to escape.

And meanwhile, this thing, whatever it was, rustled closer. Lind stood by the Mustang and listened to it approach. The sirens were getting closer, but they weren't close enough yet. The man could still escape if he was lucky.

The thing in the brush approached. Lind listened and suddenly felt calm. He held the pistol loose in his grip and waited.

208

Parkerson crept out of the brush and up to the road. Glanced back toward the lake house, the police cars clustered in the grove. There was still plenty of commotion back there.

He grinned to himself. The cops had no idea. He could hike the roadway until he found a car. He'd be on the interstate in ten minutes, with nobody the wiser. He turned away from the grove and started up the road. Then he stopped.

There was another car parked out here, on the shoulder, maybe twenty feet away. He'd been so focused on the police that he'd missed it. It was a dark, low-slung sports car, a black hole in the night. Parkerson looked and felt a sick recognition. It was a Mustang, a black one.

The asset stepped out of the shadows. Andrew Kessler. Richard O'Brien. Malcolm Lind. Parkerson watched him approach. In his right hand, the kid held a gun.

Behind Parkerson were the cops. Ahead was the asset. Parkerson stood in the middle of the road and watched the asset come closer. Gripped his own gun in his sweaty hand and knew, suddenly, that he would never use it. The asset's hand was steady. His gaze was unwavering. But there was life in his eyes. There was pain.

"I didn't want to do this," he said quietly.

He looked at Parkerson, dead calm. His eyes never blinked. Parkerson wet his lips. "Malcolm," he said. "Please."

209

Stevens followed the shoreline to the thin copse of trees. Crept to it slowly, his Glock raised. Peered inside. Then around. No one there.

Nothing moved on the shoreline. Back toward Parkerson's cabin, there was shouting now and then, but none of it triumphant. Every call was a question, and, so far, no answers.

Stevens looked around. Beyond the trees was a long expanse of land, a grassy lawn parallel to the lake. It was wide open and risky. Parkerson wouldn't have dared to cross it, no matter how desperate he was. The trees, meanwhile, continued up to the road. Stevens crouched low and started up the slope. Figured Parkerson would have maintained his cover as long as possible.

He reached the end of the trees and looked up to the road. Saw movement on the embankment and knew he'd been right.

Parkerson.

There was another man with him. Smaller. Thinner. They were just standing there. Stevens squinted into the darkness, trying to make out the second man's face. He couldn't. It was too dark to see much.

The second man stood there, his arm outstretched, and Stevens realized with a chill that he was holding a gun. A pistol, black as night, aimed at Parkerson's chest.

Stevens pushed himself forward. Before he ran more than a yard or two, though, the second man pulled the trigger. The gun roared, and Parkerson staggered back. A split second later, he fell to the ground.

210

Parkerson heard the shot. He saw the explosion. Felt the bullet catch him in the chest and reeled backward, feeling pain like a fire. He brought his hand to the hole and felt blood. Then he fell.

The asset stood above him. Parkerson stared up, at his face and the smoking gun. "I'm your only friend, Malcolm," he said, clutching his wound and feeling more blood between his fingers. "Who's going to chase the visions for you now?"

The asset said nothing. He looked down at Parkerson, his eyes all sorrow and resignation. He studied Parkerson a long moment. Then he pulled the trigger.

211

ind shot the man in the face. The man died very quickly. Lind hurried back to the Mustang and slid behind the wheel.

There was more shouting now. A man had emerged from the trees beyond the man's body. He was shouting at Lind, waving a gun. Lind ignored him. He fired up the Mustang and gunned it in reverse. Backed to the intersection and spun the wheel over until the big car was pointed toward the highway. Then he shifted into gear and stood on the gas.

212

arkerson was dead. Stevens could see that from thirty feet away. And the gunman, whoever he was, was escaping.

The shooter was already inside his black sports car by the time Stevens reached Parkerson. Stevens chased him. Wasn't nearly fast enough. The black car sped away in reverse down the road.

Behind Stevens, someone leaned on a horn. Another engine growled, and a car pulled up alongside. *"Get in,"* Windermere shouted. Stevens wrenched open the passenger door and slid inside just as Windermere stepped on the gas.

"Heard the shot," she told Stevens. "Then I heard that big engine. Figured you might could use wheels."

"You figured right," Stevens said. He looked at her as she drove, her brow furrowed, her mouth a tense line. *Instincts,* he thought. *Thank God someone has them.*

The Camry sped up and over a rise toward the intersection. The black sports car was already there. The gunman had slowed. He'd spun the wheel over and pointed the car up the road. As the Camry approached, he stepped on the gas again, launching the big car forward. Windermere cursed. "This goddamn Toyota," she said. "Next car we rent has a Hemi."

Behind them, the rest of the cops had cottoned on to the situation. The rearview mirror filled with flashing lights and sirens. The cruisers were still back at the lake house, though. The gunman was getting away, fast.

Windermere spun the wheel hard, and the Camry squealed and protested as it took the corner too fast. The car wallowed midstride, and Windermere clenched her teeth. "Go, god damn it."

The turn happened in slow motion. Stevens gripped the armrest as, finally, the Camry righted itself. Windermere stepped on the gas. The gunman's getaway car was disappearing ahead.

Windermere stood on the gas pedal, urging the car forward. The Camry howled and shuddered beneath them. Windermere ignored its protests. She looked over at Stevens. "That car up ahead," she said, "it's a Mustang."

Stevens understood immediately. "Malcolm Lind."

"Guess he had his own beef with Parkerson," said Windermere. "Wanted to stick it to the man, once and for all."

"Mission accomplished."

"Yeah. And now he's getting away."

The Camry sped forward. Felt like terminal velocity, like the damn car would break up if it went any faster. It wasn't nearly fast enough. The big Ford made more distance on the road ahead. Soon it would make the highway. Stevens picked up his radio. "Highway patrol," he said. "Looks like this guy's going mobile."

213

Lind sped the Mustang away from the lake. Made one more sharp turn and then aimed for the highway. In the distance, up a rise beyond the last stand of trees, he could see the McDonald's, the gas stations, the big-box store, all clustered around the interstate on-ramp. He'd almost made the highway. Almost made it.

And then what? Where exactly are you going?

He'd been taught to escape after he completed a mission. After he'd eliminated the target. As soon as the first objective was achieved, his new job was to get home safe.

Extricate yourself without being detected.

The first objective was complete. The man was dead. He'd seen to that. The second objective? An impossibility. He had nowhere to go. Nowhere safe. There was nothing left now but the visions. The missions were over and the man was dead, but the visions would stay with him. Lind knew they'd stay with him forever.

Ahead was civilization, a few hundred yards away. Ahead was the highway. He had a gun and a fast car. He had a good shot at escape. He would never, though—never—escape the visions.

Lind stared out the windshield at the lights up ahead. He looked at the pistol on the passenger seat. Then he closed his eyes tight and let his foot off the gas.

214

W hat the hell is he doing?" said Windermere. "His car's slowing down."

Stevens stared out the windshield at the Mustang ahead. Malcolm Lind had been a few hundred yards from Mooresville's outskirts when he'd suddenly lit up the brake lights and slowed the car down. Now he pulled over at the bottom of a low dip, still surrounded by forest and fields and the wilds.

The Mustang rumbled to a stop. Windermere slowed the Camry behind it. Stopped well back of the big Ford and kept the engine running. For a moment, nothing happened. Malcolm Lind didn't move from the driver's seat. Then the Mustang's lights died. Lind had killed the engine. Windermere looked at Stevens. "What the hell?"

"No idea," said Stevens, his heart pumping hard. He gripped his pistol tighter and studied the muscle car through the window. "This is a new one."

Behind the Camry, the cavalry was arriving. Cruisers and unmarkeds, all lit up, sirens wailing. They screeched to a halt behind the Toyota. Windermere looked at Stevens again. "What do we do?"

Stevens studied the Mustang. Lind still hadn't moved. "I guess we arrest him," he said, "but carefully."

They climbed out of the car, slow. Left the doors open and crouched behind them. Windermere looked back at the rest of the cops. "This guy's armed and mentally unstable," she called back. "We're proceeding with caution. No sudden movements, you hear?"

Stevens circled around to Windermere's side and hunched down beside her. Lind still hadn't moved. "It's like he's waiting for something," said Stevens.

Windermere looked at him. "Okay. But what?"

Stevens was silent a moment. "He's a soldier," he said finally. "He's been taking orders almost his whole adult life. Now what? His commanding officer's gone. His mission's over. He's got nothing left."

Windermere looked at him. Then back at the Mustang. "Okay," she said slowly. She craned her neck above the door. "Lind," she called out. "Malcolm. Nobody's going to hurt you. Come out of the car."

There was no response from the Mustang. Windermere glanced at Stevens. Stevens shrugged. "Out of the car, soldier," Windermere shouted. "We don't have all night."

There was a pause. Then the driver's-side door swung open. Slowly, Malcolm Lind stepped out of the car.

He was a little guy, and young, barely more than a teenager. He looked anguished, his face torn up and confused, close to tears. He hugged his arms around his frail body and stared back at Stevens and Windermere and the police cars.

At the top of the rise, more police cars appeared. An ambulance. They crested the hill and sped toward the Mustang. Lind flinched and spun around. Took his pistol with him.

"Hold it." Windermere stood and stepped out from the Camry. Waved her arms, frantic, at the oncoming police cruisers. *"Hold it, god damn it. Stop your cars."*

The cruisers sped toward Lind and his Mustang. Lind watched them, hugging himself tighter, shifting his weight, almost hopping. Stevens crouched behind the Camry's door and watched the kid's pistol dance, his own gun at the ready and a million worst-case scenarios running through his mind.

At the last second, the cruisers pulled over. Squealed to a stop just yards from where Lind stood at the base of the hill. Doors opened and slammed shut. Voices shouted, loud, insistent. A full company of police officers knelt beside their cruisers, sidearms and shotguns aimed at the Mustang.

Lind stood in the headlights, wavering, slowly circling, the gun shucking and jiving at his hip. Stevens stared out from the Camry and felt a sudden chill. *We're going to spook this kid,* he thought. *We're going to spook him, and then bad things will happen.*

215

Lind stood in the glare of the police lights, shivering, wondering what it would feel like to die.

This was the end of the game, right here. The police had him surrounded. They'd sped down from the top of the rise and slid their cars sideways, blocking the road. Now they crouched down and aimed their guns at him and screamed a thousand instructions, all of it blending together into one urgent, incomprehensible mess.

This was the end. Sooner or later someone would get antsy and shoot him, and he would die here in the middle of this lonely road.

And why shouldn't he die? He'd killed people, lots of people, without discrimination. Without knowing why. He'd killed because somebody had told him to do it. Why should he get to live?

Lind stood in the middle of the road, turning in a slow circle, seeing it all. Police on both sides. Guns drawn everywhere. This was game over. The end of the line. This was where Malcolm Lind died. And good riddance.

Slowly, he brought the pistol up from his hip. The voices were urgent now, screaming at him. Lind ignored them. He brought the gun up. Paused for a second. Closed his eyes. Then, before he could stop himself, he shoved the barrel into his mouth and searched out the trigger.

216

S *top.*"

A woman's voice behind Lind, clearer and louder than any other. Lind opened his eyes. "Don't do it," the woman said. "Don't you dare."

Lind turned around slowly, the gun still in his mouth. Found the woman staring back at him, the same beautiful black woman who'd chased him through the streets of Saint Paul weeks before, edging toward him from the first line of cars. "Don't you dare pull that trigger, Malcolm."

She approached him slowly, like he was a mean dog and she didn't want to get bitten. She bent down, halfway to him, and set her gun on the pavement. Straightened again, her hands raised, and kept coming.

Lind kept his finger on the trigger. Kept his teeth clamped down hard on the barrel. The woman came closer. She spoke softly. "Malcolm, honey," she said, "put down that gun."

217

Stevens had tried to stop Windermere when she stepped away from the Camry and started toward Lind. She was too fast. Now she stood in the middle of the road, unarmed, facing down a violent killer with a pistol and a clear mental instability. "Malcolm, honey," she said, "put down that gun."

Lind was breathing hard, his nostrils flaring. His eyes were wide and jumpy, unfocused, as he watched Windermere approach.

This is it, Stevens thought. *This is where I watch Carla die.* He inched away from the Camry, slow, so as not to alarm the kid. Circled around until he had a clear shot at the gunman. *Anything crazy and you're lit up, kid. Nothing personal.*

Windermere still had her hands up. She was five feet from Lind. She spoke to him softer than Stevens had ever heard her before, and for one stupid moment he caught himself wondering if she'd talked to Mathers that way. Then he shook his head.

Get her out of this, God, he thought, *and I swear I won't begrudge her for dating Nancy herself. Just get her out of this mess safely, please.*

"You don't have to do this, Malcolm," Windermere was saying. "It doesn't have to end like this."

Lind studied her a moment. Then he moved the gun slightly. Stevens twitched on the trigger, caught himself just in time. *Jesus Christ.* Lind backed the barrel out of his mouth. Kept the pistol trained on himself. "Let me do this," Lind said. "I need it."

Windermere shook her head. "Can't do it, Malcolm."

"I killed so many people," Lind said. "Why should I live?"

"You think blowing your head off's going to get those people back?"

Lind looked at her. Didn't respond.

Windermere shook her head. "One more body, so what? One more bullet wasted. Doesn't mean a damn thing to the people you killed."

"I'm ruined," he said. "I'm no good."

"You're sick. You're not ruined." Windermere looked at him. "You want to end your life, fine, but don't do it because you think you owe the world something."

Lind looked down at the ground. "What do you care, anyway?"

"What do I care?" Windermere laughed. "Kid, I've seen enough dying for a while. I'm sick of it. You think it's some dramatic finish, it's not. It's just death."

Lind didn't say anything. He looked at her.

"I want a happy ending for once, Malcolm. I want to bring you home, and then I want to go home myself and put my feet up and drink a beer. I don't want to deal with more death. Not today."

"I don't have a home." Lind slumped, his eyes wet. "I don't have a family. I have nowhere to go. I have nothing."

"You do so have a home," said Windermere. "You have a mother in Elizabeth City. A stepdad. They're still looking for you. They didn't forget."

Lind exhaled, ragged.

"You have that girl of yours, Caitlin—"

"Caity," he said.

"Caity, right." Windermere looked at him. "You have all kinds of family, Malcolm. Got more family than me. Put the gun down so we can go back and see them."

Lind didn't say anything. He closed his eyes tight. Kept the barrel at his lips. *This is it,* Stevens thought. *Make or break.*

Lind didn't move. Windermere didn't move. The whole damn circus seemed to hold its breath. Finally, Lind exhaled. Opened his eyes. Slowly, he lowered the gun.

Nothing happened for a moment. Then Windermere was on the kid. She wrapped her arms around him, squeezed him tight, pinning his arms to his side and talking in his ear until, finally, his whole body seemed to deflate.

Stevens watched the kid drop his gun. Watched him surrender. Then, only then, did he let himself breathe.

218

Two weeks after he'd killed Michael Parkerson, Malcolm Lind received a visitor to his treatment room in the psychiatric department of the U.S. Naval Consolidated Brig in Charleston, South Carolina.

Visitors had not been infrequent in the weeks since the Killswitch case had broken. The FBI agent, Carla Windermere, had stopped in a couple of times. She'd brought her partner with her, a quiet and unassuming Minnesota state policeman who Windermere claimed had tracked Parkerson like a bloodhound. They'd made conversation, studiously nonchalant, and then sat in silence for a while, and as they were leaving, Windermere had looked him in his eyes and squeezed his hand, tight. "I'm glad you're still here," she said.

Lind had thanked her, squeezed her hand back, but sometimes he wasn't sure he felt the same. The aftermath hadn't been easy. The military, horrified by Lind's story, had assigned their best doctors to his case, and from the way they looked at him and whispered among themselves, Lind could tell it was going to take more than a few months of rehab to fix what was wrong with him. Assuming, of course, he was fixable.

And after he was fixed? Lind didn't know. He was still a murderer. He would always have blood on his hands. Maybe, years down the road, the military would declare him fit to stand trial. Maybe they'd throw him in with the rest of the criminals and he'd spend the rest of his life behind bars. Lind didn't know, and, so far, nobody would tell him.

Still, there were good days. A few days after his internment, his mother and stepfather arrived. He'd recognized them instantly; they were older than he remembered, grayer and gaunt, but seeing them brought memories flooding back. They'd approached him shyly, hesitant. He was a murderer, after all.

They worked through it, slowly. His parents moved to an extended-stay motel a half mile from the base. They came every day, stayed as long as they could, and talked about the world news and sports and the weather. For a few hours, at least, Lind could pretend he was normal.

After two weeks in the brig, Lind received a new visitor. He followed the guard to the meeting room, expecting to see his mother again, his stepdad with the newspaper. Instead, he saw Caity Sherman.

She looked even smaller than he remembered, but just as pretty. She stood in the middle of the room, fidgeting, looking around, shifting her weight. She saw him and stopped moving. Studied his face. Didn't say anything.

"It's okay," he tried to tell her. Then he stopped. It wasn't okay. Nothing was okay. He was a killer, and she barely knew him, and nothing in the world was okay.

They sat at an empty table and looked at each other some more. Finally, she cracked that mischievous smile. "How's the food in this joint, anyway?"

Lind laughed a little, despite himself. "It's not bad."

"Better than my spaghetti?"

He shook his head. "No."

"You don't have to put up with me to get it, though."

"That's true," he said. "Thank God."

She laughed. "There he is." Then she searched his face again. "Wouldn't have made you for a Malcolm."

"Malcolm Lind," he said. "I guess that's me."

"It's a nice name. Gentle."

"Gentle," he said. "Yeah, I guess it is."

"How is . . . everything? How are the visions?"

He looked away. "They're giving me drugs. And treatment. They swear they'll go away over time."

"You getting any sleep?"

"Some." He looked at her. "You didn't have to come here."

"I wanted to come," she said.

"Wanted to. What the hell for?"

"I thought you might need a friend," she said. "I wanted you to know that you have one."

Lind didn't say anything. He couldn't look at her. He exhaled, and it came out ragged, and Caity reached over and squeezed his hand. "Hey," she said. "Hey. You're going to be fine."

Lind let her hold his hand. Relished the warmth of her skin. Kept his eyes closed and tried to steady his breathing. "I hope so," he told her. "I do."

219

A thousand miles from the Navy brig where Malcolm Lind and Caity Sherman were reuniting, Carla Windermere and Kirk Stevens sat together on their bench in Rice Park and watched Stevens's children play around the *Peanuts* statues under the blue sky of another beautiful spring day.

"So there it is," Windermere said, breaking a long, easy silence. "Another case closed for Stevens and Windermere."

Stevens nodded. "Big three."

Windermere looked across the park to where Andrea Stevens crouched behind a bronze Charlie Brown, hiding from her brother and the friendly German shepherd he struggled valiantly to restrain.

"Your daughter seems happy," she said. "All things considered."

Stevens followed Windermere's gaze. Watched Triceratops drag JJ toward Charlie Brown, where, straining and slobbering, tail wagging, he mauled Andrea with his sloppy pink tongue. Andrea giggled as she fended off the dog's advances, and the sound of his daughter's laughter, innocent and unreserved, triggered something inside Stevens.

"She's okay," he said. "The counselor says it'll take a bit of time before she fully gets over what happened, but she's a strong girl. She'll be fine."

"What about you?" said Windermere. "This stuff with your daughter sap your taste for adventure?"

Stevens shook his head. "I'm not sure yet," he told her. "Anyway, what do you need me for? You have yourself a good partner."

"What, Mathers?" She cocked her head at him. "Too young."

"Too young for what?"

"Not for what you're thinking, you big goof."

Stevens frowned. "Sorry," he said. "The Mathers stuff—I'm sorry. You caught me by surprise with it, that's all. It shouldn't have mattered so much."

She watched him. "No?"

"It was unprofessional. I'm not your husband. Why should I care?"

"Because you do care, Stevens." Windermere twisted to face him. "And I care, too. You think I didn't want you to kiss me back in Philadelphia? Get real."

Stevens blinked. Couldn't think of an answer.

"I like you, Stevens," she said. "I don't know why, but I do. And I already know that you're moony about me. But you're married—and, Stevens, I'll kill you if you ever leave your wife—and I'm not just going to carry a torch for you forever, understand?"

"Yeah," he said. "I understand. I do."

"The Mathers thing, I could have handled it better. I'm sorry. But I'm going to date, Stevens. Maybe not often, but it'll happen. And we're both going to have to get used to it."

"Of course," he said. He paused. "Lesley offered me a promotion."

"Oh, yeah?" She narrowed her eyes. "What does that mean? You get a real office before I do and I'll shoot somebody, Stevens."

"I'd get an office. That's not all."

"Oh, good God. What else?"

"Lesley figures we work well together," Stevens said. "Says I'm some kind of FBI snake charmer. I didn't bother to argue." He arched an eyebrow at her. "He wants to make me head of an FBI-BCA liaison squad. Put me in with all the interjurisdictional stuff."

Windermere stared at him. "So we'd be like partners."

"Pretty much."

"What did you tell him?"

"Told him I'd check with you first. I wanted to make sure everything was cool between us."

"And Mathers."

"And Mathers," he said. "Yeah."

Windermere sighed. "Well, Stevens, I may or may not be having dinner with Mathers tonight. Can you live with that?"

Stevens felt the familiar pangs of jealousy. He pushed them aside. "I can live with it."

"Then we won't have a problem." She grinned at him. "Partner."

"*Partner.*" Stevens shook his head. "I'm gonna have to learn to fly better."

"Damn right. I can't have you puking all over me. It's unseemly." She looked around the park and straightened. "Here comes Nancy."

Stevens followed her gaze and saw his wife crossing the park, a couple shopping bags in hand. She walked toward Stevens and Windermere, called something over her shoulder, and Andrea and JJ raced to follow.

Windermere stood as Nancy and the kids approached, and Stevens stood beside her, feeling that same niggling guilt he tended to feel whenever he and Windermere shared some kind of a moment. Andrea and JJ ran past their mother and beelined to the park bench, JJ for his father and Andrea to Windermere, though she stopped a few feet away and lingered, shyly, her eyes on the ground.

"Hey, kiddo," said Windermere, "how're you feeling?"

Andrea looked up, bashful as a fifth-grader. "Good," she said. Then she screwed up her face. "My dad told you about what happened, didn't he?"

"No shame in getting stressed out about things," said Windermere. "Happens to the best of us. Even me. You still thinking you want to be a cop?"

Andrea nodded. "Yeah. I mean, I think so."

"Good girl." Windermere glanced at Stevens. "Your dad tell you about his promotion?"

"It's not official yet," said Stevens. "I haven't committed to anything."

Nancy rolled her eyes. "Yeah, right."

"You think your dad could do it?" said Windermere. "FBI stuff, full-time? You think he could keep up with me?"

Andrea looked at Windermere. Then she looked at her father. "I dunno," she said, "but he'd better try."

Stevens looked at her. At Nancy. Andrea shook her head. "I'll be *fine*, Daddy."

Stevens swapped another glance with Nancy, caught the smile she was struggling to hide. He laughed. "Well, all right, then," Stevens said. "Guess I'd better tell Lesley I'm in."

Windermere clapped his back. "Attaboy."

"Don't get too excited," he said. "Now you're stuck with me."

"Just at the office, partner. Nancy's the one who's gotta live with you." She grinned at Nancy. "And on that note, I'm outta here. Hot date and all." She hugged Stevens tight, before he could reply. Hugged Nancy, too, and waved good-bye to the kids. Scratched behind the dog's ears, winked at Stevens, and walked off through the park.

Stevens watched her go, feeling somehow, suddenly, adrift. He stared up at the Saint Paul Hotel behind her, replaying those first frantic moments when Spenser Pyatt was shot, replaying everything that had followed. He watched Windermere walk away, headed back to Minneapolis and her dinner date, and when she'd disappeared into the city he turned back to his family. Caught Andrea's eye, felt Nancy's hand seek out his hand, warm and familiar, heard JJ laugh as he played with his dog. Knew, all at once, he was exactly where he wanted to be. "Okay," he said, pulling Nancy closer. "Let's go home."

ACKNOWLEDGMENTS

Thanks to Stacia Decker and Neil Nyren, for whose guidance, encouragement, and wisdom I remain especially grateful.

Thanks to the fine people at Putnam, in particular Katie Grinch, Ivan Held, Sara Minnich, Alexis Welby, and Chris Nelson, and to every unsung copyeditor, proofreader, and fact-checker who's ever saved me from disaster.

Thanks, also, to Tom Colgan and the staff at Berkley, who've done such wonderful things with the paperback editions of my books.

Thanks to the readers whose enthusiasm propels me forward, and to the booksellers who've been my champions.

Thanks to Court Harrington for showing me Lake Norman and his beautiful corner of North Carolina.

Thanks to Kyla McNaughton and Sarah Messenger, for getting me through the storm.

And thanks to my family, with all of my heart.